lost love found

Love in LA Series
Book One

cristina santos

Paperback: 978-1-7390407-0-3

Ebook: 978-1-7390407-1-0

First paperback edition July 14, 2023.

Cover Design: Kateryna Meleshchuk. Find out more at dongurik.myportfo-lio.com

Proofreading: Kristen at Kristen's Red Pen

To my husband and my boys. You are the reason for everything I do.

———

For all the girls who thought they were too broken for love. You are whole and you are worthy.

contents

playlist

1. Late Night Talking - Harry Styles
2. Come Back...Be Here (Taylor's Version) - Taylor Swift
3. Ur So Beautiful - Grace VanderWaal
4. New Light - John Mayer
5. Adore You - Harry Styles
6. Nonsense - Sabrina Carpenter
7. Can I Kiss You - Dahl
8. There's No Way - Lauv, Julia Michaels
9. Feelings - Lauv
10. Say It - Maggie Rogers
11. Little Bit More - Suriel Hess
12. Dandelions - Ruth B.
13. Say Love - James TW
14. Satellite - Harry Styles
15. The Few Things - JP Saxe, Charlotte Lawrence

Playlist

Get the Spotify Playlist here

a little note...

first of all, thank you.

That you have chosen this book (my debut!) as your next read humbles me to no end. I had no idea how much I needed to put such a big part of my story, feelings, and ideas of love on paper until I started reading romance novels. They truly changed my life, and though that might sound silly to some, I have a feeling that if you're reading this, you might understand what I mean. Love stories are powerful.

That being said, parts of this book may be triggering to you. I always want you to go into my stories knowing what to expect, but if you don't have any particular triggers and don't want any potential (*minor*) spoilers, skip the 'Content Warnings' page.

This is an 'open door' book, and that means that my characters have sex on the page, and things are described in detail. If that's not for you (or you're related to me), the chapters you should skip are in the 'Dicktionary'.

My wish is that this story gives you hope. That those of us who have experienced love and loss know that love is possible again. That we never give up on ourselves.

A little note…

xoxo,

-Cristina

dicktionary

Whether you want to skip it, or skip *to* it, here's where you can find the spice and whose POV it's in:

Enjoy! (Or don't…)

content warnings

Please note that this book contains the following:

- Death of a loved one by suicide (not on page)
- Death of a parent (not on page)
- Mention of a character being filmed without consent during sex
- Open door scenes of the couple being intimate (in 6 chapters as mentioned on previous page)

Reading this book should make you feel things, yes, but I never want to trigger negative thoughts or feelings, so please be kind to yourself.

1 /
did i really just write that down?

elaina

THE UPSIDE of living in LA is that it's seventy degrees on December 23rd. The downside of living in LA is that it's seventy fucking degrees on December 23rd! I feel the sweat collecting under my boobs as I pack up my shit. I curse myself for choosing a blouse that feels as though it's made of velvet and wide-legged pants I keep nearly tripping over.

This almost makes me miss Massachusetts and New York winters. Almost.

It's my last day at the studio and we've just wrapped shooting on a movie I'm super stinking proud of, despite the fact that it was supposed to wrap four weeks ago. I was so looking forward to seeing Mom and Owen, but the shooting delays have forced me to cancel my plans. While I'm relieved to be staying put, a deep pang of guilt lingers within me for how I must have disappointed them.

Owen, my older brother by four years, has been living in Marblehead for eighteen months after retiring from the Marines and has yet to come and see me. We'd been close as kids, but since Dad passed away, Owen and I haven't talked.

I know Ma has been stressing about it too, and I feel such

guilt about that. I haven't been able to bring myself to make the trip back to Marblehead. It was hard enough after Andy and impossible after Dad. But I know I need to go back. I know I won't heal until I go back to the place that hurt me the most.

The thought causes my stomach to roll and I'm thankful for the breeze sweeping through the air as I walk to my car. When I reach the trunk, dropping my bags in, I realize I didn't say bye to Manny, my favorite security guard at this studio. It's become such a part of my routine to stop and chat with him before going home, and I've been meaning to ask how his wife is doing. Poor Jen was so sick a few days ago, so I sent over some chicken noodle soup and muffins. Is cooking and baking for people a love language? If so, that's how I choose to show my love for people. Forever and ever.

I sit in the driver's seat and turn my car on, but I don't drive away just yet. I'm too busy basking in the icky feelings building up inside me. This year has been so… much. My normally optimistic and glass-half-full personality has been seriously slacking off lately. I don't know what to do to change it, but I know I need a plan.

Make Ma's moussaka recipe and take Frankie for a long walk at Runyon Canyon? Or maybe go to the wrap party? Neither. Pick up ice cream and wine, put on comfies and have a solo dance party in the kitchen? YES!

The almost smile on my face turns into a full-blown grin when I see my BFF's name pop up on my phone screen.

MAEVE

Bonnie! Are you going to the wrap party?

I hope you are. You need some fun to get out of this funk!

More than a best friend and much like a sister (though she already has a twin of her own), Maeve can always put a smile on my face. Ever the Brit, she's called me Bonnie, meaning *beautiful*, since the day we met and she proclaimed my emerald green eyes, plump ass and perky tits should be illegal all on one person. Her words, not mine. I'm about to respond when I see the three little dots flashing.

MAEVE

And if you don't go tonight and decide to go home and dance around the kitchen, I'm coming and we're having ice cream for dinner. No need for fancy meals since we have that all covered between Christmas and NYE! EEK!

I purposely ignore her mention of the New Year's Eve party she's throwing. I'm having eye surgery on the thirty-first and I hope, against all odds, that I can still somewhat enjoy the night. I need to end this year on a higher note than how it started, which was with removing all proof of my last relationship from my life.

ME

It's really eerie how well you know me, you know that? Come over. Lizzo surely has something we can shake our asses to and I'm picking up enough Ben & Jerry's to feed a small village of hormonal PMS-ing women.

MAEVE

You goddess. See you in an hour. I have wine.

AN HOUR later Bruno Mars's "That's What I Like" is coming through the kitchen speakers. I hear the door shut and Maeve's "yoohoo" as she's making her way down the hall. She is a natural-born star. You know when you see someone, and you can tell they're meant to be Hollywood famous? That's Maeve Howard.

When she speaks, everyone in the room hangs on her every word. She enthralls us all with her radiant smile and contagious laughter. Her vivacious energy and enthusiasm fill the air, and no matter the company, she is the life of the party. Her straight blonde hair always seems to fall perfectly around her shoulders, and she's got a charming smattering of freckles on her button nose. If she was a season, she would be summer: bright, warm, eternally sunny. She's singing along to the lyrics and casually grinding into my ass before I can even turn around to greet her. Man, I love this girl.

Over my shoulders, I see her aggressively biting her bottom lip, a bottle of wine in each hand, eyes closed tight. I can tell she's holding back a big smile, trying to be serious as she pushes her crotch into my hip.

"Baaaaaabe, you did it! Our first movie together with you as production designer extraordinaire and you killed it. I'm so proud so let's celebrate the shit out of how awesome you are!" She drops the wine on the countertop and hugs me, jumping up and down. I take in the scent of her lavender shampoo and yes, I really do feel better now.

I swear this girl saved my life on more than one occasion. When I moved away from home after Andy died. When my dad got so sick, I didn't even have time to go see him before *he* died. When that douche canoe Ben ended up cheating on me repeatedly during our three-year relationship. Maeve was there for all of it. She's a constant in my life and I know how lucky I am that I found my soulmate in this woman.

The kiss she leaves on my cheek is loud and proud, but when I take in her face, I can see she likely feels as tired as I do. Her eyes look more like a stormy sea than their usual sky blue. She's been working hard, too. She was the lead actress in the movie we just wrapped today. Yep, it was kind of a dream come true to have my best friend on the same set as me for four entire months.

"Why aren't you going to the wrap party? You should celebrate," I say this to her as I pour us each a generous glass of wine. Wine first, then ice cream.

"I'd much rather spend time with my brilliant BFF. We haven't been able to see one another much outside of the set and I've been looking forward to just being with you." She brings her glass of wine to her lips, swaying her hips. Even tired, Maeve exudes energy.

I smile softly at her. "I've missed you too, Maevey. And you were right earlier. You know how much I hate being in a bad mood. I don't know what it is." I take a sip of wine and she looks at me intently, taking in every word.

"Ugh. Is it because I'm not going to see Mamá for the holidays?" I pause, looking out over the backyard where my dog Frankie (a.k.a. Frank Lloyd Wright) is miserably failing at chasing a bird who is taunting my little labradoodle.

I look back at Maeve. She's waiting for me to process everything out loud, as I always do.

"Do I even have any right to be in a funk? My life is kind of great, isn't it? I bought this house. I've worked on some amazing movies. My career completely took off. What the fuck do I have to be in a damn funk about?"

As I say this, I point to the massive kitchen and look out the window again.

West Hollywood Hills is where I live. I knew I needed to stay in Los Angeles with my job, and I love it here. I'm never over nine miles from any of the major studios. Thanks to some early investing in real estate after my dad passed and left me some money, I get to live in the house of my dreams. Though I'd trade just one more day with my dad for this house, my job, and all my other earthly possessions. Fuck, I'd give it all up for one more minute. Just to hear his laugh.

Maeve doesn't answer any of my questions. She just keeps

sipping and swaying, watching me with eyebrows slightly arched as I have my freak-out. She knows I need time to process either out loud or in my head, or both, before I make sense of things.

"You're right," I say, even though she hasn't said a word. "This is stupid. I should just let it go. Must be my period or Mercury is in retrograde again or something. I'm sure after this wine and some ass shaking I'll be just fi—"

I'm interrupted by the sound of her wine glass coming down hard on the countertop.

"Oh, hellllll, no, Elaina James! No, you do not."

Oh shit, she used my full name. That's not good.

"No more of this '*it could be worse*' bullshit. Take your emotions seriously, just not literally, do you hear me? If you're in a funk, be in a funk. I know it doesn't happen to you often because you don't let it, but it's normal to just feel shitty sometimes and not have a name for it. Feel your feelings, girl. Also, maybe get some *real* dick in you sometime soon? That ought to help."

She wiggles her eyebrows at me when she says the words '*real dick*' because she knows all too well I gave up trying to date or have sex with men after I walked away from that dumpster fire of a relationship last year.

"I know you haven't been with anyone since leaving *he who shall not be named.*" Her voice deepens a little. Her disdain for Ben runs deep. She never liked him. "And I'm not saying you need a man to make yourself happy, but an orgasm or two from something other than your collection of sex toys might feel good."

I scoff at that.

"Oh, please. As if I'm guaranteed even a single orgasm from a man. No, thanks. I got it handled." I shoot her a smile that I know doesn't reach my eyes.

She looks at me, places a gentle hand on my shoulder and says, "Time to get serious. You know what I think, babe? I think you need a break to focus on yourself. Just you. You haven't stopped working since we moved here six years ago. I think you've forgotten how to do things just for you. I think you've focused on your career as a way to avoid other things too."

She squeezes my shoulder knowingly. It's no secret that my best coping tactic is avoidance.

"But before we get too deep into your coping mechanism, let me ask you... when's the last time you read a book? Or went on a non-work trip? I'm talking about no research, just for f-u-n?"

She arches her eyebrows so far up her forehead that I'm afraid she's going to lose them in that beautiful head of blonde hair.

By now, we've both emptied our first glasses of wine and I pour some more, realizing we need to open the next bottle because those were really generous pours. Lizzo is showering us with some essential lyrics as "Good as Hell" comes on. Answering no questions, I dance and sing around the kitchen and Maeve joins me. By the end of the song, I'm feeling *almost* good as hell. And that feels like enough for now.

Maeve and I eat three different kinds of ice cream, finish both bottles of wine, and are both tucked into our own beds by 10 p.m. She basically has her own room at my house, and I have one at hers. It makes BFF sleepovers way more fun when I don't have to share a bed with her. She's a human popsicle who also steals all the covers in her sleep, so I'll pass on the bed-sharing.

———

I WAKE AT 9 A.M., which is early for me when I'm not on set. Mornings are *not* my thing. Maeve's words from last night keep repeating themselves in my head. When *was* the last time I read a book? Or went on a trip just for fun? When did I do something just for me, other than cook meals? I honestly don't remember. So, I make a list of all the things I want to do just because *I* want to do them. Here we go.

·Get a manicure and pedicure - this will make me feel pretty and even if no one sees my toes, I'll know they look nice.

·Have more dance parties in the kitchen. Alone, With other people. Just generally dance more.

·Host a dinner party. Make an extravagant meal. Enjoy every second of the chaos. This is for me because being around people brings me joy.

·Visit Mamá in Marblehead. Tell her I love her. Hug her tightly. Lots.

·Make a new friend? Just at least try. But only if it feels right and good and the vibes are impeccable.

Fuck, I feel lame writing that last one, but all of Ben's friends took his lying, cheating side. I'm also not very good at meeting new people unless they're on the set design team, and then it's hard to be friends with them because I'm their boss and no one wants to be friendly with the boss. Ugh, moving along.

·Go on a trip just for fun. Pick somewhere I haven't been, or somewhere I have been and loved. Go and eat all the delicious things, see all the beautiful things and do whatever the hell I want.

·Kiss someone. Make it someone really kissable. If they suck at it, stop and find someone new. Kiss because I love kissing and because it's fun.

·Buy (and wear) sexy lingerie. Try to make it comfortable. Don't look at the price tags. Feel good about your little secret no one else can see.

·Wax my lady parts. Just because I've always wanted to try it. Because it's new. Because I want to know what it feels like.

Because Lord knows my girly bits haven't gotten any kind of TLC for more days than I care to count.

Alright, well, that's a solid start to a super-duper lame list of things normal women do fairly regularly. Great. I put my notebook down on my nightstand and head to the kitchen for some coffee. The machine isn't programmed to brew it for another forty minutes since I'm not usually up this early on a day off.

Ohhh, maybe I should go for a walk to that cute coffee stand on Santa Monica Blvd. Frankie will love that.

I turn off the coffee timer and notice a piece of paper sitting on the island. It's a note from Maeve.

Bon,

I hope you enjoy your sleep in! I'm off to see Charlie and get things ready for the NYE party, which you are most definitely, absolutely coming to. I don't care if your eye surgery makes you groggy or whatever. You're coming. Also, who books a surgery on New Year's Eve?

I love you. See you tomorrow night for prezzies!
-M

I totally forgot that Charlie—Maeve's twin—landed in LA today. She's coming to spend the holidays with us since

Maeve couldn't fly home to London thanks to this movie being so delayed.

A wave of optimism washes over me as I think about coming home and snuggling on the couch with a cup of hot cocoa to listen to classic Christmas carols while wrapping presents and seeing my best friends tomorrow.

———

NOPE. *No, no no no no. I am not feeling better about everything anymore.*

Christmas isn't the problem. It was a wonderful Christmas. For dinner, I ended up making a traditional Greek meal, all with my mom's recipes, which the girls loved. Charlie was in charge of dessert, and she made a strawberry fool, which is a delicious combination of strawberries, cream, and custard. Maeve was the bartender for the night, and served up delicious cocktails to keep everyone hydrated.

I spent the week preparing to check off items from my list. To satisfy my love of reading, I purchased two books—one murder/mystery and a romance novel—both of which were highly recommended by our resident bookworm, Charlie. As a treat for myself, I also made an appointment for a mani-pedi. Even though my toes are highly ticklish, I thoroughly enjoyed it.

So why the negativity? Well, I just found out I basically won't be able to see after my eye surgery for twelve to twenty-four hours because apparently, my eyes are extra sensitive to light. That's right. I'll be all sober and half-blind tonight, New Year's Eve, and likely unable and/or unwilling to be around a large group of drunk people. Did I mention I also can't drink? Yeah... whose brilliant idea was this, anyway?

Maeve's driver, Gary, picked me up and we're headed

back to her house where the partying will begin in exactly three hours.

"How you doing, Miss Elaina?" Gary's gravelly voice is cheery in a way I simply cannot appreciate at the moment.

"Other than the current fucked up state of my eyeballs, pretty great. How have you been, G? It's been a while."

Gary has been Maeve's driver here in LA for years. He's a gentleman, no taller than my 5'7" frame, and laughs at everything I say, which makes me feel great. Also, he doesn't bat an eyelash at my colorful language.

"I've been well. Thank you for asking. Miss Maeve told me about your plan to get this surgery before year-end no matter what. Any regrets?" I would bet money that he's looking at me through the rear-view mirror with a quipped eyebrow and a little glisten in his brown eyes. I've seen it enough times by now.

"Not yet, but the night is young, right?" I feel my face for the giant sunglasses Dr. Blau insisted I wear. They are huge, and feel more like safety goggles than anything I would ever actually wear in public. "Actually, these glasses. These might be a regret. You can see them, so tell me your honest opinion, Gary. How bad are they?"

His deep chuckle makes my lips quirk up.

"If anyone can pull them off, it's you." I can hear both the lie and the smile in his voice.

The car comes to a gentle stop, and I thank Gary, wishing him a very happy new year before I try to leave and remember I can't see. Gary takes me by the elbow and gently guides me to the front door, letting me know where each step is. I give him a hug that lasts a little too long, but I'm groggy still and maybe these drugs make me more affectionate than usual.

Ha! Not possible.

"Thanks so much, Gary. What would I do without you?" He chuckles as he knocks on the door. "I hope you have the best New Year's Eve ever. Drink some bubbly for me. Give your husband a big, juicy kiss at midnight, alright?"

Ugh, I guess this will be one more year I go without a midnight kiss.

Charlie comes to the door and takes my hand.

"Thanks, Gary. I've got her. Happy New Year!" I hear the front door close, and Charlie wraps an arm around my back. "Well, hey there, pretty girl. Lovely to see your face."

Charlie is making a joke in the most Charlie way possible, meaning it isn't obvious and I think it's hilarious. My giggling makes her snort, and my heart does a happy little somersault. I miss having her around.

"Oh, you've got jokes, Char. I know these glasses cover at least half of my face, but the doc said I need to wear them because of the light sensitivity." She takes me into the kitchen and helps me onto a stool. I hear her moving around the room quietly for a few seconds, then she's back next to me.

"I'll be right back, Lainey. I need to check on something with the caterers. I have some water here for you." I nod and run my finger down the bottle. I wish it was vodka. My eyes definitely hurt a little and I have to keep putting eye drops in them, so they don't dry up. Charlie looks at me... or I think Charlie looks at me.

"Remember, no looking at your phone. I dimmed the lights for you." She pats my hand lightly. "Back in a few." I nod as I hear her walk away.

I'm not supposed to do anything too strenuous, and I have to be very careful about light, so I guess I'm stuck with these crazy-looking sunglasses even inside. At least there's music. Maeve has one of my playlists on. I can tell because I hear "Let Me Love You" by Mario on the speakers, and '90s to early '00s music is kind of my thing. I stand up, needing a little kitchen dance. Just a little one. I take off my shoes and start to move my hips, singing along to the sexy lyrics.

can she see me?

adam

I CAN'T BELIEVE I let Rafael talk me into this. I don't do parties, let alone Hollywood parties where other actors will be present. My parents met on the set of a movie and then married in secret. He was the producer. My mom was pregnant with my sister at their wedding. As such, I grew up living as both an actress's son and in the LA spotlight. Parties were thrown nearly every weekend, and I peeked behind the velvet rope long ago. This is my idea of a nightmare.

It's 9 p.m. on New Year's Eve and I'm at Maeve Howard's mansion. Though I've never met her in person, everyone knows who she is. She made a name for herself in this town in her early twenties, but since I've been a recluse for years, we've never run into one another. We're about to become costars in a few weeks, though, so I guess this is as good a time as any.

A petite redhead lets me in. She looks like Maeve, only not blonde. She introduces herself as Charlie and sends me on my way to the backyard where the party will start anytime now, which means I didn't need to be here until at least ten. Charlie scrunches up her nose and, in a British accent, says, "You're a tad early, mate. If you fancy a drink, the bar's to the left just outside."

I thank her and take a few steps towards the backyard, but the sound of music from inside draws me in. As I make my way to the kitchen, I hear her first, her strong yet husky voice cutting through the music. Curiosity grabs hold of me and I turn the corner slowly.

A woman stands in the middle of the room, auburn hair tumbling down her back, olive skin on toned arms swaying in the air. The ripped jeans she wears fit her hips snugly, and she bops to the beat with her eyes closed.

I feel strange standing there watching, but unable to look away. Suddenly, as if on cue, she turns towards me and I'm frozen in place.

My mind races as I prepare an explanation for being caught practically spying. She has huge sunglasses on, and she doesn't seem to notice me.

Huh.

There's a smile on her face and *damn*, it's beautiful. Her lips are heart shaped and I can see a set of perfectly straight teeth as she smiles. Her moves become a little more confident, a little looser. She brings her arms up over her head and then tosses her hair upward.

I watch for a few more seconds, mesmerized by the curves of her body and her lips as she sings along with the lyrics. Her jeans are hugging in *all* the right places and she's barefoot, her black top riding up slightly to reveal a sliver of smooth skin.

The sound of her honey-soaked voice fills the room, and I can feel my heart swell in my chest. I'm pulled in by something even greater than her singing—her smile. It's wide, infectious, radiating a warmth that makes it hard to look away.

Without thinking, and because I suddenly feel a weird

lump there, I clear my throat and I catch her shocked expression when she realizes someone else is in the room.

She loses her balance as she spins, and I instinctively reach out for her, catching her by the arms before she goes down.

"Gahhh! What the hell, Charlie? Are you trying to kill me?" She hardly gets to the end of her question before she stiffens completely.

"Wait, who are you? Gary? No, you don't smell like Gary. You smell like…" Her hands wrap around my biceps, and she lifts her chin, seeming to sense where my eyes are but not quite making eye contact. I can almost see her eyes, but the glasses she's wearing are dark, and she's squinting.

Can she not see me?

"You smell like a forest and a little like soap," she continues. "Gary smells like peppermint. And you're tall. Like really tall. Gary is short. Why am I still talking and grabbing a stranger's arms in my best friend's kitchen?" She lets go abruptly.

"I'm sorry, it's just that I can't see right now and I'm a bit of a babbler when I'm nervous. Uh. Anyway, thanks for catching me, umm… who are you?"

I smile to myself at her rambling, silently wishing she would keep going. Her smile is gone and her lips are parted, her breathing is a little heavy and god, I've never wanted to kiss a stranger more in my whole life.

Wait. What? No. I don't do that. That's weird, man.

I let her arms go gently. I miss her touch the moment our contact is broken.

But why?

Before I can answer my own question, she takes a step back and I come back to the moment, clearing my throat.

"I'm Adam. I arrived a little early and Charlie let me in. My friend gave me the wrong time, so here I am very early for a party I didn't really want to come to. I'm sorry if I startled you."

Now, I'm the rambling one. What the fuck is happening?

She still seems a bit stunned and begins to respond, but no sound comes out of her mouth. A small frown forms on her face and she seems a little paler than before.

"Uh, I think I need to sit down." Her voice is quiet and a little grainy. "I just had eye surgery and I can't really see. Also, even with these ridiculous glasses on, it feels a little too bright in here. Do you think you could lead me to the living room, Adam? Please? It's just over there."

She points to the left at an open door to a darkened room. Her sweet voice saying my name and *please* playing over in my head. I want to understand what this feeling in my chest is, why the vulnerability in her voice is doing strange things to my insides. Instead, I push away my thoughts and move to help her.

I take her by the right elbow and guide her toward the living room. I want to just pick her up and take her, but that would be beyond weird and inappropriate, so I just nudge her along, making sure she doesn't get too close to any walls or bump into anything.

When we get inside the room, I don't turn the lights on, remembering they were bothering her in the kitchen. I keep guiding her toward the couch in the middle of the room. "You'll feel the couch next to your knee now. You can sit down right here."

She sits, slowly and whispers, "Thank you, Adam." And damn, I feel a tight knot tugging at my chest, hearing her saying my name like that. I want to hear it again. In an effort to snap myself out of this... whatever this is, I let go of her arm.

"I'll be right back, okay?"

She nods and sinks into the couch. I rush back into the kitchen and grab the unopened bottle of water off of the island and a bowl of strawberries someone left by the sink and get back to the living room.

As I enter the room, I see her sunglasses lying on the coffee table and her head has fallen back against the cushions of the couch. Her eyes are closed, and her face is relaxed.

"Hey, I brought you a snack and some water." I set the water and strawberries down on the coffee table. "Are you okay? I didn't even get your na—"

Huh. She's asleep.

Gingerly, I step closer, my heart thudding against my chest. The beautiful stranger is fast asleep, and her neck is bent at an awkward angle, her long lashes fluttering in slumber.

I try nudging her shoulder gently to wake her, but she only stirs slightly, so I move the pillows and carefully ease her back so she can rest more comfortably. She looks so peaceful, her breaths slow and deep.

There's a blanket draped on the back of the couch, so I put that on her and brush the hair off her face. She doesn't stir, completely still and silent apart from the soft puff of breath from her slightly parted lips. I stare for a moment too long, considering this is a complete stranger.

Get a grip, dude.

I leave before I creep myself out any further. Walking back into the kitchen, I hear a familiar voice.

"Ah, River. Have you seen a tall, auburn-haired girl in jeans and a black tank top? She's wearing very large sunnies inside, so she's hard to miss. She can't see very well at the moment and I've somehow lost her." Charlie is pacing around the kitchen, looking frazzled.

"Uh yeah, actually. She's asleep in the next room. Is she alright?"

I don't know why I'm asking. I do not know this girl and it's none of my business.

"She just had surgery and her eyes are a bit sensitive. She's probably a little loopy from the medication as well. It's all very typical for someone who's undergone this procedure." She straightens and looks at me, not quite in the eyes.

"Thanks for helping her out, River. She's like a sister to Maeve and I so she's staying here tonight, though I doubt she'll be partying out there." I see a look of concern across Charlie's face, but it's interrupted by the sound of someone else coming into the kitchen.

"Char, please tell me you've found Bonnie." Maeve bursts through the door, her eyes nearly popping out of her head.

"River, hi, you came!" Her voice gets louder with each word, and I can tell she's surprised to see me. Probably because I'm the first person to show up to her party and I'm in her kitchen, where I have no business being.

"Hi, Maeve." I reach out to shake her hand. "It's nice to finally meet you. Thanks for letting me tag along with Raf tonight."

"Lainey is asleep in the living room, Mae. Don't worry." Charlie's exasperation is balanced with the warm, kind look in her eyes that reminds me so much of my sister, Gwen. Growing up, she always seemed to know when things were beyond my control and had a way of communicating that helped me feel like I wasn't so alone. Her comforting presence was a reminder that I had the privilege of having a supportive older sister who could help me through anything.

"Oh, thank goodness." Maeve takes my hand and gives me a small smile. "Thank you. And sorry about my entrance. Lainey is my beautiful best friend who promised herself she'd finally have her eye surgery this year, so of course, she made it happen on December 31st."

She's out of breath when she finishes talking, but despite her agitation, there's a gentle tone in her voice that tells me she cares deeply for this Bonnie.

… or is it Lainey?

"I'm going to check on her quickly. I see you've met my twin sister, Charlie. Please make yourself at home! Raffy should be here any second." She smiles again and walks towards the door where I know a beautiful, mysterious woman sleeps, and I feel a little envious that Maeve gets to go see her and I don't.

My mind goes back to her singing, hips swaying to the music. I've never been so hypnotized by someone like that.

Charlie breaks my sleeping beauty daydream by clearing her throat. "Shall we head outside? Rafael has arrived. I can hear his ridiculous laugh." She frowns, like she's annoyed by the sound even from here.

I give my head a shake and follow her to the backyard where the music is now playing loudly. I see Raf's wide, toothy smile as he chats with a woman I don't recognize. "Riv, there you are!" He excuses himself from the conversation and pats me on the shoulder in a half-hug.

"Yeah, dude. I'm here. You told me nine." I scowl at him and throw a fake punch to his ribs.

"I didn't think you'd actually be on time. Sorry, bro. And I wanted you to ease into the party. I knew if you showed up and the place was packed, you'd turn around and leave before you even made it to the door." He raises one eyebrow at me, giving me a knowing look. Raf is my best friend. We've known each other since we were kids and no one knows me better than him, other than maybe my sister, Gwen.

I huff out a loud sigh. "You know me too well, man."

"You bet your ass I do. Now let's grab a drink and get you socializing with some people, preferably of the single female variety." His eyebrows dance up and down his forehead and he steers me towards the bar with an arm around my shoulder.

"Being a hot movie star should make it pretty easy for you to meet a beautiful woman, no?" I don't feel much like drinking. Or socializing. He knows that I've been questioning my purpose and place in the world, and I can tell that my friend is trying to be supportive. He keeps offering advice and reassuring me that I have a lot to offer.

And he's right about one thing. Being a well-known actor does make meeting women easier, actually. But they're never the women I want to meet. Never anyone I have any interest in spending time with. I let him take me to the bar and tell myself one drink won't hurt.

————

I DON'T EVEN FINISH that first drink. By the time ten o'clock hits, I'm so far done with talking to strangers and making small talk. On a whim, I put my drink down and walk towards the gate that I assume leads to the front of the house. I'm about to call for my car when I see the lights on inside, remembering sleeping beauty.

I wonder how she's doing. Is she awake? I hope she's feeling better.

What. Is. Happening? Why am I thinking about this girl so much? It's been years since I gave any woman more than a moment's thought.

I take a deep breath, my heart pounding as I step into the house. My feet shuffle across the floorboards with agonizing slowness, each footstep seeming to take forever.

When I finally stand outside the door, I release a deep sigh and shake my head. I have never been indecisive before, and the fact that I can't make up my mind this time is deeply unsettling. After what seems like an eternity, I finally muster enough courage to reach for the door handle.

I'm gonna have to talk to my therapist about this.

Finally, I push the door open slowly because she could still be asleep. She's sitting on the couch with her head back, feet on the coffee table, knees folded up and she's cursing like a sailor. I let out a laugh the moment I hear the profanities coming out of her full pink lips.

3 /
is the word 'lubrication' even sexy?

elaina

"...SUCKER, PIECE OF SHIT, MOTHERFU—" I sense him before I hear him. His laugh is deep, and he sounds genuinely amused by what he sees. I can imagine it's something like a crazed girl with wet spots all over her face and chest, aiming everywhere but at her actual eyeballs with the eye drops.

"I'm glad I can be of amusement," I smile and say with no cynicism in my voice.

He chuckles as he closes the door behind him. I should be concerned since I can't see a goddamn thing, but I think it's Adam—the guy who helped me earlier. At least I hope it is. He had a friendly voice and smelled so. Damn. Good.

"Sorry, I've just never heard so many swear words strung together like that before. You're a modern-day poet." I can hear the smile in his voice as he says this, though I can't even see my hand in front of me and I have no clue what this man looks like.

I snort-laugh. "Thanks. Adam?" I'm at least looking in the right direction. I can tell because I see the movement as he steps closer to the couch.

"Yeah. Sorry, I should have announced myself. Hi, *tornerose*. No, wait... Bonnie? Or is it Lainey?" My stomach does a little flip.

What did he just call me? How does he know my nickname? He's obviously talked to Maeve.

Suddenly, my mouth feels a little dry.

Get a grip, Elaina. Are you so starved of male attention you'll let a total stranger you can't even see get you all worked up? Snap out of it.

Yeah, that checks out. I need to get it together. I clear my throat. "Lainey is fine, though you've obviously met Maeve, if you know her other nickname for me. Not sure where *tornerose* came from though..." I feel the sofa shift and I can tell he's sitting next to me. Not too close, but close enough that I smell his soapy scent again.

"How did you get the nickname Bonnie, with a name like Lainey?" I feel him shift. He must have put his arm on the back of the couch. I can feel the warmth of his body closer to my shoulder. "As for tornerose, that's your newest nickname, I suppose. I'm the one who gave it you since you slept through my attempts at waking you earlier."

"Oh. Umm. Are you the one who moved me down and put a blanket on me?" I can feel the blazing heat rush up my neck to my cheeks.

Why are my palms sweating? Oh, right... because a strange, delicious-smelling guy manhandled you and tucked you in. Am I in a rom-com? The 'com' obviously being my disheveled state and temporary partial blindness. Insert eye-roll here.

He reaches over and takes the bottle of eye drops from my hand. Our fingers brush and that lava hot heat is now making its way from my fingertips to my arms.

"That's right. You passed out before I got back with your water and strawberries, which I can see you found." He must spy the empty bowl of strawberries on the table.

I was feeling around for the table and found a bottle of

water and strawberries, assuming Maeve or Charlie left them there for me. His voice is deep and gentle. It's also very familiar, but I'm almost certain we've never met.

"Oh… thank you. For the water and strawberries. Strawberries are like my kryptonite. Though that's probably not the right saying, because they can't hurt me, I just love them so much I could eat them forever. They're my weakness. They're a perfect fruit, you know? They go well with just about any other fruit and they're in all the best desserts. The seeds don't need to be removed, they look like little hearts, and they're a perfect size. They're like nature's candy."

Shut up, shut up, shut up!

He chuckles softly, and the sound sends a chill up my spine. My body is so confused. Hot, cold, ice, lava…

What are we doing here?

"I'll agree with you on this one. Strawberries are pretty perfect."

I feel a smile tug at the corners of my lips. "Hmm… something about your voice seems familiar…"

I'm now trying as hard as I can to see his face, squinting like I'm staring at the sun. I'm sure the effect is nothing short of magical for this stranger who, for some unknown reason, seems to want to be trapped in this room with me.

"Are you trying to see my face?" he asks with an amused tone.

"Uh huh… Hold still, would ya?"

"How's that going for you, squinty?" Another nickname. Another belly somersault. I inhale a deep, quick breath.

Settle the fuck down, Elaina.

There's silence for several seconds in the room until finally, he says, "Lay your head back. You need to put these eye drops in, right? And I don't think your shirt needs any more lubrication tonight."

Cheese on rice. Did he just say lubrication? And why does that do weird things to my insides? What's in the pain meds that the surgeon gave me?

"Oh, it's alright. You don't have to," I say, flustered and a little dizzy from trying to see his face. Not because of his face, but because my vision is blurry, and trying to see feels pretty fucking terrible right now.

"Come on. Put your head back. I won't hurt you. I promise." His voice and his words set off a whole world of feelings inside my body. Tingles in my arms and fingertips. A sudden weight in the pit of my stomach.

Why do I believe him when I don't even know him?

He urges my forehead down gently with his fingertips and I let him. And now he's moving again. I'm assuming he's kneeling on the couch so he can see where the drops will go. He brushes some stray hairs off of my face and I move my head towards where I think his face is.

"Hold still, would ya?" He mimics my phrase from moments ago and it makes me smile. I can feel his breath on my cheeks. It smells faintly of alcohol and mint. I swallow and keep my head as still as possible.

He puts two drops into each eye, his free hand holding the side of my face tenderly. And when some of the solution drips down my face, he catches it with his thumb, running it across my cheek. I flinch at the intimacy of his touch.

"I'm sorry. I shouldn't have done that." He almost whispers the last sentence. I hear him place the bottle on the table and he moves to get up from the couch. I reach out my hand, hoping it doesn't fall anywhere inappropriate.

"No, it's okay." Thankfully, my hand lands on his forearm. His very muscled, very hard forearm.

Not the time, you hussy.

"Thank you for helping me today, Adam. You don't even know me, and you've been very kind to me. Thank you."

"You're welcome, Lainey. It was very nice to meet you." He moves to get up again and I double down. Both hands are now on his forearm and I'm questioning how my body seems to move faster than my brain can even process just what the fuck I'm doing.

"Wait. Um… would it be awful to ask you to stay with me a bit?" My grip is still tight, but hopefully not in a creepy, desperate way. He seems to relax and sit back down. "I've been alone in here and I'm so bored with not being able to see and all. I'll even send you a fruit basket as a thank you!"

A fruit basket? Are you insane?

"I'll only stay if you make it a basket of nothing but strawberries." His forearms are rock solid beneath my touch, and I gingerly remove my hands from his arms, willing my body to relax.

"Of course. Only the best of the best for you." I try to sound casual, but I'm not sure it's working. I want him to stay. Not just because I'm now wide awake in a mostly darkened room by myself on New Year's Eve, but because something about this person has me curious. I want to know more.

His deep, low chuckle makes a comeback and I shiver at the sound. Actually shiver. I feel him settle into the couch and a ridiculous sense of relief fills me. I didn't scare him away. At least not yet.

"So, Lainey, Charlie and Maeve told me you set a goal and didn't want to miss it, hence the eye surgery?" He picks something up and pushes an object on the coffee table closer to me. "I brought you another bottle of water, by the way. It's by your right knee."

I swallow, suddenly feeling my throat dry up. "Oh. Th-thank you. You really don't have to keep doing these things for me. Honestly, you don't even know me…" I reach for the water, drinking at least half of the bottle.

"It's alright. You're kind of helping me as much as I'm helping you. I really didn't want to be with a group of drunk people tonight." After a long silence, he says, "You're not going to say anything to that? Not going to ask me why?"

"Oh. No. I was giving you time to think, in case you wanted to elaborate. Sometimes I find people react or respond too quickly to something someone says, and it just seemed like you had more to say." I take another drink. "Plus, if you wanted to tell me why, I'm giving you the chance to, since it's the natural follow-up question."

"Do you not want to know why?" he asks this with a genuinely curious tone.

"I want to know everything you want to tell me, Adam." Annnnnnd my cheeks are flushed again. To people who know me, they know this statement is 100 percent true. I am always ready and willing to listen. But he's still a stranger. I need to reel in the familiarity. Stat!

"Really? Why's that? Are you a journalist? Reporter? Work for some media company?" Now he sounds a little annoyed. Huh. Interesting. His guard is up.

I chuckle because that couldn't be further from what I do for a living. Though I do genuinely like getting to know people and understanding how they think. I haven't had the chance to do this, speak so freely and openly with someone new in… months.

"No, no. None of the above. I'd actually prefer it if we didn't talk about work if that's okay? I don't know what you do, and I'm not going to ask. If you want to keep talking in the dark with me, we can keep doing that. Just no work talk. I'm trying to focus on everything but work right now. Is that alright?"

I suddenly don't know what to do with my hands.

Is he going to think this is a strange request? Probably. Is he going to think I'm some sort of psycho? It's likely he does already.

He lets out a breath, sounding much more relaxed. "Yeah, I'm very okay with that. I don't really want to talk about work either."

"Good. So, you don't want to be around the drunk folks. What else?"

I tuck my legs under me so I can face him, even though I can't see him. I can tell he has dark hair and maybe a beard. I know he's tall, and he smells like soap and maybe pine or eucalyptus. It makes me think of fresh mountain air. He's wearing a light shirt and dark pants. And that's all I can tell from the dimly lit room and my very blurry vision.

"That's it. I just didn't feel like being around many people. I was about to leave and then I decided to come here and check on you. I wanted to talk to *you*, just not anyone else."

His voice fades away as he gets to the end of that statement. I think he's as shocked as I am that he said it and I'm pretty sure I hear him mumble something like *'fucking idiot, why did you say that'* under his breath.

I pull my lips between my teeth to keep from smiling too big. I can't help it. His honesty is refreshing, and I want to talk to him too.

I see his arm come up like he's maybe scratching the back of his head. "Anyway, you didn't answer my question earlier."

"Oh? What question is that?" I keep my tone light.

"Why get surgery on New Year's Eve?" He almost sounds like he's back to normal. The previous disgruntlement is barely present in his voice.

"I promised myself I'd do it this year. I'm always so busy with w-o-r-k and I kept making excuses not to get it done. Thankfully, my ophthalmologist was fine with a December 31st surgery and here I am."

I chuckle, but there's not much humor in the sound.

"I didn't think it'd be this bad, to be honest. I figured I'd be able to see within a few hours."

He's silent for a beat and I think he's using my 'waiting for the person to keep going' tactic.

Quickly, I prattle out, "Also, I've been meaning to do this for about two years, and my ex always hated the idea of me not being able to cook dinner for the evening. He didn't do takeout. Or his work schedule was too crazy, and he couldn't handle the stress of me being in recovery without him around. Or he had to travel and didn't want me to be alone because I might set my house on fire or something if I couldn't see. There was always a reason."

I say this all stoically because it's all true. Ben was a real piece of work.

"What a fucking asshole." He says this barely loud enough for me to hear. "Please tell me you're the one who ended it with this douche canoe." He lets out a loud breath.

"After I found out he had been cheating on me for two out of our three years together? Yes, I dumped the douche canoe." I smile proudly because this honestly doesn't even bother me anymore. Also, I really like that he used the term douche canoe.

Silence. For a long time, this time. But not awkward, which is... alarming considering we've only known one another long enough to bake a batch of muffins.

"You know I can't see you if you're making weird facial expressions at my overshare about the idiot I broke up with last year, right?" Now I'm worried. Maybe this was too much all at once. Damn my rambling ways.

"Sorry, I'm just trying to process how a guy manages all that assholery and gets away with it for that long."

I laugh, mostly because he sounds so serious and the word assholery is so perfect. "Honestly, I'm still not sure. But I don't dwell on any of it. His cheating had a lot more to do with him than it did with me."

"Hmm. You've obviously got a great therapist." He says this with zero judgment or condescension in his tone.

"Oh yeah. I've had several, actually." I smile and wiggle my eyebrows up and down. "But enough about Ben and his cheating, smaller than average, severely crooked cock. Your turn to share something deeply personal with someone you just met hours ago."

He makes a choking sound, then spits out, "Did you just describe your ex's penis to a near stranger? I think I'm a little in love with you, Lainey." And we both burst out laughing for a long time. His laugh is wonderful. It bubbles up from deep within and escapes in a rolling rumble that reverberates through me like a bass line. It leaves me feeling warm and filled with joy. I really wish I could see him laugh right now, too.

I put my face in my hands, actually feeling slightly embarrassed, but also a little free, speaking so candidly like this. Normally this is reserved for friends only, and the fact that I'm talking like this to a guy is… surprising, to say the least. "Alright, Adam. Go on."

He clears his throat and takes a deep breath. "Um… let's see." I hear him scratch his head, or maybe it's his beard? "I'm a huge Harry Styles fan. He seems like such a cool person and I really like his music."

Silence again. Because I am shook.

A strange gurgling sound leaves my mouth. "Sorry. You mean like the guy that used to be in One Direction, right?"

"Yes, Lainey. That's the guy." I like the sound of my name out of his mouth way too much. Way, way too much. "I've never told anyone about my Harry Styles admiration, so this is a big deal, okay? It's no cheating ex, but there isn't much to tell when it comes to my love life, anyway. So, Harry Styles it is."

I swear I can hear the shrug of his shoulders.

I laugh again, because I can't hold back. I hear him laugh softly, and I can feel him looking at me. Like all over me. And that crazy ice-lava thing is happening again. Chills. Heat. All at once.

"Hey Adam? I think we need to be friends." And just like that, without planning it or trying or even being able to see, I might cross another item off my list and I'm feeling damn good about it.

did i just get friend-zoned?

adam

THE SOUND of her unrestrained laughter and the brightness of her smile are contagious. My body feels lighter, and I know I made the right call coming in here instead of going home, or worse, staying at the party. I can't take my eyes off of her.

There's a dimple on her left cheek and she throws her head back when she laughs, revealing the long line of her neck. The whole thing makes me want to take a picture of her just so I can look back and see what joy looks like on someone as beautiful as her. From the tips of her black, painted toenails to the now lopsided russet-colored bun atop her head, I can't look away.

When she says we need to be friends, I immediately want to respond in two ways:

1. Yes! Talking to her is so easy and I'm not ready to stop. I don't remember the last time I talked to anyone for longer than fifteen minutes and couldn't wait for it to be over.

2. Damn, did I just get friend-zoned before she even sees my face?

So, I go with, "I'd really like that, Lainey." And the way

her whole face lights up tells me I picked the right response. "Let's see, new friend, we need to get some fundamentals out of the way."

"For fuck's sake, Adam, if you tell me you hate puppies, don't eat ice cream or think *Friends* is overrated, I am reneging on the friendship comment."

Her face is serious in a way that tells me those things are actually important to her, but also that she wouldn't actually judge me if I was lactose intolerant.

I chuckle. She's funny, and I don't even think she means to be. And I like that she swears. I'm around people who want to do nothing but be their most proper, rehearsed selves all the time, so this is refreshing.

"No, nothing like that. I love animals, ice cream is one of my favorite things and I can't hear the word 'pivot' without laughing." In true form, a snort of a laugh escapes me, thinking about that damn episode with the couch.

"But there are essential things we need to know about one another to understand our friendship compatibility."

Her eyes widen and her eyebrows jump up. Somehow, her smile gets even bigger, and that little dimple taunts me.

"Of course! You're right. There *are* essentials we need to know. You ask first because I just got three very crucial things answered nearly perfectly and I'm worried you're some sort of mind reader."

Damnit, she's cute. "Best movie snack foods?"

She scoffs. "Easy." She puts up a finger. "Popcorn loaded with butter and a glass of wine. Coke if wine isn't on the menu for whatever reason. None of that diet shit, either. For sweets, always milk duds." She slaps her hand on her lap, confident she's just aced the test. "Yours?"

"We can work with this. Though I will say the nachos with the disgusting yellow cheese are a good popcorn alternative. I've never had wine with popcorn, but I'm willing to try it." I watch her facial expressions as I respond, and she seems pleased. "Your turn."

"I know you said you love animals, but.... cats or dogs?" She holds her breath immediately after asking, so I sense there's a lot of weight on this seemingly simple question.

"Dogs. Obviously." I keep my tone flat, but I want to laugh, seeing her let out her breath loudly, another of those wide smiles taking over her face.

"Thank. Goodness. I was legitimately worried you'd say something crazy like *both*. I should also tell you I have a dog. He is perfect in every way. His name is Frankie, and he's an excellent judge of character who hates all men. So, you've been warned, for... you know... when you meet him." She smiles shyly when she finishes speaking and that adorable blush spreads from her cheeks to her neck again.

The words *when you meet him* play in my head. I want to meet her dog. I want to know this girl. Really know her. And now I'm staring at her, neither of us speaking.

"Oh. My turn," I finally say, my mind full of questions for her, but also void of any actual intellectual thought.

"You catch on quick." She shifts on the couch and inches closer to me. Her knee is now pressed against my jeans and I can feel its warmth through the thick fabric.

I clear my throat. "Where did you grow up?" *Yeah, that seems safe.*

"Massachusetts. A small town called Marblehead on the coast. I pretty much always wanted to live there, but then..." She scrunches up her face before continuing. "Then I left for NYU, spent summers in London with Maeve and Char, moved to LA and I never went back other than for a few visits to see my family, but it's been a long time." She looks down at her lap and her voice is almost a whisper when she mentions her family. "And you?"

"I've never been to Massachusetts. I grew up in California. Here, in LA, mostly. Most of my family still lives here."

Wanting to avoid any further talk about my family, I move on.

"If you could live anywhere, where would you live?" I lean closer to her, needing to take in more of her. When I talk, she looks at me like there's nothing else she'd rather be doing —even if she can't look directly in my eyes, she's focused on what I'm saying, not what I look like or what the next question will be. She's just focused on the now.

"Here. It's my favorite place in the world. It's where I feel the most at home, and the fact that it's pretty much always sunny really amps up the allure. I love New York and London, but the weather… no, thanks."

Her eyes move over me, like she's trying to see me. For a second I think she can, and I feel a slight panic. I don't want to ruin this night with her recognizing me. She takes my silence to mean she can keep talking and I'm thankful for it.

"London and New York are special to me. I found myself in those cities. And my soulmates. Maeve and Charlie… they're more than my best friends. They're my sisters. They're a part of me." She heaves a deep sigh, and her eyebrows furrow together as her forehead creases with apprehension.

"They saved me. I wasn't just broken when we started living together, I was gone. My body was here, but my spirit… it was gone." She swallows, as if it takes great effort to do so and sniffles, but I don't see tears.

"You know, Charlie said the same thing about you earlier. That you're like a sister. That's… that's really beautiful. Especially coming from someone who is a twin." I lick my lips, unsure of how to continue this. The way she looked when she talked about herself being broken makes my chest hurt. Unsure of what to say, I settle on, "You're really lucky to have found one another." That feels lame, but also true.

She shakes her head. "I'm the lucky one. Maeve knows what I'm feeling before I even do sometimes. And Charlie has this uncanny ability to see things so clearly when others can't." She pauses for a moment, takes a long breath, then abruptly looks up. "Favorite meal? Like if you could only eat one thing for the rest of your life, what would it be?"

I guess we're moving on.

"Hmm, that's easy. Thanksgiving dinner. Turkey, stuffing, cranberry sauce, the desserts… all the things. I don't recall the last time I had a full Thanksgiving meal. I was probably seven or eight." I smile at her, but the smile on her face fades. "What's yours?"

She tucks a stray hair behind her ear and licks her lips. Now I'm staring at her lips. Her plump pink lips. *Focus!* "Chicken pot pie. Ugh. God, I'm in lust with that fucking meal." She licks her lips again. She really needs to stop doing that. "It's so comforting and the flaky pastry with the mushy potatoes is the perfect texture combination, plus there's the fact that it's delicious both hot and cold so—"

"What? No, Lainey. Just… no." I make a disgusted face at her, shaking my head. But she can't see any of it.

"I don't understand. You have a problem with my favorite food choice?" Her tone is serious, but when she speaks, her lips twitch as though she's trying to hold back a smile. Her cheeks flush as she loses the battle and an impish grin spreads across her face.

"Where do I even begin? And *cold*?" I make a throwing up noise and the loud, uninhibited laugh that erupts from her is… it's intoxicating. I've got to make her laugh like this again, but I'm out to make a point about this damn pie.

"It's leftovers inside of a pastry! How can you eat that?"

She laughs even harder, wiping a tear from her right eye.

"I have never ever had anyone have such a visceral reaction to chicken pot pie before." She giggles.

"Oh, fuck, and that sound you just made. Shit, that was funny." She snorts, reliving the moment until she finally calms down. "Alright, so we agree to disagree on this one."

She leans to put her hand on the couch seat in front of her, her warm palm landing right on the back of my hand.

"And Adam? I will make you a full Thanksgiving dinner. Anytime you want." Her voice is like her touch, gentle and sweet.

I don't know what to react to first. Her hand squeezing mine before regrettably sliding away, or the sincerity and kindness in her last statement.

"It'll give me a chance to cross another item off my list—hosting a dinner party. And we don't have to wait until November. That's too far away. You need to eat your favorite meal before then." She's leaning her temple on the back of the couch and that shy, tight-lipped smile is back.

"What list?" I ask, maybe too quickly, realizing I didn't acknowledge her offer to cook me a meal. I can't remember the last time someone cooked for me who wasn't paid to do so.

"Oh, I made a list. Of things I'm going to do just for me this year. Well, next year. Maeve gave me the idea. I've been hyper focused on my career and while it's been wonderful because I love what I do, it's time for a break. There aren't any upcoming projects that need my immediate attention, so... I made a list."

A warm smile lights up her expression, but her gaze shifts downward, and she nervously fiddles with the loose thread of a pillow. I can sense her hesitation, as if she's embarrassed, uncomfortable, or maybe just unsure of herself. "Can I ask what else is on the list?" I want to know what she deems worthy enough to put on it.

What are the things she wants to do just for herself?

"Oh. Ummm n-no. Not yet. I just—I haven't shared the contents with anyone and some of it is quite... personal." She's still playing with the thread on the pillow, her squinty gaze landing somewhere on my face. "Do you have a beard?"

Another topic change. Hmm.

"Yeah, it's for a, uh—it's new."

Not me nearly telling the perfect stranger I grew a beard for a role. Idiot.

"Can I… could I… no, never mind, that's inapr—" She waves her hand in front of her face, as if erasing the thought.

I gently take her wrist and bring her hand to my cheek. "Go ahead." And the sound of my voice saying the words stuns me. I hate strangers touching me, and I just willingly put this woman's hand on my face.

Her touch is stiff at first, then her fingers tenderly curl around my face. I can feel the tips of her fingers lightly tracing the contours of my jawline and cheeks. My eyes flutter closed, and I can't help but savor this moment, my heart pounding in my chest and my breath catching in my throat.

Open your eyes.

She takes in a sharp breath. "Oh, it's shorter than I thought. And softer. Hmm." Her fingers graze my jaw one last time and she pulls away, her lower lip clamped between her teeth. I feel my fingertips twitch with the desire to pull her lip out and feel the softness of it with my own, but I clench my fists and restrain myself.

"I'm sorry. I'm not normally so forthright with people. Not being able to see your facial expressions is making me a little bolder." She lets out a short, nervous laugh. "Or maybe you just have that effect on people?"

"No, I don't think that's it. I don't know that most people are usually so open and honest with me. I really appreciate that about you, Lainey. This is easily the best conversation I've had all year."

Apparently there's truth serum in the water here. What the fuck, Adam.

She smiles. That open, genuine smile she seems to just give away so freely. The sudden thunderous sound of a countdown interrupts my thoughts. Lainey's bright green eyes widen as she seems to look right through me.

10, 9, 8...

We both sit paralyzed in the moment, straining our ears to listen.

7, 6...

My heart beats faster. My brain goes blank.

5, 4...

All I see are the shadows dancing on her face. Her breath-takingly sweet face.

3, 2, 1!

And my stupid, empty brain decides this is the moment to tell my body to move into action. My arm shoots out and my hand rests on her shoulder before my brain has time to process what I'm doing. I lean in to whisper, "Happy New Year, *tornerose*," and my lips brush the soft skin of her cheek. In an instant, the moment is over.

I'm just about to chastise myself for doing something so incredibly foolish when I feel her hand back on my cheek. She turns her face and returns my kiss. I feel the softness of her lips beneath my beard and my entire body heats when I hear her breathy, "Happy New Year, Adam."

We move in slow motion. Our departure from one another is both gradual and cautious, as if sudden movements might break the spell we both seem to be under.

She clears her throat quietly. "Well, in the spirit of honesty and the new year, I can honestly say I don't know when I last had a midnight kiss on New Year's Eve, so thanks for that." She sounds detached, and maybe a little anxious. I think she's trying to diffuse the palpable tension currently taking up residence in this room.

I make a weird noise in my throat. "Should we keep going with the questions, or are you too tired?"

"I'm a night owl, so midnight is normally early for me.

But this surgery seems to have taken the wind out of my sails, so maybe I should head to bed." She reaches for the coffee table, nearly knocking over her empty bottle of water. "Is my phone here somewhere? I can call Charlie or Maeve to help me."

"I don't think they'd hear you with the noise levels out there. I'll help." I grab her phone and place it in her hand, and she swiftly unlocks it with facial recognition.

"Um, okay. Can you text Maeve for me and just let her know I've gone to bed? Please." She's handing me the phone, and I immediately know what I'm going to do. Several seconds later, she asks, "You okay there? Still texting?"

I look up and smile. "No, I was just adding my number to your phone. Friends have one another's phone numbers, right?" I honestly don't know what's gotten into me. Less than ten people have my phone number and I just spoon fed it to someone I've known for... three hours?

She flashes me a crooked smile and says, "Well then, you might as well text yourself, so you have mine too, *friend*."

The way she says "friend" makes me uneasy. The dimly lit room seems to close in around us. I force a smile and take her hand, placing her phone back in it with a gentle squeeze.

"Wait here a second. I'll be right back to take you to bed. Uh–to take you to your bedroom. To *walk* you to your bedroom. I'll just... be right back."

I really need to get my head checked. What am I, sixteen again? Fumbling my words, getting all fired up over a kiss on the cheek? Fuck.

I open the fridge to get her some water and grab two bottles, shoving one into my pocket and rushing back to the living room. She's sitting with her hands on her lap, holding her phone, eye drops and sunglasses. Her head turns when she hears me come in, a tight smile on her face. She stands as I approach, and I take her elbow like I had done earlier.

"Which way to your room, L?" When she snaps her head

towards me, I catch the smell of her hair again. Coconut and honey. I also notice she's stiffer this time than any of the previous times I got close to her tonight.

Shit.

"You have a thing with nicknames, huh?" Her body relaxes a bit, and she turns back towards the hallway. She doesn't wait for my response. "Up the stairs, second door on the left. The lamp should be on in there, so it'll be easy to find." She stops walking and clears her throat, takes a deep breath. "Thank you so much for... for everything tonight. I hope my oversharing wasn't too much. Sometimes I can be a lot. I really had a wonderful time tonight and I'm really glad... I'm really glad you walked in on my ridiculous kitchen dancing earlier." Her playful tone is back, and she lets out a little laugh. Thank goodness.

"I had a really enjoyable time tonight, too. I like your over-sharing. And there was nothing ridiculous about your dancing." Her wide smile fades a bit and she bites her bottom lip again, sending all of my brain cells into a coma.

We say nothing else as I lead her up the stairs. When we get to her room, I let go of her elbow. She seems to know her way around now and walks over to the dresser to put her things down. "I have water bottles for you. Can I put them on the nightstand?"

"Oh, yes, please. Thank you for doing that." I set the water down and walk back towards the door. I definitely don't want to overstay my welcome or make her uncomfortable by being in her space.

She follows me to the door and when I turn to face her, she surprises me by wrapping her arms around my neck. "Thank you. Again." I barely get the chance to return the hug, putting my hands on her back for only a second when she pulls away.

"Goodnight, Adam."

"Goodnight, Lainey."

The door shuts gently and slowly, and I'm left standing in the hallway alone. My head is spinning from all that has just happened, and I can't believe tonight turned out as well as it did. I silently thank Raf for insisting I come to the party, and make a mental note to show my appreciation properly later.

5 /
what's drier than
my granny's vag?

elaina

I CLOSE the door and stand, leaning back on it for several long, long minutes. The night has been a complete whirlwind, and I'm exhausted. But my brain is having a hard time shutting off. Things keep replaying in my head. His scent, the feel of his beard, that kiss, which really should not have affected me. It was a kiss on the cheek. I kiss people on the cheek all the time. Some would even say I hug and kiss people too freely, but this felt different.

It was a sensory overload. I need to process. I need time to think and get my body to catch up with what my brain knows to be true: nothing romantic is happening here. That's not an option. He's someone I could be friends with. That's it. After Ben, I'm not even sure I want to be romantically involved with anyone. Like ever.

My bare feet glide across the familiar hardwood, and my fingers curiously explore the walls. I make my way to the bathroom, leave my pants in a heap on the floor, and shuffle my way towards the toilet. I brush my teeth without needing to turn on any lights, then slip under the blankets of the bed I know all too well, letting my mind drift until sleep comes to claim me.

———

MAEVE IS WAKING ME UP. The biatch is on my bed and she's bouncing.

Whyyyyyy?

"Good morning, Bon! How are you feeling? Can you open your eyes for your Maevey, please?" She's so cheery and wide awake, and I bet she hasn't even had coffee yet. I honestly don't get how she does this. She really is the yin to my yang. I cannot do mornings and she is like this. Every. Single. Day.

I sense the curtains are closed, and the room is dim, so I try opening one eye, and to my surprise, I can see her face.

"Maeve, I can see you," I say this loudly and immediately regret it. She's going to think I'm suddenly a morning person when, in fact, I am not.

She's smiling at me, holding a bottle of water and something in her hand. "Brilliant. Now you have to get up. Dr. Blau already moved your appointment from this morning, but I don't think he's willing to do it again."

"What? What do you mean? My appointment isn't until eleven." I'm sitting up now, taking the glass from her but not the painkiller in her hand. I don't think I feel much pain.

"Darling, it's twelve thirty. You really wore yourself out last night, I guess. I tried waking you earlier, and you were having none of it. I believe your exact words were 'shmergh-esrberhfarbergerd fuck off.'"

She giggles, and I frown, closing one eye, then the other, testing my sight. When I open them both again, my eyes feel as if a hundred needles have pierced them. I accept the pill from her and swallow it down with a gulp of water. The sharp throbbing in my eyeballs tells me the painkiller is indeed much needed.

"Aaah, eye drops, please. Oh my god, my eyeballs are drier than my granny's vag. Fucking shit, that hurts." I keep my eyes closed and lay back down. Maeve is on eye drops duty and I immediately think back to the one who put drops in my eyeballs last night.

"Spoken like a true lady. Oh, Bon, I love your mouth." She opens up the drops and pries one of my eyes open, releasing about four too many drops, but I don't even care. She does the other eye, and I immediately feel relief.

"Okay, love. Grab a quick shower, don't get those eyeballs wet with water, and meet downstairs in ten. Gary and I will take you to the good doctor. And be ready to tell me about who Adam is and why he texted me saying you were safely in your room last night." She pats me on the leg, her fingers warm and reassuring as she rises. She gives me her signature one-browed look, a silent signal of understanding between us.

Busted. I didn't think he'd text as himself. I figured he'd just send it as me. I'll have to give him shit about that later. Later... I don't even know if I'll actually ever talk to him again.

I hope so.

Oh, shut up. Go shower and stop thinking about the mystery man.

The hot spray of the shower feels invigorating against my sleepy skin, and I rush through my morning routine. I throw on a pair of black leggings and a simple white T-shirt, pulling my damp hair back into a messy bun. Dr. Blau won't mind my casual attire. I hurry downstairs, where Maeve and Gary are already waiting in the car. Maeve has her arm draped casually out the window.

Her blonde hair pulled into a sleek ponytail, a cup of coffee in the cup holder. She glances at the clock on the dashboard with a frown, as if daring me to make us late. The girl is always on time, no matter what. I jump into the seat next to her, making quick work of putting my seatbelt on.

"Alright, sleepy head, start from the beginning. Who is Adam?" That eyebrow is up on her forehead again as I tell her about him, being vague and simply mentioning that I ran into someone who was at the party, and he helped me out and we ended up talking for a couple of hours. I'm not lying, but I'm definitely omitting some details.

When I finish, she's quiet, so I ask, "Where's Charlie? I didn't see her when I came down."

"Pretty sure something happened with her and Raf last night. She won't talk about it, though. She seemed annoyed when I asked about it this morning before she stormed off to go for a run." Her tone is flat, but there's also concern for her sister in there.

Rafael is like a brother to me. He and Owen have known each other for years and now they're business partners. Raf is definitely the people person of the duo and I've never met anyone who didn't instantly like him... except Charlie. For a reason no one seems to understand, the two have never really gotten along.

"Huh. That's... interesting." They hardly ever speak to one another, so if something happened, they actually exchanged words. "Charlie hardly even looks at him when he's around and when she does, she's typically scowling. Raf just loves to get a reaction out of her." I shrug, not thinking much of it but making a mental note to grill Raf about it at some point.

"Don't change the subject, Elaina. What's going to happen with this Adam individual? Are you going to text him?"

She's facing me in her seat now, but we've just arrived, so I get away with not answering the question.

"Uh... gotta go, Mae. Be right back." I slip out of the car, and I know she won't follow because someone would recognize her. I really like my anonymity. I don't know how she does this every day, not being able to go out. I would hate it.

———

HALF AN HOUR LATER, Dr. Blau gives me the green light. Everything looks good and we'll have some follow-up appointments, but the discomfort should ease up really soon and I can look at my phone now. Hooray. I'm sure no one but my mom has texted or called, but I take my phone out of my purse before I walk out of the office anyway and freeze. There *is* a text from my mom. "Happy New Year, sweetie! Xo" But. But there's also a text from Adam. He sent it at 11:17 a.m..

ADAM

Hey tornerose. How did it go with the doc this morning?

Tornerose? Again? My eyes linger on his text as I read it again, and my stomach flutters like a thousand butterflies are taking off inside me. I can feel the heat in my cheeks and my pulse thumping in my ears.

No no no no. Stop that. Friend. We are friend-zoning him as of right this second.

ME

Hi. Just left - I slept in and Maeve changed my appointment. All good!

Thanks again for everything.

Before I even lock my phone, I see the three little dots appear. Then they stop and I feel... disappointment?

Ugh. Get over it already.

And then they're back.

ADAM

> Lainey. Please stop thanking me. I'm glad I
> was where I was last night.

> Can I call you tonight?

He's nice. Really nice.

My heart rate skyrockets as I read the last message, and my hands shake so hard I almost drop my phone. I can't remember the last time I had a proper phone conversation with someone who wasn't my mom, Maeve, or a colleague. Taking a deep breath, I force myself to focus on the task at hand and carefully tap out a response with trembling fingers.

ME

> I'd like that.

He wastes no time responding and my heart wastes no time trying to beat right out of my body.

ADAM

> Good. Call you around 8.

Good. Good? Good. Is this good? He's just a friend. My nerves must be regular friendly nerves because I haven't really taken the time to make any new friends since... well, since Maeve. And Charlie, of course. And definitely no male friends. I can safely say I don't have any of those other than Rafael, but he doesn't count. We watch soccer together and we've had no chemistry because Owen would kill him. Dead. On the spot.

Before I can elaborate any further on my mental rant about male friends, Adam, and my social life as a whole, I feel my phone vibrate again. It's Maeve.

MAEVE

> I can see you, you know? And I can hear your brain wheels turning from here.

> What's happening? Get out here!

I open the door and stick my tongue out at her as I walk back towards the car. When I get in, I don't elaborate or mention Adam's texts. Not yet.

———

GARY DROPS me off at my place after I reassure Maeve that I'll be fine on my own and the hours trickle by like a slow drip on a leaky faucet. I struggle to think about anything but the time all day because eight o'clock is coming and I'll get to hear his voice again.

It's 7:53 and I've just opened the fridge door, reaching for the can of Coke, about to pour it into a glass. My phone is now blaring its ringtone from across the room. I curse under my breath, quickly put down the can, and race to the couch. I had been checking my phone obsessively for the past ten minutes, each time toying with calling him first or sending a text or checking my email or Twitter. Now I'm running so I don't miss the call.

"Hello?" I'm out of breath. Not from running twenty feet from the kitchen, but from the sheer anticipation of this moment.

"Are you alright? Why are you out of breath?" He sounds genuinely concerned, as if I'm in any actual danger.

I chuckle, some of my nerves immediately dissipating. "Well, eager beaver, you're a few minutes early. I was pouring myself a drink, and I had left my phone in the other room. Apparently, I need to step up my cardio."

I worried about how we'd start this conversation, worried

we'd fall into a pit of small talk and never come back out. I would rather French kiss a skunk than make small talk. Small talk is the distraction while we wait for the real conversation to begin. I crave the time when the masks fall away and the awkwardness evaporates. Thankfully, he snaps me out of my internal ramble.

"Did you want me to call you back when you're ready? What are you drinking, anyway?" I can hear the smile in his voice, and I wish I could see it. I like how he does this thing where he asks two questions back-to-back, like he just can't wait to get the words out. It's kind of endearing, like a puppy who paws at your leg when it wants attention. I feel like I can almost see his lips moving, and I feel the urgency behind his words.

"No, smartass, and a Coke. I'm treating myself tonight since I feel like I've had nothing but water for days. What are you up to in your neck of the woods?"

I've made it back to the kitchen, finished pouring my drink and am making my way to the couch with Frankie.

"You want the honest answer?" he asks with a tone so earnest I want to squeeze him.

"Always," I respond quickly because it's true. I always want honesty.

"I've pretty much been waiting to call you all day. It's New Year's Day. I didn't exactly have plans. I wasn't hungover from my half a drink last night, and I nearly texted you about five times to see if I could call you earlier."

Is this guy for real? Who says this shit? He really just openly admitted to feeling the same way I was feeling all day.

I laugh, slightly relieved at this revelation.

"For future reference, you can always ask if we can talk earlier. Better yet, just call." This is exactly what I would say to any of my friends.

"Good to know. The same goes for you, L." The weird

nerves I was feeling slowly dissipate and it seems like maybe this could actually be a friendly conversation.

I can be friends with a dude. I can totally do this.

"Okay, so tell me: what did you end up doing all day? Because I walked Frankie twice, baked a batch of muffins, prepped some meals for the week and started reading a book. Oh, and then I made and ate dinner. My phone avoidance technique was to be my most productive self."

I did just about everything I could today and did it all without my phone on me to avoid the temptation of staring at it.

A disbelieving laugh bumbles out of him. "Damn, Lainey! You're making me look bad." The sound of my name on his lips, in that tone. It's so familiar. I get what feels a lot like butterflies in my stomach.

Get the fuck out, butterflies.

"I worked out and then sat around and snacked most of the day. I ordered eggplant parmigiana for dinner and then stared at my phone for like thirty minutes before I called you."

"Okay, snack monster. Next time please just call me. Where did you get the parm from? And yes, there are potential wrong answers to this question. Friendship on the line here because I take my Italian food very seriously, even if my Greek mother would disown me if she knew I like lasagna better than pastitsio." Either this man needs an education in Italian food or he knows what's up. There's no in-between.

"Bella's on Melrose," he answers slowly, confidently. Then, not even waiting for my reaction, he keeps talking. "What book did you read?" I ignore that my reaction is to be a little turned on by the fact that he didn't just get close, he said the name of my favorite Italian place.

"Wow, yes, right answer. I hope you've tried the pasta Fagioli and the ricotta ravioli. Oh, my god. Deadly. And the book… it's… uh… it's a romance novel Char recommended."

I start speaking faster now, feeling like I need to justify my book choice. "I haven't read anything that wasn't for work in a long time, so she recommended this as a... fun... read."

"Pretty sure I've had everything on that menu. Italian food is my weakness and that ravioli..." He lets out a moan that sends another funny feeling to my stomach. "So the book. How is it so far?" I hear the mischief and curiosity in his voice, and I refuse to ignore it.

I giggle at his cheeky tone.

"Shut up. It's fine. I'm only a few chapters in and so far all I know is that the boy and the girl grew up together and he's always had a crush on her. I've never read a romance novel before, so I'm not sure what to expect, but I'm pretty sure they'll end up together. That's sort of the point, right?"

"I think so. I'm gonna ask you more about this next time we talk."

Next time we talk.

A smile tugs at the corner of my lips as I try to contain my excitement. The idea makes me light-headed, a feeling I'm not used to. It's as if Adam and I have known each other for ages and not just since yesterday. For the first time in a long time, I feel a connection—a connection that's more than just physical. As if we could be just friends, nothing more.

I'm thankful when the rest of our conversation is light. We keep it simple: favorite sports teams (mine are all Massachusetts or New York-based, of course, and his are all LA), birthdays (mine isn't until February, but his is December 29th, which I feel guilty about because I met him just two days after his birthday, unknowingly), siblings (we each just have the one), then we talk about traveling and things we like to do.

It turns out he's a big reader, so he gave me many non-romance novel recommendations, which I'm thankful for. And I'm obsessed with architecture, so I recommended places for him to check out in New York since he's flying there tomorrow.

His voice was a deep rumble, like warm honey pouring through a funnel into my ear. My cheeks were sore from smiling by the time I said goodbye sometime around midnight. He has an early flight, but we promised to talk again soon.

I don't know what this is, and after just a little over twenty-four hours of meeting this man I have never seen, I feel things I'm not sure I've felt with anyone before and I don't know what to make of it all. I need to talk to Maeve. Or my therapist. Or both.

Even after four hours, I still want to know more about him. When my phone buzzes with a message from him, my heart swells with happiness and my lips involuntarily stretch into a wide, goofy grin.

ADAM

I forgot to ask you something.

ME

Sounds mysterious. What is it?

ADAM

Why does Maeve call you Bonnie?

This makes me laugh. I wonder why he's even thinking about this.

ME

Google it, you dork. It's a Scottish thing.

A couple of minutes go by and I finish brushing my teeth when my phone buzzes again.

ADAM

Yep. Checks out. She picked the right nickname.

Speaking of Googling, I'm not internet stalking you. Next time I lay eyes on you I want to see you looking back at me.

My heart skips a beat. Or maybe it beats faster. Or maybe it stops beating altogether.

ADAM

Goodnight, L.

6 /
how do i get six years back?

elaina

A WEEK GOES BY, and Adam and I exchange texts daily. He's called me twice and we've talked late into the night. Yesterday he told me about his sister and I love that they have such a close relationship. It's so different from what I have with Owen now. Hearing the way his voice changed when he talked about Gwen and her kids sent goosebumps all over my body.

It's felt a little like a secret friendship, this thing with us, because I haven't told anyone about our conversations. I don't think I'm ready to yet.

Maeve is coming over now, and she knows I've kept in touch with the mysterious guy I met at her NYE party, but she doesn't know that I'm scared.

I'm not someone who easily opens up to strangers. I always keep people at arm's length, but this is different. I'd been with Ben for three years, but it always felt like he was holding something back from me. Of course, now I know that something was his relationship with another woman. But this, with Adam, it feels different. I find myself eagerly awaiting his calls, and feel butterflies in my stomach when I think of him. Even though I've never even seen his face, I sense a connection that feels both exhilarating and terrifying. I know I have to be careful not to get too close too fast. But try as hard as I might, the more I think about him, the more I want to get to know him.

I hear the welcome sound of Maeve's car pulling up the driveway and reluctantly shake myself out of my trance-like state, dragging my thoughts away from Adam.

She's grinning from ear to ear as she enters the kitchen, her eyes immediately falling on the freshly baked muffins. Two mugs are already prepared—one of steaming coffee for me, the other with a tea bag steeped in hot water for her.

"Hello, my darling," she says, and I feel a weight being lifted off my chest. The warmth of her embrace is even more comforting than the hot cup of coffee I'm cradling in my hands.

"So lovely to see your eyes are healing so well." She hugs me tight before pulling away, and I can feel the love radiating from her.

She crosses the kitchen with a skip in her step and picks up the mug of tea, inhaling its comforting aroma. She might have traveled far and wide, but some things will never change—like her love of afternoon tea.

"Hi, Mae. I feel like a new person. A new person who no longer needs glasses." We both laugh and I settle into my stool at the island.

"I've got your favorites ready. We're ready for a full BFF catch-up." She joins me at the island and immediately reaches for a muffin. "How are you? When do you start shooting your next movie? That River guy is in it, right?" I twist up my face when I ask about her co-star. I've never met him.

"Oh, fine. Charlie left yesterday and already I can't wait to see her again. The movie starts in a few weeks, but I think I want to go to London sooner to spend some time with Char and enjoy London before it's all long shoot days."

Something feels off about her, but she's avoiding my eyes. I won't push her yet.

"And, yes, River Holm is my co-star. He was at the party the other night, but he left early." She shrugs and eats some of her muffin.

"And what else do we know about River, other than that he's very mysterious?" I don't like to gossip, but I'm curious about who Mae's next co-star is. She's had a rough go lately and I hope she gets to work with good people for this film.

"I don't know, actually. We've never worked together, but he seemed like a nice bloke when I met him." She shrugs, not seeming at all concerned that she's going to be working closely with someone she's met once.

"He's pretty hot, though. I saw his last movie. He was fantastic too. And I know you don't date costars, but I mean…" I wiggle my eyebrows at her, laughing.

She laughs. "Not going to happen. There were zero sparks when we met. We have a lot of scenes together, including some potentially steamy ones, but you know how mechanical those are. Hand here. Breathe like this. Now close your eyes. Ugh…"

"I feel like it's like that in real life too, though." I sigh because I have had exactly zero sexual experiences that would be considered mind-blowing since I was eighteen. And that's… bleak!

"Oh, Bonnie, you just need to find the right guy. Ben was selfish—in so many ways—and you need to let go a little. It's not mechanical when it's with the right person, and I think deep down you know that." She holds eye contact with me and I don't have to question that she says this out of pure love.

I can see her big shiny blue eyes sparkling with that care and understanding I always find when I look at Maeve and Charlie.

"Yeah, but I'm good, Mae. I still get mine, you know?" I

wink and we both laugh at my covert mention of my vibrator collection.

"Total subject change. I've been reading a romance novel *and* I think I'm going to go visit my mom and Owen." I look at my coffee as I say this because I'm still trying to convince myself this is actually a good idea.

"Those two things aren't related though, right? Because… weird. Also, I think both separately are great. You haven't been back for a visit in a long time. Your mum misses you. And I know Owen does, too." She touches my hand when she mentions my brother, knowing how strained our relationship has been since Dad died six years ago.

I let out a loud breath. "Yeah. It's time. And I have this break from work, anyway. Going home feels right. And Dr. Scholz agrees it's a good idea." When I spoke to my therapist last week, she was very encouraging that going home might be good for me.

"Well, you know me and Dr. Scholz are pretty much always on the same page, so… when do you leave?" She finishes her muffin and lets out a moan. Chocolate chip is her favorite.

"A few days. Will I see you before you go to London?" I pout as I ask her this. I miss her when she's gone.

"Awwww, Bonnieeeeee, you know I always miss you the most. And why don't you come with me? After Marblehead. Come and stay with me. Charlie will love it. So will I!" She's clapping now, like she's just had the best idea. And she sort of has. What else do I have to do? Might as well go to one of my favorite cities with my favorite people.

"Yes! Let's do that. Are you staying with your parents?" Now I'm clapping too.

She gasps, bringing a hand to her chest dramatically.

"Ha! That's a barmy idea even for you. No! I rented a flat in Knightsbridge. Actually, I had one for Charlie, too, but she's decided to stay at home since she found out Raf and

River are staying in the same building during the shoot." She rolls her eyes and then smiles.

"You should take it. No prying mums to worry about that way." She loves her mom, but she is definitely one to meddle. Usually, it's in the most well-meaning of ways, but that's not always the case.

"Then it's settled. You'll come to London. It'll be like old times, only better because we will not be eating ramen noodles and that awful cheap pizza from Joe's." She's smiling wistfully.

Those early summer days in London were some of our best and some of my worst.

"Okay, darling, I have to run, but we'll chat about London some more. I love you and I can't wait to spend some quality time with you."

We have a long hug, and I kiss her hair. Being a few inches taller than her makes me feel like a giant sometimes. "Love you, Mae. See you soon!"

And just like that, she's gone. And I need to plan this trip to Marblehead.

———

THERE'S a heavy brick of uneasiness living in the pit of my stomach, and it gets heavier the closer I get to my childhood home. Mom knows I'm coming, but my brother doesn't, and I have no idea how he'll take it. Plus, I called Adam when I landed, and he didn't pick up and I just thought hearing his voice would somehow help. Then I immediately felt stupid for thinking that.

Mom is sitting on the front porch and runs over to my rental car when I arrive. She gives me a tight hug and I feel tears pricking my eyes.

"Hi, Mamá," I whisper.

"*Moro mou.*" My baby. "It's so wonderful to see you!"

She's petting my hair in the way she always does, and I hear another car in the driveway. "I'm going to take Frankie in and give you two a moment." She scurries off like she has ants in her pants. That little trickster.

When I turn, I see Owen is standing next to his truck, looking at me with an unreadable expression on his face. After years as a Marine, he looks so grown up. So unlike the eighteen-year-old boy who left home all those years ago.

"Hey, O." I lift my hand in an awkward little wave and then promptly shove them into my jacket pockets. Fuck, it's freezing out here. I miss LA weather already.

He lets out a deep, rumbling sigh and strides towards me with a determined look on his face. I stumble back, but before I can react, he pulls me into a hug, dwarfing me with his immense size. His body is as solid and reliable as ever, and the warmth of it radiates around me. I'd forgotten how tall he is, and I feel a wave of nostalgia wash over me.

"Hey, little sis. I miss you." His voice is gruff and somehow soft. He doesn't let me go as tears stream down my face, hot and fast. Six words and it feels like a piece of my heart has been put back together. I keep my head buried in his chest until my toes go numb.

He walks me inside, an arm around me as we all sit down at the kitchen table wordlessly. Ma already has tea and muffins ready. As I sit down, I see a box of tissues in her hand. I turn off my phone so there are no distractions. I need to be fully present for this and I knew that the moment I walked in the front door.

When I look back up at Owen, tears run down my cheeks all over again. He takes one of my hands in his giant ones and Mom pushes the tissue box closer to me as we all sit down.

"I'm so sorry, O." I give his hand a squeeze and wipe at my tears again. "I'm sorry it's taken me this long to come back here. I miss you so much and I know you blame me for not being here when Dad got sick, and I'm so, so sorry I didn't make it back in time. I wish I had. I wish so badly that things had been different, that I hadn't screwed everything up, that we…"

I can't go on. I've waited too long to say these words to my big brother and the sheer weight of them is making my throat close up. My loud sobs take over and I hear my mom's own soft one next to me.

"Elaina, no. I don't blame you. I've never blamed you. It wasn't your fault. It happened so fast… it would have been impossible for you to get here. I thought you blamed me… for what happened." He nudges my face up with a gentle hand. "Little sis… you've thought that for almost six years? Is that why you haven't come home?"

Owen's forehead scrunches into tight lines, and his emerald green eyes are glossy with unshed tears. Even though he's been there for me since we were little, I've never seen him cry before. His jaw clenches and his arms are crossed, as if he's trying to hold himself together. I can tell he's trying to be strong, just like he has always done as the big brother.

"Lainey Banainey," Owen says with a small, sad smile on his face. He exhales loudly before continuing.

"I'm the one who is sorry. I'm sorry I wasn't there for you when you needed me." His green eyes, so much like my own and our dad's, remain steady on mine. "I know how important Andy was to you, and I wasn't here. I wish I had been. And I left a few weeks after Dad died. It killed me not to be here for you. For Ma."

I shake my head so fast I feel tears run sideways on my face. "What? Owen, you were deployed. You *couldn't* be here."

"I know," he says slowly. "But I still wish I had been. That last deployment was…" He blows out a breath and his brow creases as he remembers something so obviously painful. "Hard. Awful. The memories still haunt me. The effects of that time is something I still reckon with, in my heart and in my head. It's the kind of experience that doesn't leave, not even in the privacy of my therapist's office." He takes a deep breath and looks over to Mom before meeting my eyes again.

I nod, understanding for maybe the first time that my quiet brother has kept so much hurt inside for so long. During all those years of video calls and short visits.

He looks up at me, green eyes shining with unshed tears. "I've missed you. All these years, I've missed you. And I don't want to do that anymore."

I throw my arms around him, letting all the tears of relief flow. "I don't want to miss you anymore either." I pull back so I can see his eyes, thinking back to something he said. "And O? I don't blame you. I never blamed you. Not for a single thing. I love you. So much."

"I love you, little sis."

WE TALK FOR... I don't know... hours? All the things left unsaid are out now. Owen opens up a bit about his last deployment—as much as he can, anyway. It sounds horrific, and he's getting help to deal with it all. He and Raf started their security business almost two years ago, and it's really skyrocketed. Owen sticks to the East Coast, handling all the cyber security, and Raf has been running things in California, mostly training new bodyguards for their elite Hollywood clientele. He has a lot going on, but he seems to handle it all so well.

Grief is like walking into a dimly lit room with no windows. There's no air to breathe, and the emptiness of the space feels heavier than the objects that occupy it. Nothing can ever fill the vacancy my dad's death has created. Some days, that feeling is too much to bear, and I want to escape the pain. But being in the same room with my mom and brother, who felt the same loss as me, helps me to process my grief. I can never get back those years of trying to cope with my sadness on my own, but I know I can't dwell on that. I'm here now. *We're* here now. And I want to look forward, not backward.

I HELP MOM MAKE DINNER, and we all eat together. As we reminisce about Dad, I can practically see his hearty laughter echo off the walls, and his big hands as they fly across the old piano's keys he played every night.

MA INSISTS on cleaning up and I take a minute to explore this old house. My old house. I walk into the garage and the scent of grease and fresh sawdust linger in my nose as I run my hand over his truck's cold hood. When I return to the kitchen, I catch sight of Owen sitting at the piano bench, gently playing an old Frank Sinatra tune. Mom smiles from the sink, little droplets of water falling from her fingertips. Her eyes are full with memories of Dad.

How could I have been so blind to the pain my mother was going through? For so long, I kept my grief hidden away, never wanting to burden her with it. Yet, in the same way, I had unknowingly isolated myself from her and left her to suffer by herself. My heart aches at the thought of how much my inaction has cost us both.

THEY DON'T WANT to leave, but Owen has to get to work, and Mom has book club, which I insist she does not miss. It's been the one thing that makes her smile, so I know she needs to go.

I'm on my own for the evening. It feels nice to come into this house and not feel like I have to be on guard all the time. I'm still distracted by all of the photographs in the hall, of

Owen and me as children and teenagers, Mamá and Dad, the four of us, but I don't feel the need to run from it all. Now I feel comforted by the life that was and is lived inside these walls.

Sitting on my childhood bed, I turn my phone on and call the one whose voice I so badly want to hear. And I decide not to question that feeling. Not tonight.

7 /
what's better: her personality or her ass?

adam

IT'S 9:45 P.M. I just walked into my condo and my phone is already ringing again. Whoever it is will have to wait. This day, this week, has been so long and frustrating. My publicist has been on my ass about my image, and I'm so done. Sandra keeps telling me I need to settle down, or at least appear to do so. Apparently, no one has anything nice to say about the single movie star who doesn't date. My phone is still ringing when I look down and see *Tornerose* on the screen.

Well, this changes everything.

"Hey, beauty," I say on an exhale.

"Hi. Oh my gosh, it's nice to hear your voice," she says, sounding surprised. *Is the surprise at the fact it's nice to hear my voice, or that I finally picked up my phone?* "Hi," she says again. Her voice is a whisper, and I'm pretty sure she's smiling.

"Hi." I'm definitely smiling from ear to ear, taking my shoes off and immediately feeling the weight of the day lift off.

What is it about this girl?

"So, I'm in your time zone. I came home to see my family. It's fucking freezing here. I stood outside for five minutes and nearly froze my tits off." We both laugh, and I do my best not to think about her tits.

"Is now an okay time to talk? How's New York?" She sounds different from the last time we talked. Something about her voice is strained even though she's trying to sound upbeat.

"Now is the perfect time to talk. New York is… it doesn't even matter. I want to hear about why your voice sounds like that and why you're calling me when you're home with your mom and brother. Is your brother there?"

It's hard to keep the concern out of my voice. She's told me about how they stopped talking after their dad died. He didn't seem to handle the fact that she was away very well when he got sick, and he passed so quickly that she didn't make it back in time to see him. She said she carried a lot of guilt over that.

"Yeah, Owen is here, too. He needed to get to a work event and Mom had book club. I showed up last minute, so I didn't want to disrupt their day, but we spent like five hours talking and crying. I was so wrong about how Owen felt all this time. He never blamed me for not being here. He's just had so much of his own shit going on and we laid it all out." She sniffles once and continues.

"He apologized. He thought I was the one blaming him for Dad's death, but I would never…" I hear her blow out a breath.

"I know you wouldn't, L. Tell me more."

"We ate dinner together and talked about all our happiest memories. O played piano after, just like Dad used to." She takes a breath in and a quiet laugh escapes when she breathes out.

"Owen and I hugged, lots. I told him how much I love him and miss him. He told me the same." Her voice cracks and something twists inside my chest. "It was… incredible, Adam." She sniffles again.

"Sorry, I've cried so much today already, and I thought I was done." She lets out a little laugh as though she's releasing the day's emotions. She sounds relieved.

"Lainey, I... wow. I'm so happy to hear that." And I am. I really am. Last week, I shared with her how growing up in Hollywood was lonely.

She knows I had a lot of nannies, and my parents were away a lot. She doesn't know that I started acting at a young age and didn't have a typical school experience past the sixth grade. Thankfully, by then, Raf and I were already good friends. He's been a constant in my life. She knows I didn't have the warm and fuzzy home life she had growing up, but I had my sister. And Raf. And they're pretty much my whole family.

"Adam? Can I tell you a little more about why I've avoided coming home?" Her voice is a little unsteady and I can hear her let out a shaky breath.

"I want to know everything you want to tell me, Lainey." It meant so much to hear her say those words to me the night we met, and I hope she feels safe telling me anything she wants.

Another shaky breath from her.

"Here goes... my dad isn't the only person I lost here in Marblehead. When I was eighteen I had my first serious boyfriend. He was my first, well, everything. I was so young and so in love. So blind to so many things and naive. I had no idea what heartbreak was, and Andy he... he broke me. I'm not sure I'm quite put back together yet."

She takes a shuddering breath and I hate the sadness of it. "I was so selfish, and I stayed away for so long and then my dad... ugh, I'm sorry. This is too much, I shouldn't have—"

"No, please don't apologize." I struggle for words, unsure of what I can say to make this better. All my sentences seem so hollow, so empty. But I know I have to say something. I take a deep breath, my heart heavy with sorrow, as I try to find something comforting to say. "I understand why you hesitated to go back to Marblehead, and it makes sense, wanting some distance from a place where you felt so much hurt. I hope you know that your choice to stay away makes perfect sense. You needed to protect yourself, Lainey, to protect your heart. And that's alright. There's nothing wrong with that."

I shift in my seat, wishing she was here. "I just really wish I was there so I could hug you. This feels like the kind of thing that a hug communicates better than words and I'm pretty terrible with words, so I'm sorry. I swear I'm better at hugs."

She releases a quiet laugh. "I wish you were here, too. And you're not terrible with words. That was... that was perfect." She clears her throat. "I don't know what it is about you. I haven't told more than a handful of people about this, but I wanted to tell you."

"I'm glad you told me." I don't know what more I can say. I guess I could take this opportunity to trust her with my story, but I'm not ready.

Such a fucking coward.

"Me too. I'm going to be here for a few days and then I'm headed to London with Maeve before she starts her next movie. Are you in New York much longer?"

Her voice is lighter, and she sounds excited about London, and my temples are now throbbing. *She's* going to London. *I'm* going to London. But I have at least a week before we're potentially in the same city again. I can handle that.

"Oh, I'm sorry, Adam. I think my mom is home from her book club. I should go. Thank you for... for picking up the phone and for listening. You've been a really good friend."

"Lainey, please stop apologizing to me and thanking me. Seriously. Tell your mom I said hello and we'll talk again soon, okay?" I wish we could keep talking, but I need to sort through this publicist shit anyway and figure out what to do about the fact we're going to be in the same city soon. Really soon.

"Goodnight, L."

"'Night, Adam."

We hang up and I'm not sure I can think about what the next week will be like. I really want to see her. I really want to see her entire face light up with that big smile of hers.

With all the bullshit with my publicist, my parents acting like they're petty children and my career feeling like it's not moving forward the way I want it to, I just really want to have this one thing. This one thing that's good and pure right now. And that's Lainey. I really don't want to fuck this up.

———

THE NEXT THREE days go by so slowly. Lainey called me again two nights ago. We talked for hours about everything from our childhoods to our favorite TV shows. She told me about the recipes she tried with her mom, and it felt so good to just listen to her sounding so happy. It's so easy with her, but I'm worried about what will happen when she realizes I'm her best friend's co-star. That I withheld a lot of information about who I am. We haven't known one another long, but I don't like the idea of starting a… whatever this is… this way.

It's now Friday and after a week from hell, I'm glad to be landing in London with Raf, who slept peacefully the entire flight here.

Maeve is here already and having us over for a big dinner at the place she's renting. We're all staying in the same building during filming, and I keep wondering if Lainey is going to stay there as well when she gets to London in a few days. I feel this weird pang in my chest at the thought of her. The uncertainty of what will happen is really getting to me.

Raf has respected my need to be silent until the moment we get into our car.

"I gave you the entire flight to think through whatever shit you have going on. I even forced myself to sleep, but now it's time to talk." He's serious. Raf is rarely serious and because he knows me better than anyone, he knows I've been sulking. "Is it the shit with Sandra and your fake girlfriend? Did she find you someone?"

Sandra, the well-meaning motherly figure who has been my publicist for years, is convinced I need a fake relationship to cool the tabloids' speculations about me and the mystery of why I'm never seen dating anyone. Heaven forbid a person has some privacy.

I let out a deep breath. "No, it's not that. I mean, it *is* that because it's bullshit and I don't need a fake fucking girlfriend. But it's not *just* that."

"Yeah, what you need is a *real* fucking girlfriend and to get laid. You should really use that pretty face and your celebrity status to get yourself some. It might be just what you need after what's-her-face fucked you up this bad." He's looking at me and gauging my response. I know it. We never bring up Tiffany, the woman who nearly ruined me in more ways than one. So much so that I've been celibate since we were together. Just the thought of being with another woman has brought up so much anxiety, and no one I've met since has felt like they'd be worth it.

"You know that's not gonna happen. But I met someone. Well, sort of." Here we go. It's time to tell him about Lainey. I haven't said a word about her to anyone, and I'm not sure if he knows her or not, given that he has worked with Maeve occasionally and they're also friends.

"When? When did you meet someone?" Shit. He's onto me. He knows I go nowhere, avoid talking to people, and he's been with me the entire time we were in New York. I can tell by his tone and that one elevated eyebrow that he knows this didn't just happen, and I kept it from him.

"Uhhh, New Year's Eve, actually. But we're just friends. I can't really do more than that right now. Even if Sandra would love the idea." I scratch my forehead and look down, thinking about how much I wish I could just be Adam forever with L and ignore all the other garbage. I love my career, but this glimpse of a normal relationship has been really nice. It's not real though.

"When did you have time to meet someone? You were at that party for all of half an hour before you took off. She must have been hot if she made that much of an impression." He's turned his body and I know he's picking apart every movement of my face, every part of my body language.

"You know, it's not all about how someone looks, Raf. Maybe she just had a really great personality."

He laughs loudly, throwing his head back.

Asshole.

"Dude, you know what 'a nice personality' is code for and I have never seen you with a chick that wasn't either a model or looked like she could be one. Even if it has been a while. So, spill it." He's right. But Lainey is the most beautiful woman I've ever seen. Somehow, luck is on my side and the car comes to a stop just as he's about to keep asking me questions.

"You know this isn't over. I want to hear about this girl. You haven't even bothered to learn a woman's name since Tiffany and that was five years ago, man. Obviously, this means something to you." He puts one hand on my shoulder and squeezes, letting me know, all joking aside, he gets that this is kind of a big deal.

I try to put everything off my mind, willing myself to take this all one day at a time. For now, I'll keep my phone off and enjoy dinner. Hopefully, the jet lag and lack of sleep on the flight means I'll get some rest tonight.

Raf and I go through security, and as soon as the elevator door closes, he turns to me, elbowing me in the ribs. "Does she have a nice ass? I know you're an ass man, A. That's gotta be what hooked you, right?" He laughs, shaking his head.

"You get this one thing and nothing else. Yes, she has a fantastic ass. Like unreal. Round and full. Fucking flawless." Raf is right. I'm an ass man, and Lainey's happens to be perfect.

He laughs again. "I knew it."

We knock on the apartment door, and Charlie opens it to let us in. She frowns openly at Raf and gives me a small smile with a quick hello. We walk in and the smell immediately makes me glad I came.

"Oh my god, it smells amazing in here. What's for dinner?" Then I hear the unmistakable sound of joyful laughter. Her laughter. It's Lainey.

8 /
wait...who are you?

elaina

I GASP. "OH, MY GOD. ADAM?" I step out of the kitchen and into the hallway. "Adam?" And when our eyes meet, I know without a doubt that it's him. I take off running, the world blurring as my feet pound the floor.

When I reach him, I leap into the air, wrapping my arms around his neck. He catches me, pulling me close, and I'm hit with a wave of adrenaline so strong it's almost overwhelming. Joy rushes through my veins like a raging river, making me laugh out loud as it slams into my heart and lungs.

My eyes are closed, and I savor the warmth of his breath as his lips brush against my ear. "Lainey," he whispers, and I feel his arms tighten around me like a cocoon. His embrace is strong and gentle at the same time, and I want time to stand still at this moment.

"Oh my god, it's you. It's really you. I'd know your voice anywhere. And your smell. You smell just like… like you." I'm still laughing and in complete disbelief as he sets me down when I feel a gentle tug on my shoulder and turn to find Raf behind me. His face is scrunched up in worry. He steps forward, the sound of his throat clearing loud in the sudden silence, and wraps his arms around me for a brief moment. His eyes dart between Adam and me and he gives me a sideways glance before fully releasing me.

"Looks like I don't need to introduce you two. I'm uh… gonna give you a minute. Let me know if I can do anything in the kitchen, baby girl." He stands there with his hands in his pockets, glowering at Adam. He looks mad. And Rafael is a scary dude when he's mad.

"Oh. Yeah. Thanks, Raffy. Uh, everything's done. I just need to open up some more wine and we'll wait for Maeve so we can eat."

Raf smiles warmly at me and nods once. "I got it." When he looks back at Adam his stare turns ice cold. He walks away and I'm left feeling thoroughly confused by what just happened between the two of them. Without casting another glance at Adam, I walk into the den and motion for him to follow me. He shuts the door and when he turns around, I nearly trip over my own feet. I know that face. I know his face. Everyone knows his face because he's a fucking movie star.

Holy fucking shit!

"River?" I choke out. He looks distressed, and his eyes are wide, locked on mine. I hadn't inspected his face until right now. "What is happening? You told me your name was Adam. Are you Adam? Or are you River?"

Am I yelling? I think I'm yelling. And I'm breathing too fast. And is he just standing there shaking his head at me? What in the fresh hell is going on?

He clears his throat. "My name is Adam River Holm." All the air rushes out of my lungs as I feel my eyes widen. "Lainey, please… please let me explain. I didn't lie to you. I have never once lied to you."

I can't bring myself to look away from him. His voice is so familiar, yet his face is so unexpected. It fills me with a strange mix of emotions. I want to run away, to hide from what I see in his face. But at the same time, all I want is to stay just where I am and listen to him, to remind myself that he is still my Adam.

No, no… not mine.

"I've wanted to tell you so many times. Every time we've spoken on the phone, I've come so close to telling you, but I'm a coward." He takes a step toward me, and I step back involuntarily. He winces then looks down at his feet. "I thought you'd stop talking to me once you found out, or worse, treat me differently because of it. Not because of who I am, but because of how I deceived you."

His lips twitch, his brow scrunch together, and the corners of his eyes crinkle as if a heavy thought weighs on him. He inhales sharply and his eyelids flutter shut, as if willing himself to utter the words he has to say. "But that was never my intention, I swear. I've been honest with you about everything L, I swear it. Well, everything but this one thing. Shit, I am really fucking this up."

He takes a few steps away from me, hands running through his thick brown hair. I stay silent, not daring to move a muscle as I take in his tall frame, the broad expanse of his shoulders. He shrugs off his overcoat to reveal a navy blue Henley that hugs his fit body, emphasizing every muscle. His jeans... oh Lord, how his jeans hang low on his hips like an invitation I'm desperately trying not to accept.

You're supposed to be mad, not getting all lusty. Get back to being mad.

I'm not mad though. I'm… sympathetic. I've seen what this life of fame does to the person who's closest to me. I work in this industry, but no one *really* knows who I am. Most of the time, I have my anonymity. People like him and Maeve can't even step outside without being recognized and having cameras or phones shoved in their faces.

I take a few deep breaths. "Adam?" I step towards him.

He's still turned away and I can't see his face. "Adam. Please look at me."

He slowly turns around, and my heart races as I feel my body pull towards him with an invisible gravitational force. His blue eyes meet mine and I find myself unable to break the gaze, captivated by his chiseled jawline, the strength of his straight eyebrows and the beauty of his wide mouth that looks like it was made for kissing.

Feeling brave, I take a step closer so I can take in every detail of his face. My right hand instinctively rises, overcome by memories of the night we'd first met. I lightly run my fingers through his perfectly groomed beard, a small smile playing on my lips.

"Your beard is longer." He inhales, closes his eyes, and exhales on a long, slow breath. He opens his eyes and nods once. "And your eyes... they're so blue." Blue doesn't begin to do them justice. The color of his eyes is a stunning cerulean blue, the irises rimmed in a darker shade. His long, thick eyelashes are midnight black, sweeping gracefully across his cheeks, so unfairly long and dark that it's impossible not to stare.

Looking at his eyes this closely should make me uncomfortable. It should make me squirm and look away, but I don't. Not until he finally blinks and I come back to the moment. My hands move back down to my sides.

I can't believe this. I can't believe I didn't know who he was and that of all the people I could have met that night, I met one of the most well-known actors in Hollywood.

He swallows hard and those bright blue eyes swirl with emotions I can't name. My eyes travel the surface of his face, taking in every detail. When my gaze lands back on his eyes, I notice that his gaze is on my mouth where my bottom lip is trapped between my teeth. Righting myself, I take a deep breath and place a hand on his arm.

"I understand, Adam. Your life is so... public. Everyone

knows your face, so when given the opportunity to talk to someone who doesn't know who you are, when you're afforded that kind of anonymity, I understand wanting to take it. I understand wanting a friend who doesn't know about your fame." I look down at my feet now, feeling sick about my use of the word "friend," and unsure of what I'm going to say next. Words come anyway. "And yeah, I would have treated you differently. If I'd known that night... If I'd known who you were..." I feel my eyebrows bunching in between my eyes. I shake my head and look back up at him, unable to meet his eyes.

"I also understand, Lainey. If you're upset, disappointed, or mad. I would understand whatever feelings you might have about this. And I really am sorry." His left hand comes up, and he tucks some of my hair behind my ear in a movement so fluid, so natural, I almost forget I have only known this person for a few weeks and only just saw his face for the first time.

For reasons I can't explain, my chin wobbles, so I reach out and hug him around his torso so I can hide my face in his chest. It doesn't take long before he wraps his arms around my shoulders. I rest my head against his chest, and feel the steady thrum of his heart matching the quickened pace of my own. A sense of calmness settles over me as I feel the reassuring thump beneath my ear.

My brain chooses this moment to notice the hardness of his body. Oh. My. God. It feels amazing. His back is solid, and there is not one bit of softness that I can feel. He's all toned muscle, and what is he, like 6'4"? So tall. So, so tall.

His heart rate slows down a bit and I feel his lips on the top of my head, sending a shiver down my whole body. Trying to hide this embarrassing shiver, because apparently, I have a lot of physical reactions that need to be hidden from this beautiful man, I pull away.

"So I guess I should call you River, then?" I look up at

him, way up because we're so close now, and he flinches when I use his middle name.

"I haven't been called Adam since I was a kid. Not many people outside of my family know that it's my first name." He runs his hands up and down my arms absent-mindedly. "As soon as I started acting, it became River. I guess it's more interesting than Adam." His lips come up on one side in a crooked smile, his right hand now playing with the ends of my hair. "You can call me whatever you want when it's just us, but when we're in public... yeah, probably River. Is that alright?"

I'm sorry, come again? 'When it's just us'? I can call him whatever I want? Jesus, take the wheel.

"Uh-huh. Sure. Yeah. That's cool. Yep."

Stop talking!

The corners of his mouth turn up in a smirk, then slowly expand into a broad, ear-to-ear grin that illuminates his entire face.

Oh. My. Lanta. I may need CPR. I can't breathe. How is one person's face this beautiful? Is he real? Or is he a robot conjured up in a lab with a perfectly rugged face and rock-hard body?

His eyes crinkle at the corners as my mind spins with a hundred unfinished sentences. I try to focus on something, anything, to say. My lips part and the first words that tumble from them are, "I made a turkey dinner!" It comes out all loud and weird.

His smile fades completely, and his fingers cease their toying with my hair. "You did what?"

I'm talking a mile a minute now. "Yeah, well, this was just a practice meal. I figured it'd be great to try it out with a few close friends. I mean, I didn't know you'd be here, obviously. Raf told me River would be coming, but I didn't know you were... anyway, I decided to come to London early after everything with my family. Figured I could get a practice dinner in before I made you the real one since I've never made a whole Thanksgiving meal myself before, but you're here now, so... surprise, it's Thanksgiving in London!" My hands come up around my face with jazz fingers when I say 'surprise' and I immediately, and I mean *immediately,* regret the action.

His blue eyes are bright and wide. His smile is gone and his lips are slightly parted. Before my mouth can speak any more foolish things or my body can come up with any other dopey gestures, he pulls me into a tight hug. His hands come under my arms and around my waist this time and he buries his head in my neck.

Please let this be the way I die. Just like this. Smelling Adam, standing on my tippy toes while he holds me.

"I don't deserve you. No one does. I'm convinced of it," he whispers, but I catch every word and I hold him tighter with each one. He takes a deep breath and pulls away. All I can think is that this is the very best hug I've ever had. He pulls our bodies apart, placing his hands on my shoulders.

"I don't know how to thank you, Lainey. I can't believe you did this. For me. I—" Three quick knocks at the door cuts him off.

Dang it.

He puts his arms down and Maeve's face peeks around the door.

"Hello, darlings. I'm sorry I took so long. It seems we have a hungry bunch out there and that turkey is looking far too perfect to be eaten cold, so do you think we can get going with dinner?" She smiles sweetly, communicating *what the hell is going on* to me with only her eyes. "Hi River."

He lifts a hand to acknowledge Maeve's greeting and my nervous energy takes over again.

"Yes, let's go eat. Everything is ready. Come on, Ad— River. We don't want it to get cold." I grab his wrist and pull him out of the room and into the kitchen.

At some point, I must have let go because my hands are

free by the time I make it over to the stove next to George, who rubs my arms and gives me a kiss on the cheek.

"Dinner smells fantastic, darling." I smile up at him before I look back at where Adam is standing. He's frowning, his hands are in fists next to him and he's looking straight at George.

9 /
does anyone here know the heimlich?

adam

MY HEART LEAPT into my throat when I saw her. She's here, and she isn't angry? She, for some odd reason, understands. I had imagined this moment dozens of times, but never with a result like this: her laughing and jumping into my arms. I knew why Raf had an expression that suggested he wanted to strangle me when he heard her call me Adam. As both my bodyguard and friend, he guards my private life fiercely. He's been one of the few people to call me by my first name for so long. Even my parents switched to River years ago.

When I told Lainey she can call me whatever she wants when it's just us, a crimson blush crept over her cheeks and down her neck. I couldn't help the smile on my face as I took her in. She's so beautiful and completely unaware of her sex appeal.

My breath caught in my throat when she cupped my face in her hands. I hadn't seen the depths of her eyes until then, and they sparkled like a pond reflecting the light of the setting sun. I suddenly felt like I was standing on quicksand, sinking and unable to move. She has eyes like green jewels.

Like emeralds. Like grass on a summer's day. With rare, precious specks of gold, warm like a soothing ray of sunshine.

And now she just told me she made a practice turkey dinner. She wanted to practice before making me this entire meal all over again. I meant it when I said I don't deserve her. Really, no one deserves someone this good. Except maybe her.

She deserves everything that is good, and that sure as hell isn't me. But I'll be damned if I don't try to be everything she wants. Everything she needs.

Whoa, slow down there, partner.

She's dragged me into the kitchen, and the moment we walk in I see a scrawny blond guy put his hands on her. She's smiling one of those wide-open smiles I wish were reserved just for me. He rubs her shoulders, kisses her on the cheek, and calls her darling.

Who the hell is this idiot?

Lainey looks back at me, but I'm too busy glaring at Mr. Handsy. Maeve calls everyone into the dining room and we all head in to sit down. L is directly across from me, and I only wish I could be next to her so I could be closer, though this is second best because I can see her face and that incredible smile from here.

Raf stands up and clears his throat, calling attention to everyone around the table. "Excuse me, everyone. Before we all dig into this magnificent meal, I want to say thanks to the beautiful Elaina for putting it all together. Baby girl, you're one of a kind and we're all so lucky to have you." He winks at her, and I have murderous thoughts about my best friend.

Baby girl? Gonna have some questions for him later.

The table erupts in a cheer of thanks. I look away from my best friend's smug face to the woman across from me. Her smile is tight and forced. She's blushing, tucking her hair behind her ear, and she's looking at me with a silent cry for help. She clearly doesn't enjoy being the center of attention.

I mouth the words *thank you* and send her a wink of my own. The blush on her cheeks deepens immediately, but her whole face softens. Her eyes go hazy, her smile widens, and she lets out a little chuckle. She nods once before she looks down at her hands as Maeve passes her a dish, breaking our trance. The obvious change in her demeanor from Raf's public display of gratitude to our private moment warms my chest.

Oh, beautiful girl, I see you.

Dinner is loud and delicious. The company is actually pretty great, but the food... it's perfect. I still can't believe she made all of this on her own. We all sit, unable to move, drinking wine and talking around the table until George gets up and clears dishes away. He and his partner Jon (yes, I feel like an ass for being jealous) grab the dishes while the other guys clear the food away. I get up to help and catch glimpses of Lainey buzzing around the kitchen getting dessert set up. She laughs when Raf tries to sneak a piece of apple crumble, shooing him away with her hip. I had no idea they knew one another. And well, by the looks of it.

Once we're back at the table, everyone passes around the pies: pumpkin, pecan and apple crumble. Lainey sits silently, her olive eyes scanning each person as they chose their slices, her lips pursed in thought as if she were filing away their preferences for later reference.

"River, aren't you going to have any?" The question comes from Charlie, who is currently serving herself a slice of pecan pie.

"Yes, of course." I look to Lainey, serving herself some apple crumble. "L, can you pass me the apple crumble, please? That's my favorite." I can't help the smile that comes over my face when I see her big green eyes sparkle with joy.

She reaches out with the plate and when I take it from her, my fingers very intentionally brush over hers. I also don't miss how both Maeve and Rafael perk up at my use of a nickname. Maeve's mouth curls up slightly as Raf's gaze fixates on Lainey, searching her face for a response. He doesn't get one and passes me the ice cream because apple crumble without ice cream is a crime. My best friend might be a little pissed off at me, but he wouldn't withhold ice cream.

The apple crumble is the best thing I've ever tasted and I half groan, half moan when I take the first bite. "Oh my god. This is—" I'm midway through a bite of apple crumble when I happen to look up at her. Her thumb is dripping with ice cream and she licks it clean, her eyes meeting mine just as her tongue flicks over the tip and her lips close around it. I lose the ability to swallow. I'm so startled by the sight that I inhale sharply and start to choke. The spoon clatters against my plate and I desperately grab for my glass of water, spilling half of it onto the table in my haste.

"River, are you alright?" She's reaching her hand across the table, touching my wrist, eyes filled with concern. She has no idea. This woman has no idea of the power her simple actions hold, and my body feels like it's alive again. I've been in this dark place for far too long, and I'm not sure if I'm ready to make the leap into the light. But here she is, stirring something inside me that begs me to jump.

I make a point not to look at her for the rest of the time we're at the table and am the first to stand and start cleaning up once everyone is done. I can't get the image of her tongue out of my mind.

When Lainey gathers dishes, everyone protests and demands she go sit down. She huffs and sends everyone a glare that holds no actual menace, then promptly says thank you as Charlie hands her a cup of tea and sends her on her way to the living room.

I'm the next one to be kicked out. Maeve pulls me away from the kitchen. "Tonight, you're a guest. Next time, you're family. Take a load off and go keep my girl company. You can clean up next time." We all say goodbye to George and his family, who need to get their baby to bed, and I make my way to the living room.

I walk over to the couch and sink into the cushions next to L. Her eyes widen in surprise at first, then soften with a welcoming smile. I take a moment to take in her tired appearance; her previously vibrant green eyes are now slightly glazed over and her shoulders slump with weariness.

"You alright?" I turn so I'm facing her as she's sitting with her legs under her, much like a few weeks ago, on the night we met.

She tilts her head, and her plump lips curl into a genuine grin. Her deep emerald eyes sparkle as they move back and forth across my face, scrutinizing each detail as if trying to commit my features to memory. Although I'm initially taken aback by her intense stare, I soon feel strangely comforted by the warmth emanating from her gaze. "I can't believe you're really here."

I nod, smiling back at her. "Me too."

Her eyes widen and she brings a hand up to her mouth. "I said that out loud?" She slowly brings her trembling hand up to cover her face, the warm blush creeping up her neck and staining her cheeks pink. Her embarrassment is palpable, yet her honesty is endearing. Looking more serious, she asks, "Did you know we'd be seeing each other today? I mean, did you know I was here?"

My hands are in fists on my lap. I wish I'd told her sooner. I wish I knew she'd be here today. I wish everything didn't have to change. "No. No, I had no idea. I wasn't expecting to see you for a few more days. Please believe me. I—"

She stops me with a hand on my arm. "I do. I believe you, Adam. Ah, fuck, shit. River. Sorry. I'll work on it." She lets out a huff and shakes her head. I inwardly smile at the contradiction that is her blushing cheeks and her love of profanities. "I'm not mad. I was just curious." She sips her tea and when she sets it down on the table, her posture is a little straighter.

"Now I know what you do for work. It's not a big secret anymore. That feels kind of nice. You're an actor. And Maeve's co-star. Ugh, sorry. Is that weird? That I already know these things about you?" She moves her eyes and lips in an exaggerated frown, and I chuckle at her monologue. She's a one-woman show, and I'm fascinated. I would buy a ticket if I had any money on me.

"It's not weird, but now I want to know about you. What's this job of yours that you're taking a break from? Are you an astrophysicist? Brain surgeon? Kindergarten teacher?"

"Okay, stop, stop." She puts her hands up, palms facing me, and I have the insane urge to kiss her hands, her fingers, her wrist. *Yeah, that is insane, so you can stop now.* "Those jobs are all far more stressful than my actual job and I'm going to start feeling really bad about taking a break if you say anything else. I'm a production designer. There."

"What, like for movies?" And I immediately feel like an asshole for my incredulous tone.

She laughs. "Just movies lately, yes, but I've worked on TV shows and Broadway, too." She doesn't seem to want to go into detail about it, nor is she phased at the tone of my question. "I don't have any new projects until later this year, so I'm taking this break now because I haven't really had a chance to do that since my first… uh… since one of the shows I worked on did unexpectedly well." She clears her throat and looks up behind me.

Maeve is walking in, one eyebrow up high on her forehead. "Uh oh, Bonnie's got her *I-don't-want-to-talk-about-how-brilliant-I-am* look on her face. What did you do, River? Ask Ms. James about all the awards she's won?" *Awards? How have I never heard of her before?*

Lainey shoots her friend a serious look, but it softens when Raf squeezes her shoulder and places a kiss on her head. "Baby girl is all kinds of brilliant, but far too humble about it." She rolls her eyes but smiles at both of her friends.

I've never seen Raf kiss a woman on the head who wasn't his relative. These people kiss a lot! What the hell is going on here?

"Don't listen to them. They love to embellish." She smiles over at me, waving her hand in the air to dismiss her friends' comments.

"Wait. Raf called you Elaina earlier. Is Lainey a nickname for Elaina?" She nods quickly. "You're Elaina James. You're... holy shit! How did I not know this? You're insanely talented. Your show completely shattered records in viewership and awards... I've watched the series like three times." I could keep going and completely fanboy over how she's the youngest showrunner to ever win so many awards, but I can tell this makes her uncomfortable. She hides behind her tea as she mumbles a *thank you*. Far too humble, indeed.

Maeve and Raf are laughing at her reaction when Charlie walks in, looking over at Raf, who is seated on a sofa by himself. She spins her body, silently asking Lainey to move over. She has some sort of aversion to him, that much is crystal clear. L scoots in a bit and gestures to the spot on the couch where she had just been sitting for Charlie. Our legs are almost touching now, and I can feel the warmth of her skin radiating towards me.

The conversation moves to what's planned for the week ahead before shooting starts, and I notice Lainey is quiet. When I look over at her, her eyes are hazy, and she nearly spills her now lukewarm tea. I reach over and grasp the teacup in my hand. She leans back into me, and I can feel her body relax against mine. Her body is like a warm embrace and the scent of coconut and honey fills the air around me. Suppressing a deep breath, I shift as her head comes to rest gently on my shoulder.

"Hey, you must be so tired. Why don't you go to bed?" I whisper this to her while everyone is still debating whether we should go to the London Eye tomorrow. Raf really seems to want to go.

She shifts her head, so she's looking up at me. "No, I like this. A full house, the chatter, it makes me happy... plus, you're so warm." She snuggles closer and I'm about to lift my arm to put around her when I catch Rafael's stern look again. *What the hell is his problem?* I decide against it and just let her be.

She wraps both hands around my bicep and mumbles something I can't make out.

The warmth of her breath slowly spreads through me, and I feel her body further relax into mine. Even though I've only known her for a few weeks, I feel comforted by her presence. I can't help but get lost in the details of her face, taking in the beauty of her thick eyelashes resting on her cheeks and the way her lips, slightly parted, are fuller on the bottom than the top. When I look up, I see my best friend walking straight towards us.

"I'm gonna take her to her room. Baby girl's exhausted." I open my mouth to say I can do it, but he shoots me another deadly look. He looks over at Maeve now. "Wait for me before you talk about this. *Adam* here's got a story he needs to tell us."

Fuck. But he's right. They should know what's going on, especially since we're apparently going to be spending a lot of time together.

He picks Elaina up gently and carries her away. He comes back in just a couple of minutes, taking L's seat between Charlie and me.

Charlie quickly rises from her seat. She nods to the group, a half-smile on her face. "I'm going to let you all talk and I'll catch up tomorrow. It's late and I should really get home." Her eyes flick to her sister and she reaches out, giving her a pat on the arm. "Goodnight." With that, she turns and leaves, leaving me with Raf and Maeve.

I run my hands through my hair, then let out a deep

breath, ready to start talking. I tell them everything, except how I feel about her.

Maeve doesn't even look remotely surprised by anything I have to say. "So you're the mystery bloke she's been talking to for weeks. I knew something was up, but she was being vague. It all makes sense now." She looks at me, a serious look on her face. Then she looks at Raf, and back at me.

He takes this as his cue to start talking. "Elaina is like a sister to me. Her brother and I were in the same task force and he's one of the best people I know." He takes a deep breath and stares at me with a storm in his eyes. It all makes sense to me now; Owen is Raf's business partner, yet he only ever refers to him as James. I'd thought that was his first name. "I love you, man. You know that. But I love her, too. She's been through a lot and she deserves to find real happiness. She puts her friends and family above everything else—sometimes even herself. She has the biggest heart."

"I know, man. I haven't known her as long as either of you, but I see that." I've never heard him talk like this about anyone but his mother, and that woman is a damn angel for putting up with him and his brothers.

His expression hardens again, like he's about to say something I'm not going to like. "Just… please be careful with her, alright?" And I hear everything he's not saying. *Don't let your shit get in the way. Don't hurt her.*

Maeve says nothing, but her eyes are beseeching. "He's right. Elaina is the best, and she clearly already cares about you in case the gigantic dinner and three pies weren't obvious proof of that. Be gentle with our girl. She needs someone who can understand all the ways she thinks she's broken and be patient with her as she figures out that she's perfect just as she is."

I look her in the eyes and bow my head slightly in a gesture of respect, hoping she can see the sincerity in my expression and know that I would never do anything to hurt her best friend.

I thank Maeve before heading to my place with Raf. We've made plans to go to the London Eye in the morning. I would have said no, but Maeve said it's one of Elaina's favorite things to do when she comes to London, and she usually goes alone.

If it wasn't for the jet lag, I'm not sure I'd be getting any sleep tonight.

————

I RAP on Maeve's door and hear a muffled, "Come in!" before she scurries away. I walk through the entrance hall and see Charlie eating in the kitchen. The smell of fresh-brewed coffee wafts through the air, and I hear hushed voices coming from the dining room—Maeve and Raf are going over the security details one last time before we set off.

"You have a thing about being early." Charlie smiles at me and takes a bite of her omelet. "Your girl's right in there." She points to the living room, and I don't bother correcting her. I nod at Charlie and go straight in.

She's perched on the edge of an oversized armchair, swinging her legs back and forth. The caramel-colored knitted sweater tucked into her black, cropped pants hangs loosely off her shoulders, and the sleeves are folded carelessly up to her elbows. Her auburn hair is pulled into a sleek ponytail. She smiles to herself as she reads the book in her hands, occasionally pausing to play with the ends of her hair. Unaware of the eyes on her, she bites her lower lip in concentration.

With no prompting, she looks up, sees me, then does a double take, quickly setting her book down. A wide grin spreads across her face and sends a bolt of warmth up my entire body. "Good morning, come in, sit."

"Morning. What are you reading?" I ask, pointing to the

book on the table next to her. I can't help jumping right in. I want to know everything about her.

"Oh, ummm it's the second book in that series I started…" She blushes a little and bites her lip again.

"Ohhhhh, so you liked the romance novel? You never told me how that first one ended." My eyes follow the line of her legs up to her calves and back down. I can't help but smile as I admire her cute, exposed ankles and soft feet dangling from the edge of the couch. I'd be lying if I said I didn't appreciate a good ass, but ankles are apparently my weakness. Or maybe it's just her because I'm not sure I've ever had a reaction like this to ankles before.

That can't be normal. Ankles?

"I didn't tell you? It got steamy. Or is the term spicy? Either way, it was hot. Then he ended up moving to be with her and they lived happily ever after. Blah!" She sticks out her tongue and giggles and I laugh with her.

Raf sticks his head in the room. "Mornin' baby girl. Adam. I think we're ready to head out when you are." He doesn't seem angry with me anymore, so that's a plus. "Elaina, we have someone else coming in for security, but I wanted to run it by you first."

"Me? Why me?" She sits up, grabs her cup and stands, a confused look on her face.

"Well, the second guy is Owen." He doesn't flinch, but something in his eyes tells me he's worried about what her reaction to this will be.

"Owen? Owen James? My brother? Owen's coming to London? Like here? To work as a bodyguard to Hollywood stars?" She looks at him with the kind of skepticism that screams *no fucking way*. She laughs and gently slaps his shoulder. Lainey saunters towards the kitchen, her hands cupping her empty coffee cup as she shakes her head. "Good one, Raf." She laughs again, mumbling, "My brother… here. Ha!"

He stalks her into the kitchen, and I obviously follow,

needing to know what's happening. "His flight lands at ten o'clock tomorrow morning." She stops so abruptly that he crashes into her. "He said no the first thirty-eight times I asked, but once he knew you'd be here too, he said he wanted to do it."

She spins around quickly and I can see her eyes are glassy. "Really? He—he said that?"

His shoulders relax, and he releases a long, slow sigh of relief. "Yeah. He said he needed a change. He doesn't need to be at the office right now. Our operations manager has it all under control. I know you two worked things out, so this could be good for you?" He still seems unsure, but then...

"Ohmygodohmygodohmygod!" She impulsively jumps up and wraps her arms around him, her legs kicking up in the air as she jumps in joy. "Thank you. Thank you so much!"

So this is good.

He laughs and takes the mug from her hand before she drops it. Her eyes sparkle with joy as she quickly closes the gap between us, her arms wrapping around my neck, just like the night before. She tilts her head and whispers excitedly, "My brother's coming!" and I feel the joy radiating off of her.

When she pulls away, I hold her in place, brushing a stray hair off her cheek.

I want to be the one to put a smile like this on her face.

I just can't seem to let her go yet. "Are you happy?" I ask this, already knowing the answer.

"So happy. So, so happy." She's still whispering, like she just can't find her voice. She bites her lower lip, a big smile still in place. "Ah, this is the best day ever! I'm gonna go grab my coat." She scurries off to her room, and I immediately miss her body pressing up against mine.

Raf stares at me, then his gaze shifts to her curvy frame as she strides away. We both climb onto barstools at the kitchen island. His face is tight as he says, "Dude, you're done for. So fucked. Her brother will murder you if he catches you looking at his sister like that."

The smile on my face falls immediately. "What are you talking about?" I look at the countertop as though marble is the most fascinating thing in the world. I will my heartbeat to slow down, my body to cool off. It doesn't work.

"You're not fooling your oldest friend. Don't say I didn't warn you." He juts out his chin and points an accusing finger at me. His eyes are like two beacons of judgment.

"It's not what it looks like. She's great, but we're just friends. Nothing else." I exhale a shaky breath and lock my gaze with his. My heart feels heavy in my chest. "Plus, Sandra keeps saying she wants me to enter into some kind of arrangement-for-show so the paparazzi will leave me alone." I want to smash something just at the thought, but if the media doesn't back off soon, it's a possibility I have to consider. The constant attention is getting hard to take. And with no one bothering to ask about what projects I'm working on, and each interview solely focusing on whether I'm in a relationship or not, it makes sense to redirect the spotlight back to my movies.

He turns to look at me. "I hope you're not considering that shit." He scowls. I know it's a stupid idea. I don't want to do it. I wouldn't care so much about my image if it wasn't for the fact that I'm trying to be taken more seriously as an actor and eventually as a producer. Not even he knows about that yet, though.

I shrug, not really wanting to talk about this right now. "Let's go see if the girls are ready." We both get up and I know this isn't over, but I don't want to think about it anymore for today.

10 /
you want to kiss me where?

elaina

I BEAMED as I thought of Owen joining us soon, and in the excitement of the moment, I knew I had to take another glance at my Things That Make Me Happy to-do list. Grabbing the weathered notebook from the nightstand, I flip through the pages and sigh softly as I read it again and add a few more items.

·Go on a trip just for fun. Pick somewhere I haven't been, or somewhere I have been and loved. Go and eat all the delicious things, see all the beautiful things and do whatever the hell I want.

·Kiss someone. Make it someone really kissable. If they suck at it, stop and find someone new. Kiss because I love kissing and because it's fun.

·Buy (and wear) sexy lingerie. Try to make it comfortable. Don't look at the price tags. Feel good about your little secret no one else can see.

·Wax my lady parts. Just because I've always

wanted to try it. Because it's new. Because I want to know what it feels like.

·Spend more time with Owen. Show him the parts of my life he's missed and get to know the parts of his I've missed too.

·Sing in public. Like Karaoke? Whatever. Just sing. Sing all the songs I love most regardless of who's listening.

·Get back to doing yoga. Because it feels so good to move my body that way and because my mind needs clearing.

They all seem plausible, don't they? I didn't think I'd get to cross off spending time with Owen for a long time, and here we are. I guess I'll be staying in London a little longer. This day is really shaping up to be amazing. We're about to head to the London Eye, which is always my first touristy stop here, ever since I came for the first time.

I quickly grab my coat and, on my way back, I overhear the guys talking in the kitchen.

"It's not what it looks like. She's great, but we're just friends. Nothing else. Plus, Sandra keeps saying she wants me to enter into some kind of arrangement-for-show so the paparazzi will leave me alone."

Raf looks unimpressed at this fake relationship comment, and I'm frowning at the thought of it. "I hope you're not considering that shit."

Adam shrugs off the comment. "Let's go see if the girls are ready."

I take a few steps back and pretend like I didn't just hear all of that as I come around the corner.

"Ready!" I sound shrill and say it far too loudly, but I'm hoping they think I'm just still excited about Owen. Which I am, but now I also need to think about what Adam just said to Raf.

Maeve is at the door and I rush to her side, making sure we get into the same car before there's a chance for me to be caught in one with either of the guys.

"Let's go, Maevey. I have great news!" We step into the backseat of the first car and Charlie is already in the front seat. "Owen will be here tomorrow!" I raise my hands in the air as far as I can get before touching the roof of the car.

Charlie smiles widely and pats my leg before she turns around to put her seat belt on. "That's wonderful. Will he be here just visiting?"

"No, actually. He's coming to support Raf. I guess you all will need more security than they anticipated. I glance at her out of the corner of my eye and see a forced, unnatural smile spreading across her lips. I fasten my seatbelt, trying to make sense of her expression. There's no use in questioning Raf about the heightened security measures. He doesn't mess around when it comes to his job, and I didn't press for more information since he usually keeps it close to his chest, anyway.

"Yeah, I met with Rafael this morning. You can cross off another item, Bon." So she's fine, I guess? Looked like she was maybe a bit upset when I first mentioned it. "More time with your big bro!"

I smile as my heart flutters with happiness at the thought of spending time with Owen. Maeve and Charlie go on chatting about some meeting they have to go to later. Char handles all of Maeve's finances, being that she's sort of a math wiz and has at least two degrees in economics now. I process while they talk.

So, Adam thinks I'm amazing. That's nice. But he wants to be just friends, which is for the best. His presence definitely does weird things to me, but I'm not doing relationships. Nope. No way. Not now, maybe not ever. If I couldn't even manage a relationship with a guy like Ben who hardly ever wanted sex, traveled all the time for work and who literally never argued about anything, I don't even want to know what being with someone who isn't a robot would be like. And I'm focusing on myself, right? This isn't the right time to focus on someone else.

And the thing about his publicist wanting him to have a fake relationship? That's so messed up. I get wanting to get his name off the gossip blogs and all that, but what good would a fake relationship do?

I'm so caught up in my thoughts I don't even take in the city as we drive to the London Eye.

We arrive at the private entrance and quickly shuffle in, two well-known faces unobtrusively blending into the group. We're all inside in no time, which is so unusual for me when I visit here. There are probably some paparazzi outside, but once we're inside the pod, we're free from the public eye.

I'm immediately transported to my first time in London, and I feel the goofy smile on my face as we move up.

Adam's blue eyes are bright as he steps closer and nudges my arm. I can feel the warmth of his body radiating off him and smell his woodsy scent. His voice is low as he asks, "So, what's the story?"

"What story?" I ask, looking up at those ridiculously gorgeous blue eyes.

"With the London Eye? What's the significance?" He's turned now, so he's looking at me and not the upcoming view.

"Oh. Um, it was the first thing I did when I came to London for the first time." I shrug as I say this and he crosses his arms, raising his eyebrows as if to tell me to keep going with the story.

I sigh, happy he wants to hear more. "I waited in line for like two hours. It was spring, and the trees were gorgeous with blooms everywhere. Even the grass had come alive. I got into a pod with a group from Germany and they were so happy. They pressed their faces against the glass, mouths wide open with wonder. They asked me if I was all alone and I smiled so big when I said yes, feeling something like pride or maybe joy at the magnitude and simplicity of the moment. Everyone wanted to take pictures as we stood on the edge of the pods with the London skyline in the background. I didn't take a single photo that day. I just stood, looking out, smiling the entire time."

I keep looking out at the view now, watching as the Houses of Parliament, Westminster Abbey, and Big Ben come into view. "It was such a freeing experience that when I visited London a year later, I came back. Alone again, standing in line for a crazy amount of time again. Maeve and Charlie came with me a few times. Now, every time I visit, this is the first thing I want to do." I shake my head and let out a deep breath.

"I get to reflect on who that nineteen-year-old was, and all the ways I've changed since standing in one of these pods looking out at this unchanging city. Looking at London's skyline, with its ancient cathedrals, shining skyscrapers, and rows of terraced houses packed so tightly it seems they'll collapse in a heap. I think of my own life in the past decade— falling in love, experiencing heartbreak, losing my dad, the work I've done; the good times full of joy and the bad times of sorrow; all the lessons I've learned and the growth that has come. I feel a deep connection with this city; ever-changing on the inside, yet forever stoic on the outside. It's where I decided I wanted to pursue my career."

When I finish my little monologue, he is still in the same pose. Arms crossed, staring intently at me. I struggle to meet his eyes, and when I do, they look bluer than the unusually bright sky above us, so clear and sparkling. He's smiling at me, then he shakes his head softly. His lips part, as if he's about to say something, then he closes them again.

After a breath, he says, "Keep going."

"I always knew I would find a way to balance my father's love of architecture with mine—he saw the mathematics and engineering of a building, while I saw its heart and soul. I've crafted a career in set design, envisioning every little detail of the lives happening inside the walls. It's the details that create the story, so I pour my heart into creating sets that are multifaceted and bring the characters' lives to life. The actors, the music—those all matter, too, of course, but the little nuances of everyday life are key components in capturing an audience."

His arms are at his sides now, and there's a crease between his eyebrows. His gaze is like a hot beam of sunlight, and it warms me from the inside out. He takes a slow breath. "Wow."

The word hangs in the air for a few seconds. He holds my gaze, then he seems to snap out of a trance, holding onto the railing with both hands.

"I get it." He faces the view now, taking in the same buildings I've looked at once a year for ten years. And that's all he needs to say. He has no questions, no commentary of his own. We stand, studying the buildings, the water, and the people on the bridge in comfortable silence while our friends chat just behind us.

Half an hour later, we're all scurrying out to get back to our cars. Someone catches sight of Maeve, and before we know it, dozens of people are chasing her. Raf rushes her into a car with Charlie, leaving me to ride back to the apartment with Adam.

Good. Great. Maybe I can talk to him now about our friendship. No time like the present, right?

Once the car is moving, I quickly blurt out the words before I can change my mind. "I need to talk to you about something." I turn slightly in my seat once I'm buckled in. No beating around the bush.

He turns as well, but motions to the driver first. "Can we take the scenic route back, please?" Now he gives me his eyes and smiles. "Talk to me, L."

Ugh. I love that stupid nickname.

I smile back, wondering how not to sound like an asshat when I say what I need to say.

"I've really enjoyed getting to know you. You're easy to talk to and be around, and I don't find that with many people, and…" Oh God, his face. It reminds me of Frankie when I scold him for chewing up my socks, like he's confused and just wants to go run outside. I clear my throat. "I know we've sort of already talked about this, but I need to be perfectly clear."

Deep breath in, deep breath out.

He stares at me, eyes narrowed, and brow furrowed, as if I'm speaking a foreign language. I draw a long, slow breath, determined to get the words out.

"Look, I want us to be friends, plain and simple. No funny business. I have to know you understand that's all it can be— no hidden agenda. I don't want to lie to you about my feelings, or anything else, for that matter."

My palms are sweaty, my stomach in knots. I've barely taken a breath before the words are out of my mouth, cascading like a waterfall of anxiety.

"I don't want a relationship," I say firmly, still unable to look him in the eye. "After three years with Ben and how it ended and how it was for that whole time… I can't go through that again." I'm rambling, unable to bear the heavy silence that will surely follow my words.

"And I don't sleep around. Not anymore, anyway. That didn't do good things for me either." I finally meet his gaze and I feel my face flush with embarrassment, realizing how insane I must sound. Taking a deep breath, I try again.

"But I do like you. A lot. And I want us to be friends. What I really need is a friend."

I finish my needlessly long speech with my hands all tied up in knots on my lap. He is looking at me with a curious expression. He looks down at his lap and then back up at me with a small smile.

"So, what exactly do friends do?" He sees the shocked look on my face and keeps going. "I mean, I don't have female friends. You have guy friends, at least I see you with Raf and you two seem to have a good thing going. So, what exactly does friendship look like?"

"We do what we've been doing. We talk, we spend time together, we do things for each other." Easy peasy. I got this.

"And what are the boundaries?" He looks serious.

He's seriously asking me about boundaries right now?

"Umm, well obviously there are certain things friends *don't* do, like kiss, see each other naked, touch, you know… bathing suit areas…." I really just brought up seeing one another naked, didn't I?

Stop thinking about him naked! Now! And bathing suit areas? Are you ten?

"But you and Raf kiss. So maybe there are just certain places friends don't kiss, is that correct?" His one eyebrow dances skyward and he still seems genuinely curious about our friendship boundaries. How is he so cool about this? I'm sweating hard over here.

"Right. There are definite no-kiss zones." I wave my arms over my chest and crotch, feeling like a true idiot.

That's because you are an idiot.

He chuckles, removes his seat belt and moves closer to me. Shit. I can smell his cologne and it's delightful. That foresty scent is making my head all fuzzy.

"Raf kissed you on the head, so that's allowed, right?" He leans in and places a kiss on my temple, then my forehead as I nod. "And George kissed you on the cheek. We've done that before, so that's alright too?"

He leans in and I feel his beard on my cheek before his soft lips deliver a kiss there. I nod again.

"How about here?" He kisses my jaw, and I can feel his breath land on my neck, warm and soft.

"Ummm, sure." I chastise myself for how shaky my voice sounds, because he seems completely unphased by all this kissing.

"And here?" His nose brushes against my earlobe, and his lips leave a scalding kiss on my neck. My breath hitches and I can hear my heartbeat pounding in between my ears. He sits back so he can see my face, which is about eight different shades of red, I'm sure. "Lainey?"

Fuck, fuck, fuck. Get it together!

"N–no. No, I don't think that's a good place for friends to kiss." I swallow hard and feel his hand on my shoulder as it travels down my arm. He picks up my hand.

"Okay. I'm sorry." I see his apologetic eyes and nod. "How about here?" He brings my hand up to his face and brushes his nose across my knuckles before placing a kiss on each one.

"F-fine. The hand is fine," I say a little too breathlessly for my liking. But maybe it's because I see what he's doing next.

He puts the tips of my fingers to his lips and I can't help it, they move over his delicious mouth all on their own.

You don't know that his mouth is delicious, so stop thinking about it!

I can't tell if he says anything. The heartbeat thumping in my ears is too loud. He keeps going, holding my hand as he brings my wrist to his lips. I feel his breath against my pulse and when his lips touch down, I can't take any more. Surely he can see, hear, and feel how fast my heart is beating now.

The car comes to a stop, and I yank my hand away from his grip. "No, not there either." I fumble with my seat belt and bolt out of the car, taking in huge gulping breaths of the chilled winter air.

Seriously, what the hell just happened?

is drinking beer sexy now?

adam

MAYBE I WENT TOO FAR, but I was upset by what she said and wanted to prove that there was more between us than just friendship. I know what I told Raf, but that was bullshit. I said that to stop him from scowling at me and asking more questions. Plus, what kind of deal did she have with Ben? When she mentioned hooking up with other people, a wave of envy took over—which probably pushed me to wanting to kiss her all over. I don't want anyone else's lips on her, only mine.

Then I decided to test our boundaries. I've seen how affectionate she is with her friends, and I wanted to know if that affection applies to me as well. I'd have to be an absolute idiot not to notice how some of those kisses affected her. I know they did. Her breath changed, and her face flushed. I just about lost it hearing her gasp when I kissed her neck. And now I know her wrist is a sensitive spot. I've just learned a few important things about my girl.

My girl? Dude. No. Not yet.

I also know I need to respect her wishes. If she really

wants to be just friends, I won't force anything. I'm not that guy. I just have to be patient.

When she storms out of the car, I'm thankful for the moment to settle the raging hard-on in my pants. I get out of the car and see she's leaning against it, her face red and her body rigid with tension. We walk side by side, neither of us willing to touch, until we reach Maeve's door. I look at her to see if she's still flustered, and all that remains is a cool mask of indifference. "Do you want to come in? We can wait for them in here." Her voice is surprisingly level.

I walk in and she shrugs her coat off, hanging it by the front door. She slips her shoes off and starts walking towards the kitchen, bringing her arms up as she removes her sweater to reveal a white tank top underneath, which rides up as her sweater comes off. My eyes travel from her toned arms down to her little waist, down further…

Goddamn, she has the perfect ass.

"Do you want some water? Or tea?" She's already in the kitchen when she asks and I'm still wearing my coat, thinking about her perfect body walking away from mine.

"Wa–water's good."

Why is my voice hoarse?

I step into the kitchen, and she stands on one side of the counter with two glasses already filled. The glint of the glassware in the light catches my attention. I grab a tall barstool from the corner, its metal legs clanking as I pull it up to the opposite side of the counter. We both meet each other in the silence and take a sip of cool water.

"Alright, so now we have kissing and touching boundaries. Do you have any other questions?" She's serious and seems fully recovered from the car kisses.

"What kinds of things do you do with your friends? Is going out for meals allowed? Or spending time together alone?" Because I want to spend so much time alone with her. So, so much time.

"Of course. There's no *allowed*. We can always talk about things as they happen, so if either of us is uncomfortable with something, we just say so." She's holding on to the countertop with both hands, elbows locked and eyes on me. "For example, if someone you're dating doesn't like us spending time together, we talk about it." She grabs her glass to drink some more water, her eyes widening as she realizes it's empty.

"Well, we don't have to worry about that. I'm not dating anyone, nor will I be." I hear myself and feel genuinely surprised I've just admitted this. But it's true. I will not be dating anyone. No way. Not when I know the exact shade of pink her neck turns when she's flustered from my kisses... or was she turned on?

"What kinds of things do you and Raf do?" I really want to know, because he says she's like a little sister, but I'm still a little jealous of how freely they hug and that nickname he has for her. Even though I know he has nicknames for everyone.

She turns around and gets more water from the dispenser on the fridge door. She lets out a little laugh.

"Well, we used to do this thing where we would pretend to be dating." She turns around, smiling, and her eyes go big when she sees the stupefied look on my face. "Oh no. No, no, no. Not like that. If he saw a guy hitting on me and he could tell I wasn't into it, he'd walk over, throw an arm around my shoulder and scare the dude away. It helps that his nickname for me definitely has a double meaning." A giggle escapes her lips as her eyes light up and she lets out a content sigh, as if recalling a pleasant moment in time.

"Oh? And what did you do? I can't imagine Raf wants girls scared away that often. He seems to give them all equal attention." I get up now to pour myself another glass of water and she turns, resting her hip on the countertop so we're facing one another.

"Oh, the same. Cling to him, run a finger down his chest

and call him baby in my most obnoxious voice," she says this quickly. "And you'd be surprised. He can be very picky. I have a signal. I pull on my left ear when I'm not into the guy. He isn't as subtle. He's not subtle at all, actually. Usually, he'll just send me a look when, as he says, *a girl is just tooooooo thirsty.*" She deepens her voice to sound like Raf at that last part, and we both burst out laughing.

That feels good. Seeing her laugh. Laughing with her. "Okay, that's good. You look out for one another. What else?"

She bites her lower lip, thinking as she looks down at her feet for a second. "Oh! Maeve and I used to share a music playlist, adding whatever song we were loving at the time. In the end, we got this wild mix of music and we both still listen to it, even years later." She shrugs, looking at me like maybe she's second-guessing what she just suggested.

"I really like that. Can we start our own playlist?" I mimic her stance, leaning on the countertop, taking another drink and taking in the sight of her in these tight pants and tank top.

"Really? You want to?" She stands up straight, her pony-tail bouncing as she does. I nod at her once. "Oh, my gosh, yes. Let's do it. I'll send you one tonight. Is that okay?" Her genuine excitement about this one simple thing is contagious. I may want to be more than friends with her, but if being *just* friends, as she put it, is what she needs, I'm actually willing to do it. It's worth it to see her this happy.

"Yeah, that sounds great. We can try to add a song a day for now, so we get a solid list going." She's still smiling wide and, unsurprisingly, I smile right back at her.

Our moment is broken when Raf, Maeve, and Charlie storm into the apartment.

"Wow, those guys were tough to get rid of," Charlie says as she plops herself down on a stool. "Good thing Owen is getting here tomorrow. Looks like word is out that River and Maeve are in town for this movie."

"Yeah, about that, we're going to have to switch some things around." Raf has his bodyguard voice on. It's a little deeper and much more serious than his usual tone. "I'm going to be here with Maeve. Owen is going to stay with Adam, so that means you get an apartment for yourself, baby girl." He quickly glances at Charlie, and she flinches. "Chuck, if you need a room when you visit, there's an extra in Elaina's flat." Charlie's scowl grows when Raf uses his nickname for her.

"Whoa, wait, why are we leaving Lainey on her own? That doesn't seem right," I pipe up immediately, because WTF, Raf?

He smiles at me, that sideways smile that tells me he heard everything I didn't say. "Alright, Lancelot, you can put your shining armor away. This princess doesn't need your rescuing." He glances over at Lainey, who has her arms crossed and is giving me an inquisitive stare, her eyebrows lifting high towards her forehead.

"That's right. I'm not a famous movie star so I don't need a bodyguard. I'll be fine." She stares at me with a glare that quickly melts away into an expression of understanding. Her ability to forgive quickly is something I had noticed about her before. "I'll be coming and going anyway, so it makes sense that I have my own place. With your hectic filming schedules, we probably won't even see each other much."

Oh. Coming and going? Won't be seeing one another much? Hmm. I don't like that.

I let out a low growl and try to cover it up with a cough, but Raf definitely hears it.

"Fine." And now I look like a pouty toddler.

Lainey giggles, then reaches up and kisses me on the cheek. She repeats the move almost identically with Raf and walks off.

"Thanks, boys. I'll go pack up and make sure the room is clean and ready for O tomorrow."

I'm not sure if I love or hate that Raf and I just got the same treatment. On one hand, I like that she felt comfortable enough to kiss my cheek after everything else today. She recovers quickly, that's for sure. On the other, I don't want to be forever friend-zoned along with Raf. No fucking way!

———

LAINEY MOVES into an apartment on the floor below ours, and I see little of her over the next few days. I wanted to give her space to spend time with her brother, and it looks like he brought her dog, which she's very happy about. She texted me a selfie of her and Frankie, and I may have looked at it about a hundred times already. Per day. We've started our playlist, and looking back at our text exchanges this week makes me laugh.

TUESDAY

TORNEROSE

Okay, I sent you the playlist. Song number 1 is in honor of your motherland. Enjoy.

ME

"California Love" - classic.

Also, we're starting with the '90s, huh? I like it.

TORNEROSE

Glad you approve. Looking forward to your contribution!

"Yellow" is such a great song!

ME

Well, we are in Coldplay's motherland now. Felt appropriate.

> How do you feel about a '90s and '00s playlist?

> How's Owen liking London? You two seem to be busy tourists this week!

TORNEROSE

I feel very, very good about that!

He's falling in love with London, as everyone does. We went to Tower Bridge today. Did you know there's a secret chamber down there?

WEDNESDAY

TORNEROSE

Gave the East Coast some love today on the playlist today ;)

ME

> I didn't know that about Tower Bridge! We'll have to go back sometime.

> "Mo Money Mo Problems" - Okay, I see you, L. '90s rap is your thing

TORNEROSE

A few songs in and you don't know what my 'thing' is yet! I'm full of surprises!

ME

> I don't doubt it.

> Your song is ready.

TORNEROSE

OHHHH MY GOSHHHHH! "Let's Get Married" is a whole jam! Definitely a kitchen dance song.

ME

You better not be having a dance party without me.

Hope you and Owen are having a good day.

THURSDAY

ME

Ready for you, L. I added "21 Questions" by 50 Cent - it's a classic.

I also added "Let Me Love You" by Mario to the list. Seemed appropriate ;)

TORNEROSE

I'm sorry, I haven't looked at my phone all day!

Added "Feelin' So Good" by Jennifer Lopez

Booked a trip to Paris for a few days on my own. Crossing things off my list! Leaving Sunday!

ME

I don't think I had heard that song before.

Why Paris? You better make sure I see you before then. Don't leave without saying bye!

TORNEROSE

Excuse me, do not insult queen J-Lo like this!

Because I love it there and it's close and you all are going to start filming anyway. I don't want to be in anyone's way while you're all busy working.

ME

You're never in the way.

How about a goodbye dinner tomorrow? I'll order and come down at 7.

TORNEROSE

I'd love that. I miss your face.

———

I'VE WORKED OUT, showered, read through lines, and I've just ordered Indian food to be delivered to Lainey's, so I head down to meet her. I rap my knuckles twice on the wooden door, and I hear a high-pitched bark followed by the sound of tiny paws scratching against the floor. A snuffling sound comes from underneath the door, and a deep growl emanates from the other side.

Frankie.

"Oh Frankie, relax!" The door creaks open, and I see her standing in the frame, her russet-colored hair cascading down her narrow shoulders, her fair skin bare of any makeup. Her perfect lips tilt up in a heart-stopping smile, and her bright green eyes sparkle with warmth and curiosity. Beside her, Frankie sits, his small body tense, unsure what to make of me. With a gentle wave, she welcomes me in.

"Hey, Frankie!" I can't believe I'm greeting the dog first, putting my hands down low, palms up to invite him in. Lainey's reaction tells me somehow I did the right thing though, as her smile gets even bigger and Frankie sniffs my hand, giving it a lick.

"Oh, my gosh, he likes you! He doesn't like any men." She scratches behind his ear and bends to kiss his head affection-ately. Then she does what she does. Lunges into my arms and I unhesitatingly catch her around the waist.

"Hi! It's so good to see you." She pulls back and her hands linger on my chest as she gazes up at me. "Hi."

"Hey, L." My eyes move over her whole face, taking in

every detail, like the way her eyes look extra emerald green today.

Her eyes and hand land on my beard at the same time.

"It's even longer! Are you playing a yeti in this movie?" She scrunches her nose and then pulls away, smiling. She walks into the apartment, and I take her fully in. Her leggings, cropped T-shirt, and bare feet.

Is she trying to kill me?

I reluctantly look away from her body and take in her apartment. It's much smaller than my own, and Maeve's identical one, but it feels much more inviting. A dog bed lies on the floor and books I had recommended to her line the coffee table. Brightly colored flowers are placed in a vase on the kitchen counter, and a small smile creeps onto my face as I react to her joke about my beard.

"I wasn't sure how long they needed it, so I just let it grow. It's so itchy." I follow her into the living room.

"Ugh, I bet! I tried to let my leg hair grow once and I couldn't. Everything rubbed against it and it got so itchy. Not my thing. I enjoy being hairless, thankyouverymuch!" She blushes and looks down at her dog, petting his head absent-mindedly. "Anyway, how has your week been?"

Now I'm thinking about how smooth her thighs probably feel under those pants.

Damn it. Already?

"Uh, good. The week's been good. I've been re-reading the script, and Raf and I got to spend some time together before he's officially on security duty." She smiles at the mention of my best friend. "What have you been doing these last couple of days?"

"Owen and I have been playing tourist all week and we've been squeezing in all the sites. Of course, I'm also throwing in some gems I know of after visiting so often. It's exhausting but in the best way. I almost didn't make it into pajamas last night after my shower. I was so ready to pass out." She blushes again and I'm pretty sure I do, too, now picturing her in nothing but a towel, getting into bed.

Is this what being her friend is like? Having to hear about her being smooth and falling asleep with no clothes on? I'm fucked.

"Anyway, he's loving it. And he brought me Frankie, which was such a nice surprise. There's a dog walker right in the building, so he's gotten lots of attention while I'm gone all day with O."

"Good. Good. I'm glad you two had a chance to spend time together." I'm doing my best to think about Owen now, to keep the images of a towel-clad, hairless Lainey at bay. "I met him yesterday. He's ummm…"

"Huge? Intimidating? Serious?" She laughs as I nod at every adjective she's throwing at me. "He's a big giant teddy bear. I promise."

"He seems like a great guy. Had nothing but nice things to say about you." I don't mention the absolutely terrifying look he shot me when I said I was friends with her. Protective big brother. I understand. And I appreciate why, but I'll have to win him over.

There's a knock at the door and she gets up. "I'll get it. Mind making sure Frankie stays put?" She points to his bed, and he obeys, going to lie down but never taking his eyes off of her.

I get it, little dude.

I crouch down to pet him and he flops onto his back, giving me his belly to rub. After a minute, I get up and walk to the kitchen.

"Thank you so much. I hope your night turns around. Bye, Pat." I hear her from the kitchen as she closes the door and skips to the spot next to me.

"Did you know the delivery guy?" I take one of the bags and start opening it up.

"No, but I asked his name and how his night was going. He's had a couple of difficult customers, so I left him an extra juicy tip." She opens up a container and inhales a deep breath as the smell of butter chicken fills the room.

"You know that was paid for with a tip, right? Maybe he was just playing you and was after the extra tip?" I'm not as trusting as she is, she sees the kindest parts in everyone.

"Well, then he really deserves it. Plus, it's gotta be hard carting food all over this busy city and I'm sure he gets some shitty attitudes thrown his way, so why not make his night?" She's bouncing around the kitchen, getting plates, glasses, and cutlery for us. "I don't care if he lied. Though I really don't think he did."

She flashes me a bright, toothy grin and walks over to the beverage fridge. I feel the heat spread from my cheeks as my gaze drops to her shapely backside. She grabs something from the bottom shelf and rises slowly, balancing herself with one hand on top of the fridge.

"Do you want beer, wine or water? Thanks for getting dinner, by the way. I love Indian food."

"Umm… whatever you're having is fine."

Think of Owen, her giant, scary brother. Do not think of her perfectly round ass. Do. Not.

She pops back up with two beer bottles.

"Beer it is. Does that work?"

My chest swells with anticipation as I nod in reply, and I feel a thrill of pleasure race through me as I imagine doing this night over and over, sharing beers and takeout with this kind-hearted, gorgeous woman before carrying her over my shoulder to the bedroom for…

Nope. Focus. Fuck, man, what is wrong with you?

We dish out our food, and she heads to the table.

"Sorry, I don't trust myself to eat this on the couch. It will end up all over me." She waves a hand across her chest and then opens our beers. "Cheers to our first beers together." She smiles, touching her bottle to mine and taking a drink from it.

How is she even sexy when she drinks beer?

. . .

THE NIGHT SPEEDS by while we're seated on the couch, talking just like we did when we first met. She's able to see me this time, and the room is brightly illuminated, so I can take in every detail of her. We both stop at two beers, and our conversation is easy—as it has always been.

We touch on our high school days, differences revealed now that I can open up more freely. She recalled how she'd dominate the basketball court with her tenacity, while I remembered the pungent scent of menthol cigarettes that my tutor would take smoke-breaks to have. She stayed up late, always ready to work at the local diner that was run by Betty, a tough-loving old lady, who took everyone under her wing. I, on the other hand, would often wake up early and perfect my technique in the swimming pool alone. It felt good to reminisce like this; to be so close and so open.

"So what about boys in high school? I bet you were asked out a lot." I smile, thinking of her driving all the boys crazy as a teenager.

Her lips are in a tight, straight line and her brows scrunch together. She looks down at her lap.

"Andy was my only high school boyfriend."

Shit. Fuck. Shit, shit, shit.

"I'm sorry. I'm so sorry. I'm an asshole—" I'm grabbing my hair and doing my best not to pull it all out. What a dumb-ass move.

"Stop. It's fine. You couldn't have known that." Her hand is on my knee, and she's lowered her head, trying to get me to look at her.

"I didn't start dating until I got to NYU. I hated high school boys. They were all so stupid and immature." She shrugs and opens her mouth, then closes it again like she's not sure she wants to continue. "When I started college and met the twins, I made it my mission to date as much as possible. I wanted to erase all proof of the girl I used to be. And I succeeded."

"So it was the college boys you had swooning every night of the week, then." I should really learn when to shut the fuck up.

Was that it? She dated lame frat boys?

There's a long silence as I think about how she told me she tried sleeping around and that didn't work for her.

"Just ask." She smiles at me, resting her cheek on her knuckles as she sits sideways.

"Ask what?" I do my best to look confused. I'm an actor. I should be able to handle this, but she sees right through me.

"Ask me about my days dating and sleeping around in New York." She's completely calm and looking at me with those deep green eyes.

I pause. I don't care what or who she did. It doesn't matter. But I want to know why. The curiosity is eating away at me.

"Why did you feel you needed to date so much when you moved there?" There. That seems safe.

"Like I said, I wanted to erase the girl I used to be. I was inexperienced, sheltered, even, and wanted to be the opposite. I'd also just had my first real relationship, and it ended... traumatically. I needed to see what regular dating was like." The words roll off her tongue so casually, like she's discussing the mundane details of her breakfast. She says it with finality, implying there's nothing else to be said and this is the truth.

"And what was regular dating like? I'm honestly curious because I'm not sure I've ever experienced it."

She runs her hands through her hair as she lets out a sigh and looks up at the ceiling.

"Let's see. A slew of unmemorable boyfriends, a few one-night stands because... why not? A lot of awful first dates. Not everything it's cracked up to be. Once I graduated, I was done with all of it. Something changed. What hadn't changed was how heartbroken I still was over Andy." Her eyes soften when she says his name, and her face seems to glow just thinking of him. "Before I knew it, I was in therapy again, trying to figure out how to let go of everything that had been holding me back. Then we moved to LA, and my dad died that same year. A lot changed."

"You can talk to me about them, L. You can talk about Andy. You can talk about your dad. You don't need to hold back. It won't make me uncomfortable, and I won't try to console you when you talk about them. I can just listen."

Her eyes fill with tears, and she looks down quickly, brushing a tear off her cheek before looking up at me again.

"Thank you. That's… thank you." She hesitates, a sadness clouding her face.

"Andy didn't break up with me." Her eyes meet mine and she must see the slight confusion on my face, so she keeps going.

"He, um, he died." She nervously chews her lip and glances away from me as she speaks. "I feel so guilty when I bring them up. People don't really like to talk about someone who's gone… but they're still so alive in my heart, in my thoughts, in my memories." She looks off into the distance, her eyes misting over with tears.

"Of course, they are. You should talk about them whenever you want to. At least know that with me you can." I'm taken aback at how naturally the words flow out of my mouth when I talk to her. It's as if I can say what I'm feeling without putting up any barriers or walls.

That's new.

Her eyes are glistening, so I try to think back to my last words, looking for a sign of what has upset her. But then her arms circle my neck and she pulls herself up on my lap, her lips pressing against my shoulder. She shifts her head slightly so that her warm breath spreads over my neck.

"I'm so happy that I met you. You're a wonderful person."

Her voice trails off into a faint whisper, and her breath hitches from her quiet sobs.

We sit in silence for what seems like an eternity, with my hand gently tracing circles on her back. When she finally pulls away, I tenderly grab her hands in one of mine, and when she tries to pull them away, I hold fast. Her gaze meets mine, her eyes wide and red-rimmed with tears. I tenderly use my thumb to wipe the salty droplets away from her cheeks, and she responds by leaning into my touch before closing her eyes.

"The last person to wipe my tears away like this was my dad." A few more tears escape and I cradle her face in my hands. I place a kiss on her forehead and bring our foreheads together, moving my hands back to hers. Our breaths mingle and my thumbs draw lazy circles on her knuckles, almost as if by instinct.

She's the first to pull away again, and I can see how tired she is now.

"You should get to bed, L." I bring one of her hands to my lips and kiss the back of it.

"Yeah. Yeah, I'm pretty tired." Nodding twice, she tucks some hair behind her ear and shifts away from me. "Thank you. For dinner, for talking, for listening. Just… thank you." Her chin wobbles and she takes a deep breath, as if to stop herself from crying again.

"Thanks for sharing another piece of yourself with me. I'm always here for you. Always." And I know at this moment that I really mean that. "Now my *tornerose* needs to get some shut-eye. Paris awaits!"

Her smile is small, but it reaches her eyes as we both get up from the couch and walk towards the door. We stand there for a few seconds just looking at one another before she says, "I'll miss your face."

I smile at her, committing this moment to memory. Her

slightly puffy eyes scanning my face, lips curved into a smile, telling me she'll miss me.

"Goodnight, L."

"Goodnight, Adam." I walk away and hear the door close, feeling both lighter and heavier. Lighter for having spent hours with the girl of my dreams, heavier knowing I won't see her tomorrow or the day after.

12 /
does this feel friendly to you?

elaina

I WAKE up to my alarm telling me it's 10 a.m. and I need to go to the airport in a couple of hours. I'm glad that Yesterday Elaina thought of packing ahead of time rather than leaving things to the last second. Today Elaina is grateful. I hear someone moving around the apartment and have a minor panic before remembering that my best friend has a key and wanted to come say goodbye before I fly out today.

"Good morniiiiing!" Of course, she's wide awake. Charlie walks in behind her mouthing an apology and lifting a very tall cup of coffee towards me. Maeve settles on the side of my bed. "Are you excited about Paris? You haven't been in years."

"I am excited. Last time I was there for research and there was so much I didn't get to do, but I'm going to miss being here. These last two weeks have been… so good. Just so good." I sip my coffee, thinking about Adam and Owen.

"It's been nice to spend time with your brother, huh?" Charlie smiles that small, secret smile of hers.

Maeve looks at me with narrowed eyes. "And River.

Adam. I don't know what to call him." She huffs and throws her hand in the air in a dramatically frustrated gesture.

"It's been really nice. Owen's really changed, and it finally feels like we're friends again. I missed him so much." I sip my coffee again, looking down at my cup, hoping we can avoid the elephant in the room.

"Uh-huh, that's wonderful. Owen is nice to you now. You're a family again. It's adorable and makes me so happy for you." Maeve shifts, so she's facing me on the bed. "But don't think you're getting away with avoiding the unavoidable, Bon! Talk to me about Adam."

"Oh, I don't know, Mae. We're friends. I like him a lot and he's so easy to talk to, but that's all it is."

Lies. You liar. Big fat liar, liar, pants on fire!

"Liar. Try again." Her face doesn't even twitch at my flimsy excuse. Charlie scoffs. They understand me too well, even when I don't want them to.

"It's too complicated. I already told him we can't be anything but friends and he agreed, so that's where we are now. Friends. Forever." Maeve laughs. She actually laughs at me. I just sit there staring at her gorgeous smiling face because I'm too stunned to do anything else.

"Oh, my love. You've got it bad. Pushing him into the friend zone isn't going to change that." Maeve looks to Charlie for confirmation of her latest statement.

Charlie shoots me another apologetic look. "Come on, Lainey, you know this could be something wonderful. Why are you pushing him away?" That's exactly what I'm doing and of course she is the one to call me out on it. "He's obviously enamored with you. Have you seen his sparkly blue eyes move all over you when you walk into a room?" She wiggles her eyebrows at me and lifts my chin so I can see her eyes.

"No, it's not like that. I overheard him telling Raf we're

just friends. And that he has some shit to sort through." I can feel my chin getting wobbly now.

Damn it, why am I so emotional these days?

"And I just can't get into another relationship. I wasn't happy in a long-term relationship, and I wasn't happy casually dating. And what did I learn from the whole experience? That I had a lot of growing up to do, that I needed to stop looking for someone else to make me happy, and that I wanted to be whole on my own. I think I had my one big love and maybe that's all we get in life." I shrug, not wanting to make a big deal out of what I've just said out loud.

"You know I think you're wrong about this. But I won't push you to do anything you don't want to do. You deserve to be happy. You deserve it more than anyone else I know." Maeve reaches for my hand and Charlie places a warm palm on my leg, and we all sit, just looking at one another for a while in quiet understanding. Maybe being in Paris will be good. I can brainstorm how to make this friendship work, how to stop all lusty thoughts of Adam. Because I really do like him, and I would rather be his friend than nothing at all.

"I love you, Maeve. I love you, Char," I say, reaching out to hug them both. "You know that, right?" I don't do well with saying goodbye to my people.

"We know, Bon. And we love *you*." Maeve grabs my face and kisses my cheek loudly, diffusing the emotional heaviness in the air. "You know, there's probably a perfect country song about this." She smiles at me as Charlie scoffs loudly and I'm immediately thankful for their ability to take me out of my spiraling thoughts and for Maeve's weird love of country music.

We all laugh and finish our coffees, talking about what the week is going to look like; with filming starting for Maeve and Charlie starting some work for their dad. Shooting will happen in London for six weeks, then back to LA to finish at the studio.

We say our last goodbyes and the day goes by in a blur of taxi rides, with a short flight in the middle. Once I reach my hotel in Paris, I immediately feel lighter. First things first: a crepe and a cup of coffee before people-watching over a glass of wine.

I'm on my second glass of red when my phone dings.

ADAM

Bonjour, ma belle! How is Paris?

Your song is ready. I see you already added one.

ME

Oof. You went for it with Aerosmith. Not sure I can top it with "Crash Into Me".

I guess we were both feeling the sappy love songs today.

Hope you have a great first day tomorrow. Call me when you can. Anytime.

I wait to see if he'll respond, but nothing comes through.

Though that doesn't stop me from checking my phone every two minutes for the rest of the time I drink my wine.

ADAM DOESN'T CALL. And I don't want to bother him, so I do my best to just enjoy my first night in Paris. Of course, that means a fabulous meal, more wine, and a long walk back to the hotel, taking in the city lights.

He also doesn't call the next day, though I think about calling him far too many times.

I SPENT the first few days doing a lot of walking, and last night I went to dinner with some old colleagues who live in the city. I woke up to a string of texts. I read Maeve's first.

MAEVE

Having the best time? You better be.

We've been on set nonstop, but the location is gorgeous. You'd love it.

xoxo chat soon

I check Adam's messages next.

ADAM

Sorry I haven't called. The days have been long. We hit the ground running.

Maeve is incredible to work with. I'm really starting to see what you mean about her being small but mighty!

Miss you already.

Bonsoir beauté

I send Maeve a selfie of me in bed with a bottle of ibuprofen and water to paint her a picture of how much I enjoyed the wine last night.

My fingertips tap the screen of my phone as I read Adam's message about Maeve. His enthusiasm for Maeve being cast in the movie is impossible to miss, and I knew she was going to be great. A wave of jealousy I can't explain courses through me. This is my best friend, and she deserves the best co-star in the world. So why does my chest tighten at the thought of them together? Then he said he misses me, and my chest swelled with a whole other mix of emotions. Somehow, I manage to push them away as I contemplate what a bit of distance might do for us. With a deep breath, I type my response.

ME

Feeling this song today, maybe because I
had a hard time waking up.

Miss your face.

I didn't expect him to respond right away, but he does.

ADAM

LAINEY! "Pony?" Really?

My stomach is in knots.

Why the hell did I pick this song?

I cannot think about riding Adam's pony. Nope, nope,
nope. Not even gonna think about it a little bit. Okay, maybe
later when I'm not so hungover...

ADAM

Added "Hey Ya" for you.

Maeve said you're hungover. She showed me
the picture you sent her. Are you being safe
over there? And why aren't you sending ME
pictures?

ME

Is Maeve spilling my secrets? I went to
dinner with friends. Very safe. And here
you go.

I send a picture someone took of me last night. I'm looking
off to the side, glass of wine in hand, laughing so hard that
my eyes are closed. It's not a very flattering picture, but it's all
I've got.

I don't hear from him for the rest of the day, which is fine.
I only have a couple more days left in Paris and I'm braving
the Louvre today, spending the day there.

•   •   •

I DON'T HEAR from him the next day either, and I'm headed back to London tonight. It felt good to do things on my timeline, but I'm looking forward to snuggles from Frankie tonight and hopefully seeing Maeve, Owen, Raf, and Adam tomorrow.

BY THE TIME I get back to the apartment, it's 2 a.m. and I'm wiped. I immediately take my pants off—right after kissing and hugging Frankie, that is. I've just taken off my bra when I hear a knock at the door. It's gotta be Maeve.

What did she do with her key?

"Just couldn't wait until morning to see me, huh?" I open the door only to be mauled by a giant of a man, who pushes into my apartment. Adam kicks the door shut, and then he's hugging me tight around the waist and lifting me off my feet.

Oh god. He smells so good. So, so good.

He holds me close, and I feel his heartbeat thudding against mine. His warm breath tickles my ear as he speaks in a low voice.

"No, you're right. I couldn't wait. I asked Casper to let me know when you came in." His confession catches me off guard. I didn't think he knew the overnight doorman's name.

Is that what's really important here?

The warmth of his hands seeps into my bare skin, and I melt into his embrace. My lack of clothing should bother me, but I find myself wishing there was even less of a barrier between us. I want more of his heat, more of his calloused hands on me, more of his warm breath on my skin.

But I can't. We're friends. We can't be more than that.

The thought snaps me back to reality, and I pull away, feeling a blush spread across my cheeks. His eyes linger on my body, taking in my white tank top that clings too tightly and barely keeps my underwear from view. His eyes seem to drink me in and I feel like I'm standing here naked, my heart racing as if I'd run a marathon. Just like the night we met, I feel his gaze all over me. The heat of it as his eyes rake over every inch of my body. I don't cover myself up. I let him look.

This doesn't feel very friendly, now does it?

Oh shut up. I don't care. Not one bit.

"I… it's late. Sorry, I… I'll see you tomorrow. Goodnight, L." He looks at the wall, the floor, the dog, his shoes. Everywhere but back at me and then turns towards the door so fast he nearly runs into it. And just like that, he's gone. And I'm leaning back on the wall, knees weak, knowing I'm going to need a battery-operated companion to join me in bed if I'm going to get any kind of sleep tonight.

———

DAYS GO by and I don't hear a peep from him. Not even a text. I know they're having crazy long days because Maeve just told me, and she's barely had time to text me as well. We're sitting on the couch in her apartment eating nachos. She has tomorrow off, so we're taking the opportunity to catch up.

"How's everything been on set? Have you filmed any of the love scenes with River yet?" It feels easier to use his stage name when asking my best friend if she's kissed or had fake sex with the guy I've been having wet dreams about.

Can girls have wet dreams?

"No, I haven't. And it's River now, is it? Weird to think of me snogging with *Adam*?" She gives me that one eyebrow lift and studies my face. I'm blushing, and I have no idea why. This is my best friend I'm talking to!

"I have something to confess." I take a deep breath because she is going to give me so much shit for this. "I imagined it was him when I was Lone Rangering the other night. And again, last night. And I've been having dreams." I put both of my hands to my face and shake my head because even I can't believe what I'm saying. I don't tell her about the nightmares, only about the pleasant dreams.

"What you're saying is he gets you hot. So hot that you're having sex dreams about him. So hot that *you*—the girl who could win an Olympic gold medal in masturbating without attachments to any specific fantasy or person—have been fantasizing about Adam? Did I get that right?" She picks up a chip and crunches down loudly as if this isn't the single most ridiculous admission I've ever made to her.

"First of all, that's an incredibly specific Olympic sport and we clearly know way too much about each other." I've moved my hands back to my lap, but I can feel my face is flushed. "Second of all, yes. That's exactly what I'm saying." My knee is bouncing like crazy and I'm shoving enough nachos into my mouth to make sure nothing stupid comes out of it for at least another few minutes.

"Called it. You're so into him. What are you going to do about it?" She keeps casually eating. Again, it's like she doesn't get how huge this is. How insane this is. How not okay with it all I am. "And you can stop freaking out. I know this is a big deal for you and that overactive brain of yours, but this is what us mere mortals go through when we have a crush, Bon."

"I'm going to do nothing about it. I have to get over it. End of fucking story. Remember when he told his best friend that we're just friends? Yeah. That's all I need to move on." And I know I can do it. This is just a silly crush, nothing else. And I'd know what to do about it if I'd been someone who had any crushes in the last decade, but I haven't. Not really. Not since Andy.

"I have a brilliant idea. Come to the set tomorrow. River's supposed to be doing a scene where a bunch of women hit on him. I'm only in it for a minute and I'm not one of them, so it won't be weird. See how you react to that?"

It would be sort of like exposure therapy. I'll surely get

over this whole stupid thing after seeing a bunch of girls fawning over him.

"Hmm. Okay. What time should I be there?"

She nearly chokes on her chip, eyes all bugged out of their sockets.

"What? You'll do it? I was half-joking, you know?" She takes a big gulp of her drink and I feel a little bad for catching her off guard.

"Yeah. I think you're right. Seeing him surrounded by women who will probably hit on him in real life might do the trick, especially if he flirts back. And he might." I feel a little sick thinking about that scenario, so I may just make sure I don't eat anything tomorrow in case I get barfy.

"Okay, Bon. Just come with me in the morning then. I'm sure it'll be no issue having you there. You can be my assistant for the day." She winks at me as I plot what I'll wear tomorrow.

———

"IT'S TOO EARLY for this, Mae." I'm in the backseat of the town car and she's trying to put mascara on me. "And I've already had eye surgery. I don't need another. You're literally going to poke out my eyeballs with that thing."

"Then either stay still or do it yourself. It's just some mascara and lip gloss." I know she means well. She wants me to feel good when I see Adam today, who has still yet to text or call. But I'm doing my best to be cool about it. He's had a lot of late nights on set.

"Hand it over. I'd like to not go blind today." I put on some of the mascara and the lip gloss, which I know will come right off as I sip my coffee. Makeup just has never been my thing, and I'm fine with that.

Maeve is off to hair and makeup almost as soon as we get there and I end up having to fill out a bunch of paperwork just so I can be on set today. What a pain. Try as I might, I don't see Adam, but then again, the actual shooting location is not that close to where the trailers are.

Hours go by and I have a chat with the director, who is a colleague. That makes getting onto the set far easier than all the paperwork! It's been a couple of years since I've worked with Mitch, but he's just as funny as I remembered. He's in his mid-thirties and has curly brown hair, which is kind of adorable on him. It sticks out of his baseball cap charmingly and he looks more like a college student than an accomplished director. He's only slightly taller than me and definitely seems to be on the other side of his divorce, which he was in the thick of when I was the production designer in his last film.

When it's time for lunch, I find an empty table and make small talk with some of the crew. I don't end up eating anything because I have no appetite, but it's nice being in this kind of environment with none of the pressure to be working. Maeve and Adam are off somewhere so I sit with Mitch, who is definitely probably flirting with me.

Huh… isn't that something? Maybe Maeve was right about me coming today. Having a guy flirt with me could be a great way to not think about you-know-who whom I am most definitely not thinking about right now.

Mitch doesn't stay for long, saying they have to get to the next scene right away. He said a few changes had to be made and they're shooting an alternate scene today. When I asked if I could come, he didn't hesitate, so I'm tagging along.

Maeve and Adam both walk on set, laughing and talking casually. They can't see me because I'm too far away. I had grabbed a baseball cap from my bag to hide my hair. I take a few uncertain steps into the film set and immediately notice it's a bar, with its cozy booths and shelves filled with liquor bottles. I hear the melodic laughter of actors and actresses as they greet each other.

It all seems innocent enough until the scene begins and I lock my eyes on him. The guy who has been giving me a lady boner. He has his arm around a Victoria's Secret model, their lips inches apart. Maeve's character is watching from the other end of the bar, her face scrunched up into an expression of jealous rage. Before I know it, he's kissing another actress, and then another. Every new lip-lock makes my heart squeeze a little tighter in my chest.

Adam is locked in a passionate embrace with two women. His hands rove over one of the woman's curves and then her breast spills out of her top. I gasp in surprise and begin to cough uncontrollably, which earns me angry glares from the surrounding crew. I want to look away, but my eyes are glued to the spectacle and my brain is jumbled up with confusion, jealousy, and a hint of arousal. My lady bits are equally confused. I can't help but imagine it's me standing there with him, instead of those beautiful women.

I need to get away from the chaos, so I tip-toe out of the door, trying my best not to draw unwanted attention. The cold air is a welcome embrace, and I close my eyes for a few seconds, savoring the calm. When I open them, I silently make my way back towards the building in search of the security guard, intent on finding out if the "sexy shit" has been wrapped up yet. Just as I'm about to ask her for help, the door bursts open, and Adam comes barreling out with such force that he sends me tumbling backwards.

"Oww. Well, that's gonna bruise." I grab my arm where it's been hit by his elbow and wince in pain.

"Oh no. I'm so sorry. Are you—" He stops when he sees it's me, eyes wide with surprise.

"Hey, River." At least I have enough sense to use his stage name. His face moves from concern to surprise to panic. He holds my eyes for several long beats. Long enough that the security guard surely suspects I'm some kind of intruder.

"Lainey. What are you—when did you—were you in

there?" His blue eyes look over my whole face. "Did I hurt you?" He doesn't wait for me to answer and takes me by the elbow, walking away from the door, away from other people.

"Uh. Maeve invited me. I came with her. And yes, I was. Earlier. And also yes, probably, but I bruise easily, so it's not really your fault." I can feel my eyebrows twitching, my mouth puckering, and my lips quivering. I try my best to repress the emotional chaos that's playing out on my face, but I know there's no hiding it.

The air between us feels thick, electric with anticipation, but I'm too busy focusing on the fact that we haven't hugged—something we've done without fail every time we meet up. Suddenly, the door of the building bangs open and everyone that had been inside comes streaming out, laughing and talking. My best friend skips over to us with a bright smile.

"We're finished for the weekend and going for drinks. Come with us, Bon! River, will you come too?" She looks up at Adam with hopeful eyes, but he appears to be ready to decline her invitation when Mitch speaks up.

"Hey, gorgeous. You're coming for drinks, yeah? I'll save you a seat next to me." He winks at me playfully, completely unaware of the murderous glare Adam is sending him. I have to bite back a smile; poor Mitch is so oblivious.

"Yeah."

"Yes."

We respond simultaneously, only I'm grinning while he's frowning. Maeve quickly snatches me by the arm and pulls me aside, waving her hand over her head as she does. "See you soon, boys! Play nice!"

In Maeve's trailer, she insists I change at least my top. She has a few things there and I settle for an emerald green cashmere sweater that falls off of one shoulder. I keep my jeans on and thankfully already had cute heeled boots on. I freshen up my hair, opting for loose curls and Maeve makes sure to slap some more makeup on my face.

After a short drive, we pull up outside the restaurant. We're welcomed inside and led through to a private room, Raf lingering close enough to jump into action, but far enough away that it doesn't feel like he's hovering over us. About a dozen people from the cast and crew gather around a large table, talking excitedly. Candles flicker on the tables, throwing soft light across the room.

My stomach contracts as I make my way to the bar, eager to dull the images of Adam and female models that have been seared into my consciousness. I order a glass of pinot noir, the liquid providing a momentary comfort. I drink it far too quickly and as I set the glass down, I notice a familiar figure entering the room. Sea-blue eyes dart around the place, and Adam's gaze eventually lands on me. Before I can turn away, I feel a hand on my shoulder and hear Mitch's voice utter a cheery greeting. It seems like nothing is going my way today.

"There you are. I got you a drink." Adorable Mitch offers me a fluorescent pink concoction that glows like a neon sign as he plants a soft kiss on my cheek, leaving it wet and sticky. I feel nothing, not a spark of electricity or a knot in my stomach. I smile politely and thank him, wanting to wipe the dampness away with the back of my hand.

We talk about the usual topics—work and life—while I fidget with my left earlobe and search the room for any friends who can save me from this dull small talk. Raf must be here somewhere. Just as I'm about to make a run for it, a strong hand curls itself around my waist, making every cell in my body come alive as goosebumps spread like a wildfire. This is not an innocent gesture, but one with a possessive weight that seems to promise something more. I'm paralyzed by a thrill that is both exhilarating and terrifying.

"Hey, gorgeous." Adam's voice is husky in my ear. He echoes Mitch's earlier words and this time, I definitely feel things. He takes the pink drink from my hand and sets it on a nearby table, replacing it with a glass of red wine. One hand gently settles back on the curve of my waist, his thumb drawing a languid circle that sends a chill up my spine.

His rough fingers brush my hair to the side, and I shiver as his scorching lips graze my bare shoulder. His kiss trails up my neck, lingering just behind my ear.

"I've been looking for you," he murmurs. My heart races as my body leans into his of its own volition.

Fucking fuckity fuck. Focus, Elaina.

"You don't mind if I steal my girl away, do ya, Mitch? Good to see you out, dude."

My girl. Oh god. I'm going to have to revisit that later.

Adam grabs my hand, his grip tight and urgent, and pulls me away from the clueless director.

What's his name again?

Everything is a blur until we stop moving and his hands are both gripping my waist. I guzzle the rest of my wine, feeling the warmth of it travel down my stomach. When I look up, his eyes are two stormy seas of blue, full of anger and heat.

What the hell?

"What are you doing?" I hiss as I set my empty glass on a table next to us.

"Pretending to be your boyfriend, or whatever it is Raf does when you're not interested in a guy. You pulled on your left ear. I saw it." He hasn't taken his hands off of me yet. "Mitch is a total creep. He hits on every woman on set."

Oh. Well, that… sucks.

"So? Maybe I don't care about that." I cross my arms over my chest, doing a great job of looking like I'm about to throw a toddler-sized tantrum. "I'm sure every woman on set is too busy hitting on you to even notice adorable Mitch, anyway. You walk around with your sparkling blue eyes and perfect ass and no one else stands a chance, so what does it matter?"

My propensity for word vomit seems to grow exponentially with every glass of wine I foolishly drink in lieu of lunch or dinner.

"Yes, you do care. And adorable Mitch? Perfect ass? We obviously need to talk more." He has the audacity to smirk at me, and I am not having it.

"I care, but only a little. Mitch is like a lost puppy dog with his curly hair and big brown eyes." I roll my eyes, intent on continuing my tangent. "Have you honestly never turned while looking in the mirror? You have a perfect ass. The most perfect. Like tight and round. It's fucking unnatural."

Must. Stop. Talking.

"And *we need to talk more*? Maybe when you're done ignoring me we can talk, you dumbass." I scoff and shove his shoulder but he doesn't budge.

"God, I miss you and that mouth." His eyes move over my face again and his stupid eyes sparkle.

Ugh.

"I gotta go. Nice to see you, River." And with that, I push him away from me and walk back to the bar, immediately requesting a shot of vodka and another glass of wine. If you ever wanted to know what regret tastes like, this is the recipe.

13 /
how did i get here?

adam

ELAINA IS DRUNK. She must be. She has had far too many drinks, though no one seems concerned. Not Maeve and not the bartender. Just me. I've never seen her like this. Then again, I feel like I haven't really seen her at all lately. After she got back from Paris and I barged into her apartment and she was wearing white lace underwear, I needed space. The thought of her exquisite tits under the thin white tank top, of the heat that was radiating off of her skin… every night since then I've been dreaming about her under me, on top of me, in the shower… I think I've made my point.

My stomach tightens thinking about running into Lainey on set today. I hadn't expected her to be there, and I still don't know how much of the scene she saw. I'd been dreading shooting this alternate scene, where I had to make out with three different women. It was Mitch's stupid idea, and it made me hate him even more.

When I saw her with Mitch, I felt a surge of anger. She looked so gorgeous in that tight sweater, and the thought of him touching her made my blood boil. So, I did what she said Raf did when creepy guys came around—I pulled her in close and pretended she was mine. Hearing her talking about my eyes and my ass only intensified my feelings. But where did that come from, anyway? I'll need to ask her about that when she's not busy guzzling wine.

Wait… did she just stumble? Oh, hell no. She's out of here.

Like the absolute caveman I have apparently become, I walk to her and place a firm hand around her waist. "I think it's time to say goodnight. Have a great weekend, everyone." Maeve gives me a small nod and Lainey doesn't fight me, but I see the fire in her eyes.

"What do you think you're doing?" Her voice is low. She's drunk, but not enough to make any kind of scene. I should have expected that she's in control even when she's inebriated.

A short walk outside later and we're both in the back of a town car. I put the privacy window up and buckle her seatbelt while she tries to fight me off.

"Elaina, I'm taking you home," I say this as calmly as possible, then buckle my seatbelt and give her a second to calm down before saying anything else.

"I'm so mad at you. And you never call me Elaina," she growls at me, crossing her arms and huffing out a loud breath. I would notice how adorable her pout is, how she looks about as angry as a bunny right now, but I'm a little pissed off, so I put those thoughts aside. I narrow my eyes and cross my arms as I glare at her. She sways a little, even as she's sitting.

"Oh, you're mad at me, are you? Please, tell me more." I can barely contain my sarcasm as I ask the question; she's just nearly caused a scene and now she has the audacity to be mad at me?

"Yes! I'm so mad. You show up at my apartment when I'm in my underwear and get me all… whatever. I thought you were Maeve, by the way. I never would have come to the door like that if I knew it was you."

She narrows her eyes back at me and then almost instantly looks horrified at what she's just said. "Because you're my friend, and I don't walk around in my underwear in front of my guy friends, for the record." She's breathing fast, but if I know anything about this girl, it's that she's not done with her rant.

"And then you ignore me. No texts, no new songs, no sign of life. And I miss you. I fucking hate it, but I miss you so much when you're not around." She closes her eyes tightly, like she's concentrating on what to say next. "I couldn't wait to see you today, and when I see you, you're making out with *three women*, which is fine. Whatever. It's your job. But the boob? Ugh! Oh my god, I could have lived without ever seeing your hand on a supermodel's fucking perfect tit!" Her breathing is heavy, but she hasn't given me the signal that she's done yet, which is eye contact. She'll look at me when she's done.

She presses her forehead against the window, her breath fogging the glass. My stomach churns as I consider how she must have felt watching the other actors and me during that scene today. All of it is so carefully choreographed, but still intensely intimate. I wouldn't be okay watching her do any of it. I don't care if that makes me a hypocrite.

"What makes me the most maddest of all is that I didn't even know how to feel watching that whole thing unfold. A little grossed out? Curious? Turned on? Like what the fuck am I supposed to feel when I see my *friend* in this situation?" My brain can't decide what to focus on first. Her voice is high pitched and the fact that grammar has gone out the window tells me a lot about just how inebriated she is. But the thing that stands out is that she sounds jealous. She had a hard time processing her feelings after seeing me today. After she came back from Paris.

"I've never done this before. There's no hand job... book description... hand description? Ugh." Her hands come to her lap with a slap. "Handbook. Job description. Those don't exist for how to be a friend in these situations."

I can't help the chuckle that escapes me. Thank fuck she doesn't hear or see it. That would really make her mad. And now her eyes finally come to mine. "You all done now?" I take a rogue curl and tuck it behind her ear, needing to see her face more clearly.

She nods. "I'm done. I hate being drunk. I'm so stupid when I drink, and I hate it."

"Why did you drink so much, then?" The car stops and her door opens a few seconds later. I get out on my side and meet her on the other side to get her into the building. She hiccups and nearly trips on the last step up to the doors.

I hold her elbow, but she keeps tripping over her shoes. "Fuck it." I put one arm behind her knees, the other at her back, and lift her. She doesn't fight me. Her hand comes to rest on my chest, her head on my shoulder.

When we get up to her apartment, I unlock her door and set her down. "Go get changed. I'm going to get you some water and painkillers. Have you eaten tonight?" She shakes her head so hard that her hair flies all around her face and then sashays away towards her bedroom.

This girl is too much.

I take these few minutes to process what she said. Even if it might be the alcohol talking, something is happening here. Maybe my feelings aren't one-sided. Maybe she feels everything I've been feeling too. Well, not everything.

I've just finished getting water, pills, and some toast with butter so she can soak up some of this alcohol when she comes into the kitchen.

"I don't wear pants to bed. You can't make me. I put on some shorts, though, so you're welcome. You won't be seeing my ass or my tits this time." She waddles over to me and grabs the pills and a glass of water.

Her comment about not seeing her ass is debatable. The

hem of her baggy T-shirt barely reaches the bottom of her tiny shorts. I say nothing, just watch her finish her glass of water and then refill it for her. I definitely do not look down at her long, smooth, toned legs.

"Is this toast for me?" She leans over the counter to reach for the plate and sure enough, her shirt rides up and there's half her perfect ass straining against her tight shorts. Deep breath in.

She's your friend. And she's very drunk.

"Mmmm. This is so good. Thank you so much." Great. Now she's moaning and licking her lips. Just perfect.

She finishes her toast and beelines for the bathroom. Uh oh. I hope she's not going to be sick. When I walk closer to the bathroom door I hear her humming a song. I'm pretty sure it's "Yellow"—the first song I added to our playlist. The song that I knew would always make me think of her and her bright smile. I guess she's been listening to it. I have, too.

"Adam?" She peeks around the door, and I walk further down the hall to meet her. She's standing in the doorway with her arms crossed. Her face is clean and I can smell her face wash. She's perfect like this. Messy hair, pajamas and no make-up on. "I can answer your question now. Can I tell you why I drank too much tonight?"

"I want to know everything you want to tell me, L." We smile at each other for a few seconds, and it feels like we're back to being ourselves. Just friends. Friends who tell each other everything.

"I've been having nightmares. Again. I thought a few drinks might help me, because I'm so tired I don't know what else to do. I've even tried to just not sleep at all because as soon as I close my eyes, the nightmares come. Well, more like night terrors. And they're awful. I either relive Andy's and my dad's deaths or it's Owen and Raf being hurt or killed overseas. I haven't told anyone yet and I wanted something to just knock me out, but I'm afraid it's not going to work."

She's looking down at her feet, playing with the hem of her shirt.

I swallow and lift her chin with my index finger.

"I'll stay here and make sure you don't have nightmares. Would that help?" She nods twice and smiles a crooked little smile. I take her hand and walk her to her bedroom. She gets under the covers, and I tuck her in with a kiss on the forehead.

"Goodnight, L."

"Goodnight, Adam." She closes her eyes as I turn off the lamp and head to the living room. Maybe I'll just stay here tonight, or wait until she's been asleep for a while to make sure she doesn't have nightmares.

Half an hour passes, and Frankie and I both jump off the couch when we hear her screaming. I sprint into the bedroom and skid to a stop in front of the bed. She's curled up in a tight ball, her eyes are squeezed shut and tears stream down her cheeks. Sobbing uncontrollably, she screams out my name in terror.

I rush over and scoop her up into my arms, feeling her body quivering against me. I brush away the strands of hair that are matted onto her face and whisper her name. Her eyes flutter open and as soon as she sees me, her arms wrap around my neck tightly.

"Adam? Adam! Oh my god. You're okay?" Her voice is shaky and trembling with emotion, sending a wave of pain through me.

"Yeah, baby. I'm okay. I'm right here," I reply reassuringly, stroking her back to calm her down. She releases her grip on me slightly but still keeps me close, her body shaking with sobs. I place a finger beneath her chin to tilt her head upwards so that she can meet my gaze. The fear in her eyes nearly breaks my heart.

Knowing there isn't much else I can do, I tuck her back into bed and slip in beside her, allowing her to snuggle up against me as if seeking protection from whatever had scared her so much.

"Please stay," she murmurs into my chest.

"I'm not going anywhere," I reply softly, rubbing circles over the top of her head. "No more nightmares, L. I'm right here." Gradually, the trembling of her body stops and the rhythm of her breathing syncs with mine, indicating that she's finally drifted off to sleep, safe and sound in my arms.

———

MY EYES FLUTTER OPEN, and I squint against the bright sunlight streaming in. Elaina is lying beside me, her head tucked into my chest and our legs entwined. The soft strands of her hair tickle my face as I inhale her sweet shampoo scent. I revel in the moment, savoring the feel of her body pressed against mine. Suddenly, she begins to move and wriggle, her hands roaming over my abs as a low moan escapes her lips. A thrilling shiver runs through me.

"Mmm, Adam." A gasp. "Oh, shit. Adam?" She goes stiff and her grip on my shirt loosens as she tries to extricate herself from the tangle of sheets holding us together. "I'm so sorry. I'm so, so sorry." Her face is burning with embarrassment as she apologizes. I kiss her forehead lightly, untangle our limbs, and let her put some space between us.

"Good morning, *tornerose*. No more nightmares?" I sit up on the bed, arms behind my head.

"No, no more nightmares. I don't think I've slept more than a couple of hours all week." She huffs out a humorless laugh. "Wow. Thank you. Thanks for staying with me." Finally, her eyes meet mine and again, we're back. It's just us, eye to eye for a few seconds until she looks away.

"I'm gonna make us some breakfast. Why don't you take a long shower and relax?" I reach over and kiss the top of her head again, then get up.

"You don't have to. I'm so sorry about last night. I don't know how to thank you." Her fingers are in knots on her lap. I wish she could just relax, just be and not feel like she needs to always thank me.

"Please stop apologizing and thanking me. Now go. Shower. I'll see you soon." I walk out of her room shaking my head, wondering whether I'll ever be able to get her to stop overthinking, stop needing to say the perfect things and just trust me. Fully.

I make eggs, bacon and toast. The coffee was already programmed to be brewed at 10 a.m., and it doesn't surprise me that she left the house yesterday with her coffee machine all ready to go for the next morning. My girl doesn't mess around with her coffee.

I smell the coconut and honey before I see her walk in. She has black leggings and a cropped sweatshirt on because she must want to torture me with her flawless backside. I take everything out of the oven where it was staying warm, and before I can turn to grab plates, her body is pressed against mine. I feel her fingers run through my hair, face is tucked into my neck, and the warmth of her breath on my skin. Every inch of her is against me, down to our toes.

"I don't deserve you." And as quickly as she was there, she's gone.

"Yeah, no. We're gonna talk about that just as soon as we both have some food in us. Then we're gonna talk about last night. Then we're gonna talk about Mitch, that asshole…" I'm just about to launch into another rant when my phone vibrates in my pocket. I glance at the screen and groan—it's Sandra, my publicist. I send her call to voicemail, but before I can stuff my phone back in my pocket, the angry buzzing starts up again.

"Pick it up. Go ahead. She wouldn't be calling right now if it wasn't important." Lainey is right, but I don't want to talk to Sandra in front of her. I don't want any talk of this fake relationship she's suggested to come up because I haven't told Elaina about any of that—mostly because I don't want it to happen at all.

"Hey, Sandra."

"River, you brat, I've called you five times this morning. Do you have any idea how early it is here? Why are you ignoring me?"

"I was just making breakfast. I wasn't ignoring you." Except I was.

"You know I wouldn't call unless it was important, so get your head out of your ass and get ready to listen." If she wasn't the absolute best publicist out there and our family hadn't known her for so long, I would never stand for this shit. But she gets away with it. I don't even mind.

"I know, I'm sorry, Sandra. I won't ignore your calls again." Elaina's eyes widen in surprise and her mouth twitches into a smirk as I grovel to my publicist. She hastily bites down on her lower lip to stifle her laughter.

"Have you seen any of the gossip sites this morning? Has Lainey?"

"I haven't seen anything, no. What now?" I take a deep breath as I listen to her. "Lainey? Why?" Now she's really perked up. Lainey's lips move in a silent whisper as she mouths something to me. I try to focus on her, but it's useless —Sandra has launched into a story that's impossible to ignore. I strain to hear what she's trying to tell me, but I can't make out the words.

"We're going to need to talk to her, River. It's you two all over every gossip blog this morning. Is she there? Put me on speaker." How the fuck did she guess I was with Lainey?

"Hang on. Just... don't say anything embarrassing. *Please.*" I put the call on speaker so Elaina can hear.

"Lainey, honey, are you there?" Sandra is already far sweeter to Elaina five words in than she has been to me in all of our fifteen years together.

"Yeah, hi Sandra. I'm here." Her eyes widen and she looks at me for a clue as to what's going on. I shrug my shoulders and lift my hands in the air, my lips forming the words 'I don't know'. She nods slowly in understanding.

"I'm going to get right to the point. There's a video of you two from last night. The first part is of River kissing your neck, and you look like you're quite enjoying it, my girl. But who can blame you, right?" Sandra laughs and clears her throat. Elaina's face turns red with a mix of rage and embarrassment. I'm now mouthing *I'm sorry* to her, already worried about what's going to come from Sandra next.

"And the next part is of you walking out of the bar and getting into a car with River. The tabloids are going crazy making up stories about your relationship." She pauses, while Elaina gasps, bringing her hands to her mouth. "Lainey, I don't know how much River has told you, but he's been getting a lot of heat lately for how secretive he is about his love life. Or lack thereof." I clear my throat loudly, letting Sandra know to shut up already. "Studios are threatening not to bring him onto projects because of the negative publicity. They don't want movie premieres to become more about his personal life than about the project. I had suggested he find himself a nice girl to pretend to date, since he's as picky as they come."

"Sandra, come on!" My voice is gruff.

What the fuck is she saying?

"So what can I do to help?" Lainey is still looking at the phone as though I'm not here.

"River isn't going to like this." Sandra knows this isn't an option. No way.

"No, Sandra. We talked about this. If I wouldn't do this with a stranger, what makes you think I'll be okay doing it with someone I actually care about?" I'm already saying too much, but I need to be clear that I will not bring Elaina into this.

"I don't know what else we can do here. I know you two are just friends, but the video speaks for itself. Riv, the way you kissed her neck…"

"Tell me, Sandra. Tell me what I can do, and I'll do it," Lainey cuts in, swatting my hand away when I reach for the phone.

"We're gonna need you to pretend to be River's girlfriend, sweetheart." A heavy silence hangs in the air. I watch as her gaze slowly shifts, her eyes finally meeting mine. She pauses for a moment.

"Okay."

"No."

We both answer at the same time. She grabs my phone from the table and types something.

"Sandra, I just texted you my number. Please call me so we can discuss what exactly I need to do. I'm going to talk to River about this now, but please call me later, okay?" I'm stunned. My brain does not compute what is happening in front of me right now.

"Thanks, kid. You really are as great as he says. One more thing, there was a flood at your house in LA, River. Kelly called me when she couldn't get a hold of you, either. You'll need a place to stay when you're back in a couple of weeks while it's being dealt with. Let me know if I can help in any way. Talk soon, kids." And the call disconnects.

A flood? What. The. Fuck?

I take a moment for my brain to catch up. "Elaina, no. I'm not asking you to do this." I get up from the table and begin pacing. This can't be happening.

"You're right. You're not. Sandra is, and she knows what's best for you. She wants what's best for you. And for your career." I keep pacing the room, my hands clenching and unclenching as I shake my head. She remains seated, her fork slicing through a crisp, golden-brown piece of bacon and placing it delicately in her mouth, her expression unchanged, as if we were discussing the rainy day outside. "You took me away from two bad situations yesterday. Creepy puppy Mitch and potentially drinking far too much, which I'm sure would have ended with me flat on my ass. I got you into this. I'll get you out."

"No, that's not how this works. This is not something I can ask of you. I don't even know what Sandra wants in order to guarantee some sort of semblance of a relationship." I've stopped pacing now because I really am hungry and watching her eat is making me hungrier. I sit so I can eat too. Might as well figure this out on a full stomach.

"We're friends. This is what friends do for one another, right? Pretend to be each other's partners to get out of a sticky situation? That's all this is. I'll be River's girlfriend out there to the cameras. Adam and I can still be just friends." She smiles, but it doesn't quite reach her eyes.

We can't do this, can we? No. No, this is too crazy.

"Oh, and come stay with me when we get back to LA. I have plenty of room and it'll make us being seen together even easier if we're coming and going from the same place. It's very safe. Raffy made damn sure of that before I moved in. Besides, I'm super close to the studio so your commute will be nice and short." She picks up her coffee cup and brings it to her lips, winking at me. "Don't argue with me. This is exactly how friendship works and you know it. You would do the same for me if the tables were turned."

I can't really argue that last point.

"We have a lot of things to talk about. We'd better make a list." And now she laughs a beautiful, bubbly laugh and it diffuses the situation just enough for me to relax my shoulders, which have been wound tight since Sandra broke the news of the video.

"We'll have lots of time to talk, roomie." She pops a last piece of bacon into her mouth and winks at me again. Maybe this will actually be okay. Maybe.

14 /
is this real life?

elaina

I NEED to get my head checked. I'm pretty sure yesterday I agreed to let Adam live with me while I pretend to be his girlfriend after he slept in my bed holding me all night because I was downright schnookered Friday night thanks to my nightmares. *What the actual fuck is my life?*

After Adam left, I talked to Sandra and I'm not sure if I feel better or worse about the whole situation. She basically told me we need to make this thing look like we're Noah and Allie and there are *The Notebook* levels of romance at all times. No, that's not basically what she said, that's exactly what she said. I think she's half expecting that we'll be making out in the rain at some point.

Adam is coming over any minute so we can sort through the details of this fake romance and our future living arrangements. We spent the day apart yesterday. I think we both needed to process all the ways our relationship has changed and all the dumb things I probably said or did while shitfaced.

I hear the soft knock on the door and Frankie rushes to it, tail wagging. He knows it's Adam and doesn't even bark anymore. They have an annoyingly adorable bromance going on.

"Hey, beauty." He shoots me that deadly smile, leaning on the doorway and my body parts all start remembering the ways they betrayed me Friday night. I wanted to be as covered up as possible today, so I've got a long cowl neck sweater on over leggings and thick wool socks. There will be no neck kisses today, no sir. No sexy vibes happening here, though he didn't get the memo, proven by his low-slung jeans and blue Henley that only makes his bright blue eyes stand out even more. I can see his six-pack through his shirt and my fingers tingle as they remember what they felt like the other morning. Damn it. *Traitors.*

"Hi. Come in." I'm trying too hard to just be normal, but I'm not even sure what that entails at this point. He hugs me, because that's what we do, and I melt a little when we pull back and he tucks my hair behind my ear. "Hi."

"You look great. Cozy. Cute." Does he have to speak? Seriously, it's like the man wasn't affected at all by all the crazy things that have happened in the last thirty-six hours.

"Thanks. Have a seat. I made you tea." I sit at the far end of the couch, and he again misses the memo, sitting smack in the middle so we're close to one another. "So, did you actually make a list?"

He chuckles. "Sort of. But only because I didn't want to leave anything out. Is that alright?" His earnestness is inconveniently endearing and so I nod, doing my best to not show my internal panic. "Let's start with Mitch. What's your story with that bag of limp dicks?"

I nearly spit out the tea in my mouth. "Oh my god, couldn't you have waited until I wasn't drinking?" We both laugh and I'm thankful he chose humor to start with because now the tension seems to be minimal, and that's just how I like it with us. "There's no story. We worked on a film a while back. I ran into him on set and he seemed to think we hit it off. We didn't. He's a nice enough guy, but I'm... I'm not interested."

"He's not a nice guy. But okay. Next thing. I wasn't ignoring you, and I'm sorry I didn't call or text after you got back from Paris. That's on me, and I'm sorry." He sure knows how to apologize. Of course, I've forgiven him before he even finished what he was saying, because that's just what I do, but I also realize it feels nice to actually get an apology. I don't think Ben apologized once in all the years we were together. I smile and nod at him, waiting for him to continue.

He sighs, runs his fingers through his dark hair and somehow the aftermath is better than whatever he could accomplish by actually styling it. "The scene yesterday. It's... I'm... that shouldn't have happened." His eyebrows come together in a deep V, and he shakes his head. "It's not going in the movie. I'm still so pissed off that Mitch tried to pull that off, and I'm really sorry that you were there for that."

Though it wasn't my favorite thing to witness, it feels so far away now after everything else that happened that night.

"It's fine. I promise. I've seen plenty of sex scenes being filmed and I know that it's all very... mechanical. It just took me by surprise. That's all." I smile and pat his hand, and he links our fingers together before I can pull away.

"Okay. Can you tell me about your nightmare?" When I look into his eyes, all I see is kindness. I know I can trust him with this, but it's hard to relive those very vivid visions.

"The nightmare Friday night was about you. Someone took you away and threatened to hurt you, but I couldn't get to you." I feel my chin wobble and will my tears not to spill. "I could hear your screams..." The tears come anyway, streaming down my cheeks, and blurring my vision. My hands shake so badly that I have to grip Adam's arm for support as I tell him the rest of the dream. "I couldn't find you. I ran, and I ran, and I tried so hard, but I couldn't reach you, and then the screaming stopped and I knew you… you…"

Before I can finish, his arms are around me, pulling me onto his lap knowing how much I need the contact right now. His firm grip around my waist is comforting, his hands tracing circles up my back while his lips press against the top of my head.

"Shh. That's enough. You don't need to tell me anymore." I press my ear to his chest and feel the thumping of his racing heart beneath my cheek. He wraps his strong arms around me and pulls me close, as if he needs to be comforted as much as I do.

We sit like that for a few minutes, neither of us wanting to move, until he places a gentle kiss on my forehead and guides me back onto the couch. I curl up into a ball, my arms locked around my knees, dreading what else could be on his list.

"Are you okay?" His voice is so soft, it makes tears burn the backs of my eyes. I nod and he continues. "You said something the other day that really bothered me." He really is just plowing through this. He's efficient. "You said you don't deserve me, and that's… I don't want to hear you say that ever again." He's so serious and I've never seen this stern look on his face before, so I don't respond. "You deserve everything good in this world. I just want to try to be a small part of that for you, so please let me try. You do so much for everyone around you. Let other people do things for you, too."

I feel tears pool in my eyes again, knowing that this man sees me in a way maybe no other has before. That knowledge sends a bolt of fear up my spine, reminding me that this can't go beyond friendship. That my heart is too broken to live through another loss, another man I love exiting my life, whether it's done intentionally or not. Ben left a crack in my already fragmented heart, mostly filled with insecurities and bullshit I didn't need. Adam, though… he could obliterate the pieces that remain and leave me with nothing. I can't go back to that shell of a person I became after Andy. I won't allow it.

I nod because it's hard to respond with words, so I deflect. "Are you going to take your own advice and let me help you with your situation then? I already spoke with Sandra. She also knows you're staying with me. She loved the idea."

He lets out a loud breath and musses his hair again. "I know. She called yesterday. Who the hell are Allie and Noah? I didn't understand half of what she was talking about." He looks genuinely confused. I laugh, which feels good after more tension. We seem to do this a lot. It's a well-balanced dance, and it feels easy. Somehow talking about the hard stuff, then joking around, crying, then laughing, it all feels normal. It feels safe with him.

"Well, this might mean you've never seen *The Notebook* before, which we will remedy when you're my house guest next week." This is where I should have stopped talking, except my stupid mouth loves to get me in trouble. "But no pressure to see it with me, or do anything with me just because you're staying at my house. I've arranged to have the back bedroom ready for you. You have your own bathroom and there's even a side door in the hall, so you can come and go as you please. I don't want you to feel like I'm going to be all over you. You'll have as much privacy and space as you want, especially while you're busy shooting. I'll be working in my office anyway, and it's all the way on the other side of the house with my bedroom, so you won't even have to see me if you don't want to."

You had to stumble through the dance, didn't you? Way to make it awkward, loser.

"L. Stop. Stop that. Of course, I'll want to see you. Be all over me. I don't want space from you. Please don't say that." His face is a little flushed, and he takes a few deep breaths. I'm pretty sure I've stopped breathing altogether. "I just mean… if I'm going to stay with you, I want to see you. I want to spend time with you. Please don't ever think that I don't."

He takes another deep, loud breath. My stomach does roughly a dozen flips. My face feels hot. "Thank you. Thank you for letting me stay with you and for helping me. I appreciate everything you're doing. More than I can say."

"You're welcome." I'm not sure I'm breathing yet.

Be all over me. I don't want space from you.

Those words are flashing in bright pink neon in front of me, taunting me. Thankfully, the torture doesn't last very long.

"Now we need to talk about Sandra's plan." He's looking everywhere but at me. His eyes scan the whole room and land on Frankie, who is laying next to the couch. "She wants us to be seen together before we go back to LA. Do you think you have time to come to the set this week? We can go get dinner somewhere after I finish shooting."

I swallow, willing myself to do what he did and just move on from the weighty words hanging in the air between us. "Yeah. I can do that. Any night you want." I smile at him, wishing I could think of a single funny thing to say to diffuse the tension again.

"Okay. I'll look at the schedule and text you. Is that alright?" I hate how unsure he sounds about everything he's saying.

"Perfect." Silence. Followed by more silence.

Somebody say something.

"I have to go to a meeting, but I'll talk to you later." He gets up, pats Frankie on the head, and I quickly make my way off the couch as well. I follow him out to the door where he turns, lays a kiss on my forehead and reaches for the door handle.

"Bye, L."

"Bye." I stand with my forehead on the door for so long that Frankie comes to check on me.

———

EARLIER TODAY, Adam texted me details of when we'd have dinner, but things have felt weird between us since the weekend. I need to fix this before seeing him.

ME

Today's song is "Fantasy" by Mariah!

ADAM

Original Mariah or ODB remix?

ME

ODB remix, obvs!

ADAM

I added "Nice & Slow" today by none other than Usher Raymond

ME

I swear, if you didn't spell out his name in your head when you typed that, we're no longer friends

Can't wait for dinner tomorrow!

ADAM

Good thing I definitely sang it in my head then ;)

Me too, L.

With our weird vibes somewhat fixed, I can focus on reading a new book. And that's exactly how I fall asleep, a book on my chest and Frankie on my feet. And I dream of Adam. Happy dreams. Too happy, in fact.

———

IT'S TUESDAY NOW, and by the time 7 p.m. hits, I'm a ball of nerves. I've paced in front of Adam's trailer for about six minutes, and I just can't force myself to go in. He's probably alone in there, and I don't think I'm prepared to be alone with him just yet. I don't have time to get ready though, because he comes out of his trailer, all bushy beard, wet hair, smelling like a man should.

"*Tornerose*, you're here. Why didn't you come in? It's freezing." He pulls me into a hug, and I close my eyes when I feel his beard tickle my jaw as he kisses my cheek.

"Oh, hi. Um, I wasn't sure if you were dressed, so I waited out here. It's fine." I smooth the front of my coat down as he keeps one arm around me, leading us towards the exit. He looks down at me with those sparkly eyes, and I melt a little into his touch.

"Hi." The crooked little smile on his face could literally set ice on fire. And panties. I'm pretty sure it just incinerated mine.

He waves goodbye to a few people, including Sierra, the friendly security guard that witnessed our collision a few days back. He opens the car door for me and we sit quietly for a few minutes as I chew on my bottom lip.

"Are you nervous, L?" I didn't even notice his body had turned towards me.

"Huh? Oh…maybe a little." He moves closer, eyes on my lips as his hand moves to hold my chin. His thumb pulls my lower lip from its cage then moves over it slowly, deliberately.

"You'll hurt yourself biting down so hard, *tornerose*." His gaze locks on mine, now. "Nothing to be nervous about. It's just us, okay?" I nod, willing my nerves to settle.

Our driver, Tom, gets us to the restaurant quickly, and I'm grateful for it. During the short drive, we mostly talk about the movie and how we both can't wait to get back to LA weather.

As we walk in, the hostess seems to expect us, but her eyes still widen when she lays eyes on Adam.

Uh-huh. I know, girl. I know.

He helps me out of my coat, and I feel his knuckles travel down my arm, making me shiver. I try to cover it up by quickly turning around.

"Thank you," I murmur, before he hands the coat off to the hostess and his hand lands on the small of my back. His gaze travels slowly up my body, taking in the details of my outfit—starting at the heeled booties, then tracing up my legs, hips and waist, lingering on my breasts and lips before finally meeting my eyes. He's admiring the red long-sleeved sweater dress I almost decided not to wear, but ultimately chose over everything else in my closet. The dress hugs my curves perfectly, without being too tight, while a small slit at the hemline shows just the right amount of skin.

"Wow. You look… wow. You're stunning, Elaina." I take the opportunity to take him in, too. Light blue cashmere sweater layered over a striped dress shirt and black pants.

Yum. Now stop licking your lips. He is NOT on the menu.

We're seated in a private corner, which is great because I don't want all eyes on us for our first fake date. Though I suppose eyes would be good since the point is sort of for us to be seen together. The waiter comes around and asks what we'd like for drinks and Adam orders a bottle of my favorite red. If this were a real date, he'd probably get to second base tonight. Make that third. But I better not think too much about that, lest my body betray me again.

15 /
what's your favorite muffin?

adam

FUCKING HELL, *Elaina in this goddamn dress. How am I supposed to function with her looking like that and licking her lips?*

Thank fuck we were seated quickly. I already knew they had her favorite red wine here so at least I didn't need to use my brain to order.

"Is it okay that I ordered wine? Not sure you'll want any after the other night." I chuckle and smile at her and I'm glad to see she's smiling back.

"No, wine is fine. If you had ordered vodka, I might have had to leave though." She giggles as she reads her menu. "I'm lucky in the sense that I rarely get badly hungover, but I had an awful headache the next day."

"You did?" I place my hand over her menu, so she'll look at me. "Why didn't you say anything?"

She cocks her head to the side and lifts her shoulders in a lazy half-shrug, the corners of her lips turn down in a smirk.

"Like I said, no big deal," she says nonchalantly, as if being hungover when she agreed to be my fake girlfriend wasn't at all significant. "It should have been much worse. The toast, water and pain killers saved me. That and the greasy breakfast you prepared." She places a warm hand over mine and squeezes. "I was fine. I promise. You took great care of me."

The anguish on her face is palpable at the mere mention of that night, and I feel a pang of guilt for dredging up her nightmare. I take her hand in mine and kiss each one of her knuckles, savoring the way her breath hitches slightly at my touch. We sit silently together, our eyes locked in a meaningful gaze, until we're disturbed by the clinking sound of our wine glasses being placed on the table by the waiter.

DINNER CONVERSATION MOVES from our ongoing playlist to the movie Elaina will be working on later this year. She talks excitedly about being back home and how she's looking forward to having her kitchen back. Apparently, I will be well fed—her words, not mine—while I live with her. I would never expect her to cook for me, but she's very enthusiastic about doing it.

"What's your favorite kind of muffin?" Her eyes have their sparkle back as she's hanging on every word I say next.

"Um, probably something with lots of fruit in it. Like raspberries or strawberries?" I don't know that I've ever been asked this question before. "What's yours?"

"A fruity muffin. Noted. Mine is lemon-poppy seed. My mom always makes it for me and hers are the best." She smiles and looks down at her lap before looking back up at me. "No one has ever asked me what my favorite muffin is before."

"And my guess is you know what everyone's favorites are and you make it for them, right?"

She blushes and bites down on her bottom lip. "How did you know?"

"Because that's just the kind of person you are." I reach over and tuck her hair behind her ear, letting my knuckles run down her neck. "You think of everyone. You want to know these little details about them so you can make them feel special. And you do."

Our waiter comes by to ask if we want dessert and I'm thankful she does, since it prolongs our time together. Every second I get to spend looking at her, listening to her talk and learning new things about her, is a gift. And I don't take any of it for granted.

As we prepare to leave, I step behind her and carefully slide the coat over her shoulders. As I do, I notice the dozen or so people waiting outside of the restaurant for us, cameras ready. I step in front of her, doing up the lowest button of her coat as I lean in to kiss her cheek.

"Paps are outside. I'm sorry." I wince as I take in her reaction. She smiles up at me easily.. Of course she does.

"That's okay. It's why we're here." I continue to do up her coat as she watches me.

Taking her small hand in mine, we walk out of the restaurant. The paparazzi give us a bit of space, seemingly wanting to capture a candid moment—as candid as possible when there are several cameras pointing right at you, anyway.

I'm used to this, but she's not. I feel her hand grip mine tighter as the first few flashes come. As we approach the car, I stop and face her rather than opening the door.

I pause to take her in, tucking a strand of hair behind her ear and then she knocks the breath out of me when she whispers, "Kiss me." I don't know what to say. I want to kiss her. I've wanted to kiss her since New Year's Eve. I want to kiss her more than anything, but I didn't want it to be like this.

Willing my heart to slow down and my dick not to betray me, I lower my lips to her neck and place a gentle kiss there. "Are you sure?" I ask low enough only she can hear.

"Yes," she breathes as her hands come up to grasp the lapels of my coat.

I run my nose up and down her slender neck and she sways, fingers tightening their hold on my jacket.

If anyone is listening, I need self control. A lot of it. Right now.

She raises her chin, eyes locked on mine. I breathe in as I lower my lips to the corner of her mouth. Then she turns into me and our lips finally connect.

It's a soft, tentative touch at first, but my body reacts faster than my brain and in the next second, my hands are cradling her face as my tongue seeks entry into her mouth. She tastes like dessert and when I nip her bottom lip, I feel her body mold into mine then hear her whimper.

Fucking damn it, I need to hear that sound again.

Though it pains me to stop, I pull back before I can get too carried away. I take a second to look at her, rubbing my nose against hers. She has a lazy smile on her face and I know my own face matches hers.

The flash of paparazzi cameras cuts through the air as we intertwine our fingers together and I reach for the door handle, helping her inside first.

"Do you think they got what they needed?" Her voice is flat, and she's looking out the window.

Shit.

I clear my throat and take her hand in mine. "Yeah. I'm sorry about that, Elaina."

She links our fingers together and looks up at me. "Don't be. That's what tonight was for, right?" Our fingers remain linked, but we don't exchange any more words during the drive.

My mind is reeling.

What is she thinking? Did she feel the same spark between us when our lips touched? Damn it, all I want is to lean over and take her face in my hands again and really kiss her. That wasn't enough. I want so much more.

My thoughts are so loud, I'm afraid she can hear them, but she seems unaffected.

When we get to our building, I walk her to her door. Before I can think of what to do, she reaches up and hugs me.

"Thanks for tonight. I had fun." She pulls away and smiles brightly. "Goodnight, Adam."

"Goodnight, L."

———

WE DON'T GET to see one another much over the next few days since we're wrapping up on location. I'm sure to text to check in on her.

WEDNESDAY

ME

"Your Body Is a Wonderland" is my addition for today

I talked to Sandra today. Did she call you? Tell me your thoughts, please. All of them.

TORNEROSE

John Mayer feels appropriate. ;)

I can't believe I hadn't added No Doubt until now! "Underneath It All" is one of my faves.

Oh, and I did talk to her. She seemed very… excited… about the photos. I don't have many thoughts about this, tbh.

But I have other thoughts. I have been thinking that it's weird how we eat pizza from the inside out. Crazy, right?

Your turn. Tell me all your thoughts.

ME

You're so weird. I love it.

> My only thought: the picture of us smiling at one another when we walked out of the restaurant might be my favorite photo ever.

TORNEROSE

Yeah. We're cute.

THURSDAY

TORNEROSE

"Tearin' Up My Heart" because '90s *NSYNC. Nuff said.

ME

> Your love for the '90s knows no bounds.

TORNEROSE

You have no idea.

ME

> "Wonderwall" by Oasis

> Are we flying out together tomorrow?

TORNEROSE

Yes! I'm sitting with you whether or not you like it. Because I miss your face.

FRIDAY

ME

> See you soon!

I'M thankful for the chartered flight, so we all get to fly together. When I get to the plane that evening, Owen and

Lainey are already inside. I hear her laughter as I walk in, and when she sees me, her whole face lights up. A rush of warmth travels from my toes to the tips of my fingers, all the way up my torso, just from looking at her.

There's no way this is normal, is there?

No time to answer that. Elaina's giving me one of her incredible hugs.

"Hi! It's nice to see your face. You must be exhausted after this week. You doing okay?" Of course, she has to check on me. I bet she's going to repeat some form of this with Maeve and Raf, too, checking in on how they're doing. Her hand smooths over my beard and our eyes meet. "Hi."

"Hey, beauty. I'm good. Better now. Thank you." I smile and she disentangles herself from me much too quickly, reaching for something next to her. I don't even have time to ask her how she's doing and I think she does this intentionally.

"Raffy, I brought you some more of the soup I made. Is your throat any better?" She hands him a glass jar as he walks in and reaches up to give him a kiss on the cheek, pausing to get a good look at his face. I didn't even know Raf was sick.

"Almost all better, thanks to you, baby girl." He pulls her in for a side hug and takes the jar. "Liquid gold, right here." He points to it smiling. She's already on the move again as Maeve walks in behind us.

"Hi, Maevey! Charlie is coming to tomorrow's spa day. And I even requested your favorite masseuse." She leans in to give her friend a kiss on the cheek. She takes Maeve's hand and squeezes it to her chest as if comforting her. This kind of genuine affection isn't something I'm used to getting from anyone, but it's hard to imagine being without it now. Being without her.

"Lainey Banainey, everyone is here and sufficiently taken care of now. Please sit down and relax." Owen's baritone voice booms across the plane, but his tone is gentle. The last few weeks have really changed his relationship with his sister. I don't think I've heard him use a nickname for her until today.

She smiles warmly at her brother and then turns to me with a gleam in her eye and takes my hand, our fingers intertwining as we make our way towards the back of the plane. We settle into two seats that are side-by-side, the way she wanted. I can't stop thinking about what this fake relationship and proximity to her over the coming weeks are going to do to me if she insists on remaining just friends.

I run my fingers gently through her hair as she dozes off on my shoulder, feeling a sudden pain in my chest at the thought of my life without her in it.

Raf walks over and sits across from me, resting the soup that's been transferred to a bowl on the table.

"Hey, man. You alright?" he asks.

I hear the change in his voice now. It's hoarse. I can't believe I didn't realize he was sick. "Yeah. How are you doing? I didn't realize you weren't feeling well. Sorry, dude. That was shitty of me."

"You've been preoccupied." He shrugs and glances at Elaina, who is still fast asleep. "Have you told her yet?"

I look down at my lap and huff out a breath.

Of course, Raf knows.

"No. No, I haven't. We're just friends, remember? Nothing to tell, right?"

Raf slurps his soup and shakes his head.

"You two have *never* been just friends. You both need to get that shit straight and stop dancing around what's right in front of you." He lifts his eyebrows at me and brings another spoonful to his mouth. "Mmm. I swear it's worth getting sick just for Elaina's soup. I'll deny it *and* cut off your balls if you ever repeat this, but it's better than my mom's." We both chuckle and Elaina stirs on my shoulder. "I'm here when you need me." Raf gets up and pats me on my free shoulder before walking back to his seat.

She's been the one insistent on us being just friends, but I have yet to tell her how I feel. Maybe that needs to change soon. She needs to know I'm not interested in just pretending, but what if that makes things awkward between us and we can't recover? Fuck it. I can't think about this right now. Better close my eyes and hope sleep comes.

I WAKE to Elaina sitting sideways in her seat, reading a book. When I grunt and stretch, I look up to find her smiling at me.

"Who's the sleeping beauty now?" She taps me gently on the nose and now I know she's translated the Dutch nickname I gave her. Nicknames aren't my thing, but I know my Gramps would have some sort of Dutch term of endearment for Lainey as soon as he met her.

"Still you, *tornerose.*" I smile and stretch my legs, thankful I managed to sleep a bit. "Are we landing soon?" I honestly have no idea how long I've been asleep for.

"In about thirty minutes. You slept a while. Good luck getting to sleep tonight." She chuckles, knowing the time difference is going to mess with me. She tucks her book away, giving me her attention.

"Hey, I've been meaning to ask you if you think you can come to a wedding with me. It's a couple of weeks from now when we break from filming." I wipe my eyes and run a hand down my face, feeling more awake. "It's my cousin's wedding and Sandra asked me to see if you could go with me."

And I want to ask if you want to go as my date. For real. So, I can touch you and kiss you all I want.

"The resort is very private, but there will definitely be photos of the event since the groom is a famous drummer.

Sorry I haven't asked sooner." She's grinning at me, probably because I'm stumbling all over my words. I'm asking to put her life on hold so I can attend a fucking wedding.

This is so stupid.

I don't want this to be weird for her. She'd have to meet my whole family and pretend to be my girlfriend in front of them too. They don't know this isn't real.

"I know. Sandra already asked me. And I already said yes. Hawaii will be fun!" Her eyebrows shoot up her face and her grin widens. Of course, Sandra already talked to her. "Kelly booked everything already. She called me yesterday to confirm our flight time. I'm surprised she didn't tell you." She's completely unphased by the fact that my publicist and assistant have both called her about this.

This girl.

"And before you ask, yes, I'm sure. This isn't messing with any of my previous plans. Also yes, I do *want* to go with you. So, you can stop thinking of questions to ask me about it." She sits up and kisses my forehead then walks away, completely unaware of the way my heart is beating violently against my ribs.

16 /
how smooth are your hardwood floors?

elaina

IT FEELS great to be home. As soon as I step inside, I feel the weight of six weeks in London lift off my shoulders. I love London, but the chill was getting to me—and I'm from Massachusetts, for Pete's sake. California winters have spoiled me.

Adam follows me into the living room, stopping every few steps to take in the details: the taupe velvet sofa, bookshelves stuffed with records and books, the soft vintage rug beneath our feet. He smiles and says, "I love your house" at least three times before we even make it out of the room to continue the tour.

"This place is amazing. It's exactly how a place would look if someone took all the best parts about you and made a house. It's warm, inviting, insanely beautiful." He's running his hand over the fireplace as he says this and I feel myself blushing.

"Well, I take that as a compliment, especially as a production designer. Designing this house has taken some time, and it's not quite done yet." I smile, looking at the collected antiques mixed with new modern pieces that have taken me years to pull together.

"You've done this on your own?" he asks, incredulously, but there's no ill-meaning behind it.

"Yeah. I decorated it on my own. Now come on, let's go see the rest of the house." I shove my hand into the crook of his elbow and take him through the kitchen and into his room, making sure to show him the side door again. We walk over to the other side of the house where I show him Maeve's room and mine. He lingers in the doorway to my bedroom but doesn't go inside.

The urge to pull him in, pull him close, is sitting right there on the surface of my absurdly brittle self-control.

Walking down the hall, I open up my would-be office and let him into the dusty space.

"This is where my office will be." I smile even as I look at the unpainted walls.

"Wow." He walks straight towards the windows. "The view from here is amazing, L. Why didn't you make this your bedroom?" He turns to look at me.

I shrug. "I didn't see a point in my bedroom having the best view. I spend most of my time there with my eyes closed, anyway. I wanted my office to feel light and inspiring if it's where I'll be sketching and coming up with new ideas."

I walk over to the window he's next to. "I want a big desk here, facing out." I turn to the left, waving my arms up. "These bookshelves will be repainted to hold all my favorite things." I head to the right now. "Here, there will be a couch. Something deep and comfortable, probably in creamy linen to keep everything light and bright. A vintage rug to warm things up and plants by the window."

When I turn back to him, he's standing in the middle of the room with his hands in his pockets, beaming at me, nodding. I feel a little flutter in my belly. I haven't shown anyone this room, other than the girls. Sometimes I come in here and just stare at it, thinking about the day it'll finally be finished.

Adam puts his arm around my shoulder and kisses my temple.

"It's going to be amazing, Lainey." I smile up at him as we walk out, and that little flutter dances around my belly some more. We head back into the kitchen and I grab us some water before heading outside.

"We can order something for dinner if you're hungry. There's no food in the fridge, but I'll go to the store tomorrow. If there's anything special you want, just let me know." I smile at him as I sit on the edge of the pool, folding the hem of my jeans so I can dip my toes in the water.

"I don't need anything special, but please let me take care of groceries while I'm here." He sits next to me, mimicking my earlier motions and folding his pants up to his calves.

I scoff and give him a sideways look. "Not a chance. You're taking me to Hawaii, so I can handle groceries, thank you very much. Plus, you're my guest. Plus, it doesn't matter because we're friends and *this is what friends do, Adam.*" I cock my head to the side and stick my tongue out at him.

"There's no arguing with you, is there?" He smiles and laughs, that gorgeous rumbly sound I love so much hitting me square in the center of my chest.

"Nope." I flash him a wide smile. We sit, looking at each other for a few seconds. He reaches up and tucks a strand behind my ear, and I'm delighted. I lean into his touch and take a deep breath. "I'm glad you're here."

"Me too, beauty."

All I want is to tell him that I hate this being friends bullshit, that I've wanted to kiss him every day since the day we met. But I don't.

We end up moving to some loungers, eating sushi and drinking wine until it gets too cold and we head inside. Frankie is already snoring in his bed when we head in, and we both chuckle at how loud he is.

"Let me know if you need anything, okay?" I reach up

with a hand on his shoulder and kiss his cheek. We both linger, noses nearly touching. "Goodnight," I whisper.

"Night, *tornerose*." He places a kiss on my jaw, then my cheek. My grip on his shoulder tightens and my lips part as I hiss in a breath. *Kiss me. Please, please, please kiss me.* Then Frankie barks and comes barreling over towards us, immediately murdering the moment.

Fuck you, Frankie!

We both force out a strained chuckle and I motion for Frankie to follow me. I won't sleep for quite some time, so I am thankful I'm reunited with all my battery-operated friends.

———

I MAKE myself scarce the following morning, heading to the grocery store early, picking up coffee at my favorite place and taking Frankie for a walk. I leave Adam a note on the countertop next to some muffins I baked. Yeah, I got pretty much no sleep last night, but I made sure my time was productive.

> A,
>
> Enjoy the muffins. There's an iced coffee for you in the fridge along with lots of other food! Make yourself at home. I'll be back from the spa around 4 and I'm making chicken for dinner. The gang's coming over at 6. I hope that's okay.
>
> -E

I arrive at the spa before Maeve and Charlie, so I sit in a plush chair and open my book. I hear the automatic doors open and glance up from my reading to see them both walk in. We smile, eager for our spa day to begin. We're handed our thick white robes and slippers, then directed to the pedi-cure chairs. Gentle music plays in the background and I feel my shoulders loosen as we all relax into our chairs.

The spa attendant returns with a bowl of warm water for us to soak our feet in. She sets up a pedicure station for each of us, complete with fragrant foot scrubs and lotions. We take turns talking about our plans for the week. Charlie has been in LA for a few days already, so she tells us about some cool restaurants and stores she's visited so far since this was her first time here without us.

Once we've finished our pedicures, we're led to a cozy room with massage tables side by side. A thick blanket of lavender scented steam fills the air as the masseuses enter and start working on each of us.

Our time at the spa flies by, that is, except for the forty-five minutes in which I have all of the hair ripped off of my lady parts. That was… torture. But I have to say, I really like how it looks. And how it feels. I wonder if Adam would like it.

Slow your roll, dude. Jeez.

When I get home, Adam isn't there, but he's left me a note on the back of the mine from this morning.

L,

The muffins were perfect. Thank you! I'm training for a bit this afternoon, but I'll see you for dinner. I'll bring home more wine.

xx,

A

I read the note five more times. *Home.* I shove the little flutter I feel in my belly far, far away. Shove it down, down, down. I take a quick shower and change into my favorite jeans and a cropped tee, keeping my hair down.

By 5 p.m. I have the chicken cooking and everything else

is ready for dinner. Raf, Maeve and her stylist Taylor came early, so we turn on some music because any chance to have a kitchen dance party is welcome in my house. We're all dancing to Lizzo's "About Damn Time" when I feel eyes on me. I turn to find Adam standing in the doorway with a bottle of wine in his hand, eyes moving all over my body as he licks his lower lip.

Oh, Lord… am I dreaming?

Without thinking, I glide across the kitchen towards him, my hips swaying in time to the beat. As I dip with my back arched and sway my hips, I notice that his shirt is soaked with sweat and essentially glued to his body. His breathing is heavy, and I feel his chest moving against me as he gently grabs my elbow and pulls me closer. We stand there, the air thick with anticipation, until I finally break the silence.

"Uh, hi." The room is silent but for the music and the sound of my own heartbeat in my ears.

"I gotta go shower." He lets go of my arm, hands me the wine and takes a step back, then turns to walk down the hall towards his room. I stand there like a fool and as the song ends, I hear a throat being cleared.

"There ain't enough room for us *and* the sexual tension in this room, honey." Taylor fans himself as he walks over to his glass of wine. "Was that River Holm? He is far hotter in person than on the screen. Damn, get it, Elaina." He snaps with his hand high in the air and I take in Maeve's face. Her jaw is about to hit the floor and Raf's eyes look like they're about to pop out of their sockets.

"Okaaaay. Anyone need a refill?" I walk to my wine glass and take a few big sips, mostly because my mouth is bone dry. I know the people around me are talking, but I can't hear a thing. My brain keeps replaying the scene from a few minutes ago. The heat in Adam's eyes as I danced, the rise and fall of his chest, the way he pulled me in.

It finally registers that someone is talking.

"How was the spa today, ladies?" Taylor, blissfully oblivious to the magnitude of what just happened, moves right along. We talk about how lovely it was and I'm thankful for the subject change. Maeve goes on and on about her massage because the masseuse there really has magical hands.

"And I hear someone got herself a special something today?" Taylor wiggles his eyebrows at me and laughs. "How smooth are your hardwood floors right now, Elaina?"

"Oh my god, Taylor!" I shriek at him and Raf plugs his ears. "Leave my *floors* alone, okay? Fucking hurt like hell though, jeez." I grab my crotch ever so slightly, remembering that my lady parts are mad at me right now.

"What hurt like hell?" I freeze at the sound of Adam's voice.

Goddamn it, whyyyyy?

"Oh, Elaina had her first *Brazilian blowout* today." Taylor motions to his own crotch as he says this. "Hope you enjoy it, big guy." Taylor winks at Adam and sets his empty glass down. "Anyway, boys and girls, I have to go, but it's been lovely to see you all. Later!" He walks out, blowing us all kisses. A little Taylor tornado just ripped through my house.

Adam's eyes go wide as understanding of what Taylor was talking about hits him. He clears his throat and looks around a little nervously. "Who is that?"

"That was Taylor, Maeve's trouble-making stylist." I get the words out as quickly as I can and finish my glass of wine. I walk over to the stack of plates. "I'm going to set the table quickly. The wine's open and there's beer in the fridge."

And with that I leave the room, taking at least a dozen deep breaths, which either help me with my lightheadedness or make it worse. It's hard to tell right now. I hear Raf's cackle as I set down the plates.

I so did not need this today.

By the time I get back to the kitchen, Owen has arrived, and everyone has moved on from the shitshow of ten minutes ago. Dinner goes by quickly, but I feel Adam's eyes on me the entire time. I avoid looking at him like I avoid the 5 south after 3 p.m.

If you know, you know.

By eleven, we've all got full bellies and we've all laughed enough to almost work off the cheesecake I made for dessert. Almost.

When Raf, Owen and Maeve leave, Adam is standing behind me as I wave to them from the front door and I can feel the heat coming from his body.

"I'm pretty tired. I'm gonna head to bed. I'll clean up tomorrow." I kiss his cheek, but make it quick. "Goodnight, Adam."

He kisses my forehead and lets out a deep breath I feel on my cheek. "Goodnight, L."

———

THE NEXT MORNING, I wake up to a perfectly clean kitchen and a warm feeling in my chest knowing Adam did that for me.

His schedule is full and he leaves early most mornings. Occasionally we get to have breakfast together and it's so easy being around him. It's like he fits here. He picks up where I leave off, washing the coffee pot and taking Frankie out in the early mornings.

We hardly see each other between his training and shooting schedules, and I haven't been shy about taking on some commitments. From a possible project to guest lectures I've been invited to give at different colleges.

Apparently I'm not that great at taking a break from work, but these feel different. I've wanted to pursue lecturing but never had the time for it.

. . .

I FIGURE the only way to keep my mind off him this week was to do something girly and indulgent, so I headed to a lingerie boutique on Melrose. I picked out sheer black stockings, a lacy lingerie set in ivory, and a corset with velvet straps. I couldn't help being drawn to the lingerie's soft textures and sensual cuts. By the time I got to the counter, my arms were overloaded.

Just as I was leaving, Sandra called asking Adam and me to make a public appearance together. Despite how little time we've had together lately, I assured her we'd do our best.

ME

Hey, want to go get some ice cream when you're home tonight?

Sandra needs us to be seen together and there's a great spot we can walk to on Sunset.

ADAM

I'd love that. I miss your face.

And your hugs.

I do my very best not to read into him using my line back on me, or that he misses my hugs. Hugs *are* friendly, after all.

I run a few more errands to make myself not count down the minutes until I see him, and by the time I get home he's just pulling in as well. I leave my bags in the car, not wanting him to see the giant bags of lingerie. I start to walk toward him, and he breaks into a full run towards me, scooping me up in a hug that has my feet dangling off the ground.

"My *tornerose*. I missed you so much." His beard tickles me and I can't hide the giggle building up inside me. I also can't ignore the bubbly feeling that builds in my stomach and travels up to my chest.

My tornerose. My. My.

"Hi. How do we see each other less living in the same

house?" He sets me down and I take in his face. His hair is longer, his beard is shorter. So short I can see his dimples underneath it. "Hi."

"I know. It's not fair. I need to see more of you. Notes on the kitchen counter won't do." He's smiling, tucking my hair behind my ear as he scans my face like he hasn't memorized it already.

"Well, no need for notes tonight. Let's go grab that ice cream. I'll just get Frankie quickly."

17 /
why?

adam

THE SMELL OF HER, the sight of her in that sundress, the feel of her body against mine and her hands in my hair... I want to drown in this moment, live in it forever. I've missed her voice, her sweet giggle, and the way she smiles up at me with those golden flecks shining in her green eyes. How she always says *hi* quietly the second time after we hug.

We've had such long shoot days and in between shooting there have been so many meetings, trying to make this next project work. I haven't told anyone about taking on a producer role in a movie because nothing is official yet, so I've had to be a bit mysterious about what all of these meetings are about. I want to tell Elaina though. I've been dying to talk to her about it.

She comes skipping out with Frankie on her heels, smiling and reaching for my hand. How can she think this is just friendship? She's it for me. I don't want ice cream with any other girl. I don't want anything with anyone that isn't her.

"Alright, so Sandra was pretty adamant that we look... um... affectionate. I'd rather not have anything specific planned because I'm not very good at acting, so are you okay if we just… improvise?" Her brows are furrowed and she's looking up at me, nervously biting her lower lip again.

"Yeah, Lainey. Let's do that. Let's just have fun, okay?"

Let's just do what we always do, except I want my lips on your lips regardless of who's watching or not watching.

She smiles and nods, seeming satisfied with my answer.

We walk hand-in-hand, looking at the signs of spring popping up all over the city, which in LA is basically just what people wear, since there really isn't much of a winter to speak of. We both laugh when Frankie hides behind one of us at the sight of anyone who isn't a woman or child.

We get to the ice cream shop and she orders something with strawberries in it. Of course. I go for the mint chocolate chip.

We sit at a table outside and I try not to lose my shit as she moans while licking the side of her ice cream cone.

We're sitting on a bench and she's leaning against my arm, her laughter lingering in the air. As she looks up at me, I notice the smudge of ice cream under her lip. She licks it away before I can, and I'm transfixed by the sight of her tongue just like that first night in London.

"Lainey?" I whisper in her ear.

"Hmm?"

"I'm going to kiss you now, okay?" I wait for her response, but one doesn't come. I pull back, doing my best to hide my concern. When I tip her chin up towards me, I see her small nod as she licks her lower lip again.

How the hell I'm supposed to pretend she's my girlfriend while wanting her to be my actual girlfriend while also pretending that I just want to be her friend?

"Fuck," I breathe out as I lean down and press my lips to hers, swiping my tongue against where the ice cream was. Her eyes close and lips part, like a soft invitation. She melts deeper into my body, her free hand holding tightly to my forearm. I don't push for more than just tasting her lips, and when I feel her open up for me, we both hear the sharp click of a camera shutter. She jerks away, her cheeks now tinged pink, her lips still parted as she breathes heavily.

I hide my disappointment, kissing her temple while she busies herself with her ice cream cone, as if nothing out of the ordinary had happened.

So much for not being very good at acting.

This shouldn't be so easy though, leaning down to kiss her. It shouldn't feel this natural to be with her. I shouldn't be fucking my fist in the shower nearly every day to the thought of her in my bed. But it is easy, it does feel natural, and I am most definitely doing that.

After this many years of celibacy, without so much as kissing another woman, I expected all of this to feel foreign. But everything feels right with her and I only want more of it.

A cool breeze blows in and Elaina shivers. I slip off my sweater and drape it over her shoulders. I take Frankie's leash, and we start our walk back. Elaina talks animatedly about the romance novel she's reading, her deep green eyes lighting up as she describes the characters and plotlines and how she can imagine it playing out on the big screen. Her excitement is infectious, and I find myself completely absorbed in her words.

I want to savor every moment with her, while at the same time willing away my own feelings that have come flooding back after our kiss earlier.

———

THE FOLLOWING day I wake up to music. "Fantasy" by Mariah Carey is coming from the kitchen along with the unmistakable smell of L's chocolate chip muffins. When I walk in, she's singing into a wooden spoon, one arm in the air as the messy bun atop her head bobbles and her body sways in that irresistible way of hers. She's in her typical leggings and a cropped T-shirt—what I recognize now as a true Elaina uniform for yoga, baking, or hanging out at home.

"This is just like the night we met," I say over the music, not wanting to scare her, but also unsure of how to let her know I'm here without doing so.

She jumps back, putting the spoon down then quickly swatting at me with it.

"You scared me! What are you doing home? I thought you'd left already."

I chuckle, walking towards her.

"Sorry, I didn't mean to." I kiss her on the forehead, leaning to grab a mug for the coffee that is, of course, already made. When we see one another at home, it's always with this easy, natural way of moving around one another. I reach around her to pour myself the perfect amount into my mug and take a deep breath of the freshly brewed aroma of the coffee. I sip my black coffee while she guzzles her beige-colored one doused in creamer. No doubt there's also half a pound of sugar in it.

I grab a cloth, scrubbing the sides and bottom of the pot as she takes a step back to reprogram the machine for the next day. I let Frankie out early in the mornings before my workout and she takes him for a walk in the afternoons. Even when we don't see one another, that's how it goes. We perform these routine acts without ever having spoken about them. They just happen.

I finish washing the coffee pot, remembering that she asked me what I was doing home. I turn back towards her, looking into her eyes as if I want to say something more than "I don't have to be on set today." But that's what comes out anyway.

"Oh. Well, I hope I didn't wake you." The wrinkles around her eyes deepen and her brow furrows as she studies my face with obvious concern. I can almost feel the weight of her worry, like a heavy blanket draped over me.

"You didn't," I immediately reassure her. "But even if you had, there are worse ways to be woken up than with your singing and baking, Lainey. Both of which are fantastic."

I walk towards her again, brushing off some flour on her cheek with my thumb. "What are you doing today?" This is my lame attempt at diffusing the tension that's already thick in the air.

"Maeve is going to her beach house for the weekend to decompress, so I was going to take these muffins and a casserole up for her so she has some of her favorite things with her when she gets there." She smiles a shy smile, like I just caught her doing something she's not supposed to.

"Want company?" I don't think, I just ask because I don't actually care what she's doing today. I would have wanted to go with her anywhere.

Her eyes brighten and she stands a little straighter. "Really? You really want to come?"

"Really. I really do." I hardly finish my sentence before she's hugging me, nearly spilling my coffee all over us.

"Okay, I'm gonna shower and change and we can leave. I don't want to take up your whole day, so we can be quick." When she looks up at me with that wide smile, I know I would say yes to absolutely anything this girl asks of me.

"I'll do the same. And my day is yours, beauty. Whatever you want to do, I want to do it with you." She scrunches her nose at me, smiling even bigger.

She lets out a little squeal. "This is the best surprise. You're the best!" She scurries off down the hall and I go off to my bedroom, doing a terrible job of ignoring that she's naked and in the shower at the same time as me.

TWENTY MINUTES LATER, we meet back in the kitchen. Elaina's auburn hair is falling down her back, half up in a little clip. She has a white dress shirt half tucked into denim cutoffs and white sneakers. She's all toned muscles and long legs and the coconut honey smell that is entirely hers traps me in place. She's just finished packing the food when she turns to me, smiling. "Ready?"

I nod, twirling my keys on my finger. "I'll drive. Come on, Frankie." The pup slips and slides all over the floor, running towards me and out of the house to my car. The whole scene is so natural and comforting. It feels like we all belong like this. Together.

In the car, she insists on listening to our playlist, which is such a mess of all different songs. We laugh as 50 Cent and *NSYNC mingle, but we also sing along to nearly every song. Her hair blows in the wind and her long legs bounce with the music.

When we get to Maeve's house in Malibu, Elaina leaves the box of muffins and a note on the kitchen counter along with the fresh flowers we stopped along the way to buy. I take her wrist and pull her towards me, wanting nothing more than to kiss her. Willing my self-control to kick in, I settle for combing my fingers in her hair. "This is really nice, you know? What you're doing for Maeve?"

She leans on the counter next to us, swaying into my touch. "It's nothing. I know she's really stressed out and tired. She deserves this."

I shake my head, fingers still in her hair. "It's not nothing. You're a good friend. The best. You put in a lot of effort. And you deserve stuff like this, too." I wonder who in Lainey's life does things like this for her. Who takes care of her?

"Yeah, well, I like to do these things for the people I love. It doesn't feel like effort." I don't know if she's noticed, but our bodies are closer, hers leaning further into mine.

"I know you do, *tornerose*. The people you love are very lucky people." I run my thumb along her chin, angling her face towards mine. Her lips part and she shakes her head softly.

"I'm the lucky one," she whispers.

The suddenness of the barking and the loudness of it completely rips the moment to shreds, and she steps away from me before I can even think of holding her in place. I swear Frankie has something against men getting close to Lainey, which I don't mind. Unless I'm that man.

"Um, we should head back. We can stop and get lunch on the way if you're hungry? Or I can make us something at home. Whatever you want. I don't mind either way." She's moving quickly around the kitchen, grabbing her purse and Frankie, heading towards the front door. This is *not* how I wanted things going today.

"Let's grab lunch somewhere. That sounds good. And, hey, if you want to come by the set on Monday, we're filming a really cool scene. I think you'd like it." Let's hope that gets her out of rambling mode.

"There won't be any boobs involved, will there?" She turns to look at me with a smirk on her face. Her eyes flash with amusement and I smile in response. The air between us is tinted with relief as we share a brief laugh, each of us now standing a respectful distance apart.

"No boobs. But you can see what I've been training for." If I tell her it's bare knuckle boxing, she might not want to come, so I omit that little detail.

"I'd really like that." Her shoulders are relaxed as we walk to the car and we drive to the restaurant in Malibu in comfortable silence, hair blowing in the wind, the likes of Ginuwine and Oasis now keeping us company.

———

WE ARRIVE BACK at the house with full bellies and the usual feeling of familiarity between us. The sexual tension has somewhat dissipated, but I know it's still there, lurking just beneath the surface.

"What else did you have planned for today?" I put away Frankie's leash and take off my shoes as she sets her purse down.

"Honestly, not much. I was going to do some yoga, order Italian for dinner, and maybe watch a movie." I nod and tilt my head while she lays out perfect plans for an evening at home.

Her eyes widen as she catches on. "Want to join me?" And then, as if a literal light bulb has come on, she lights up. "We can finally watch *The Notebook*!"

I laugh, walking beside her with a hand on her shoulder. "That sounds perfect. Where are we doing this yoga?" And this is the part of the plan I might have regretted if I were a better man.

She slips back into tight black leggings and a hot pink sports bra, her muscle definition stretching the fabric of both. I watch as she gracefully flows through the poses with ease.

During our session, we are intimately close, and I can feel her soft skin brush against mine as she adjusts my body into some of the deeper stretches.

I find myself entranced by her movements, and although she gives no indication of being affected by our contact, I can almost feel an electric spark between us. It makes me wonder if this is all one-sided. If she's just really good at pretending when we need to, but that maybe she meant what she said. We're nothing but friends. The thought makes my temples ache and I store it away for another time. I want to focus on today.

WE ORDER MORE food than we could possibly need and bring it all into the living room to eat on the couch. She bounces around and puts *The Notebook* on, and her enthusiasm is contagious. I'm even excited to watch Ryan Gosling now.

As I watch the movie, my gaze often drifts away from the screen and towards her. A single tear runs down her cheek at a particularly emotional scene, and she openly laughs or gasps at others. It's impossible not to feel a little of her emotions too, and by the time the movie ends, I find myself wiping away my own tears.

She turns on the couch, legs crossed. "So? What did you think?"

"I liked it. It was sad but beautiful." The smile on her face tells me I answered correctly. "But I want to know something." Her eyes widen as she waits for my question. "Have you ever watched any of my movies with this kind of enthusiasm?"

She smiles, looking down at her lap, and I prepare to hear that she hasn't watched any of my movies.

"Yes." She clears her throat and looks up, not meeting my eyes. "I've watched every single one of your movies with this level of enthusiasm. Most of them more than once, actually, and quite a few of them recently."

I pull her closer to me, setting her legs on my lap, and lower my face so she'll meet my eyes.

"You've watched *all* of my movies?" She nods. "More than once?" My voice is high, and she giggles, nodding again. "I don't know what to say." I pause, amazed at her admission. "Why recently?"

She gently smiles, her eyelids fluttering a little before she leans her head back against the couch, closing her eyes as she speaks.

"Sometimes because I missed you. Sometimes because I wanted to see you before I knew you. But really, I think..." Her voice trails off and she opens her eyes, gazing down at her folded hands in her lap.

Taking a deep breath, she raises her gaze to meet mine and blushes as she continues. "I think I just wanted to feel closer to you." She gives a small shrug before biting her bottom lip in shyness. *Fuck, this girl drives me crazy.*

She swallows and closes her eyes again briefly. "Have you… um… ever watched anything I've worked on?" She bites her lip again, looking down at her lap.

I move closer to her, taking her face in my hands so she can see my face when I answer her. "Every single thing, Lainey. More than once. All of them recently."

Looking into my eyes, she whispers, "Why?"

I brush the hair off her face tracing her nose, lips and jaw with my fingertip.

"Because I want to know every part of you. Because you matter to me. Because what's important to you is important to me."

Her eyes fill with tears, and she takes a quick breath in through her mouth.

"Thank you for telling me." I wipe the tears from her cheeks with the pads of my thumbs. "I should get some sleep, and you too." She kisses my cheek and lifts herself off of the couch. "Goodnight, Adam."

"'Night, L."

I sit there for a long time, replaying the last ten minutes in my head. Her words, the way she bit her lip, how her eyes filled with tears. Why did I agree to be just friends? Why won't she give in to this?

We nearly kissed twice today. Away from prying eyes and cameras. This pull between us isn't just for show and as much as I want to, I'm having a hard time understanding her reservations.

I want her.

I want all of her.

18 /
is that adam or river?

elaina

THERE IS no sleep happening in my bed tonight. None. I was certain my confession that I've watched all of his movies would be one-sided. I was not expecting him to admit the same thing. I wasn't prepared for *I want to know every part of you. You matter to me. What's important to you is important to me.*

Maybe there's something to be explored here. Even if it's temporary. Even if it's just for the duration of this fake relationship, because it's getting harder and harder to draw the line between what's real and what's pretend. My body is pulled to his in a way I know I've never felt before and my brain fights with it daily, not wanting to ruin a perfectly good friendship. But can we be friends with this much tension between us? Wouldn't it be better to just see where this goes than to live forever in this game of tug of war?

I take the opportunity, since I can't turn my brain or my body off, to check my list. I only have one thing to check off. I obviously need to add more since we're only a few weeks into the year.

·Sing in public. Like Karaoke? Whatever. Just

sing. Sing all the songs I love most regardless of who's listening.

·Try a new recipe. Bake something new for me or for someone else. I already do this, but this is my reminder to keep doing it.

·Do something that scares me. Not like skydiving or anything involving near or potential death, but something that scares me deep down. Something my soul will remember. Something I'll be glad I did when I'm old and wrinkly.

·Have more than one orgasm in one day. Try to make it with something other than a plethora of toys, but no pressure. Just have more orgasms in general. I've gone long enough without them.

·Masturbate in the bath because it sounds like fun. If it's not fun, don't do it. Bonus points for bringing snacks for afterwards.

These all seem like things I can do. It's not hard to know where my brain decided to go given the last two items added. I'm up for the challenge though.

I don't know how long exactly it takes or how many times I replay every part of today in my head, but eventually, very very late into the night, I fall asleep.

THE WEEKEND GOES by in a flash, and I don't see Adam once. We keep missing each other as he has training and I had made plans to see Charlie and Raf (separately, of course) while Maeve is in Malibu.

Monday comes and I realize Adam and I didn't discuss

details of when I'd meet him at the studio today. When I walk into the kitchen I see a note next to the coffee.

> *L,*
>
> *I had to leave early to meet my trainer, but you can come by the studio when you get this. They know you're coming and someone can direct you to my trailer. I'll probably still be in there by the time you wake from your slumber. Just be there before 11, okay?*
>
> *Can't wait to see you.*
>
> *xx*
>
> *-A*

I read the note five or six times, absentmindedly touching my lips as I do and then I look at the clock. It's 9:57.

Shit!

I rush to shower and figure out what to wear, settling on a black pleated skirt, a cropped caramel-colored sweater with my white sneakers. I put my hair in a low bun and put some mascara on. Good enough.

I make it to the studio at 10:37 and find Manny, someone who thankfully recognizes me. It's nice catching up with him and it settles my nerves as he gives me a ride to Adam's trailer. I thank him and say goodbye, then I'm left pacing outside the trailer, working myself up to knocking when I hear my name.

"Elaina?" Oh shit. Shit, shit, shit.

How is this happening again? It's puppy-dog-eyes Mitch coming over to talk to me.

"Hey. Nice to see you here. You coming to watch River's next scene?"

"Hi, Mitch. Uh yeah, I'm just waiting for him." And with

impeccable timing, Adam opens the trailer door. His hair is a disheveled mess, and he has some very tight pants on, which is making me exceptionally curious about what kind of scene they're filming today. His beard is nearly gone, and he looks downright edible.

"Hey, beauty. You're here." I feel his eyes move over my whole body, and his smile sends happy feelings straight to my belly. He places a lingering kiss on my temple and his hand on my lower back.

"Mitch." He nods once. "See you in there." And with that he starts to walk away, moving his hand to my hip, pulling me closer, adding a kiss on the crown of my head. "I've missed you," he whispers in my ear, and I melt into a puddle of pathetic lady goo.

I'm dizzy by the time we make it onto the set. Nothing has happened, but I'm loopy with lusty thoughts for two reasons.

The first is that Adam is very good at acting like we're dating. The nickname. The forehead kiss. The sweet I've missed you, which I didn't think anyone could hear, but made the whole thing very convincing, nonetheless.

The second is he's now removed the hoodie he had on and is currently shirtless with those very tight pants on. There isn't much left to the imagination and watching his muscles move as he boxes with a man similar in build is making me so hot I'm regretting this sweater. I think we should revisit the boxing attire of the nineteenth century.

To be honest, I couldn't pick out the guy he's fighting with out of a lineup. I haven't taken my eyes off Adam's abs. And butt. And biceps. And that butt. It's been four hours and it's safe to say most women and a few of the men in here don't mind that this scene is taking a long time to shoot. Adam and his boxing partner are putting on a mouthwatering show for us all.

I don't know the complete story, but I know this movie is set in the 1800s and follows the life of an American who moves to England and eventually becomes a famous bare knuckle boxer.

Before the next set of lusty thoughts about running my tongue along the ridges of his abs can take over every useful brain cell I possess, it registers that something has gone wrong. The other guy throws a punch at Adam's face and it unintentionally lands. Hard! Adam goes down and I jump out of my seat.

Several people rush over to him, and I can't see anything. I'm too far away. He hasn't gotten up. He's bleeding, and I hear someone say he'll likely need stitches.

Stitches?

They rush him out to the medic, and I'm left standing next to a small pool of blood. His blood. I feel myself start to panic a little as I make my way toward where they took him. I push through a few people and finally, *finally* I get close enough to see his face through the crowd outside of the first aid tent.

My heart is beating in my throat. In my ears. In my temples. I step closer, barely managing to keep my feelings at bay. He's perched on the edge of a table, and a medic is carefully taping a bandage to his right eyebrow. The blood has been staunched. Our eyes meet and my heart races even faster. He slowly raises an arm towards me, and I step into his space. His grip is firm when he grasps my hand and pulls me closer.

His gaze is intense, and I can feel the tension radiating from his clenched jaw.

The medic seems to be done and has moved somewhere out of sight. I come to stand between his legs, heart pounding against my ribs. I bring both of my hands to his cheeks, inspecting his face, moving it from side to side.

"Are you okay?" I kiss his right cheek and then the left. "What can I do?" I kiss his forehead and his chin. "Does it hurt?" I kiss as much of his face as I can while avoiding the cut above his eye. "I was so scared."

His eyes search my own before his head straightens and his lips meet mine. They're like two halves of the same puzzle finally finding their place in the world. Hot sparks erupt in my chest and spread throughout my body like a fireworks display, igniting a sense of belonging and assurance I haven't felt before.

One of his arms wraps around my waist, and a hand runs up my back, pulling us desperately closer. His tongue brushes over my top lip as I melt into his hard body, opening for him and then I'm tasting him and he's tasting me. He's salty and minty and the combination shouldn't be so delicious, but it is.

His kiss is slow, methodical, like he's taking his time learning every inch of my mouth. The feel of his beard against my chin sends a shiver of excitement up my spine and my thighs tense as I imagine that delicious scrape against them.

He holds me tightly, as if I'm made of sand and could slip between his fingers. I am delirious, high on the lust coursing through me, hoping and praying it never ends and knowing I would chase this feeling forever.

My fingers tangle in his hair. My skin burns everywhere we touch, and my lips already feel swollen. Time stops, or it speeds up. What even is time? There is nothing but this, no one but us as our mouths explore with frantic desperation. His grip on me is so tight, I'm sure he's the only reason I'm still standing upright because I can't even feel my feet.

All thoughts blow apart on the wind, like dry leaves on a street in wintertime. I'm drowning in his warmth, a quiet moan escaping me as I feel my now heavy breasts press against his bare chest.

Someone clears their throat and it might as well be a bucket of ice being dumped on my head. He pulls away with a dissatisfied grunt. My eyes are still closed as I catch my breath and he places a final lingering but tender kiss on my lips. I force my eyes open.

"I'm okay, baby." I'm met with blue eyes so dark I hardly

recognize them. The cerulean ocean is now a stormy, raging sea. It's not a look I've ever seen in my friend's eyes. On my fake boyfriend's beautiful face. As our surroundings come into focus, I take a step back, smoothing my skirt. I see a hand holding a phone move into a back pocket and I hear whistles, maybe even a few claps. Understanding hits me like a cannonball to the gut.

This was River kissing Elaina. Not Adam. River.

"That's a wrap here. Let's move on," the faraway voice says. The place clears as I stand there a few seconds longer gathering all the pieces of me scattered in this tent. The scared pieces, the confused pieces, the very, very, *very* turned on pieces.

I touch my fingertips to my now definitely swollen lips while he puts on the same hoodie he had on earlier. Wordlessly, he takes my hand, and we walk out towards his trailer. I hear the faint sound of voices and whispers, but they eventually fade away and it's just us.

Or is that still River?

We walk into his trailer, and he drops my hand as if my touch has burned him. Because that was all for show, after all, right?

"I'm going to have a quick shower, then we can go get something to eat. Are you okay here?" He's already taking his hoodie off and I look away because I simply can't handle seeing any more of his body today.

"Uh-huh." And he's gone.

Fuckity fuck, fuck, fuuuuuuuuuck! I am so royally, monumentally, totally screwed.

That was the hottest kiss I've had in my adult life and it wasn't even real.

Tell that to your throbbing lady bits. They didn't get the memo.

I sit staring at the wall until I hear him come out of the back of the trailer. His hair is wet, and his jeans look like they were made specifically for his body. His gray T-shirt fits him perfectly and does nothing to keep his bulging biceps out of sight of my greedy eyeballs.

"You ready?" He's standing in front of me all smelling like a dewy forest and shit, with his hand out for me to take. Which I obviously do. When I stand, he does a slow perusal of my body and suddenly everything feels tight. I sense his eyes everywhere and it sends tingles all. Over. Me. How does he do that without even touching me? "You look amazing, by the way. Hungry?"

Very, so go ahead and lay down so I can nibble on your delicious body all night, please and thanks. Ugh. Stop it. Just. Shut. Up.

"Uh-huh." Yep. These are the only words left in my vocabulary. I still haven't said actual words to him since that fake kiss that felt very real to all my body parts, including my brain, for a hot second.

Once we're in the car and he's driving, I'm once again struggling to find words. I don't normally have this problem, so this feels very... new.

I blow out a breath. "That was some kiss, River." I turn my head so I can see him and the moment I say his name, he flinches and I feel as though I've made a terrible mistake.

"Um, right... sorry. Was it too much?" Okay, so maybe not a terrible mistake. He seems fine. And didn't correct my use of his stage name.

"No, no. Not at all. I'm sure Sandra will see it soon." I give him a crooked smile because I don't know what to do with my face at this moment. I want to scream. I want to jump his bones. I want to run away.

He turns his face towards me. "Elaina, I'm sorry. I wasn't thinking." He takes my hand and draws a couple of circles on my knuckles before speaking again. "I need you to tell me if any of this is ever too much. I don't want to overwhelm you or make you uncomfortable in any way. You have to know that." Those baby blues are beseeching and steady. So very steady, as he has been since the first moment we met.

"I know that. I do. I trust you." My voice cracks and I feel a twinge in my gut as I say the words, because I don't even believe myself. I want to trust him, this, but something in me just can't. Not completely. "I promise I'll tell you if it's ever too much." That I can commit to.

He lets out a loud breath and looks down at our hands. "Okay. Good." He squeezes my hand as he stops the car. "I trust you, too. Completely." And I believe him.

The valet attendant opens the door for me, and I slip out quickly. Adam takes my hand into the crook of his elbow and smiles down at me as we walk into a dimly lit restaurant.

19 /
does everybody know?

adam

WE'VE MADE it to dinner, but before getting here I needed a cold shower. The colder, the better. I can't believe I fucking kissed her like that, but goddamn it, the worry in her eyes felt like a punch to the gut, and before I knew it, she was pressing her lips on my forehead, my nose, my cheeks.

I was overcome with the need to feel her lips against mine, to taste her. Our mouths collided and my heart swelled with a wave of emotion that was more intense than anything I've ever felt before. This kiss wasn't soft and timid like the others.

Any worry I had that she didn't feel what I felt vanished when her body molded into mine. I just wasn't thinking about how quickly people would be pulling their phones out to take pictures and videos of the whole thing. I turned my phone off because I can't bring myself to see what's already out there an hour after the fact.

As we walked back to my trailer, a chill ran down my spine and I couldn't recognize it. It wasn't the usual fear or anxiety that came in the past when I even thought about being with a woman. No, this was more like awareness that the fear wasn't there. It was the awareness that this felt like something we should be doing every day. That I want more. That I will always want more with her.

She's been quiet and distant since the whole thing happened and I was afraid I'd overwhelmed her with the kiss, and then she said, *That was some kiss, River.* Fuck. She called me River. That felt like a punch in the nuts. Did she think I did that as River? That I was just faking it? Is that what it was for her? Was the concern nothing but her playing the doting girlfriend? I have so many questions.

"So… I have questions." She peeks up at me above her menu, her long lashes almost touching her cheeks before she looks up. I lean back in my chair, raise an eyebrow, and motion for her to continue. "How's your eye? Does it hurt? Did anything else get hurt?"

"It's fine. It's a small cut, and doesn't need stitches, but it'll probably bruise. Head wounds bleed a lot, so it looked worse than it is. It doesn't hurt much, and I didn't get hurt anywhere else. I think you did a pretty good job of checking for other injuries to my face earlier." I smile at the memory of her leaving kisses on my face and she blushes.

"Yeah, I guess I did." She bites her lower lip before continuing. "Where did you learn to fight like that, anyway? And do you work out every day? Because I've never seen you work out, but there's obvious proof that you do because… holy fuck… abs and biceps and more back muscles than I've ever seen on one person before."

She blushes again and I savor this little rant of hers. I love her potty mouth and that it works faster than her brain, so she says things without fully thinking them through.

I laugh, but I don't hate that she noticed. "I've been training for the last eight months for this role. Yes, I work out every day. I have for years. And don't forget my perfect ass. I recall you telling me I have a remarkably good butt."

She scoffs. "I don't think I said th—Oh my god, I did. When I was drunk. I said you have a perfect ass." She covers her face with her menu. "Oooookay, I'll just be over here behind this menu all night, thanks very much."

I pull the menu down.

"None of that. I tell you that you're beautiful all the time. It was about time you said something nice about me, even if it's not about my face." I can't help my smile because nothing feels more like 'us' than this kind of easy banter.

"You don't need to be told." She rolls her eyes, and her voice has a mocking tone to it. She puts her menu back up and then brings it back down a second later. "That ass *is* pretty tight, though." And that's when we both burst into laughter. I take hold of her slender fingers and bring them to my lips, pressing gentle, reverent kisses against the back of her hand. When I slowly flip her palm up, I see her emerald eyes widen and her laughter fades away.

"You two are adorable. Would you like more time with your menus, or have you decided?" Our waiter is back, smiling at us with an expectant look on his face. She seems to have forgotten how to speak, so I clear my throat, quietly urging her on.

"I'll have the burger, please. Thank you." She calmly hands him her menu, smiles at him, and takes a drink of her water.

"Same for me, please." The waiter leaves and I place our hands on the table. "You okay?"

"I'm great. This is... lovely." She traces the shape of my knuckles with her index finger, then frowns when she looks at my hand. "You did get hurt. Your knuckles." Her eyes come back up to mine and she stops the movement of her fingers.

"You don't have to stop doing that. They don't hurt." She frowns at me again. "It was just from the last two days of shooting. No pain. Promise." She smiles at me, and her hand remains on mine, but she stills any movement.

"Thanks for inviting me today. And I'm sorry if I overre-acted and made a scene. It was just a little scary when you went down like that." She swallows, biting her lip, her eyes not leaving my knuckles. *So that was real?*

"Lainey, I'm alright. I promise. We were done shooting anyway and I won't have to do any more fight scenes. You don't have to worry, okay?" I lift her chin towards me and kiss her lips once, then her jaw and neck. I feel her body relax a little more with each kiss.

She lets out a shaky breath. "Okay. I'll stop worrying."

We eat in comfortable silence, but her eyes don't meet mine for the duration of our time at the restaurant. I sense her lingering concern and kiss her temple throughout the meal, hoping to soothe her fears. This girl of mine and her great big heart.

―――――

FOUR DAYS LATER ON SET, I'm a ball of nerves. We're flying to Hawaii in a couple of days, and we've missed one another every day since that kiss.

She's been busy with something, but we haven't even had a chance to talk about it. We'll be in Hawaii for a week, and she'll be meeting everyone on my dad's side of the family. That's over twenty cousins, my parents, my sister, niece and nephew, and Gramps. It's a lot, and I hope it doesn't over-whelm her.

A familiar ping comes from my phone, and I turn it over, seeing the picture she sent me when she was in Paris. She's so beautiful, laughing, with her hair blowing in the wind. It's exactly the way I picture her in my mind.

TORNEROSE

Hey Sugar Ray. How you doing?

Today's song: "Kiss Me" by Sixpence None
The Richer.

ME

Sugar Ray? Lol nice

Great song, but my song for today is "U Got
It Bad" by Usher.

I miss you.

Her response doesn't come right away and I get a little nervous. *Was that too much?* Fuck it. I don't care. She just shared a song with me called "Kiss Me." She can't be surprised I'm basically admitting to her that I have feelings for her by choosing that song.

Fuck, this is the longest wait ever!

Finally, I see the three little dots.

TORNEROSE

You have a thing for Usher I should know
about, Holm?

I miss you too.

"Who's got you smiling all goofy like that? Kidding, I already know it's Lainey." My best friend walks into my trailer with a big goofy smile of his own. "Have you talked to Owen yet about what's going on with you two?"

I sigh. The mention of talking to Owen about me fake dating his sister doesn't exactly bring on warm and fuzzy feelings.

"No, I haven't seen him much, but I know L's talked to him."

"Who did Lainey talk to?" And in walks the man of the

hour. Owen and I are both 6'4" but he's even wider than I am, so his presence feels significantly more imposing.

"Oh good. You're early. I'll see you guys later!" Raf just about skips out of the trailer, mouthing *good luck* to me before he disappears. Of course, he set this up.

"Hey, Owen. Uh, I know Elaina talked to you about this whole fake dating situation." I scratch the back of my neck. "I wanted to talk to you about it too and clear some things up." He scowls and crosses his arms, but continues to wait for me to speak. "I know it's not ideal. She insisted, even though I didn't want her to do it. And we've talked about boundaries. She knows I will never do anything she's not comfortable with. I need you to know that, too." His eyes remain on me, but he uncrosses his arms.

"I know, man. She only has good things to say about you. And I've worked with you long enough now to see for myself that you're a decent guy." He takes off his baseball hat and puts it back on. "You've been a good friend to her. I just need you to be honest with me about something. Can you do that?" He furrows his brow and holds my gaze, his green eyes unblinking. I feel like he can see right into my soul. It's fucking terrifying.

"Of course."

What am I getting myself into?

"Do you have feelings for my little sister? More than just friendly feelings?" He's scratching his chin and still looking at me like he's reading every micro expression of mine. He and Raf are a lot alike that way.

I let out a deep breath, scratch the back of my neck again and look back up at him.

"Yes." No use in sugar-coating it.

We just stand there, both stunned by my admission, or not stunned at all, just unsure of what should come next.

"Good. Okay. She probably won't make this easy for you, but that's only because she has a hard time letting people in.

Just... don't give up on her." He opens his mouth to say something else but seems to change his mind.

"I won't, Owen."

He nods, rubbing a hand across his jaw and looking slightly awkward. "I haven't seen her this happy in a long time, and I know you have a lot to do with that." He nods, as if to himself.

"It has a lot to do with you, too, Owen. She admires you so much. You being around... it's made her really happy." This conversation might be going into uncomfortable territory, but Owen is the most important man in Lainey's life. He should know that.

"I guess we both better make sure she stays happy then." He raises an eyebrow at me and extends his hand. "None of this leaves this trailer."

"You got it. Thanks, man." We shake hands and he turns, walking out without another word.

Now I really just want to get the fuck out of here and get to Elaina.

OWEN, Raf, Maeve and I all share a car to a nearby shooting location. We've had to have Owen and Raf with us often because there have been so many paparazzi around during the filming of this movie. I get in the car and see that Raf is driving, Owen is upfront, and Maeve and I are in the back.

"Hey, has anyone checked in with Elaina lately?" I look around, hoping that with all of their busy schedules, they haven't forgotten about the one person who never forgets about anyone else.

"I saw her yesterday," Maeve says. "I brought her those donuts she adores to say thanks for the things you two dropped off at the beach house. Thanks for going with her, by the way." She smiles softly at me.

"I stopped by two days ago and I brought her lunch from Bella's." This comes from Raf.

"I talk to her almost every day. We just had dinner the other night and FaceTimed our mom together." Owen turns around to look at me as he answers. "Don't worry, big man. Your girl's alright." He shoots me a crooked smile and I hear Maeve giggle.

"Bloody hell, Adam. Bon's really done a number on you, hasn't she? It's really nice to see how much you care about her, though." She smacks me on the shoulder and laughs again.

"Does *everyone* know?" I lift my hands in the air in an exasperated motion and slap them down on my thighs.

"Yes."

"Yup."

"Uh-huh."

All three answer together.

Fuck.

Am I really that obvious? I guess that's what I get for not being in a relationship for years. I have no clue what I'm doing.

"Great."

"Everyone but your girl, that is. She's a stubborn one. You're going to have to reeeeeally work for it." Maeve shoots me a sympathetic smile. "And that's all I'll say on that. But she's worth it. She's worth every bit of effort. That I can promise you."

"I know. I know she is. Did she tell you I kissed her on set the other day? I completely lost it. Forgot where I was. Fuck." I rub my eyes with the balls of my palms, trying not to relive the moment too much even though it's pretty much all I've thought about for days.

"She didn't have to tell me. We all saw your snog fest and we all needed cold showers after, thanks to you two." She laughs again. It's nice that Maeve makes this feel a little more lighthearted, especially when I'm having a hard time processing all the thoughts and feelings going through me.

"Enough about that though. It's bad enough I had to hear about my little sister doing… that… from half a dozen people already. Not you, too, Maevey." Owen's tone changes when he says Maeve's name. It's somehow softer and she blushes when he says it.

Huh… that's weird.

Raf is pretty quiet for the ride, but I see him look back at me through the mirror a few times. He's sympathetic and concerned. I think the sympathy is for me, and the concern for Elaina.

20 /
you miss me?

elaina

THE DAYS GO by in a blur. I'm thankful for Raf and Maeve's visits, and talking to Owen is one of my favorite parts of the day. A few months ago, I would have thought it impossible that my brother and I would be this close again.

My brain is a jumbled mess. All I think about is Adam, but I don't know where we stand right now. I haven't fully processed the kiss. Kisses. Mostly the kiss at the studio. I'm still in knots over the whole thing.

After I dropped Frankie off with the dog sitter, Taylor came over to help me pack some outfits for Hawaii and help me pick out a dress for the wedding. I feel much better knowing he's helping me. With the way my thoughts have been in a scramble of lust and confusion, I might pack myself a parka and forget all my underwear.

I'm all packed and ready to head out when I get a text from Adam.

ADA

Hey, I'm swinging by to pick you up in 10, okay?

ME

See you soon.

This is just about all we've said to one another this past week other than the occasional text or hello/goodbye as we see one another in passing. I hate it. I miss him. And we're living in the same house. But it all feels different now because of the kisses.

When I hear the car, I rush out the door with my suitcase and he is standing outside, arms crossed, leaning on the car. Damn, he looks good, and all he's wearing is jeans and a T-shirt. Not fair. I want to jump up and hug him, but I don't, worried that it'll make things even weirder. The driver takes my suitcase and I reach for the door, but Adam stops me.

"I don't get a hug today? I haven't even seen you all week. I miss you, L." His eyes are searching mine and I struggle to keep my emotions in check.

"You do? Really? You miss me? You've hardly even texted me!" I cross my arms and stand with my feet set apart.

"You're adorable when you're mad, Lainey. That's not fair." He reaches to tuck my hair behind my ear, but I flinch. My stomach does several somersaults and my knees wobble. This is too much. He's hardly even touched me and my body is turning to jello.

"No. Don't do that. Don't be all cute with me when I'm mad at you!" I reach for the door, but he holds it shut, not letting me run away from this conversation.

"You're mad because we haven't seen each other all week." It's not a question, so he knows.

"You said you wouldn't shut me out again. I know you're busy, but damn it, we live in the same house." I might be yelling a little now, not realizing just how mad I was about all of this.

"You're right. I'm sorry." He puts his hand on my cheek, but I move away again.

"You're not forgiven. It's not right that I have to sit with all these feelings and not be able to talk to you about them. And now we're about to go to this wedding and pretend like we're dating in front of your whole family and it's a lot." He needs to know that I can't just hear the word sorry and be okay with whatever dumb shit he wants to pull. Even if all I want is to forget about it and climb him like a tree.

"I get it. It was just a busy week. I promise. And I was trying to give you space because you could hardly even look at me during dinner the other night." He reaches for my cheek again, and this time I lean into his touch. "I wasn't ignoring you. I was trying to make sure you weren't uncomfortable, and that you had time to process whatever has happened."

"I don't want space from you. Not unless I ask for it. Do you understand?" I did not mean for that to come out, but here we are. But I mean, he said those words first…

He swallows hard and links a hand with mine. "I do. I understand. Maybe we just need to find a better way to talk to each other. Like by *actually* talking to each other." He chuckles and I immediately feel lighter about all of this.

"Are you still mad at me?" He asks this as he brings our foreheads together and my hand comes to rest on his forearm. I shake my head. "You really are very cute when you're angry, so it's okay if you want to go back to pouting and crossing your arms."

I smack him on the arm and we both laugh.

Ahh… there we are.

"I'm not mad. Can we do that hug now?"

"I'll do anything you want. Anything." He leans down, placing a gentle kiss on my forehead. His arms wrap around my shoulders, and I nestle into his warm chest. It feels like the most natural place to be in the world.

When we finally pull away, I can see the driver's lips stretched tight in the rearview mirror—he's doing an admirable job hiding his amusement of our little show.

We ride the rest of the way quietly, and Adam holds my hand every step of the way from the car to the private plane. We sit next to one another and once we're taking off, he turns to me with furrowed brows. "So you know you're going to be meeting my whole family, right?"

"Yes. Is there something you need to tell me about your family? Any cheek-pinching aunties I need to stay away from? Actually, I did want to ask something. Should I call you Adam or River? How much do they know about me? Are we telling them the real story of how we met?" I pull my lips between my teeth to stop talking. I have more questions, but I'm trying to keep my rambling to a minimum.

"You have more questions, don't you?" I nod and he smiles softly, his lips just barely curling up at the edges. He takes one of my hands and holds it in both of his. His fingers are gentle as they trace the lines and curves of my skin, the calluses on his hands providing a slight friction that seems to soothe him.

"They're mostly normal. Loud and nosey, but normal." He pauses for a moment before continuing. "Very few of them still call me Adam. Mostly Ash and Gramps, sometimes Gwen. So, I guess probably River. And we can tell them the real story. They don't know much about you, though they've all asked a million questions. I just figured it'd be easier to answer them all at once and in person."

"How are you feeling about spending the week with your parents?" His eyebrows come together as he considers his answer. "We probably won't see them much. I see my dad occasionally for work, but he's not usually present for family stuff. I think he has a new girlfriend, and that usually keeps him pretty busy. He prefers to keep his distance. Especially from my mom." He continues to look down at our hands.

"Has it been like that for a long time?" I keep my comments about what a jerk his dad sounds like to myself.

"My whole life. Gwen got a few good years with my parents being together, but they divorced before I turned one." His face relaxes a bit, but I feel like there's more there.

"And your mom? What's she like?" I link our fingers together to support him through telling me about his family.

"She'll be focused on the wedding, micromanaging details and whatnot. Even though this is my dad's side of the family, my mom remained close with them. I'd say that was for our sake, but I think it had more to do with making sure the divorce seemed amicable to the public." He pauses and rubs his thumb across my knuckles. "Maintaining her image has always been the most important priority for her. Bethany Holm is a household name, after all, right?" His voice is bitter, detached, and I don't like it one bit.

I have to literally bite my tongue to keep myself from saying something rude. Yes, everyone knows who Bethany Holm is. She made a name for herself playing a doting mother on one of the longest running TV shows ever. She was America's sweetheart. But it sounds like the doting stopped on set.

"Hmm. Okay.. Now let me see if I have this right. Your dad is Karl. Your sister's name is Gwen and her two kids are Liam and Emma. They're seven and four, and their dad is Callum, right?" I hope I got that all right. When I look up at Adam and see his big, bright smile, I have a feeling I did. "Your cousin is Ashley, and she's marrying rock star Ryan?"

He brings my hand to his lips and kisses my palm. "And they're all going to love you."

21 /
what did you just say?

adam

OUR FLIGHT and the travel time to the resort feel carefree and we burst into fits of laughter often as I tell her some stories about my family and things that have happened on set throughout the week. When we get to the resort, our concierge shows us to our suite, and everything is fine until we're both standing in the bedroom alone, looking at one big bed in the middle of it.

"I'm sure I asked Kelly to book a suite with two bedrooms. Shit, Lainey. I'm sorry." I pick up my phone to call her and get this changed, but she stops me by taking my phone from my hand.

"It's fine. Probably best that we don't change our room. If anyone gets wind of us booking a room with two bedrooms, it won't look good." She smiles tightly at me, puts my phone down on the nightstand and walks to her suitcase. "I'm just going to change quickly and we can head down to meet your family. You said we're the last to arrive, right?"

"Yeah, um, I guess I should do that too. You can take the bathroom if you want. I'll just change in here while you're in there." Okay, so we seem to have a solid plan for how not to see each other naked. Something I hadn't needed to think of until this very moment. Great.

After a few minutes in the bathroom, she emerges with her eyes cast downward, her steps slow and unsure. She tucks her hair behind her ears and nervously adjusts her collar.

"Is this okay? I have all these new clothes thanks to Taylor and I'm second-guessing at least half of what he packed for me already." She looks down at herself and smooths the fabric of her white romper down. "And I'm about to meet your whole family. While wearing a bathing suit. Ugh."

It's adorable that she's a little nervous. I should probably be feeling some of that too, being that it's been five years since I brought anyone around to meet my family. Instead, I feel calm, steady, certain.

"You're perfect. Don't be nervous." I reach for her hand, giving it a quick kiss and we walk out. The sun feels good, and she seems to relax once we're outside. My sister texted to say they're at the beach, so we head there. I hear a chorus of "Riveeeeeer" as soon as my cousins spot us. Everyone flocks over, but I know the attention is not for me. They're all dying to meet Lainey.

She smiles at everyone and jokes about how she won't be able to remember all their names but that she swears she'll try. I catch a few of my male cousins checking her out a little too closely and place my hand on her lower back to guide her away from the crowd. She smiles up at me, laughing at the rambunctious bunch we just left behind.

When she turns into me, I pull her face towards mine and kiss her, nibbling on her bottom lip then kissing her chin before I pull away.

"That was nice," she says, biting the same lip I just did. Kissing her is so much better than nice. It's everything.

"Uncle Wiver! Uncle Wiver!" Emma's voice pulls us away from our quiet moment, and I'm glad I kept the kiss PG. I kiss

Elaina's hand before letting it go, knowing Emma is about to jump up. I catch her just in time and twirl her until she begs me to stop and we're both good and dizzy. I hear Elaina giggling as she watches us.

"Okay, Uncle Wiver. That's enough! I wanna meet your girlfwiend."

I put Emma on my hip but she begs to come down. She's getting so big. Elaina watches as Emma gets closer then leans down.

"Oh, you must be Princess Emma!" And this is the moment she wins over my niece. She curtsies, head down, pretends to fan out her invisible long dress and everything. Emma gasps as Elaina says, "Your highness" and then stands back up.

"How did you know I was a pwincess?" Emma brings her little hands to her heart.

"Everyone knows! And it was one of the first things your Uncle River ever told me. I could never forget." She smiles at my niece and holds out her hand, crouching down to meet Emma at her eye level. "It's very nice to meet you, Princess Emma. I'm Elaina."

Emma struggles to say her name a few times. "Your uncle calls me L. Or sometimes Lainey. You can call me whatever you want." Oh, she's good. Emma is enamored.

"I wike Wainey. I will call you dat." She gives L a thumbs up. "You're beautiful, Wainey. Your hair is like a mermaid's!" Elaina blushes at the four-year-old's compliments.

"Thank you, Emma. You're very beautiful, too." Elaina smiles and looks up at me. I can't take my eyes off of her.

"Hey, Uncle Riv." Liam comes over and gives me a fist bump, already a little too cool for hugs at seven years old. "Hi, Elaina. I-It's nice to m-meet you. I'm Liam."

"Oh, I know who you are, Liam. Your uncle tells me you're really into Legos, is that true?" She puts out her hand for a fist bump, though he probably wouldn't say no to a hug from her.

"Uh-huh. Yeah, I like to build stuff," he says shyly, blushing. I think the kid's got a crush.

"Well, when I was your age, I built an entire city out of Legos for my hamster. It was awesome! Right up until I had to clean it up that is." She makes a shuddering sound. "Then it was the pits. The poop pits! I bet you build way cooler stuff!"

Liam laughs, appreciating a good poop joke. "Yeah, I can show you some later, if you want?" And it's confirmed. The kid's got a big, huge crush on my girl.

Get in line, little man.

"I'd love that!" She looks at me again and her smile widens in excitement that my niece and nephew seem to like her. My sister and mom walk closer, catching up to the kids who ran over to us earlier.

"Hey, you two! You made it!" Gwen gives me a kiss on the cheek and a bear hug. "Hey, little brother!" And she quickly moves to Elaina, bringing her into a bear hug of her own. "Elaina! We've heard almost nothing about you because little brother withholds all information from us." She shoots me an exaggerated scowl. "We're so happy you're here and we finally get to meet you!"

While Gwen is busy telling Elaina about my shortcomings, my mom gives me a quick hug and kiss on the cheek. She takes a step toward Elaina and proceeds to look at her from head to toe. "Nice to meet you. Based on that little kiss we all witnessed just now, I can see you two are taking your roles very seriously."

Shit.

She knows this isn't real. Of course, she does. Somehow she got information out of Sandra, and it makes my blood run hot hearing my mom talk to Lainey like this.

"It's wonderful to finally meet you, Ms. Holm." I know

Elaina is nervous, but she doesn't show it up until this very moment. Her hand shakes ever so slightly as she reaches out to shake my mother's.

"Bethany, please, dear." Mom's smile is too wide and her voice is too sweet. It's unnatural. Maybe she's not as great of an actress as everyone thinks.

"Bethany. Okay. Thank you for having me." Elaina's smile is warm and genuine—quite the contrast to my mother's. No doubt everyone here will be in love with her by the time we leave.

"Volleyball game! Who's playing?" I hear Kyle, one of my cousins shout over to us. Elaina looks at me expectantly and I can tell she's game, even if just to get out of this uncomfortable meet and greet.

"We are!" she yells out before getting a verbal response from me. I hear someone say *I like her already* as we walk towards some lounge chairs to put our things down. I notice several sets of eyes all staring at the same spot behind me, so I turn around to see what they see. I'm met with Elaina shimmying out of her romper, revealing a white string bikini underneath. She tosses the romper onto the chair and shakes her hair out, reaching up to put it into a bun. She has a tattoo on her rib cage that starts right under her left breast. I want to get closer to see it, but instead, I turn around and scowl at all the lingering eyes on my girl's heart-shaped ass.

I knew having her around these idiots was a bad idea.

I pull my white T-shirt up and over my face, and when my eyes meet hers, I can feel the electricity between us. Her bright green eyes travel from the waist of my shorts, to my toned abs, pecs, and then up to meet my gaze. She chokes out a sound before clearing her throat.

"Ready?" Her voice cracks, her feet falter and I grab her by the waist for reassurance. We take our positions opposite of each other on the same team for the volleyball game.

Her movements are graceful as she moves around the

court and I find myself caught up in watching her. The ball is heading right toward me and yet I can't tear my gaze away from Elaina's bouncing butt cheeks while she jumps. The other team gets the point because of my distraction.

Now she's moving back to try to get the ball and walks right into me, pushing us both back into the sand. The back of her body is pressed against the front of mine until she turns to face me.

"Are you okay?" I silently wish she'd start kissing me all over like last time she thought I was hurt, so I pretend a little, groaning. "Oh, gosh, I'm so sorry!" She starts to lift off of me, but I grab her by the waist and switch our positions so I'm on top of her, tickling her just a little.

She wiggles and laughs. "Ah! You little sneak! I'll get you back for this!" She's softly pounding on my chest with both fists but when I lean down and kiss her neck, she stops.

"I hope you do." We're nose-to-nose, my heart racing with anticipation when someone shouts, "Get a room!" From the corner of my eye, I can see Elaina's cheeks are stained bright red. She bolts from her spot, and the game resumes without us. The other players don't seem to be affected by our little display. Once the game ends, we walk back to our chairs.

"I'm gonna go for a swim." She doesn't look at me as she rubs her hands together to dust off some sand and heads towards the water. I'm sensing she's maybe a little over-whelmed and needs a few minutes alone.

Garrett, another one of my cousins, elbows me in the ribs. "Damn, dude. You did good." I hear several other similar comments from behind me. Not wanting to entertain my cousins' comments about Elaina, I grab a drink of water and go build a sandcastle with Liam and Emma.

When we're just about done and I'm pretty much ready to call it a day because there is sand absolutely *everywhere* on me, I see Elaina walking toward us.

"I thought you could use a special finishing touch on your

castle." Elaina kneels down across from me. Water is dripping down her body, several droplets rushing to the haven under the thin fabric of her bikini top. She stretches out her flattened hand and presents us with a starfish. Her lips slowly turn up as Emma gasps in delight. Her eyes come up to mine and she beams, flashing me a toothy smile that I can't help but return.

I wonder if my heart will ever not beat a little faster every time she looks at me. I wonder if this feeling of wholeness I feel when I'm with her will ever fade. My gut says no. Not ever.

"It's perfect!" Emma beams, claiming that Elaina shall be the queen of her castle. I snap a quick photo of the girls and their castle before we start to clear out.

Everyone packs up their beach towels and bags, preparing to meet for dinner in a couple of hours. Elaina throws on her romper, not realizing that her still-damp bathing suit is making the fabric cling to her skin, becoming see-through. When we walk back to our room, I feel dozens of eyes glued to her, but she doesn't seem to notice any of them.

As we enter the room, a chill rushes over us. I can tell the air conditioning temperature was set too low, and when I turn to her, she is already shivering. I can't help but take notice of the goosebumps that form on her skin and the way her nipples peek through two layers of clothing. In an attempt to warm her up, I run my hands up and down her arms and she shuts her eyes tightly in response.

"Umm, I'll open the balcony door and let some warm air in, okay?" I let go of her arms, and she nods and goes to the thermostat to arrange the temperature of the room.

"Do you want to use the shower first?" She walks to her suitcase and tucks her hair behind her ears, not looking at me.

"You go ahead, L." I try to keep my tone light, but I can tell something has clearly shifted with her. Was it one of my loudmouth cousins? Did my mom say something? I need to talk to her. We can't let this linger.

"Hey, wait." She stops in front of the bathroom door and turns around, but her eyes stay on the floor. "What's going on? Did something happen?" I nudge her chin up with my index finger, needing to see her face.

She squeezes her eyes shut, her lashes fluttering. Her breath is a stifled gasp and her shoulders tremble with a deep exhale as she shakes her head slowly.

"I don't know if I can do this," she whispers. She opens her eyes but looks at a spot behind me. My stomach drops to my feet. "All this pretending… you're so good at it, and I… I just can't. I can't do it." She walks around me, sets her clothes down on a chair and puts her hands on her hips shaking her head. "You get to be River when we're in public. When you kiss me, when we hold hands, when you get all sexy in the sand on top of me. You're someone else and I'm still just… I'm just *me*. *You* get to be someone else, but I can't do that. I don't know how to separate who we are in public and who we are when we're alone."

She still hasn't looked at me, so I keep listening. "And I like it all too much. I like the feel of your hands on me. I find myself looking forward to when we get to pretend again because it feels so good. I wonder when you'll kiss me again and the anticipation borders on painful. But then reality hits and I remember you're just being River." She's still looking at the wall. "And you do things when it's just us that stirs up… feelings. A lot of feelings. I don't know what to do with those. I'm not used to feeling this much with… *anyone*." She paces around the room, brows furrowed as she pinches her bottom lip with her thumb and index finger. "And I'm not saying I want a real relationship. I don't want that. But I also don't want to ruin our friendship." Her voice lowers but she doesn't slow down. "The only thing I do want is you. I want *you*. And I don't know how to stop. I've tried, but I don't know how." Finally, she looks at me.

I lunge forward, my arms caging her in as I press my body

against hers. She stumbles backwards, her shoulder blades scraping against the wall as I lean in and take a deep breath. Our noses nearly touch as I stare into her eyes, my grip, now on her waist, tightening. "You *want* me?" I whisper. She nods, not breaking eye contact. This woman is my every dream come true.

"I have never pretended with you, Elaina. Never. Every kiss, every touch has been because I don't know how to stay away from you. You own my every thought, every dream, every memory. All of it belongs to you. Only you." Her hands come to the nape of my neck, and she pulls me down to her so slowly that her breath becomes my breath.

"There's no distinction between Adam and River. I'm just me, too. There's no pretending. There's no agenda when I reach out to touch you or to kiss you other than because I want to. Because I can't help myself. Because every part of me is drawn to you." Her breath hitches and I can see her breathing quicken. "Do you understand?"

"Yes," she pants. She leans in, her eyes searching mine for a moment and then closing as our lips meet. My hand cups the back of her head to pull her closer, feeling the familiar warmth spread between us both. I hold her close as our tongues explore each other, tasting the salty sea air that lingers on her lips. A sigh escapes her mouth as my hands roam down over the curves of her body. I firmly grip her hips, and then move lower until I'm cupping her ass, pulling her up, closer against me. Her legs wrap around me and when she moans, I feel myself grow impossibly harder. She feels it too and arches her back, grinding into me, a gasp escaping her as I move my lips down to her neck then to bite and lick her shoulder. I want to taste every inch of her. My hand moves up her body and when my thumb flicks over her nipple, she moans so loudly it seems to pull her right out of the moment.

"Wait. This is too much. I can't—" She's breathing heavy,

eyes closed and hands are on my shoulders. I immediately bring my hands to her hips and set her down, putting some space between us.

"I'm sorry. Fuck. I'm so, so sorry," I pant, taking a step back but keeping my hands on her hips.

I can't believe I've already fucked this up.

She steps forward and puts a hand on my cheek. "No, no. You did nothing wrong. I told you, I want you, and I do. I want you so much." There's a *but* coming, I'm certain of it. "But we need to talk. I want to be honest with you. About everything." She steps closer and nudges my nose with hers, laying a tender kiss on my lips. "Okay?"

When she pulls away, I pull her in for a hug and hold her close. I have no clue what she needs to tell me, but I'm pretty sure there isn't much she can say that will convince me to stay away from her.

"Why don't we shower … um… separately…and get dressed? Then we can talk, okay?" I run my thumb along her jaw as she nods before walking away towards the bathroom again.

When she comes out, she has nothing, but a towel wrapped around her. Her hair falling in wet waves around her face sticks to her shoulders and she bites her lower lip when she looks up at me. "I'm sorry. I rushed in and forgot to bring my clothes with me."

I nod, doing my best not to dwell on the fact that she is, indeed, naked under that towel. I take a shower so cold that my lips turn blue, but thankfully when I come out, in jeans and a T-shirt, she's also fully dressed.

"Hey." She's still biting that bottom lip, sitting on the edge of the bed. Her hair is starting to dry into loose curls.

"Hey, beauty," I choke out. Because, damn, she really is the most beautiful woman I've ever seen. I sit on the chair next to the bed, facing her.

"I'm gonna try really hard not to ramble, okay?" She

smiles shyly, tucking her hair behind her ears. Seeing my nod, she takes a quick breath and closes her eyes for two seconds. "I'm very attracted to you. Your body, your brain, your heart. It's a whole package deal." She looks up at me quickly, then clears her throat.

"If we're going to do this, whatever *this* is, I need you to understand a few things about me. First, I need to know that we'll always be friends first. I know that we've only known one another for a few months, but I consider you a good friend, and your friendship is more important to me than whatever amount of attraction I feel towards you. So please hear that. You're important to me. Okay?" I nod again, struck by her words, unsure of how to react.

"Second, I told you I'm not looking for a relationship and that's because I have a hard time with big feelings. I'm pretty broken when it comes to relationships with men, and I know that. So, I'm going to suggest that we explore whatever this is between us for the duration of our fake relationship. Obviously that was never going to last forever anyway, so I'm proposing that when that ends, this..." She waves a hand between us, " also ends." She looks up at me now and a tight smile forms on her face.

An uncomfortable feeling in the pit of my stomach twists its way up my chest and stays there. I know she has been pushing for us to be just friends, but I thought that would change once this thing between us grew into something more. I know she feels it, too. The way she responds to me isn't just friendly and I know that now that I've seen her interact with Raf and other men. I've never wanted this to be just friendship, but I need to tread carefully. I don't want to push her away. But how am I going to show her it's safe for her to fall for me? That *I'm* safe? That she can trust me?

Slowly. Patiently.

I can do that.

"There's more," she says quietly, looking down at her

hands. "I want to tell you how Andy died." Her eyes lock on mine and I give a small nod, urging her on. "I know you've never asked, but I think it's important for you to understand me and how I feel. How I am now. Because there was the me before Andy and there's the me after." Her throat bobs, but she doesn't swallow and I can feel the strain in her next words already.

"He committed suicide. While we were dating. He never broke up with me, he just…" Her eyes fill with tears and she pulls her lips between her teeth. "I didn't know he suffered from depression. I had no idea he was struggling so much and a few months into our relationship he killed himself. Fuck, it never gets easier saying that out loud." She takes a deep breath, words coming out quickly, like she needs to get this out as soon as possible. "It crushed me. The weight of the guilt, the shame, the loneliness—it was all-consuming. I couldn't stay at home. I was suffocating under my mom's well-meaning attention and smothering, so I left. Before I moved to New York, I went to Cambridge with my dad. Looking back, I wish I had enjoyed that time with my dad more. I wish I'd been less numb. I didn't know just four years later he'd be gone, too, but I was so sad and mad and confused about everything that had just happened. I fell in love and had my heart broken and realized that I didn't really know Andy at all. It rocked me to my core. It felt like the most cruel, grueling, traumatic way to be left by someone, even if I know his decision likely had nothing to do with me. It doesn't matter. The feelings still linger. And I know this is a lot. What I'm sharing with you, it's heavy, and it's messy. I understand if it's too much for you. If being with the broken girl is too much for you."

I pause, trying to think of which part of this to react to first, all the while aware that I can't be silent for too long. "First of all, thank you for opening up to me about this. That you trust me with this means everything, and at the same time I'm crushed that you lived through this kind of sorrow and heartbreak. Please know that I'm here for you and I will always be on your side. You are never too much, regardless of how heavy or messy you think your situation is. I'm right here. Understand?"

She nods, eyes glossy. I reach over and take her hand in both of mine, looking up at her bright green eyes.

"Now, I need you to hear this next part really clearly. You are not broken, Elaina. Your experiences have been traumatic and awful, but you are whole, and you're here, and you have support in whatever way you need it." A single tear falls down her cheek and I catch it with my thumb. "You're important to me, too, L. You know that, right?"

Her eyes sparkle as they fill with more tears. She nods once, smiling at me.

"Good. As for the other thing, your proposal... yes. Okay." I shake my head in pure disbelief that I just agreed to her terms, but I will honestly take whatever she's willing to give me. "Now I need to tell you something." I know I need to be honest with her too. I need to tell her. "I'm celibate." *Way to just ease into the topic, dumbass.*

"Sorry, what? What did you say?" She moves her torso forward, closer to me, in a quick movement. Her eyebrows shoot towards the sky as she stares at me.

"I've been celibate for a while. I was in a relationship when I was twenty-five with a woman who took videos and pictures of me—of us—without my consent. I thought I was in love with her, and she just wanted a paycheck. Since then, I haven't been able to trust anyone. I haven't even wanted to be with anyone else since. Kissing you, touching you, it's the closest I've been to a woman in a very long time." It's surprisingly easy to say this out loud and to trust her with this information. Especially since she's already trusted *me* with so much.

"Adam, I... I'm so sorry that happened to you. Thank you

for telling me. For trusting me." She looks up at me with glassy eyes and moves to get off the bed. The sense of relief I feel when she moves to sit on my lap is irrefutable. She takes all the heavy things and makes them weightless.

"Can we both promise to always be open and honest with each other? To go as slow as we need?"

"I promise, L. We can take it slow. I'll never push you too far, okay?" I smooth down her hair with one hand and draw circles on her hip with the other. "And we'll talk to each other. I'll tell you what I need and you tell me, too."

She's got her legs curled up on the chair and I feel her nod on my chest. We've both just laid all of our cards out on the table and now we can move forward.

We sit, holding one another in silence for a while until it's time to go to dinner. We seem to both wordlessly agree that we've said enough for right now.

22 /
who sets an alarm on vacation?

elaina

SITTING HERE, feeling Adam's heartbeat beneath my hand is exactly what I need right now. We both said a lot of words. I hit him with some pretty heavy stuff and he hit me with that celibacy bomb that feels like it's still detonating slowly inside my brain. He's been so careful with me this whole time. I had no idea I should have been careful with him too.

Five years with no sex. No kissing. No touching.

We've sat on the chair quietly for a while, and now we're finally peeling our bodies away from one another so I can finish getting ready for dinner.

As I walk away, he takes my hand and brings me toward him, so my back is to his front. He hugs me tight and his breath on my neck makes me teeter, so I lean back into him. His lips leave a trail of kisses from my ear lobe to my shoulder and my moan draws a groan out of him.

"Okay... dinner." He lays one last kiss on my shoulder.

"You are very good at making my knees feel wobbly. Very, very good." I feel his smile on my skin before I once again peel my body away from his.

I finish getting ready and we leave to meet his family for dinner. As we walk into the restaurant, he puts his hand on the spot on my back where my skin is exposed, between my crop top and my skirt and his thumb slips underneath my shirt, drawing little circles. The action is so familiar but so new. We sit at a table with two of his cousins and their significant others. The conversation is effortless, and the food is fantastic. His arm rests on the back of my seat for the majority of the time and he's generous with his affection, kissing my cheek or temple a few times and even sneaking a chaste kiss on my lips when I tell our table the story of how we met.

As we walk back to our room, his hand returns to my back, the lazy circles under my shirt sending shivers up my spine. As soon as we walk in, I let out a loud yawn, the day's events catching up to me quickly. "Oh my gosh, I'm sorry!"

He kisses my shoulder and laughs. "Nothing to be sorry about, L. It's late. Let's go to bed."

And my panties are wet.

His deep voice saying, *let's go to bed* is all it takes. My whole body goes stiff at the thought.

But we're taking this slow. But also sleeping in the same bed. But he's celibate.

"Just to sleep, Lainey. I can hear your inner meltdown from here." He chuckles, and it makes me laugh, too.

We head into the bathroom to brush our teeth and wash our faces. Adam takes the bedroom to get changed in and I stay in the bathroom. When I come back into the bedroom, I shiver at the sight of him in a white T-shirt and gray track pants.

For fuck's sake, not the gray sweats. I have to sleep next to that? And not hump him like a dog in heat? How?

I bend over to climb into bed when I hear his grunt. "Really? Are you trying to kill me?" I turn quickly at the sound of his voice, and he raises his hand to cover his eyes with a growl. I look down and laugh in understanding when I see that my very perked-up nipples can be seen through my thin tank and I have pink lacy underwear on—one of my fancy purchases.

"I had pajamas but I can't find them. I'm sorry. Should I put something else on?" I pull my lips between my teeth to keep the laughter at bay. I know Taylor had everything to do with my missing pajamas.

He walks to the other side of the bed, getting under the covers.

"No, you're not. And no, you should absolutely not. Get in here."

I get in next to him and he motions with his head for me to get closer. I lay my head on his shoulder and let my hand move from the side of his torso, over one rock-solid peck to the center of his chest.

"Mmmm. What a day… we really don't know how to just do things the normal way, do we?"

Adam reaches up to turn off the light, and a low chuckle tumbles out of him. I ascertain that I don't only love the sound of his many laughs, I love the feel of them.

"No, we do not. Maybe we can try for normal tomorrow?"

"Sure. Let's see how long that lasts." I giggle and he laughs, and we move closer to one another as the sound of our laughter dies out.

"Goodnight, beauty." He leaves a lingering kiss on the top of my head.

"Goodnight."

———

I ALWAYS WAKE up in the same way: slowly, with a long stretch that tends to start with a wiggle of my butt and a drawn-out moan. This morning is no different, except for the wall of hot man pressed up behind me. It doesn't register right away, but my butt wiggle is met with some groans and the big hands around my waist move up my torso so I arch into the feel of them hoping they reach a nipple when the hands abruptly move to my hips and hold me down.

"Elaina." Adam's rusty morning voice hits me right between the legs. "Please stop moving." I giggle and move my body away from his, not wanting to tease him, but he pulls me right back.

"No, stay here. Just… stay still. Please."

But I can't. His morning voice and his morning wood are both calling to me and I *must* answer, so I turn around. I put my hands on his abs and delight in the way they flex for me. Then I reach up and lay a kiss on his stubbly chin, his jaw, his cheek.

"This reminds me of something." He smiles at the memory, and I do, too. "I'll never forget the feel of your lips all over my face like that. The look in your eyes. I forgot all about where I was. It was like it was just you and me." His eyes are closed.

I kiss his nose, his other cheek, and his eyes. "It *is* just you and me now," I say on his lips. His hungry mouth is quickly on mine, our tongues mingling, his hands skimming the skin underneath my tank top—it's all essential and I'm not sure how I've lived without this, him, us.

BEEP… BEEP… BEEP!

We both jump up at the sound of my alarm going off.

"Fucking shit on a stick!" I grab for my phone to turn the agonizing noise off and when I turn back around I feel the bed shaking with Adam's silent laughter.

"I love your foul mouth, you know that?" He pins a chaste kiss on my lips and gets up off the bed. "Come on, *tornerose*. I know you don't want to be late for what we're doing today." He puts both hands out to help me up. "It's just you and me until the rehearsal dinner tonight. Is that okay?"

Standing in front of him with so much of our bodies

touching, the moment hardly feels real. "That's perfect." I smile up at him, biting my bottom lip to keep the excited squeal building up inside me from escaping.

We move around one another with unpracticed ease just like we do at home in the kitchen. Except now we're stealing affectionate touches as we pass one another on the way in or out of the bathroom and we brush our teeth side-by-side. It's a level of intimacy I haven't shared with anyone, ever. My stomach swirls at the thought and I quickly push the funny feeling down, allowing myself to just feel joy and remain present here, with this dreamy, beautiful man.

OUR DAY IS nothing short of magical. We spend it on a boat, have a beach picnic for lunch and swim together where we steal a few steamy kisses. By mid-afternoon, we're so spent from the time in the sun that we crash and nap all tangled up in one another. We wake up a heap of sweating bodies, but smiling and content. Adam chats with Ori, the boat captain, for a while and when we leave he promises we'll come back one day. Ori invites us to not only come back but to have dinner with his wife and two kids. I smile at the sight of Adam's easy demeanor and friendliness. It's hard to believe he's the same guy who had kept people at arm's length until recently. He's made every effort to learn people's names, talk to them and make actual eye contact. I take no credit for it, nor do I want to think it's because of anything I've said and done. It just feels nice to experience this new openness in him, especially after understanding a bit more of why he's been so distrusting.

BACK IN OUR ROOM, we have more of that easygoing feel from earlier. We laugh when we bump into one another, and I keep the mystery alive by getting changed in the bathroom again. When I emerge, I nearly gasp at the pornographic sight of him in a dress shirt with the sleeves rolled up to his elbows.

What the fuck is it about forearms?

He's sitting on the edge of the bed and when he looks up, I cover up my drooling face by doing a little twirl for him. "Is this okay?"

The blush fabric of my dress is silky and falls in graceful swoops, the neckline low and the back scooped even lower, barely skimming my waist. I didn't bother with a bra; no one will be able to tell, anyway. The skirt of the dress hits midthigh and I have to keep my hands tightened into fists to keep from tugging it down. Taylor talked me into packing it, though I'm slightly unsure about it now, seeing Adam's eyes widen. My hair is secured into a low bun at the nape of my neck, wisps falling against my cheeks. The heeled sandals that complete the outfit are tan and reach the middle of my calf.

"Christ almighty, Lainey." He rubs both of his hands up and down his face, snatches the room key from the dresser, takes my hand, and walks out the door. "You have everything you need?" He asks this even though we're already out in the hallway and I nod. "Good, because I can't be trusted in a room alone with you when you look like *that*." He looks at me from chest to thighs and I bite my bottom lip, reminding myself to thank Taylor when I get home. As we wait for the elevator, he leans down and puts his lips to my ear. "You look good enough to eat, beauty. And I bet you taste like fucking strawberries."

Goosebumps travel from my neck down to my ankles, and I have to squeeze my thighs together to keep the pulsating feelings down below at bay.

Whoa! Obviously any concern I might have had that celibacy messed with Adam's game is completely obliterated!

I'm grateful for the young family sharing the elevator down with us because we might have gotten arrested for indecent exposure otherwise.

By the time we're walking into the restaurant, we've both settled down slightly, but he keeps his hand on me with those little circles on my lower back, making me shiver even though it's Hawaii and notably warm. Tonight, we're seated with four of his cousins, three guys and a girl. I don't remember any of their names and none of them hold it against me.

"So, I thought this was a rehearsal dinner. Don't you need to rehearse something?" I lean into Adam, genuinely confused.

"Yeah, they did all of that already. I didn't need to be there since I'm not doing anything for the ceremony, just at the reception. No need for me to rehearse." He looks down at me as he places his napkin on his lap.

"Of course, the Hollywood megastar doesn't need a rehearsal." I wink at him and grab my napkin as dinner is about to be served.

When the first course is served, Adam places his left hand on my knee. His thumb traces some imaginary pattern that sends a delightful shiver up my spine. When the main course arrives, his hand moves up further so that it's at the hem of my dress and his fingers graze my inner thigh. Thank god the tablecloth keeps his wandering hands hidden.

"How's your pasta, L?" He moves his fingers in lazy circles on my inner thigh, pulling it closer to him so my legs spread further apart. "Do you like it?" I know he's not talking about the food. I can tell by the little gleam in his eyes. I nod my response and his grin is nearly wolfish. "Do you want more?" he asks loud enough for only me to hear. I nod again and his hand travels up, until it's under the hem of my already short dress.

The moment the dessert plate touches the table, he grazes

the lace of my underwear. I let out a moan, which I cover with a cough, and I see the smug smirk on Adam's face.

"You alright, L?" Of course, he feigns concern, taking the opportunity to sweep his knuckles up and down my center. My knee jerks up so fast I'm afraid I'll knock something over. I can feel my face flush and I excuse myself, rushing to the ladies' room.

23 /
what do you want?

elaina

I'M in there no longer than thirty seconds, bracing myself on the sink when I hear a soft knock on the door.

"Lainey, it's me. Are you okay?" I open the door and his eyes are dark, brows furrowed in concern. "I'm so sorry. I-I-I shouldn't have pushed. I thought you liked it, I—"

I grab a fistful of his shirt and pull him inside, locking the door and backing myself up against the sink as I pull him towards me.

My mouth goes for his neck first, licking and biting its way up to his mouth which now tastes like cheesecake, since he obviously managed to get in a bite of dessert before coming here.

"I liked it," I whisper as I bring my leg up around his hip and arch into him looking for the friction my body needs right now. He grabs a handful of my ass, lifting me onto the sink and grinding into me. I feel his hardness and whimper at the contact.

"Fuck, Elaina." We simultaneously moan or groan or both and his other hand feels its way up my ribs, his index finger and thumb pinching my nipple lightly through my dress. I gasp into his mouth. A warm feeling spreads from my abdomen up to my chest and I start to feel that familiar ache right before the blissful release, so I arch my body to get closer to him, but that's when he starts to pull away slowly, putting space between us.

No, no, no! I was getting so close!

"You were close?" Fuck, I guess I said that out loud. His hands go to my waist and his eyes dart all over my face.

I sigh, an exasperated sound. "I-I think so. I don't know. It hasn't happened in so long, but if that was too much for you, it's okay. I'm sorry." I hide my face in my hands and feel his strong arms wrap around me.

"Hey…none of that. Obviously, I moved too fast and I'm sorry. All I wanted was to make you feel good. No pressure for anything else, okay?" His hands are soothing as he runs them up and down my back and he kisses the top of my head.

I look up at him, still embarrassed but willing to let him see me in this vulnerable moment. "It wasn't too fast. I want this…I want this with *you*." I feel my cheeks flush, but I continue. "You did make me feel good. You do. All the time, but that just now and the stuff at the dinner table… that was… really, really good." My cheeks grow warmer still as I tilt my head up and smile, meeting his eyes. I hope he can see the appreciation in my eyes and the affection I feel for him in this moment.

He smiles back, a radiant grin he doesn't seem able to contain splaying across his face. "Good. Because it was really, really good for me too." He kisses my lips and cradles my face in his hands. "You have no idea what you do to me." We stay silent for a few seconds, our breaths blending together, warm and sweet. Our foreheads touch and the world slows down around us. "I'm gonna go out there but you take your time, okay?" I nod, and he closes his eyes, taking a deep breath. He adjusts his pants quickly, kisses my cheek and slips out of the bathroom.

I stand in front of the mirror fixing my dress as I take in the reflection before me. When was the last time I felt this turned on by a man? Looking at my own face now, cheeks flushed and lips swollen, I hardly recognize this woman and the feeling is oddly freeing, not terrifying, as I would have expected.

I smooth out my hair and head out of the bathroom. I turn the corner to go back to our table and catch Adam in a clearly unpleasant conversation with his mother. His blue eyes, the same ones that had been bright and dilated minutes ago are now dark and intense. His arms are flexed at his side and his shoulders are slumped as if he's equally angry and... defeated? I feel an immediate need to go to him, but I'm suddenly unsure.

No, he needs you. Even just as his friend, you should be there for him.

I see Adam's lips move and I can see that he's saying, "Let's not do this right now, Mother." My heart skips a beat as I step closer to him, my feet moving of their own volition. His skin is warm, his muscles taut under my fingertips as I slide my hand down his arm and intertwine my fingers with his.

"Hi, Bethany! It's so nice to see you again." I look up at Adam, but his eyes remain on his mom. His arm relaxes and his spine straightens, so I feel like that's at least an improvement.

"Hi, dear. Are you having a good time? I hear River treated you to a day away yesterday. Did you have fun?"

Something about her tone isn't sitting right with me, but I'm going to go ahead and stamp down the urge to fight bitchy with bitchy.

"Yes, it was amazing. I had never done anything like that before." I grin brightly and she struggles to force her face into a tight expression that almost resembles a smile.

"Oh, that's nice. River, please remember to check in with the wedding planner to make sure she has your notes. I'll see you both at the wedding in a couple of days." She doesn't take her eyes off Adam, and he nods once and then looks down at his feet, taking a deep breath as she walks away.

"Hey…" I step in front of him, toe to toe and link his other hand with mine. "That looked like it sucked. Wanna get outta here?" His eyes dart open and hold mine. "Sorry if I overstepped by coming over, by the way."

He shakes his head once and his blue eyes do that thing where they dance all over my face like he's constantly memorizing every freckle, every detail. "I'm glad you did. I need to check in with Ashley about the wedding but then we can go."

We unlock our hands and he runs his hand from my lower back to my neck, where he rubs lightly as we walk over to Ashley's table. I get the sense that the touch is comforting to him as much as it's wonderful for me. Upon seeing us, she jumps up to greet me.

"Oh my gosh, Elaina! I can't believe we haven't even talked yet. Sit, sit, sit. I want to know everything about the girl who stole my favorite cousin's heart." I wonder if she's always this ball of energy or if it's just wedding jitters and excitement. Either way, I think it's sweet.

"Ash, is everything good for the big day? Do you need anything?" Adam pulls out a chair for me to sit next to his cousin and then takes the seat next to mine.

"Oh, everything's fine. I want to talk to your beautiful girlfriend, not about wedding stuff." She twists her face into an exaggerated scowl and proceeds to ask me all about how we met. She laughs with such delight when I tell her the part about him putting eye drops in for me. "Addy here's always had a soft spot for a damsel in distress. He used to love being the prince charming to my princess when we were little."

The fact that she calls him Addy sends a warm feeling up my sternum and I immediately fall a little in love with Ashley.

"Ash, come on!" Adam's voice is deep with mock anger.

Ashley responds with a laugh. "Don't worry, I won't embarrass you. I'm sure Lainey already knows all about your big, mushy-softy-tender heart." She looks at me and takes one of my hands in both of her small, warm ones. "He's one of the good ones, L. Like the best. And the way he talks about you… well, I can tell you're a good one too. He deserves to be this happy." Her eyes go all glossy and she shakes her head lightly. I feel my eyes widen, unsure of how to react so I do the only thing I can think of. I hug her. She giggles and sits upright, wiping her face.

"Okay, honey. I think it's time you get some rest. What do you say?" Ryan's gentle voice comes from behind her as he places both hands on her shoulders.

She lets out a long, wistful sigh. "Yeah, okay. Elaina, you're coming to the bachelorette party tomorrow night. Don't deny a bride her one wedding wish!" She winks at me, and I can't help but smile and nod at her. "It was so good to meet you." She hugs me tightly, then repeats the move on Adam. "Goodnight, Addy." She whispers something to him I can't hear, and he grins, cheeks blushing a little. Ryan scoops her up in a gentle embrace before they walk away all wrapped up in one another. Gosh, they sure are sweet.

"I think I love her," I say to no one as I sit back down, but I hear Adam chuckle behind me as he turns and pulls my chair toward him so my knees are in between his.

"She has that effect on people. Kind of like someone else I know." He smiles at me, and his baby blues sparkle again, which makes me so thankful we didn't leave after that ugly situation with his mom. I'm glad he got his sparkle back.

I can't hide the giddiness in my voice when I talk about Ashley. "She calls you Addy! And she called me Lainey. And did you see her and Ryan? They're so cute, it makes my insides all warm and gooey." I clasp my hands together and rest my chin on them watching as Adam's chest shakes with a laugh.

"She's never been okay calling me River. And she's heard me call you L or Lainey for weeks now."

He's talked about me that much?

His hands come to rest on my hips so I lower mine to his forearms. "Ryan is a great guy. I'm really happy for them." He looks off behind me to where they just were and smiles. I sit forward and kiss him because I just can't not kiss him. He makes it impossible. I feel his grip tighten on my hips, his forearms flexing. We both seem to pull away at the same time. The tension from earlier is like a fog around us, heavy, thick, and difficult to move through now. We sit with our foreheads together for a few seconds before he lets out a breath. "We should get going too."

I nod, and stand, linking his fingers with mine. We walk in companionable silence to our room, but I hear him sigh a total of three times before we get there. His brows are furrowed like he's trying to work through something, so I give him the space to do that.

When we walk in and the door clicks shut, I tug his hand, willing him to turn toward me. I kick off my shoes and then trace his jaw with my fingers, traveling to his temples.

"What's going on in here?" I tap gently twice with my index finger and rake my fingers through his hair. He shakes his head twice and lets out a huffed breath.

"Is it anything I can help with?" My fingers continue softly scratching and massaging his scalp and he relaxes some more. His head shakes again and when his eyes meet mine, I believe him. "Would you tell me if I could?"

He swallows and his gaze softens as he nods his response.

"Promise? And I'm going to need your words for this one." I smile at him, hoping he understands I just want to be sure he's okay without pressuring him to talk.

"I promise." He leans down and kisses my shoulder.

"Thank you." My grip around his neck tightens and I hold his face down close to mine, my nose brushing his earlobe.

My other hand splays up his abdomen to his hard chest and I feel him tense everywhere I touch.

"Tell me what you want, Elaina." I swallow as the air rushes out of my lungs, his request taking me by surprise.

"I… I want…" I swallow again. I know exactly what I want, but not how to ask for it. And I don't want to push his limits.

"You can tell me. You can ask for anything and it's yours." He runs his hands up my bare back and fists his hand in my hair, gently tugging my bun loose, causing my pulse to quicken. I can tell he notices because he licks the very spot on my neck.

"I want to finish what we started earlier." My shockingly steady hands start to move to unbutton his shirt from top to bottom, eyes darting up to meet his again. "I want to feel your skin on mine." I pull the bottom of his shirt out of his pants and continue. "What do you want, Adam?" My hands slide up his chest to his shoulders and down his arms, forcing his shirt down to the floor. When my hands reach for his belt, he doesn't stop me and once his pants and socks are tossed aside I steer him toward the sofa.

"I want to hear all the little noises you make when I touch you." His hands slip under the hem of my dress, fingers slipping under the lace covering my ass. "I want to know what your nipples taste like on my tongue." He presses his hardness into me and I whimper, needing more. "I want to know exactly how wet you are for me under these lacy panties." I squeeze my thighs together and he gives my ass a final squeeze and moves his hands to my waist.

"So fucking wet." Like embarrassingly wet, but I don't care one tiny bit. I pant when he bites down on my shoulder and then soothes it with a swirl of his tongue. His hands travel up my arms to my shoulders and he hooks his thumbs under the thin straps of my dress. His fingers slide back down my arms bringing the straps with them, revealing my breasts to him.

I gasp.

He groans.

My dress pools on the floor.

He backs away, pulling me with him. He sits on the couch and I take my time kneeling above his lap. His hands travel from the backs of my thighs to my ass as his mouth works sweet torture on one of my nipples.

My fingers thread into his hair, holding his head in place before he moves on to my other peak, readily waiting for him. He sucks and licks and I start to feel the build-up inside me just as he pulls away, trailing kisses up my chest as I slowly lower myself onto his lap.

"You're so beautiful," I say in a whisper, not meaning to, and I feel the blush creep into my cheeks.

"Finally, she compliments something that isn't my ass." He smiles up at me and my body melts onto his.

I feel the wetness of my panties against the hardness of his erection, and my desire floods through me as I try to stifle a whimper. With a gentle rocking motion, I move against him, letting out a low moan at the exquisite pleasure radiating through my body. His hands grasp my hips and I whisper in his ear, "I can think of at least one thing I like more than your ass right now."

"Elaina, fuck." His fingers dig into my hips, stopping my movement. "I'm not going to last long if you keep this up."

His lips are on my neck again and I can't take it. I need to move. Need to feel him.

"I don't care about that." I start a slow but steady grind on him again. "I'm so close already. You feel so good." I kiss him deeply as his hands move up my back, one tangling into my hair.

We find a rhythm and when I roll my head back and close my eyes, he calls me back to him.

"Open your eyes." When I do, I see his dark blue eyes on mine, and something shifts inside of me. The intimacy of the moment, the pressure building inside me, it all feels too over-whelming. I bury my head in his neck as I pant, feeling my body shake. But it's not from my climax, it's something else. Panic? Fear? I don't have time to figure it out as I feel his body convulsing once, twice, three times as he finds his release. And me? I find myself in this same place I've been before, where my brain takes over and rather than allowing myself to feel, I shut down.

did you...you know?

adam

DID THAT REALLY JUST HAPPEN?

I'm about to feel embarrassed, but everything about being with her feels natural, even dry humping like a horny teen. Her head is still buried in my neck and her body feels stiff, very unlike mine which feels more relaxed than it has in a long time. Did she not...? I felt her body tense up, but maybe...?

Running my hands up and down her arms, I gently nudge her away from me so I can look at her. "Hey..." The moment I see her face I know it. She didn't come.

Fuck, how could I have missed that?

"Did you...?" Her eyes shoot up as I start to ask her the question, but they don't meet mine and her eyebrows bunch together in confusion. "Hey, look at me." When she does, all I see in her big green eyes is worry and I hate it. That's not how this is supposed to go.

"I'm okay, Adam. That's how it always is for me."

Wait, what?

She looks back down at my chest and a small, sad smile

tugs at her lips. "It's my own fault. I just can't shut my brain off. Ben did always say I was a bit stiff and frigid, so—"

"I'm going to stop you right there. First of all, let's never speak his name when you're nearly naked in my lap again, deal?" I nod, and he repeats the movement. "Secondly, there is *nothing* frigid about you and that was one of the hottest experiences of my *life*. Hell, I should be embarrassed I just came in my underwear, but I'm not because that's what you do to me." I tug at her chin so her eyes will meet mine again. "Understand? You drive me absolutely wild." She pulls both lips between her teeth as she nods again.

"Can you tell me what happened? What changed? Twice tonight you said you were close, so help me understand." I tuck her hair behind her ear, playing with the ends of her hair.

"I just... I haven't... that doesn't happen unless I'm by myself." Her cheeks flush and she licks her lips, as if giving herself more time to continue. "You took me by surprise. You keep doing that, actually. When I said I was close, I meant it, but it was like once I was aware of it, I froze up." Her sheepish smile tells me it's okay for us to talk about this now.

"I can't believe I'm saying this, but we're about to make an exception to the rule we just set."

As much as I hate to do this, we need to talk about this asshole.

"So, for three years. With Ben. You never...?" I ask, unable to stop the words from tumbling out.

"Never. Not with anyone. Not for about ten years, actually." Her voice is quiet, almost a whisper, and it takes all of my self-control not to show the shock I feel on my face.

"But you and Ben, you loved each other. Or at the very least you loved him…"

"No. I didn't. Ben was... uncomplicated. Simple. We never fought and I thought that after Andy, and dating as much as I had, that he was what I needed, even if he wasn't what I really wanted." Her eyes flick away for a moment before returning to me again. "I thought if I had someone like him, I could maybe grow to love him. But I never did. On paper we were great. Perfect, even. But it never felt quite right. Physically or emotionally."

I clench my jaw, fighting back the desire to proclaim the words I've been dying to say. I want to tell her how right it feels with us, like this has been designed just for us. I was made to be hers. And I am. But she needs more time.

"Thank you for telling me, L." I lightly kiss her forehead and hold her tightly in my arms, her head resting on my chest as I inhale the scent of her shampoo and kiss the top of her head.

When our bodies part, I'm acutely aware of the cold wetness between my legs. She pulls away from me, her eyes heavy and cheeks flushed. We hurry to the bathroom, taking turns stripping out of our clothes, and changing into soft T-shirts and clean underwear.

Returning to the bedroom, my body moves towards hers, our limbs intertwining naturally. We settle into bed in peaceful silence, our breaths even as we drift off into a deep, restorative slumber.

———

I WAKE up to the sound of my name, but what jolts me out of my dream is the feel of her ass on my crotch. I still her movement with my hands again.

"Morning, my *tornerose*." She scoots even closer to me.

"God, I love it when you call me that." I kiss her earlobe then lick circles in the spot right below it. "Mmm, and I love it when you kiss me there." She arches into me, and I run my hand over her stomach, sliding it under her shirt until I find her breast. "And the way you touch me…"

I pinch her nipple as I bite down on her shoulder gently. I

don't want to push her, but fuck, if I'm not dying to make her come. To see her. Hear her. So when the idea comes to me, I just go for it.

"Show me." I whisper in her ear then keep kissing her neck.

"W-what? Show you what?" Her breathy voice tells me just how into this she is and that only urges me on more.

"How you touch yourself. How you make yourself come. I want you to show me." I take her hand and slowly start guiding it down below her belly button. She doesn't stop me, but I don't miss the way she holds her breath, like she's too nervous to even breathe. I stop, our fingers right at the hem of her panties. "You don't have to—"

"I want to," she whispers. "B-but maybe just me? Just my hand?" I nod and slowly run my hand up her torso, moving her shirt over her breasts.

As her fingers slip between her thighs, she gasps and I watch as her fingers work in a slow, circular pattern. I palm her breast and work her nipple in the same tempo as she's working her clit.

"Is this okay?" I watch closely as her face turns towards me, a whimper leaving her sweet lips that makes my cock twitch in my shorts.

"Yes. Feels so good." She moans and the sound travels right through me. I want to see more of her, so I move so she can lie on her back.

"Can I kiss you?" I can tell she just put a finger in her pussy by the way her back arches and it's taking every last ounce of willpower not to replace that finger with my tongue, my cock, my own finger. Anything so I can be the one feeling how hot and wet she must be.

"Yes. Please," she says between moans and when our tongues collide, I feel the thrust of her hips as she tries to get deeper. I move my mouth down to her pebbled nipple, working one before I move to the other. Her movements become more frantic, the moans a little louder.

"Oh god, Adam." With one last flick of my tongue, I lift my head. As much as I want to lick and taste every inch of her, I can tell she's close and I need to watch her.

"You look so fucking gorgeous, Elaina. So beautiful like this." Her breathing speeds up while I talk to her, her eyes glued to mine as she pants. "Next time it'll be my fingers inside you. I can't wait to feel how wet you get for me, baby."

She moans loudly, telling me just how much she's enjoying having me talk to her. "Do you want it to be me next time, Elaina? Do you want to come all over my hand?"

"Yes! I want that."

"I can't wait to feel you. Taste you. Bury myself inside you." Her movements are desperate now and it sounds like she's about to climax at any moment.

"Oh fuck, yes. Yes!" Her back arches further as her hand works frantically.

"You're so fucking sexy, Elaina. You have no idea how many times I've fucked my hand thinking about you. Your body on mine. My tongue in your tight pussy."

And that does it. The dam breaks and she shuts her eyes tightly as her body convulses. Her movements slow and I take in every moan, every gasp, every drop of sweat beading on her chest.

She is perfection, and though all I want to do now is grab that hand and lick her orgasm off her fingers, I want to give her space.

What we just did is so intimate, and I need to show her I don't take her trust for granted.

As her breathing slows, she opens her eyes and moves her hand to rest on her belly. I pull her shirt back down and lay a soft kiss on her lips.

"That was the hottest thing I've ever seen." She smiles,

biting her bottom lip in that shy way of hers, but I can see she's at ease now. Fully relaxed and sated.

She turns into me, slamming her mouth into mine and pouring everything she isn't saying into the kiss, so I do the same. I will my kisses to tell her how perfect she is. How thankful I am that she trusted me.

Her hands move from my chest down to my abs, fingers exploring every ridge. Just then my phone starts vibrating on the nightstand. We both ignore it as she grinds into me, moving her hand lower. She's so soft and warm, and her quiet moans are driving me insane. Her hand is just about to reach my cock when her phone starts ringing, too. We ignore it until mine starts vibrating again. And the moment is gone.

Fuck!

We both groan as we separate and reach for our phones. She shows me hers: Maeve. I pick mine up.

"Hi, Sandra. Please let this be important."

We have our respective conversations, mine being much shorter than hers as Sandra just needed to update me on a few changes to a contract we're negotiating and to check in on the *fake* relationship. She's happy with what's been made public, and I don't give her any further insight into what's going on with us because we haven't defined what this is. I head into the shower to give Lainey some privacy.

When I come out, Elaina is just finishing up with Maeve, laughing.

"Mae, you're my girl, but there's a beautiful half-naked man who is freshly showered walking towards me and I must go smell him and kiss him immediately. I love you so much. Byeeeeeee!"

She tosses her phone on the bed and walks toward me, a bright smile on her face. Her body melts into mine and she kisses me sweetly, moaning softly.

"You smell fantastic."

She pulls away from me, scrunching up her face. "But I do not. I need to get in that shower. Be right back." She pecks me on the nose and walks away, that ass taunting me with every step she takes.

SHE COMES out of the bathroom already dressed and I reach for her, but unfortunately, before we can tangle ourselves up in another kiss, my sister calls to remind us we're meeting at the beach.

We leave our room to get breakfast and meet my family. As usual, Elaina takes this all in stride, even seeming excited to spend the day with my rowdy cousins.

IN A BLUR of cool dips in the ocean, telling stories about our childhood, a few stolen kisses and far too many hours in the sun, the day ends and we are blissfully exhausted by the time it does.

"I don't know if I'll make it to dinner." Elaina is laying face down on our bed, freshly showered in my track pants and a tank top. "*And* the bachelorette. I don't think I can do both. Am I becoming an old lady?"

I chuckle and sit next to her, rubbing her neck. "Why don't we order room service, have a little nap and then go to the parties when we're refreshed?"

"Adam Holm, you really do say the sexiest things to me." She turns over and I scoop her up while we both laugh.

————

I BLINK awake to the familiar sounds of her singing in the bathroom and the sweet smell of her honey and coconut shampoo on the pillow. I smile to myself, rising from the sheets. When I peer into the bathroom, I see her body swaying in time to her melody as she pulls her locks into a high, tight ponytail. She's changed into a red jumpsuit, with an open back and wide legs. Her skin glows against the fabric and my gaze immediately falls to her chest—noticing that, once again, she isn't wearing a bra. My dick twitches in my shorts at the sight and I must make a noise, because she spins around.

"Hey, you. What do you think?" She does a little twirl. "How do I look?" Her make-up is heavier than usual, and she has red lipstick on.

I stalk towards her, wrapping an arm around her waist. "You look like you should be spending the night with my mouth all over your body." She shivers and leans her head sideways, giving me her neck. Naturally, I kiss it. "Exactly how many outfits do you own that don't require a bra, Miss James?"

She giggles but doesn't answer me. I trail kisses up and down her neck as she sighs. The way she reacts to my touch will never get old.

"I have to go. The girls are waiting." I groan, not wanting to let her go. She runs her hands up my arms, resting them on my face. "Be good tonight. Those rowdy boys will surely get wild!"

I release my grip on her and give her a kiss on the forehead.

"I'm always good. You be careful. My cousins like to party, and they'll try to drag you into their shenanigans."

She laughs and swats my shoulder. "I'm the old lady who just took a nap before going out, remember? I'll be surprised if I have more than two drinks tonight." She runs her knuckles over my cheek and across my jaw. "I'll see you soon?" I nod because if I talk I'm going to say too much. She grabs a clutch and walks out the door. And I miss her instantly.

BY MIDNIGHT, Elaina has sent me two texts:

> **TORNEROSE**
>
> I'm adopting Ashley. She is the cutest human I've ever met!
>
> Wow! You weren't kidding. Your cousins like to party!

The next one comes shortly after:

> **TORNEROSE**
>
> I miss you and your cousins keep feeding me shots. Help!

Garrett walks over to me and slaps me on the shoulder. "The girls are doing karaoke. We're going to go watch and crash their party."

Great. At least I'll be closer to Elaina.

We follow the distant beats of the bass and quickly find the bar two blocks away. Through the crowd of clapping, swaying bodies and hazy smoke, I easily spot Elaina. She stands on stage with a commanding presence, one hand grasping a drink, the other confidently holding the mic. Her voice is strong and soulful as she sings Shania Twain's "Man, I Feel Like A Woman" with seductive moves. Her jumpsuit hugs her curves while her legs move gracefully, captivating the entire audience.

I hear Kyle's whistle behind me. "Damnnnnn. You get to take that home tonight? I hope you know how fucking lucky you are." *Oh, I do.*

The other girls aren't hard to find; their raucous laughter and swaying on their feet hinting at the level of intoxication. I stay rooted to the spot until I see Elaina's head peek through the crowd, her gait steady as she holds Ashley up. Elaina's eyes light up when she spots me and a wide grin spreads across her face.

"Adam!" She barrels towards me, nearly knocking me over as she wraps her arms tightly around my neck. Her hands move to my hair, and she looks up at me with a softened expression.

"Hi," she whispers.

"Addy, please tell me you saw Elaina on stage. Did you know she could sing?" She throws her arms out, almost hitting a stranger on the head. "Oh, my gawwwwd, she's amazing! Like Shania, but somehow even sexier. Ugh. Marry her already, or I will. Don't tell Ryan." Ashley giggles as she walks to where the other girls are. Elaina is now giggling in my arms.

I tuck a strand of hair behind her ear. "Are you okay?" I wrap an arm around her waist as she leans her head on my shoulder.

"Much better now. I missed you." Her green eyes are bright and sparkling.

My heart beats a little faster at her admission.

"I missed you, too, *tornerose*." She bites her bottom lip and smiles. It feels different, this smile. It's not like the one she shares with the world. It feels like it's just mine. *She* feels like she's just mine.

I take in her flushed cheeks and wonder exactly how many shots my cousins have given her. She must somehow read my mind.

"I switched to water a couple of hours ago. Everyone else is so drunk they haven't noticed me not actually taking any shots. But I have definitely crossed the border into Tipsy Town."

I laugh, knowing all too well how rowdy my cousins can get.

"They're animals. You sounded great up there, by the way. Looked great, too." She blushes and buries her head in my neck, shaking her head. "You did, baby. I knew it was you the second I walked in. I couldn't take my eyes off of you." I still can't.

She lifts her head, emerald eyes meeting mine. "Can we go home now?"

Fuck. Yes.

I take her hand and wave to Ash and Ryan, letting them know we're leaving. She tells me all about the shots my cousins fed her early in the night and reiterates how much she loves Ashley and everyone else.

I feel that familiar tug in my chest now as she talks about how well she's gotten along with the girls. The guys are also enamored with her, not just because she's gorgeous, but because she calls them on their shit and can hold her own. I haven't done this in a long time, but I know no one else has ever fit this well before. No one else ever will.

When we reach our suite, she takes off her shoes right away, tucking them under a bench neatly. When I turn around she has stripped off her jumpsuit and now all she has on is a silky red thong.

Goddamnit. This woman.

She tugs on one of my shirts, the cotton fabric baggy and soft. As she steps into the bathroom, the light casts a faint glow onto her face. She washes her face and brushes her teeth, the sound of the running water filling the room with a calm hum. I watch her go through her routine, leaving a water bottle on her side of the bed. By the time I've put my track pants on and brushed my teeth, she's nearly asleep, curled up on her side.

I kneel down beside the bed and carefully undo her pony-tail. Strands of hair are knotted and I take my time to gently untangle them with my fingers. When she opens her eyes, they're bright with tears that threaten to spill over.

"I'm sorry. Did I hurt you, L?" She shakes her head,

though one tear escapes and falls down the bridge of her nose.

"That was the tenderest thing any man has ever done for me." I cup her cheek and she leans into my palm. "You are the sweetest, sexiest, most wonderful man I've ever met, Adam River Holm. I don't know what I'll ever do without you."

Her eyes are closed and she's drifting off to sleep before I can ask her what she means.

you trying to steal my girl?

adam

I MISS her butt wiggle and her soft moan in the morning because I have to sneak out of bed early to make sure Ashley and the wedding planner have everything they need from me. Ashley had asked me to officiate the wedding, but I didn't feel good about doing that.

Being in the spotlight for work is one thing, but for my little cousin's wedding? No. I didn't want to take anything away from her big day by putting myself in the middle of the action. So, we agreed I'd give a speech—the only speech—at the reception. And I also agreed I'd help keep the guys on task because Ryan's groomsmen are a group of rowdy bros with little concern for things like punctuality or simply doing what you're supposed to.

Before leaving the room, I leave Elaina a note on my pillow.

> L,
> Sorry I had to take off so early. I didn't want

to wake you when you were sleeping so peacefully...
and snoring so loudly!

  I can't wait to see you later. Save me a seat -
I'll be there once all groomsmen are safely standing
next to the groom.

  Yours,
  Adam

My mother is already at the reception space when I arrive there and I greet her with a kiss on the cheek.

"Good morning, darling. I trust you slept well. Ready for your speech?" She raises one eyebrow at me as she asks this and I can't believe after thirty years of life, my mother still feels like she has to make sure I'm ready for anything. We've hardly even lived in the same house since I was fifteen.

"I did, thank you. And yes, Mom. I'm ready." I dismiss her tone. I have to pick my battles with this one.

"And your little girlfriend? Is she here?" She looks around absentmindedly, pretending to look for Elaina. She knows she isn't here.

"Elaina is sleeping. I didn't think she needed to be here for this, so I didn't ask her to come."

"Sandra reassured me that this woman is the right person for you to do this with, but I want to hear it from you." I hate that she knows about our arrangement.

"Elaina is one of the best people I know, Mom. I trust her. We've been friends for a couple of months and she's close with Rafael, too. Not that she needs a character reference, but there you have it anyway." I really don't like where this is headed. At least Sandra doesn't seem to have told her I've been staying with Elaina.

"Hmm. I hope you're right. I'd hate to have our name dragged through the mud again because another simpleton is after a little bit of money." She rolls her eyes as she says this, and it takes me several deep breaths before I can respond to her.

"Elaina is an award-winning production designer. She is sought-after and incredibly talented. She does very well for herself, and I can assure you, she's not after anybody's money." I catch sight of the wedding planner on the other side of the room and figure now's as good a time as any to get the fuck away from this conversation.

"Excuse me, Mother. I have to go. I'll see you at the wedding." I don't wait for her response, nor do I look at her for any indication that she heard what I said. I can't believe she would say that about Elaina.

———

THE REST of the day goes by slowly. So slowly. I've texted Elaina several times, but hanging out with a bunch of hungover dudes is really making the day drag.

TORNEROSE

I do NOT snore. How dare you.

Otherwise, thank you for the sweet note.

ME

You do, but I like it.

I wish I could have stayed.

TORNEROSE

Me too. What are you doing now?

ME

Making sure all of the groomsmen shower and shave. Keeping them away from any alcohol. These guys are absolute beasts.

TORNEROSE

> Such a responsible lad you are. Ashley picked the right man for the job.

> I've been listening to our playlist. When did you add "Iris"? Gosh, that's such a great song.

ME

> The night Mitch got you that disgusting fruity drink and I rescued you.

> Kidding. I know you don't need rescuing.

TORNEROSE

> Ugh. Don't remind me. That thing was repulsive.

> And I don't, but I didn't mind seeing you get a little protective.

> I just added "I Try" because Macy Gray is underrated!

ME

> Agreed. Great song.

> Shit. One of the groomsmen found the minibar. Gotta run. See you in an hour!

TORNEROSE

> Go get 'em, Tiger. xx

Finally, about twenty minutes before the ceremony is due to start, I leave the groomsmen in the hands of the best man, who seems to be the least hungover and most capable of the bunch. I walk out into the garden for some fresh air and immediately I'm hit with the most beautiful sight. Elaina is throwing her head back, laughing with her eyes closed as her curls fall low on her back. Her hand is gently and casually placed on my grandfather's shoulder as he looks at her, pure joy on his wrinkled face. She leans down to say something in his ear and in turn he lets out a belly laugh. The scene is so unexpected it takes my breath away.

Before I can make my way to them, she tucks his hand in the crook of her elbow and guides him towards the chairs set out for the ceremony. I rush through the path, intent on getting to them as quickly as possible. Gramps sees me first, and stops.

"Adam, my boy. Your lady here found me in the garden and took pity on an old man." He removes his hand from Lainey's arm and reaches out to me, embracing me in a tight one-armed hug.

As I come out of the hug, I see Elaina smiling sweetly at us. "Oh, that's not true at all. I was walking around the garden alone and Gramps rescued me like the true gentleman he is." She winks at me then looks back over at him, green eyes sparkling.

"Well, the important thing is that we found each other, isn't it, *min skat*?" Gramps takes her hand and kisses it as he calls her *my darling*, a term I haven't heard him use since we were kids. Elaina's cheeks turn deep pink as she looks up at me.

"Gramps, are you trying to steal my girl?" I pull her closer and kiss her temple, taking in her floral floor-length dress, not missing the slit that comes up above her mid-thigh or the way it hugs all her curves.

The deep belly laugh I love and miss comes out of Gramps again.

"Oh, no, I couldn't even if I tried. She's quite smitten with you, this one. Hang on to her, *min dreng*." He pats my arm as I take in his sky-blue eyes. "Now, would you two come sit with me? It seems fitting to be surrounded by love on a day like today. Come on, Elaina. You'll sit by me, won't you?"

Her blush deepens as she smiles sweetly at him.

"How could I say no to you, Gramps?"

And with that, the three of us walk to the second row and

take our seats with Elaina between us. Once we're seated, she turns to me, taking my hand with a look of uncertainty in her eyes.

"Is it okay that I'm sitting here? Aren't the front rows just for family? I can move. I can go sit further back, I just didn't want to upset your Gra–"

"You're right where you belong, Elaina." I squeeze her hand and lean in, taking in that coconut honey scent I love so much. "And you look absolutely gorgeous." I brush her hair off her shoulder and kiss her there, feeling her body shiver at the contact.

She turns her face, so we're nose to nose.

"Okay. And thank you. You look *very* handsome in this suit." As she pulls away, her eyes meet mine and she smiles that smile that feels like it's just for me.

We hold hands for the duration of the ceremony, and I catch her wiping away a tear when Ryan says his vows. The rock star drummer took us all by surprise with his heartfelt words. The ceremony is beautiful, short and low-key, which suits Ashley and Ryan perfectly.

MURMURS and whispers and hushed laughter fill the room as the guests gather for the reception. Garrett, one of Ashley's older brothers, gives me a sideways glance as he takes his seat at the table beside Elaina. He, like me, begged Ashley not to be sitting at a table with our parents. He taps my shoulder and motions to my face as he looks at Elaina.

"Nice beard, man." He quickly moves his focus, and I don't miss the way his eyes linger a little too long on her exposed thigh. "You must be the now infamous Elaina. Even Gramps is talking about how awesome you are!" He puts his right hand out towards her, flashing a wide smile. "I'm Garrett. Riv's best-looking cousin."

She giggles and places her right hand in his. He doesn't

miss the opportunity and turns her hand to kiss her knuckles. I'm about to punch Garrett in his pretty face. He's got the true Dutch genes, all blond-haired and blue-eyed where I got my mother's dark hair.

"Oh, well I see you learned your charm from Gramps. You Holm men are a dangerous troop!" As she lowers her right hand, she moves her left one to my knee and I feel some of the tension in my body release.

Garrett laughs, throwing his head back.

"I like you, Elaina. I can see why Gramps and Ash have been singing your praises. You must be some kind of special to get this guy to come out of his dating hiatus. Though I'd be surprised if he still remembers what to do after so long."

Her eyes widen in surprise, but she's quick to respond to Gar's less than witty remarks.

"Oh, I can assure you his memory is intact, as are his manners, which is more than I can say for you at the moment." I nearly spit the water out of my mouth as a laugh bubbles out of me. Leave it to Elaina to put Garrett right back in his place with a smile on her face.

I'm still laughing when I feel the wedding planner tap me on the shoulder, handing me a microphone. I guess it's time for my speech. I give Lainey's hand a squeeze before I stand. The music stops and I feel all eyes turn to me.

"Good evening, everyone. My name is Adam, but perhaps you know me as River. I'm Ashley's favorite cousin, which is why I'm up here tonight." There's a low chuckle from the crowd and I hear a faint *you wish* from somewhere in the room, causing more laughter.

"When Ashley and Ryan asked me to stand here, in front of all of you, and speak about their love, I was speechless. As I stand here now, I can't help but be filled with a deep sense of admiration for them and the love that has grown between them.

"Marriage isn't exactly something I know very much

about. Being in a relationship isn't something I know much about either, to be completely honest. I have been fortunate in life with wise examples of what it means to have a long, strong marriage. Grams and Gramps were the epitome of such a relationship for sixty-two years. Ashley and Ryan, I hope for you the same resilient, unwavering love."

"Ash, you've seen firsthand the power of love with your own parents, where communication, openness and the ability to laugh have kept them together despite any obstacles. I hope you and Ryan always find it in yourselves to openly talk to one another and laugh often—even when it's difficult."

"From my lack of experience, all I can offer is that you remember to always see one another as best friends, each other's greatest cheerleaders and, most importantly, put each other first. To find the love of your life in your best friend is an incredible gift, and I'm certain you have that. Here's to the happy couple!"

I raise my glass and as I sit to clink glasses with Elaina, I see she has tears openly streaming down her face. I put my glass down, cradling her face in my hands to wipe her tears. I kiss her softly once, twice, three times.

"That was perfect," she whispers. "Now go hug your cousin because you made her cry, too."

She smiles up at me and I let her face go. "Okay, pretty girl. I'll be right back." I make my way to Ash, who gets up quickly to hug me, scolding me for making her cry.

The only thing on my mind is the taste of Elaina's lips on mine. How soft her skin feels when I touch her. The smell of honey and coconut ingrained in my memory as my favorite smell.

That speech was for her. She's my best friend and the love of my life. There's no doubt in my heart. Now I just need to erase any doubt in hers.

26 /
how could you do that?

elaina

ADAM'S SPEECH left me a little shaken up. It was so earnest, and when he said *To find the love of your life in your best friend is an incredible gift*, well, I lost it.

Each time I'm around Adam, I discover something new about him and I can't help but be drawn in. My chest tightens knowing that whatever this is between us can't last. I can't handle another broken relationship.

I can't handle being left again. I don't think I'd survive that, not with Adam. But try as I might, I can't stay away from him. No matter what the outcome, I need to savor every moment we have left.

I'm glad for the bit of space to process this while he goes to hug Ashley. She really is such a sweet and beautiful bride. Garrett does a great job of snapping me out of my deep thoughts.

"Need me to dry your tears while Riv's gone, Elaina?" Garrett is looking at me with that shit-eating grin of his. He is equal parts charming and annoying. I'm not sure what to make of him yet but I'm thankful for the distraction.

"I think I'll be okay, but if you can tell me whether or not I have makeup running down my face, that'd be great!" I lean in closer to him and he grabs my chin, inspecting my face with squinty eyes and I see his are the same sparkly blue as Gramps and Adam's.

"Nah, you're all good. Beautiful." I manage a weak smile at Garrett as he relaxes in his chair. Adam's hand gently moves the hair away from my neck as he takes a seat and kisses me softly in the area where my shoulder and neck connect.

My heart beats faster as I lean in close to him. His warm breath tickles my cheek, and the beard on his jaw line brushes my skin. My pulse quickens when my lips graze his ear. "I really like it when you do that," I whisper, before pressing a soft kiss beneath his earlobe. I pull back and dare to meet his gaze, feeling a bit brave. His lips curve into a smile, and his eyes sparkle, letting me know he enjoyed my bold move.

DINNER GOES BY IN A FLASH, and we have lots of laughs with everyone at our table. I excuse myself to go to the ladies' room and when I leave the stall to wash my hands, I catch Adam's mom's eyes in the mirror.

"Oh, hi, Bethany," I say with as much warmth as I can muster, which is about the equivalent of the ice buckets with champagne sitting at each table.

"Hello, dear. Having a nice time?" Her smile reminds me of the Grinch as it slides up higher and higher on her face.

When I look back up to dry my hands, I see her reach for the lock on the bathroom door and I still my movements in shock.

"I wondered if perhaps we could have a little chat? Woman to woman?" She slithers closer to me as I clutch the paper towel in my hands.

"Oh. Sure."

"I know this little performance with my son might look

real to everyone, but I'm his mother. I know it's all for show." Her gaze moves over my face and the air suddenly feels chillier. "I also know River needs to move attention away from his relationship status and back to his career, so I'm hoping you'll be willing to help me with that."

"What exactly does that mean?" There's a bowling ball in the pit of my stomach. This feels all kinds of wrong.

"I think that if we can create a scandal big enough, the magazines will get what they want and River can move on, and so can you." She must read the look of confusion on my face because she keeps going.

"Nothing too shocking, of course. Perhaps you'll be caught with another man... or woman... sometime after shooting is done for this film. It'll keep people interested in him, gain some sympathy. He can choose not to speak about the *heartbreak*," she says the word with a scoff and air quotes, "and when the film is released, no one will need to bother asking about why he's not dating. They'll just assume he's still getting over you and the focus can be back on his acting career."

"No." My voice cracks. It sounds so small as the word leaves my lips, but all I can hear in my head is *no, no, no, no, no.*

"I'm sure you realize this would be completely staged, so you don't have to actually do anything you don't want to do, Elaina." I'm shaking my head, trying to wrap my brain around what she's saying. "And I understand now that money may not be an incentive for you, but I am very well connected in Hollywood. I'm sure we can come to an understanding and help escalate your careen even fur—"

"No!" The sound echoes in the empty bathroom. "Stop. Stop it!" The paper towel in my hand is turning to dust, I'm clutching it so hard. "This conversation is over, Bethany."

She stands impossibly straighter.

"I'm sure you can't mean that, dear. Everyone has a price.

And I'm nothing but a concerned, loving mother. This is just how things are in this business. I did it once and I'll do it again for him without any regrets."

I ignore her last quip, biting my tongue. Understanding sets in that Bethany set up the situation with Tiffany, making my stomach turn.

"Surely you can appreciate where I'm coming from. If I don't look out for his career, no one will. I only want what's best for my boy."

The serpentine smile on her face surely wouldn't win her any acting awards. She is the furthest thing from a loving mother.

"How could you...? Adam deserves so much better than this. So much better than you." I look down at my white knuckles and back into her soulless brown eyes. "I'm going to walk out of here now and pretend this never happened. Not for you. For him."

I crumple up the paper towel with more force than necessary and hurl it into the wastebasket. My hand shakes as I turn the lock and open the door with a creak. I step outside, my vision blurring from the angry tears threatening to spill. I stumble down the dimly lit hallway and lean against the wall for support, my chest rapidly rising and falling as I try to control my breathing.

I cannot believe that just happened.

With the resolve not to cause a scene or ruin a happy day, I wipe my face and head back to our table. Ashley and Ryan are having their first dance and the lights lower as I take my seat. Adam looks at me and immediately takes my still shaking hand into his, bringing it to his lips.

"Everything okay, *tornerose*?" I take in a shaky breath, but I can't quite meet his eyes yet.

"I guess weddings make me emotional." I attempt a laugh, but the sound comes out screechy and forced. "I'm sorry."

He pulls me close and brushes a gentle kiss on my temple, and I feel all the tension evaporate from my body. His arm stays wrapped around me as we watch his cousin and her new husband, spinning around the dance floor in blissful adoration. I try to push away the memory of Bethany's cruel words, focusing instead on the warmth emanating from his embrace.

ONCE THE COUPLE'S dance and dances with parents have ended, the lights lower further and the DJ starts to play some Top 40 hits. Despite my attempts to get Adam on the dance floor, he seems very against the idea. I don't push it, but that also doesn't stop me from dancing with his cousins. I need to blow off some steam and perhaps this is the best way for me to do that without Adam catching on that something is wrong.

I'm in a group with Garrett, Ashley and Ryan when the DJ slows it down, playing "Change the World" by Eric Clapton. I smile, wanting to walk back to sit with Adam, but Garrett quickly pulls me into him, one hand on my back and the other holding my hand.

"Let's see how quickly Riv gets here when he sees me with you, shall we?"

"I don't like playing games, Garrett. If he doesn't want to dance, that's fine with me. I won't resort to making him jealous for a dance." I give him a stern look as I watch him glance over my head, no doubt looking for Adam.

"Listen, I don't want to piss him off, but he should be out here dancing with his girl. I've never seen him like this with anyone. You're the real deal, Elaina. I've seen Riv like girls before, but this? What you two have? It's way more than that and the quicker you both realize it, the better." He meets my eyes then, and I see that he's, for once, serious. "Gramps called it. And Gramps is never wrong. About anything."

I smile at the mention of Gramps and then feel a hand on the back of my neck. I'd know that touch anywhere and when I turn, I see his scowl pointedly directed at Garrett.

Huh. So Garrett was onto something. This did make him jealous! Weird.

"May I dance with my girlfriend, please?" His husky voice is loud enough for the surrounding couples to hear.

And that's the first time he's called me his girlfriend. Don't freak out. Don't freak out. Don't freak out.

Garrett removes his hand from my back and places my other hand in Adam's.

"Bout time, Riv. Elaina, it was a pleasure." He does a little bow and walks away backwards throwing me a wink, which makes me laugh.

"May I ask what's funny?" Adam's hands are on my lower back, not as respectfully high as his cousin's were.

"Just Garrett. He's really quite the character." I place one hand on his shoulder and the other on the back of his neck, looking up at his sapphire eyes. "He was trying to make you jealous, you know?"

"Yeah, well... it worked." This makes me giggle and I move my hand into his hair, pulling our bodies closer together. "I added this song to our list today and I wanted to dance with you."

"Thanks for coming to dance with me." I smile up at him and his face softens, his eyes landing on my lips. We sway to the music, eyes locked together while my fingers twist in his hair and he draws little circles on my lower back.

He lets out a long breath and brings our foreheads together. "You drive me crazy, you know that?" I shake my head, smiling. "You do. You're all I thought about all day. And now all I can think about is getting you back to our room and out of that dress."

My breath hitches as I look up at him.

"Okay. Let's do that." His lips crash onto mine and I don't

know if we're still dancing because all I can feel is his tongue on my tongue, his growl in my mouth and his hands wrapping around my hips. Before our kiss can deepen any further, I hear clapping and hoots and hollers.

We just did that in front of his whole family!

We both look out quickly before I bury my head in his chest.

"What a bunch of assholes," I hear him whisper into my hair. But I don't care. Everyone around us seems so genuinely delighted. Adam pulls away from me.

"Are you laughing?" I can't even form words, I'm laughing so hard. In no time, I see the corners of his eyes crinkle and feel a laugh rumble deep in his chest. We stand there looking at one another, laughing while the music changes back to something poppy and upbeat. And then Adam is there, dancing with me, twirling me around and holding me as he rolls his hips into mine and it is glorious because it turns out he *can* dance.

AN HOUR later I'm so ready to leave and have Adam make good on his promise to get me naked. I excuse myself to the ladies' room, pushing out all thoughts of what happened a couple of hours ago in here.

When I come out, Adam is leaning on the wall waiting for me, hands in his pockets, looking like a goddamn snack.

"You ready to get out of here?" The question is enough to send my lady bits into a frenzy. I nod as he takes my hand and links our fingers together. "Let's go."

"Shouldn't we say goodbye to everyone first?" I may be horny and in a rush to get this beautiful man naked, but I'm not going to be rude to his family.

"Nah. Ash and Ryan already slipped out and we'll see everyone else tomorrow." He puts our hands on my lower back, trapping my arm.

"Would you rather stay?" I shake my head quickly. Probably too quickly. He lowers his mouth and kisses the tip of my nose.

"Good." And just like that, we're walking out of the building, into the warm night air. Anticipation for what's to come is bubbling up inside me and all around us.

WHEN WE WALK into our room, he is cool as a cucumber. He takes his shoes off slowly, removes his tie and hangs up his jacket in the closet. I manage to take my shoes off, but suddenly I don't know what to do, so I just watch his steady movements. He removes his cufflinks and doesn't break eye contact with me as he sets them on the nightstand and walks slowly toward me.

His hands come to my neck, moving my hair off my shoulders—a move I've come to adore, a touch I now deem intimately ours because I know what comes next. His lips are on my shoulder. I feel the swirl of his tongue as it moves further towards my neck, and I lean my head back to give him more access.

"Have I told you today how gorgeous you are?" His breathy voice sends shivers down my spine as it mingles with his wet kisses on my skin.

"I don't remember. I don't remember anything before right now." I feel his chuckle and his smile on my skin and my hands begin absentmindedly undoing his shirt buttons. I feel infinitely sexy knowing his muscles are flexing at *my* touch.

His mouth continues its venture to my ear lobe where he bites and sucks. His shirt falls to the floor and my hands set out to explore the ridges of his abs, the hair on his chest, the feel of his collarbone and his quickening pulse.

When my fingers reach his jaw, our mouths finally meet. The now familiar dance our tongues perform together pulls a long, drawn-out moan out of me. His hands move to undo the zipper at my side and my dress falls to the floor.

"Fucking hell, Lainey." It's barely there, but I hear his groan as his eyes and hands skim over my lacy black panties and the matching strapless bra. "Do you wear these just to drive me crazy?"

I smile knowingly as I reach for his belt and he lets me undo it.

"No. I wear them for myself. That you like them is a perk we both get to enjoy." I slide his zipper down, slip my hand into the waistband of his underwear and wrap my hand around his erection.

Holy fucking shit, he is huge!

At the sound of his strangled moan, I clench my thighs together.

The other night I was able to feel how hard he was, but not how big, and now... now I feel his size and my pulse is beating fiercely at my core thinking about how he would feel inside me.

He makes quick work of removing his pants and socks as I walk out of my dress.

His hands are soothing, caressing my back and arms. I bury my face in his neck, smiling in disbelief that we're here and how right it feels. When I lift my head up, he brushes the hair off my face, taking in my smile.

One of his hands grazes my inner thigh, my knees happily spreading wider apart in the process. When his fingers skim the top of my panties I feel my knees wobble. He wraps an arm around my waist to steady me and his other hand slides further down until I feel his finger parting me open.

His breath is hot on my neck, his thumb presses down lightly on that spot that makes my blood run hotter, pulling a gasp out of me. I see his small, smug smile and my legs wobble further. I bring my hands up to his shoulders for purchase. "Fuck. Do you only wear these sexy lacy things?"

He drags a finger down to my opening and back up, circling that spot again and again.

"It's something new I'm trying." It should also be embarrassing how close to panting I am when I answer him.

"And you're so smooth. Are you always this smooth?" I feel a finger push inside and arch my back and grind into it, a loud moan spilling out of me.

"That's new, too." And now I am panting. "Do you like it?"

Seriously, who am I?

Adam's groan and the way he grinds into my hip are all the answer I need, but I feel the heat of his words when he responds while pumping his finger into me. "I like everything about you, Lainey. Every," pump, "single," pump, "thing," pump.

There's a fire starting inside of me. A flame that's been put out for so long, I didn't think there were any embers left. Yet here Adam is, lighting me up in a way that feels so new. His finger is moving in a slow, steady rhythm and I can't take it. I need… "More. I want more."

A second finger joins the first and they pump into me faster, his palm applying the perfect amount of pressure to my clit as he moves in and out. His mouth is busy licking and biting my neck, ear lobe, and shoulder. He finally makes his way back to my mouth, but when he curls his fingers inside me, my head falls back against the wall, my eyes closing tight.

"Don't hide from me, Elaina." His deep voice sends a shiver up my spine. "I want your eyes on me when I make you come." I straighten and look into his now indigo eyes and I see desire, but also a level of adoration I've maybe never beheld before. "I want to witness every second, *tornerose*." His fingers curl again and his palm rubs against me just so. "I want you to be here. Be with me. Always." And it's then I feel myself fall.

His eyes never leave mine. His steady hand holding me

never wavers. And at his steadiness, I stagger, stumble, and fall right over the edge. I come apart so ultimately, I don't know if I'm whispering or screaming, but it's his name on my lips over and over. When I finally crash, his fingers slow to a gentle caress, his palm no longer rubbing against my now most sensitive spot.

The swirl of emotions inside me threaten to take over as my breathing slows and the realization that a man hasn't brought me to orgasm in a decade hits me. I'm bombarded with relief, guilt, affection and awe all at once and the blow is powerful.

His kisses are sweet, covering my temples, my cheeks, my chin and my jaw, catching the tears I didn't realize were falling.

His whispers are soothing. "You're so beautiful." Relief washes over me that I am able to connect with him on this level.

His hands stop their movements. "Thank you for trusting me." Guilt threatens to drown me as I realize Andy was the last person I fully trusted with my body.

An arm at the backs of my knees, one at my back. "You felt amazing." The fondness I have for him fills me with a warmth that I didn't know was possible, and I find myself feeling more for this man than I've ever felt before.

My body is gently placed on the bed, covers pulled over me. "You're perfect." Awe descends over me for a lover whose tenderness has left me speechless.

His arms wrap around me as I lay my head on his chest. "Lainey, baby, please stop crying." Fingers thread through my hair and more kisses land on the top of my head. "I'm sorry. I'm so sorry." And that, those words, they sober me up.

"W-what?" I sniffle and wipe at the tears blurring my vision. "No. Please don't say that." I struggle to pull myself up and Adam rolls us so I'm on my back and he's on his side. I reach up to cradle his face. "Please don't be sorry. I'm sorry.

For crying. It's just…" My bottom lip trembles, and I feel the sting of tears on my cheeks. He gently brushes them away with his thumbs, and then cradles my face in both palms and kisses me tenderly.

Through the warmth of his lips, I feel an infinite level of comfort that halts my tears in an instant. I rest my forehead against his and search for the right words to thank him for being so steady and patient with me through it all. "It just… you just…" I feel my eyes well with tears again.

"We don't have to talk about this right now." His voice is gentle as he tucks me closer into him and kisses my head.

"Thank you. For being so steady. For holding me up. For letting me fall. You… this… means so much and I just… I don't have the words quite yet."

I see his throat bobble as he swallows. "Those words will do just fine, my Lainey."

27 /
are you happy?

adam

I WILL NEVER, for as long as I'm breathing, be able to erase last night from my memory. Elaina's moans grew louder with each passing moment, her body writhing in pleasure beneath me.

Suddenly, her breath hitched, and she began to whisper my name. Her hands clawed at my shoulders and then her body went rigid before going limp. Tears streamed down her cheeks as she opened her eyes and stared into mine, her quiet whispers reduced to quiet sobs.

My fingers moved in slow circles on her back, and my voice tried to fill the void in her heart. I scooped her up in my arms, and she clung to me like a life preserver. Her skin was soft and damp with tears, and her breath shuddered with each sob. I pulled her close, gazing into her tear-streaked face —and I saw something surprising behind the sadness. There was relief, as though she had found in me something she had been searching for.

She looked up at me and murmured a thank you that seemed to come from deep within her soul. In that moment, I knew there was no way I could ever let her go.

———

I'M AWAKE BEFORE ELAINA, as usual, and I smile when I witness her little stretch and butt wiggle. My name is the first thing she says in the morning, and I wonder how I ever woke up without the sound of her raspy voice calling out to me.

We linger in bed, all soft kisses and touches until we're tangled in the sheets laughing.

"I like seeing you like this," she whispers to me as her index finger traces the shape of my nose.

"Like what?" I scoop her up so she's straddling me, sitting on my stomach. Her perfect breasts are pushing against her shirt, hair falling all around her face in wild curls. Somehow, she looks even more beautiful at this moment than I've ever seen her before.

"Happy." Her finger traces the outline of my lips and I catch it gently between my teeth, letting go when she gasps.

"I am happy. I'm the happiest." I trace circles on the insides of her wrists, watching her smile grow. "Are you happy, *tornerose*?"

"Yes." She closes her eyes when she answers, and something shifts in her demeanor.

Before I can question it, she lowers herself and brushes her lips on mine.

"And I'm also very, very hungry." A soft giggle echoes in my ears as she rises from the bed, her T-shirt slipping off her body, revealing her toned stomach and the curves of her hips.

She struts towards the bathroom, glancing back with a mischievous smile before disappearing behind the closed door.

The shower starts running, and I want nothing more than to join her, but I know that wouldn't be right. Elaina is still apprehensive around me, and I'm scared that if I tell her how I feel too soon, it'll scare her away.

Before I can do much more thinking about this, she comes out of the bathroom in a towel, wet hair hanging down to her lower back.

"All yours," she says with a sweet smile. I know she's talking about the shower, but I wish she was talking about herself. I steal a kiss as I walk past her.

BY THE TIME I come out, she's dressed in a short jersey dress that hugs her body all over. I stop, openly looking at her ass as she bends over to put something in her suitcase. When she turns, she bites her lower lip, smirking as she glances towards what's underneath my towel. She walks into the bathroom to dry her hair and I make quick work of getting dressed.

I step into the bathroom, intent on fixing my hair, when I see her open a tube of lip gloss. I move quickly before she can apply it, trapping her against the sink with my hands. Sweet coconut and honey assaults me as I breathe in her scent. I press my lips to hers with a possessive hunger and feel her body relax into me. Her delicate hands roam up my chest as my fingers find the curve of her backside.

"Why does it feel like you're not wearing underwear?" I murmur against her lips.

She moves her hands up to my neck and whispers in my ear, "Because I'm not wearing any."

"Fuck me, Elaina." And my fingers are already moving to the hem of her dress.

"I'd love to." I love her breathy voice, and the way her soft gasp sounds when my fingers skim her thigh.

I shake my head, pulling away so I can look into her eyes. "No, baby. You know that's not what I meant. The first time I'm inside you isn't going to be a quick fuck in a bathroom. I'm going to make love to you slowly. So slow, you'll be begging me for release. I'm going to worship every inch of your perfect body." I slide my hands up her ribcage, running my knuckles over her nipples. Her eyelids flutter as she whimpers at the touch.

"Then I'm going to fuck you so hard you won't just whisper my name when you come, you'll scream it. I'm going to take my time. I'll make sure you feel exactly how gone I am for you. How you've ruined me. And if you let me, I'll never stop."

Her eyes widen and her breath quickens with every word I say and just as she's parting her lips to respond, but then they close again. I love being able to render her speechless.

"You make me feel like a teenager, you know? I've never wanted anyone like this." I'm combing my fingers through her hair gently while she twirls her fingers in mine.

"You make me feel..." she whispers. I wait for the rest of the sentence, but it doesn't come.

"Make you feel what, *tornerose*?" My other hand is drawing circles on her hip, inching higher and higher up her dress.

"That's it. You make me feel." She swallows hard, eyes darting away from mine. "I haven't felt much of anything with anyone in a very long time, and with you..." She hesitates.

"Tell me, baby."

"With you, I feel everything." She looks down at her hand on my chest as she speaks. I move my hands to cradle her face, pulling her in.

"Me too, Elaina. Me too." I kiss her to keep myself from saying the thing I've known to be true for a long time. It's sitting right there, on the tip of my tongue and as I deepen our kiss, there's a loud knock on our door.

"Yo, Riv. It's Garrett. Open up, man. And you better not be naked. Elaina, totally cool if you are."

She shakes her head and chuckles as Garrett disrupts our otherwise perfect moment with his foolishness. She rests her forehead on my chest for a second and I kiss her head before I walk to the door, rearranging my erection to avoid Garrett's further commentary.

I open the door and he just barges right in, looking around the room, likely trying to see if he can actually catch a glimpse of Elaina in the nude.

"Sup, bro." He turns just in time to see Elaina come out of the bathroom. "Damn girl, that's a *dress*!"

"Lovely to see you again, Garrett." She shoots him a look that would intimidate anyone who is *not* Garrett as she puts on a long dress shirt over her dress.

"River, man, your dad just showed up with his new girl-friend and your mom looks like she's about to lose it. I can't find Gwen, so that's why I came to get you. You should get down there." He looks back over at Elaina. "I can stay and keep your girl company, though."

"That's okay. I'll come with you. Maybe I can help." Elaina doesn't miss a beat. "Come on. Let's go." She takes my hand, and we walk out together.

Moments later, the three of us are in the hotel lobby, and I notice my mother's face turning bright red as she addresses a woman who appears to be somewhere in her early twenties.

Fuck.

I walk over to them as Garrett and Elaina hang back. My mom immediately turns to me. "River, you need to speak to your father about this."

"I'm not sure what there is to speak about, Mom. Dad, nice to see you. You, uh, missed the wedding." I nod at the woman next to him who looks terrified of my mother, rightly so. Bethany Holm is not to be trifled with. And yes, she kept my father's last name even after the divorce.

I look back to see Garrett walking towards the elevator. Gwen has now joined Elaina with the kids and Callum.

This isn't going to be good.

Gwen and Callum make their way over to us and Gwen quickly takes control of the situation, as she always does.

"Okay, we're going to take this to our suite and chat privately. Elaina, being the angel that she is, volunteered to take care of the kids while we resolve... whatever the hell is going on here. Let's go."

I don't have time to react. I look at Elaina and she's smiling, giving me a thumbs up and then blowing me a kiss just before she takes Liam and Emma by the hand and skips off with the two of them. All three of them are laughing.

What did I do to deserve this girl?

Gwen ushers all of us towards her suite and I think of ways I'm going to make this up to Lainey.

————

MOM AND DAD sit as far away from one another as they can in the large living room of the suite. Dad seems completely unphased by the fact that his ex-wife and his current girlfriend are in the same room, but something tells me this is about more than my dad dating another young gold digger.

"Well, Karl, what do you have to say for yourself?" my mother asks incredulously.

"Listen, Beth, I know you own part of this business, but I can hire whoever I want. It's never been an issue before." Dad openly runs his hands up and down his girlfriend's leg as he speaks. We don't even know her name yet. "Cassie here is perfectly capable, and I think she'll be great as my new assistant."

"Dad, Mona has been your assistant for twenty years. You can't just replace her with a temp." Gwen rubs at the spot between her eyebrows like this is literally painful for her to endure. I get it.

"No offense, Gwenny, but I can do what I want. I still own thirty percent of the company, and I believe you have a measly twenty."

God, he's so fucking arrogant.

Karl Holm is the CEO of Holm Productions, which he started with my mother. Gwen and I became shareholders when we each turned twenty-one and we are likely the reason the entire company hasn't collapsed. The animosity between my parents seemed to be the driving force behind every decision made for the company, which, as one can imagine, is terrible for business. What my parents don't yet know is that I sold my shares to Gwen, making her the majority shareholder. Dad's head is about to explode.

"Actually, *Dad*, since we're all on the board of your company and we decided years ago that executive positions require an in-depth interview process, you can't!" The tips of Gwen's ears are red, but that's the only giveaway that my sister is angry. Her voice is eerily calm and even. "Especially not when you're sleeping with the person you want to hire."

"I still have final say in anything that happens as the major shareholder and I say Cassie is my assistant from here on out. She'll be accompanying me on any and all trips as well." Dad gets up, as if he's just going to walk away from this conversation.

"This isn't how I wanted to do this." Gwen looks at her husband, who's been rubbing her back since we all sat down. "You're no longer the major shareholder, Dad."

Mom and Dad's heads snap up simultaneously. I can feel the shock radiating from them. Dad's eyes narrow as he settles back into his chair like a boulder dropping from a cliff.

"That's right. Gwen bought my shares. I'm officially out of the family business. I don't even need to be here, actually…" It's my turn to stand and excuse myself.

"Oh, River, sit down," my mother snaps. "Is this the little

bit of drama you're drawing up to get your career back on track?" She points a finger in my direction, and I see nothing but animosity in her eyes. "Is this because your little *girlfriend* didn't agree to my plan?"

I don't sit back down, I can't move. What the hell is she talking about?

"Explain." It's all I can manage.

"Oh, what? She didn't tell you? I proposed we create another minor scandal. We ran into one another in the ladies' room and…"

She continues, telling me all about what she proposed to Elaina and how she reacted, how she walked away and suggested they pretend the conversation never happened. She said another.

Another minor scandal.

Like the first one that… she caused?

"I figured she'd go running to tell you. She seemed quite furious with me when she left. She'll be tougher to crack than Tiffany. That girl didn't even pretend to be shocked when I offered to pay her to film you. This one is putting on a good show as devoted girlfriend, though."

My stomach churns as I listen to my mother's bitter words, my heart beating loudly in my temples. The anger coursing through my veins is molten hot and I feel myself about to snap.

Gwen, who had been sitting next to me, must sense my fury as she stands and places an assuring hand on my shoulder.

"I'll handle this. You should go," she whispers in my ear. I shake my head. This isn't hers to handle.

"We're done. Me and you." I point to my mother. "We're done. You had no right to ask this of Elaina. You have no right to make these decisions about my life. You didn't have the right five years ago, and you don't have the right now." My mom has the gall to look shocked at my words. "She's the best person I've ever met. Generous and loving, honest and hardworking, strong and soft. She's everything I want to be. She's everything I... she's everything. And you tried to ruin that. But you can't. Because she's too good. And you have no idea what that's like."

I turn to Gwen, who has tears in her eyes. I whisper so only she can hear, "I'll make some calls and expedite the transfer of the shares." She hugs me tightly, nodding as she takes a deep breath in.

As I walk away from my family, I hear Gwen's even voice say to my parents, "I'm not finished with you two yet."

Give them hell, Gwen.

I WALK BACK to the suite I'm sharing with Elaina, making some calls, and sending a few texts along the way to see how quickly we can get this transfer made. I also need to know how quickly I can get paperwork done for my production company, which is the major reason I wanted out of Holm Productions in the first place.

I sink into the couch in our room, feeling the cool of the fabric through the thin cotton of my shirt.

My mind drifts back to Elaina, her eyes red and puffy when she returned to our table last night. She'd bitten her lip, trying to suppress the tears, and I'd assumed she was just feeling emotional. Little did I know that my mother had just offered a disturbing proposal that Elaina had firmly rejected.

I knew my mother had gone to great lengths and done more than her share of questionable things to advance her own career, but I had no idea she was capable of this.

My stomach turns as I think of what she took from me when she paid Tiffany to take those videos. At the same time, I might never have met Elaina if I hadn't shut myself off from women for the last five years.

Now, as I think of her walking away from my mother's

offer, my determination is stronger than ever. I need to show Elaina that we're forever.

I send a text to find out where she is.

ME

> I'm so sorry that took so long. We just finished up. Where are you?

TORNEROSE

> Sorry, can't talk. Busy going down the funnest water slide everrrrrrrr!

She follows this up with a photo of the three of them at the kids' water park, so I quickly get changed and make my way there to meet them.

When I arrive, I have no trouble finding them. Emma's squeals of joy stand out among the buzz of animated voices, and she runs over to me when she spots me waiting for her at the end of the slide. Elaina comes running out after her in her tiny bikini, and I wonder if it's normal to be envious of triangles of fabric and string.

"Uncle Wiv, Waina is the most coolest pwincess! She can curtsy *annnnnnd* knows twicks, like going down the water slide backwards!"

"Oh no, no, no, we don't need to tell Uncle River that. It was our secret, remember?" Elaina is blushing, and I see Liam laughing behind her.

"Yeah, Elaina is the coolest. She almost got in trouble for doing that, but it was sick, Uncle River. You have the best girlfriend. You should totally marry her." Liam looks at Elaina like he wants to be the one to wed my girl. *Sorry, little dude, but she's all mine.*

I look up and see Elaina's cheeks, now a deep rose color.

"Sounds like you all are having a great time. Can I join in?" A cheer rises from the trio, but my attention is solely on her. She's wearing a white swimming suit, her wet hair curling around her face and dripping down her bare shoulders. Her eyes sparkle with that secret smile just for me. I know we can discuss my family drama afterwards. Right now, all I want is to take in this moment with my favorite person.

One hour, 750 trips down the slide and four cones of ice cream later we're all exhausted, and we happily drop the kids back off to Gwen and Callum, who thank Elaina profusely. As soon as their door closes, I back her up against the wall and kiss her, taking in the smell of her sunscreen and the taste of strawberry ice cream still on her lips.

"You were incredible today." I kiss behind her ear, licking a trail down her neck. "I need to find a way to properly thank you." My hands travel over her nipples, and she gasps, making me even harder. I love the way she reacts to my touch.

"Adam..." Her breathing quickens as her hands find my hair. "Someone will see us." I slow down my movements and kiss her gently on the lips.

"Okay. Let's go." I take her by the hand, and we walk quickly back to our room. Just as we're walking in, my phone rings.

"Hi, Kelly."

"River, you need to leave in an hour. I got you a plane back to LA and then you need to leave in the evening for New York. If you don't go now, you'll have to wait until tomorrow."

"Thanks, Kelly." She says a quick goodbye and we hang up. *Fuuuuuuuck!*

Unsurprisingly, Elaina senses my mood, even though I only said four words on the phone.

"You should tell me what happened today. And what happened just now." She sits on the couch and pats the spot next to her. "As much as I want to make out with you and finally get you naked, we gotta do this."

I let out a long breath. "That's not helping, L. But yeah.

Yeah, we do." I proceed to tell her about my dad's transgressions, selling my shares to Gwen and how I now need to speed up the process so Gwen can do some damage control at Holm Productions.

"Kelly got a plane for today, but it leaves in an hour. I gotta get to LA for a few meetings, then Raf and I will fly to New York tomorrow." She takes this all in stride, nodding along. "You can stay. Enjoy the beach and the spa, and relax. I can see you back at home."

"What? No, absolutely not. I'm not staying without you. And you're not leaving without me." She's not mad, just stating the facts.

As quickly as she's processed this, she starts to pack a few things. "I'm hopping in the shower quickly. I can be packed in ten minutes." She winks at me and closes the bathroom door.

ELAINA STEPS out of the car onto the tarmac, her posture perfect as she strides across to the awaiting plane. She adjusts the strap of her carry-on bag, brushing a few loose strands of hair out of her face before reaching the airplane stairs. Her expression is calm and determined, not a trace of worry or hesitation in her step as she climbs aboard for our private flight.

Once we've taken off, we move to sit on the couch, and I feel Elaina's gaze on me. She reaches out to cup my jaw lovingly, her touch sending a shiver down my spine.

"You should get some rest. It's been a hectic day, between everything with your family and the water park chaos," she says softly. Then she pats her lap and motions for me to lay my head down.

Without giving it a second thought, I do. She tenderly strokes my hair as I drift off into a peaceful sleep.

Hours later, I drop Elaina off at home after she reassures

me she is fine. It's amazing how my not texting her for a few days angers her, but babysitting two kids she just met and being asked to leave a vacation early warrant essentially no negative responses. She's an enigma, this girl.

28 /
is it the tan or the orgasms?

elaina

WELL, this vacation certainly took a turn. That was some Drama with a capital D!

After Adam dropped me off, I unpacked and got back to my usual routine. I did some yoga, had a shower and now I'm baking pies—a chicken pot pie and an apple crumble. Comfort food feels appropriate after the last two days.

I feel bad that we had to leave in such a hurry and texted Ashley to apologize for not being able to say goodbye. I really like her. My phone pings with an incoming text.

ASH

> Hey babe! Don't even worry about it. I know there was some drama with my aunt and uncle. Addy said you were a total trooper about it all.

> Speaking of my favorite cousin, look at these photos of you two at the wedding!

The first photo captures the exact moment when Adam's lips meet mine on the dance floor, our lips pressed together in a passionate kiss. We're surrounded by bodies in motion, oblivious to the surrounding commotion.

The next photo shows us a few moments later, with our arms still wrapped around each other. Everyone is cheering, but all I can see is Adam's face, bright and filled with joy as he looks down at me. In that moment, it feels like I'm the most important person in the world. I don't know that I've ever seen someone look at me that way before.

ASH

Now do you see it? You two are so in love it's sickening. But in the most adorable, wonderful way. Ah, I love love!

I can't bring myself to respond.

In love? No. No, no, no. This isn't love. It can't be.

I need to distract myself. I will not overthink this. We have an expiration date, and that's how it's going to stay. What's the best way to ignore any deep thoughts? Turn on some music and have a kitchen dance party. Also, cleaning up the giant mess I made in this kitchen should keep me busy for a while.

AFTER CLEANING UP, I pick up the romance novel I brought to Hawaii with me but didn't actually read. This series is completely addicting! I could totally see this being made into a movie or a TV series.

Searching for further distractions, I immediately start dreaming up what it would look like. I run up to my office and come back with my iPad so I can sketch out a few ideas.

I know it's not happening, but it feels really good to just be creative for fun, without an agenda or a producer and director to please. They're just my ideas free-flowing. I'm sketching out the hero's bachelor pad on the couch and the next thing I know there's an arm under my knees and I smell that familiar soapy, foresty smell.

"Adam?"

He lays a kiss on my temple. "Hey *tornerose*. It's late. Go back to sleep." He's walking into my room and putting me on my bed and I feel the sudden heat in my core. Adam. My bed. Mmm. *Ugh, No! Focus!*

"No, wait." I sit up as he sits on the edge of the bed facing me. "How did everything go? Tell me what happened." He looks so tired, so defeated, so not like the Adam in the photo I definitely didn't look at 200 times tonight.

"The lawyers are on it, but it looks like I'll be in New York for a few days. All I want is to produce my own movies, you know? Without being under my dad's thumb. I need off of this board and away from his bullshit." His voice has a weariness to it that is unmistakable as he exhales loudly in frustration.

"Adam. That's wonderful! You're going to produce a movie?" I beam with pride, and my eyes light up with enthusiasm. I can't help the huge smile that spreads across my face at the thought of his accomplishment.

The corner of his lip turns up slightly. "Hopefully more than one...but yeah." He looks down at his lap, brows furrowed.

I take his face in my hands, so he meets my eyes. "Of course, you are. I'm so proud of you." His blue eyes widen as he takes my words in. "Will you tell me if there's anything I can do to help? Please?"

He exhales a single chuckle, his breath warm and soft on my skin as he nods. His lips brush against mine with a gentle reverence, completely devoid of the frenetic rush that usually accompanies our kisses. As he pulls away, I feel something deeper than before, a tenderness and admiration that means more than anything else.

He takes my hand in his, kissing my fingers, my palm and

my wrist. I fight the moan trying to escape me by biting my lip. "I have to get going." He looks down at me. "I'll miss you. I'll call you tomorrow, okay?" He tucks a strand of hair behind my ear as I nod. "Now you get to sleep, my sweet *tornerose.*" I lay down and he tucks me in. Like actually tucks me into my bed, kisses me softly again and turns off the light before he walks out.

———

I WAKE up to the sun shining brightly outside and a series of missed texts. I start with Maeve, because duh.

MAEVEY

Bon! I miss you. Come over tonight?

Of course, she sent this at 7:32 a.m. I texted her when we landed yesterday letting her know I was back in town. I respond at a much more appropriate time, 9:46 a.m., letting her know I'll bring the pies I made last night.

Next is Sandra:

SANDRA

Hi sweetheart. Award season is coming up and I'd love for you to attend some with Adam. Will you think about it and let me know?

ME

I attend many of them already, and I suppose it'd be strange for us to go to the same events separately, right? I think you already knew that though, you little sneak ;)

SANDRA

You got me. You really are the best!

I guess I better get ready for a lot more cameras at these red-carpet events. Usually, I fly pretty low since no one really cares who I am. I like it that way, but Adam doesn't have that option. I saved his message for last.

ADAM

Landed safely and missing you already. P.S. I saw the sketches you were working on last night and we are definitely talking more about those later. They're amazing, L. I thought you were taking a break - is this a new project?

ME

Glad you're safe. I miss you, too.

I was just sketching for fun, basing it on the books I've been reading.

Did you sleep? Have you eaten? Please get some rest today before you call me. xo

His response comes in immediately.

ADAM

I have more questions about these sketches. Later though.

I slept a bit on the plane. And yes, I ate. Your concern is adorable and appreciated. xo

Call you in a couple of hours?

ME

Can't wait to hear your voice.

Oh god. 'Can't wait to hear your voice?' I am so cheesy. What's wrong with me? Ew.

I let out a frustrated groan and fling myself out of bed. I need to get it together. I make the bed, get some workout clothes on and make myself a smoothie before taking my yoga mat outside. The morning is crisp, and I need the cool air to snap me out of this Adam frenzy I'm in.

I've just finished my practice when I walk into the kitchen

to see my phone is ringing. All the work I've just done to focus on stretching and *not* thinking about Adam is undone as his name flashes on the screen.

"Hi...you."

So unnatural. What the hell was that?

"Hey, L. You okay?" I hear the hum of traffic and horns being honked in the background. So very New York.

"Yeah, sorry. Hi! How were your meetings?" I walk into the kitchen and grab some water to give my jittery limbs something to do. I don't know why I feel nervous.

"Good. We're trying to decide on what project to take on and Judith and I can't agree on anything. So...not that good, I guess." He lets out a humorless laugh. "Anyway, we'll sort it out. I'm going to be here for two more days and then I'll be back in LA to finish filming."

"Is Judith the director you're working with?" Adam has had a lot on the go lately and this seems like it's been much more involved than I realized after he told me about it last night.

"Yeah. Keller. We worked together a while back and hit it off. She's been really great so far, but we haven't found a story we can both agree on." The sound of stubble being scratched fills the air as he speaks. I feel the urge to reach out and feel the coarse hairs on his chin, remembering how it feels to run my fingers through his beard.

I force myself to focus on the conversation. "Judith Keller. Wow! She's such a powerhouse." He hums in agreement. "Well, if I can help with anything I'm here, okay?"

"Thanks, L. I know. So tell me about those sketches. What made you want to start them?" Of course, he's switching topics and not telling me about the situation with his dad. Fine. I'll play. I also respect that he maybe just needs the distraction.

I go on, telling him about how the characters in these books are richly drawn and highly relatable. The characters stumble through missteps and mistakes, but also experience moments of self-discovery and growth.

Ultimately, the reader can relate to their journey of redemption from their worst qualities. There's a complexity to their relationships that brings the reader into their lives in such a way that it seemed like a movie was playing out in my head even in the first few chapters.

I felt like I had gotten to know each character so well that I could almost see them interacting with each other, and it felt natural to start imagining the sets and scenes for this imaginary movie.

He listens intently as I break down how I see these characters, imagining how great it would be to give them life by adding in details like their favorite coffee mug with a little chip on the handle, and how that would look on camera with the right lighting against moody kitchen cupboards.

An hour passes and he hasn't said more than a few words. He just keeps making reassuring noises, encouraging me to keep going. I finally stop and he remains silent for a few seconds.

"Do you think you could come to New York, L?"

Uhhh what? Did he even listen to what I was saying? Why would I go to New York?

He senses the confusion in my silence. "Could you just come and repeat all of that to Judith and me in a meeting? Because you've sold this movie to me, and I've seen one sketch." He sounds serious, but he can't be, can he?

I laugh because there's no way he means it. "I mean it, Elaina. This sounds like exactly what we've been looking for. Something real, raw, but ultimately with a happy ending. A real love story."

I take a deep breath, my throat tight with anxiety, and try to make my voice steady.

"You're serious?" It still comes out high-pitched, so I clear my throat before asking the question again. "You're not joking?"

I hear him move into a quieter space, somewhere indoors.

"Of course, I'm not joking. I understand if you don't want to potentially work with me, so if that's your hesitation, I—"

"No. No, no. I... I don't have a problem with working with you. Of course, that's not it. I've just never pitched a movie before. I'm usually just brought on by people who already have ideas of what they want it to look like." I take a breath, pacing around the kitchen. "Are you sure about this?"

"I'm sure that you're one of the most talented and passionate people I know, yes. I've already got Kelly reaching out to the author so we can talk about buying rights to make this happen. I called her after your text earlier out of curiosity, but your retelling of the story is what sold me." I make a weird choking noise and he pauses. "Lainey. I'm sorry. Did I overstep?"

I laugh in complete disbelief that this is my life right now. "No. I'm just in shock, I think. I don't have anything ready to show... I..." My pacing quickens.

"There's no pressure, L. I'd just love for Judith to see your enthusiasm for this story. It's just a meeting. No commitment. Okay?"

He makes it sound so easy, and I mean, I've done this before—had meetings that didn't go anywhere—and it's not a big deal. Not all movies get made, duh. But I've never pitched it with my vision, always with someone else's. Having this much creative freedom? This is a dream.

"Okay." I hear myself say it before I really think it.

"Really?" Adam sounds so happy that I let out a laugh. "I'm going to have Kelly set up your flight. You'll come and stay with me. Is tomorrow too soon?"

Now I really laugh. I don't know that I've ever heard him this enthusiastic about anything before.

"Tomorrow's fine. I don't exactly have anything going on."

"This is fantastic! I have to go to another meeting, but I'll see you tomorrow?" There's definitely a slight edge in his question like he doesn't quite believe I've agreed to this.

"You'll see me tomorrow," I promise.

"Okay. Thank you. I'll talk to you soon?" He's so hopeful, I don't think I could have said no even if I had wanted to, which surprisingly I didn't. I don't.

"Talk soon." We hang up and I finally stop pacing. Thank goodness I'm meeting with Maeve tonight.

———

I ARRIVE at her house at 7 p.m. on the dot and she greets me with a glass of red wine. "My Bonnie! You're here! Look at you and your Hawaii tan! You're glowing!"

"Must be the orgasms," I joke, and she nearly spills her wine everywhere. "Yeah let's just get right into it, shall we?" She takes my hand and leads me to the couch, not saying a word.

"I swear I just need to get this out and then we can talk about real life things like the strong, independent women that we are. But right now, I need to talk to you about a guy." She tucks her legs under her, big, bright eyes locked on me as she nods. She makes big, sweeping motions with her arms, urging me to get on with it, already.

"So Adam managed to pull two orgasms out of me, and we haven't even been properly naked together yet."

Maeve has a wicked smile on her face as she clutches her wine glass with both hands. She's downright giddy. I had told her about us kissing when we last spoke, but I had made no mention of anything else. Now she's hearing it all and enjoying it far too much, as far as I can tell.

"This is the best thing I've ever heard. You're falling in

love and it's wonderful." She's so genuinely happy, smiling at me like she's just announced a diehard fact like baby rabbits are called kits, and not at all the stomach-turning, brain-exploding proclamation that has me in a full-blown melt-down. She sees my eyes nearly bulging out of my head and quickly backpedals.

"Oh, no, Bon. Don't freak out. Come on, you must have known these feelings were growing into something more than just *like*, no?" I start breathing heavily, sweat is building up on my forehead. "Oh, shit. You really didn't, did you? Oh, come here."

She pulls me into a tight hug. "I don't love him, Mae. I don't. I can't. I haven't…" She just keeps hugging me until my breathing slows.

"So you don't love him. But you have feelings for him, yes?" I nod, swallowing hard. "And he has feelings for you. That much is crystal clear, yeah?" I nod again, wiping the sweat from my face. "So just be happy, babe. This is a wonderful thing. He's a great guy and you're the best person in the world. You deserve to be happy. Do you hear me?" I nod again, numbly. "Say it, Elaina. Say 'I deserve to be happy.'"

I look at her, incredulously, but she's not budging.

"I deserve to be happy," I mumble. She's still looking at me disapprovingly, clearly not satisfied. "I deserve to be happy," I say again with more pep. She smiles and sips her wine.

"Good girl." She gives my hand a squeeze and I relax my shoulders a little more.

"There's more," I say before taking two giant gulps of my wine, nearly emptying the glass. "I'm flying to New York to meet him and the director he's working with for a new movie he wants to produce. Oh god, I shouldn't be telling you this. He hasn't told anyone. I just found out."

"Bon. It's me. You know my lips are sealed." I exhale

loudly. Of course. She's my best friend. Of course, I trust her. "And Adam wants to bring you in?"

I nod and tell her all about the books, how I've been telling Adam about them since I read the first one, how he saw one of my sketches and this is just the kind of story they want to tell. This time Maeve's bright smile makes me smile, too.

"This sounds exactly like what you were looking for. Something you're passionate about. It's perfect."

"Yeah, I'm excited about it. And the director is Judith Keller. She's a complete renegade and such a fucking talent. Like major bucket list person to work for. I'm a little nervous about meeting her, actually." I take a couple of deep breaths because it feels like I haven't breathed since I got here. "But I'm not putting pressure on it. It's just a meeting." I smile, almost believing my own bullshit. I'm going to stop talking now. I want to hear what's happening with you. Are you feeling any better after those few days in Malibu?"

Maeve's cheeks flush and she fidgets with the hem of her shirt before looking at me.

"Yeah. I'm much better. It was just a stressful few weeks and I think my body was trying to tell me to slow down." She takes another sip of wine and I swear her eyes well up a little. "Thank you again for the flowers and all that food and the muffins. You really are the greatest friend in the world, you know?"

"Nah. You know I'm always down for a batch of muffins anyway." I smile at her, taking her hand in mine this time and squeezing. "You can tell me, you know? Whatever it is, Maeve. You can tell me." She nods, looking down at our hands. "I won't pressure you, but I want you to know that no matter what's happening in my life, it's not more important than what's going on in yours. Not now, not ever." She nods again, meeting my eyes this time as she wipes a tear from her cheek.

"Can we please cut into whatever you brought with you now? The smell is driving me crazy. Is it chicken pot pie?" Her eyes brighten and she stands to pick up the food I set down on the coffee table. Adam may not get the chicken pot pie obsession yet, but Maeve sure does.

"Yes! Let's eat. Chicken pot pie and apple crumble. It seems we both need all the comfort foods right now, so let's get to it!"

We rush to the kitchen to grab plates and end up just digging into the pies with our forks, moving on to chatting about Charlie and Raf, the charity she's working with, and what she's wearing to an award show next month.

We're sprawled out on the living room floor, talking about anything and everything in between mouthfuls of pie. The easy familiarity between us makes me feel comfortable and happy.

Just before I leave, I get an email from Kelly with my flight details for tomorrow. I'll leave late in the morning and be there for dinner with Adam and Judith. Perfect.

29 /
are you kidding me with that skirt?

adam

THANK GOD, Raf was able to come to New York with me. Being here on my own after having to deal with the board and lawyers and my mother's tantrum over dad's new girlfriend would have been too much. Pile that on top of everything that's happened with Elaina in the last few days and my brain is mush.

We promised one another to take this slow, to see where things go because she doesn't want to get into a serious relationship again, and I respect that, but it doesn't change the fact that I'm having a really hard time following through on the whole going slow part.

We're sitting in the living room at my apartment when Raf breaks me out of my thoughts. "You're doing it again, A."

"Huh? What am I doing? I was just sitting here." I look down at my glass of scotch, swirling it around. Raf laughs, openly calling me on my bullshit.

"Right. As if I don't know you. What is it this time? Your parents? Elaina? Judith?" He raises one eyebrow when he says Elaina's name. We haven't talked about what happened in Hawaii. "All of the above?" I look at him and give him a sideways smile. Even if we can't talk about Elaina, we can talk about the other two things, so sure... why not?

"Well, you have lawyers dealing with your parents now. They made their bed and now they can lie in it. You've got one foot out the door of that board anyway, so what do you care?"

He has a point. I don't really need to think about my dad's drama. Or my mom's. That was easy. "Judith just needs the right story. I've been reading the first book in that series Elaina won't shut up about. She bought me a copy after I kept stealing hers. It's good, man. And you know she is going to make that shit come to life like no one else can." His one eyebrow goes back up and we both know which topic he's about to tackle next.

"Apparently, you've figured out more of my life than I have. That's great, Raf." I roll my head back on the chair I'm sitting on, waiting for his next words of wisdom.

"Yeah, that much is clear." He chuckles as he leans in, resting his elbows on his knees. "What's the deal with you and Lainey? You haven't said anything about Hawaii, but you're different. You've been different for a while. Did you tell her how you feel?"

"Different how?" I wonder if he'll let me avoid the topic of feelings.

"Well, for starters, you smile all the time. You're a pretty cheerful guy, but this shit is next level." He puts up two fingers now. Oh good, he's counting. "You get all spacey all the time, and I know you're thinking about her because you get a goofy, sideways smile on your face." A third finger goes up. *Shit.* "You're nice to people. You ask drivers and assistants what their names are. Two weeks ago, you brought a whole ass bakery to the studio. You're a nice guy, but again, next level."

When a fourth finger is waved in my face, I get the distinct feeling I'm not gonna like what he says.

"And lastly, even though I could go on, you will go to any length to bring her into your day-to-day. Yesterday you asked me, 'Have you noticed how Lainey closes her eyes when she takes the first bite of food?' and when a PA asked you how you take your coffee and you said 'two sugar, three cream' even though you take it black, and I *know for a fact* that Lainey likes her coffee to taste like dessert and not a shade darker than beige. But my favorite is the fact that you've watched every single thing she's ever worked on and you bring up her movies in literally every conversation possible."

"I do that? Fuck." Apparently, subtlety isn't my thing.

"So, did you tell her or not?" he pushes, even though he likely knows the answer already.

I straighten and look at the drink in my hand.

"Not really. Not completely, that is. But we're not just pretending anymore." I look at him as I say this, attempting to gauge his reaction. A small smile plays on his lips.

"Well, it's about time. She knows you've been celibate?" His face is serious. Despite never being shy about his busy sex life, Raf has never made me feel bad about my choices. I nod my answer. "Good. And she told you about her... ugh, fuck..."

He runs a hand over his face.

"She told you she has a hard time... finishing... with guys?"

I feel the blood drain out of my face as I nod. How the fuck does Raf know about this?

"She blurted it out one night years ago when she was a little drunk. Believe me, I wish I didn't know."

He finishes his drink. Talking about this is clearly difficult for him, considering Elaina is like a little sister to him.

"And you're all shaken up over the fact that she didn't with you either? Because this isn't about you, you know?" Raf refills his glass and mine. We both need a little liquid courage for this conversation.

"No. That's not it." His eyes narrow at me and when I don't say anything else, his eyes widen as realization hits him.

"Holy. Fucking. Shit." He places his glass down on the table loudly.

"We, um… we haven't had sex. That's all I'll say about that." I shoot him a sympathetic look and I can see the appreciation on his face. "It's not the physical I'm worried about. She's…incredible. Everything I could ever want. Better."

Raf clears his throat, clearly uncomfortable.

"You're worried about how she'll react when you tell her you're in love with her." It's not a question, and this says everything about how well Raf knows both me and Elaina. When I don't respond, he keeps going.

"Honestly, I'm not sure when she'll be ready to hear a man say that to her." He scratches his head. "She freaked out when I told her I loved her for the first time, and our relationship is one million percent platonic. She started having crazy nightmares afterwards."

I jerk my head up at the mention of nightmares and Raf doesn't miss the movement.

"Fuck. She's had them about you."

"The night I took her home when she had too much to drink. She had one that night and she told me she'd been having them again." I huff out a breath, not knowing what to do with this information this late at night and this many glasses of scotch in. "She doesn't seem to be having them anymore though, thank god."

"Just…tread lightly, Adam. I know you're a patient guy. And you *are* in love with her, yeah?" Raf's glare is tenacious. He knows the answer, but he wants to hear me say it.

"I'm fucking crazy in love with her, man." I run both hands in my hair, a little discombobulated at the fact that I just said it out loud. "She's the best person I've ever met."

Raf's smile stretches from ear to ear. "Fuck, yeah, bro!" He slaps my shoulder and shakes me a little, drawing a small smile out of me as he laughs. I don't feel much better about where things with Elaina will go, but it at least felt good to talk it out.

————

I'VE BEEN PREPPING for the meeting with Elaina and Judith tonight. The author of the books we want to buy the rights to seems interested, so we're booking a meeting with her when we're back in LA. Things are looking good. I just need Judith to believe in this story as much as L and I do.

Elaina lands at 5 p.m. and when she texts me, saying she's headed to my place, I know I won't get to see her before dinner. *Fuck.* The magazine interview Sandra squeezed in today ran long.

Now I'm in Brooklyn, Elaina is at my place in Tribeca, and Judith is supposed to be there in an hour.

Raf and I walk into my apartment and, like always, the sound of Elaina's voice and laughter hits me square in the chest. She comes around the corner and runs to me, wrapping her arms around my neck. I kiss her shoulder and our lips come together in a chaste kiss as Raf clears his throat next to me.

Elaina laughs and quickly goes to hug our friend. "Hey, Raffy. I've missed you!"

"I've missed you, too, baby girl. You look beautiful." A fleeting smile dances across her face as she runs her hands down the sides of her skirt, a figure-hugging black pencil that ends just above the knee. She adjusts the hem of her thin cashmere sweater, a light gray that clings to her curves and shows off her silhouette. Her shoes are at least three inches high and the red bottoms match her lipstick. She looks downright edible.

We walk further into the apartment as Kelly finishes

setting up dinner. Once Judith arrives, Kelly takes off and Raf makes himself scarce, taking his dinner upstairs. We eat first so Elaina and Judith can get to know one another and I can tell Judith immediately likes her.

"You know, River has said some really nice things about you, Elaina. But I have to say, I already knew who you were before he mentioned you." Elaina's blush carries to her chest when Judith compliments her on a recent project.

"Well, Judith, if we end up working together, it'll be a dream come true. Woman to woman, you're such an inspiration in this business and I'm just so glad I'm even getting to meet you." They smile at one another, sharing some secret female communication I'm not privy to.

After we finish the last bite of dinner, I lead us to the living room.

We take our places on low armchairs and couches as Elaina pulls out her iPad from a nearby desk. She shows us the sketches she's been working on and they're stunning.

She uses just a few lines to outline the heroine's home and bring the space to life, and each stroke is perfect. As Elaina talks about the heroine's bravery, I glance at Judith, and I can tell she's enraptured. To reassure Elaina, I give her knee a gentle squeeze.

We end the evening all feeling optimistic about the potential of this movie. I still can't believe Judith actually agrees with me on this one, but I'm not fooling myself here. I know that Elaina was the one to sell this to her. Between the way she told the story and the sketches she had to show, Judith was hooked.

We make plans to meet back in LA in a few weeks once we have the green light from the author and we can get started on a script. The meeting couldn't have gone better.

The second the door clicks shut, my hands are on Elaina. "Are you fucking kidding me with this skirt and those shoes?"

"Oh, you like them?" she mocks.

"Goddamn, Elaina, that ass has been taunting me all night." I wrap one arm around her waist as my other hand tugs her ponytail, gently bringing her lips up to mine. She whimpers into my mouth, and I feel her body relax into mine as her fingers grip my shoulders.

"Wobbly knees," she breathes as our tongues mingle and I taste wine and strawberries. "Hey, so the meeting—" I kiss her again, my hands traveling to grip her ass. "I was just thinking—" I pinch her nipple through her sweater and she yelps.

"Baby, as much as I want to talk about this meeting and how fucking sexy you are when you're working, or how hot it was to watch you present this movie better than anyone else could, I'm gonna have to stop you."

"But it went well…" She gasps as I kiss her neck, but she's clearly enjoying this little game. "Don't you think?" I take her mouth and she moans, but pulls away again. "I really like Judith, she—ahh!"

I toss Elaina over my shoulder and stalk towards my bedroom. She giggles all the way down the hall, and I silently hope Raf is out of earshot. I kick the bedroom door shut and her giggles stop as I give her ass a smack and set her upright again, her body brushing against mine as her feet reach the floor.

"The only thing I'm capable of right now is thinking about how I want to taste every inch of you. How hot and tight your pussy is gonna feel when I'm inside you."

Her cheeks are flushed and her breathing is heavy like mine.

"So are you going to talk about the meeting again?"

She shakes her head as she licks her bottom lip.

We stand close as we slowly undress one another. First, I run my hands up her torso, over the swells of her breasts, pulling her sweater over her head. Her hands sit gently on my shoulders as I unzip her skirt and she tosses her shoes off. I slide it down her body, running my hands over her hips. Of course, she has a matching bra and panties set on. Of course, they're lace and see-through.

My fingers skim over her nipples as I pull her bra down and she shivers. I love that I have this effect on her. I hook my thumbs into her panties and slide them off, watching as they drop to her feet. She's perfect like this. All soft curves and creamy skin, swollen lips and hooded eyes.

Her hands are steady as she slides them down my chest, over my abs and beneath my sweater. She spreads her fingers wide, as if to touch as much of my body as possible. I pull the sweater over my head, and she lays a kiss on the middle of my chest. I wonder if she can feel the speed and force of my heart beating for her. Only her.

She unbuckles my belt, taking her time, running her finger along the waistband of my pants before she works the button and zipper leisurely, her warm breath landing somewhere over my heart as she watches her hands work. She follows the line of hair beneath my belly button with her index fingers, hooking them into my boxer briefs and pulling them out and over my hard cock. She doesn't touch me, but I feel the heat of her stare as I go even harder.

Out of desperation for her, I take hold of my erection and stroke it once. The shaky gasp that comes from her, followed by the way she licks her lips, nearly knocks me off my feet.

"You like seeing me touch myself, L? Like seeing what you do to me?"

"Yes," she whispers.

I groan and spin her around, dropping her gently onto the bed and climbing on top of her. I slowly kiss all the way down her body, tasting her soft round breasts, her hardening nipples. I lick all the way down her tattoo, reading the script for the first time. *It's easy to halve the potato where there's love.*

She told me about this one night. It was one of her dad's favorite Irish sayings.

I continue, licking down to her belly button, not missing the way her knees spread a little wider for me.

"I need to taste you, Elaina. Can I?"

"Yes. Please, yes." She gasps when I kiss the inside of her thigh and her hips buck up when I slide my tongue up her sex. I hold her hips down with one hand as I take her clit into my mouth and suck. I could lose myself in this woman, in this moment, only to find myself in her all over again.

Her hands grip the sheets, and she moans so loudly it makes me chuckle. I suck again, harder this time, and she screams as I feel her body tense. She shudders as she comes on my mouth and I lap up every drop.

Before she comes down from her orgasm, my tongue is inside her, working her towards another climax.

She gasps, trying to speak.

"Adam. Oh, god. I can't. I've never..." I push two fingers into her, curling them into that spot I know drives her crazy.

"You can and you will, baby. Now give me another." When I look up, she is watching me with bright eyes and parted lips.

"Oh fuck. Oh shit. Damn it. Ah! Adam!" she screams out again as her body shakes and I slow my movements to allow her to recover.

As her legs relax, I soothe her with kisses on her thighs, then her stomach, traveling up her chest to her neck.

"I was wrong," I say into her ear. "You taste so much better than strawberries."

She groans and turns her face to kiss me, wrapping her legs around my hips, and pulling me onto her as we both taste her on my tongue.

"I want you. Please..." she whispers into my mouth.

"Tell me what you want, Elaina."

"I have an IUD. I trust you. Adam, please... I need you

inside me." She kisses me, grinding onto my cock and I feel her warmth, how wet she is. I feel how much she wants me, but hearing that she needs me as much as I need her, that she wants us like this as much as I do… my chest tightens, and I hear my heart beating in my ears to a steady rhythm of *I love you. I love you. I love you.*

I pull back so I can see her eyes. They're bright green and full of desire. For me. After five years of avoiding any kind of connection, five years of being afraid to give anyone the opportunity to wreck me again, I know with every part of me that this is right. That I've just been waiting for her this whole time. It had to be her.

I line myself up to her core and enter her slowly, like I promised her I would. It takes every last ounce of my strength, will and self-control to not immediately come.

She's so tight. So warm. So perfect.

i do, you know?

elaina

I MUST BE DREAMING. There's no way this is real. Adam just gave me two back-to-back orgasms. With his mouth! I must be in an alternate universe where things like this actually happen. And now I'm asking, no, begging him to have sex with me.

He fills me slowly. So slowly, just like he promised he would. When I feel his hips nudge mine and I know he's fully inside, I circle my hips, asking with my body for him to move. He doesn't. He takes a deep breath, still looking at me as he pulls almost all the way out, pushing himself inside again as he shifts my hips, slightly changing our angle. I feel the air rush out of my lungs as if I need to make more space inside me for this beautiful man. I want him everywhere. I want to be consumed by the feeling of him and I like this.

I use every pelvic exercise I've ever read about to my advantage and squeeze him from the inside.

"Oh, fuck... you feel amazing." He keeps his eyes closed as he buries his face in my neck. His hands fist in my hair and his lips brush my earlobe, sending a shiver through my body. I tilt my head back and exhale heavily, feeling the warmth of his skin against me, the hardness of his body pressed against mine. His eyes open and meet mine, a deep, electric blue that seems to penetrate me to my soul.

"Do you feel how perfectly we fit? How you take my cock so well?" At his reverent but filthy words, I feel a burst of pleasure course through me as every inch of him touches me, and I know I'm close to a third orgasm. "Hmm?"

He pulls out excruciatingly slowly again and waits for my answer.

"Yes, I feel it. It's so good, Adam."

He's slams into me, faster this time and I scream. The pleasure is nearly too much. I feel every solid inch of him and still I want more.

"It's better than good, baby. This pussy was made for me like my cock was made for you."

I swear I feel his words move through me. Every filthy thing pulling me closer to the edge yet again as he picks up speed, thrusting harder into me with inexplicable control.

He leans down and takes a nipple in his mouth and the hot, burning sensation takes over from the tips of my toes to the tips of my fingers. He's relentless, slamming into me and I relish the sight of him like this, sweat on his forehead, groaning with every thrust as if he can't control his noises any more than I can. When I scream his name over and over, I know I've gone over the edge again.

I feel the soft pad of his tongue on my pulse point as my orgasm washes over me. "There's nothing sexier than you coming on my cock, Elaina. I want to do this forever."

Forever.

Tears prick at the backs of my eyes, the truth slamming into me all at once. I've never come like this before. I've never responded to a man's touch like I do his. Never. His words make me wild with desire, stoking a fire I didn't know was burning inside me.

Before I can process and before any tears can fall, Adam

moves us around, his arms around my back, our lips and tongues dancing in time to the music of our movements. He sits up with his legs spread beneath me and I'm straddling him, my own legs wrapped tightly around his waist.

"You're gonna give me one more, *tornerose*." My eyes go wide as I shake my head.

There's no way I can come again. Right?

As if reading my thoughts, he smirks, grabbing my hips to pull me down harder onto him. He rocks up into me, and I grind down onto him, each movement more delicious than the last.

Our breaths become rapid and shallow in sync with our movements, and I feel the heat building deep inside me again.

How is this happening?

I tilt my head back as he trails soft kisses along my neck, his hips grinding into me in time with each stroke. Every second with him seems to fill me with a little more bliss until I feel I'm glowing from the inside out.

"Elaina," he says into my mouth as our eyes meet again. "I love you. I love you so fucking much."

I can't manage words or thoughts. All I can do is feel. I feel everything. The sweat dripping down my chest, my hair stuck to my forehead, his shallow thrusts as he comes inside me, his steady hands on my back, my orgasm rippling through me again, his breath on my lips and the twin tears racing down my cheeks.

We're both slick with sweat and we move together as if our bodies are dancing to an unheard rhythm, both of us panting heavily. As our movements slow, he tenderly tucks a strand of hair behind my ear, a small smile playing on his lips as he leans to kiss me softly. He then carefully lays me down and pulls out of me, and I miss our connection instantly.

"I'll be right back," he whispers before getting up.

When he returns, he has a warm washcloth. He cleans me up and lays next to me, lifting my upper body onto his chest.

I kiss his neck, tasting the salt of his sweat, our sweat, probably.

"I think you broke me. I... I'm speechless."

His rumbly chuckle is quiet, but I feel it in his chest. With his strong arm around me, as I listen to his slowing heartbeat, I fall into a deep sleep.

———

I WAKE SUDDENLY as his words replay in my mind.

Elaina, I love you. I love you so fucking much.

I nearly choke as air struggles to creep into my lungs.

No. No, no, no. Oh god, no.

I climb out of bed as quietly as I can and run to the bathroom to splash some water on my face. I feel sick. Shaky. I slip into the bedroom to gather up my clothes. Back in the bathroom, I get dressed, but I lose my balance by putting my heels on and knock over the soap dish, which clunks loudly in the sink.

"Elaina?"

Shit. Shit, shit, shit.

I don't have time to react. He's standing at the bathroom door. Thank fuck he threw his boxer briefs on. I do not need to be swayed away from my decision to leave by his beautiful, perfect cock.

"Are you okay? Wait, what are you doing? Why are you dressed?" I'm panting, borderline hyperventilating as I try to come up with better words than *I am freaking the fuck out*! His brows are furrowed, his hands on his hips.

"I'm so sorry. I just... I can't. I have to go." My hands are shaking, and I can't look at him. He moves towards me and I take a step back.

"Baby. What happened? Look at me. Please." I nearly break in two at the agony in his voice. He walks toward me again and I don't move. His hands come to my shoulders, then he cups my face, moving it until our eyes meet.

"Please don't leave. Talk to me." His blue eyes are pleading with me and I have to look away or I might just stay.

Would that really be the worst thing? Yes. He doesn't love me. He can't. I can't.

I shake my head. "I... I can't, Adam. I'm sorry. This is too much." I blink back tears. I can't cry right now.

"Then we slow down. We take a step back." He pulls me in close, so my head is on his chest. "Please, Elaina. Please don't leave like this in the middle of the night."

"We won't. We won't slow down. We haven't been able to do anything slowly." My voice is surprisingly firm considering I am crumbling inside. I pull away and take in the look on his face. "It's not your fault. It's mine. I let this go too far..." I see the hurt in his eyes and it's killing me to be the one causing it.

"No." He shakes his head. "I'm not letting you run away from me." His hands each hold on to one of my elbows, keeping me in place. "Just... let's talk through this. Is it because I said I—"

"Stop. Please, Adam. Stop." I'm pleading with him a lot tonight. I take two steps back, needing the distance from him. I can't hear him say it again. "You need to let me go." Tears fill my eyes, but they don't fall.

"It's the middle of the night." His lips are in a tight line. He's still standing in the doorway, so I can't leave.

"Your doorman will get me a cab. I'll be fine." Of course, he's worried. And I won't do anything stupid. I just can't be here. "I'll let you know I'm safe. I promise. I need you to let me go. Please."

He moves aside and I rush past him, my shoulder brushing his chest, sending sparks all over my body.

"Elaina," he calls as I grab my suitcase and walk towards

his bedroom door. I stop, but I don't look back. "I do, you know? I love you. That's never going to change."

I don't believe you. I almost say the words, but I walk away instead. Out of his room. Out of his apartment. Out of his life.

I get downstairs and ask the lovely middle-aged man at the door to help me with a cab, which he happily does. I get in and ask the driver to take me to JFK.

It's not enough to be out of his home. I need to get out of this city. And I know exactly where I need to go.

Of course, there are no flights to Boston at 1 a.m. The earliest flight leaves at 5:30 a.m. and I could drive to Marblehead in that time. It's not like I'll be able to sleep tonight, anyway.

Rental car, it is. Before I drive away, I quickly text Maeve to let her know where I'll be, and my mom to let her know I'll be arriving first thing in the morning.

And when I turn on the car and Harry Styles's voice is singing to me about being a bluebird, the tears come. Fast and hot, they stream down my face. I don't think I stop crying until I reach Marblehead.

It's just after six in the morning when I pull into my mom's driveway, and I can see the lights are still off inside. I don't want to wake her, so I sit in the car and wait.

I must fall asleep because the next thing I see and hear is my mom in her housecoat tapping on the car window. I take the key out of the ignition and exit the car slowly.

My whole body is stiff from driving all night and I really need to pee.

"Honey. What are you doing out here? It's cold. Come on. Let's go inside. I have the kettle on." She doesn't ask anything else. Doesn't comment on why I have a tear-streaked face and puffy eyes. She puts her arms around me and guides me into the house with a calmness only a mother can possess.

We sit at the kitchen table, and she floats around getting the tea and some muffins she just happened to have ready. I notice she has banana, Owen's favorite, and lemon-poppy seed, my favorite, which I never make myself because she won't give me the recipe. I wonder at that moment how I never noticed that she just always has these here. Like she's always ready for us to walk in and have tea with her.

I sit and pick at my muffin, not actually eating it. She sips her tea quietly, still not saying a word.

"I'm sorry for just showing up like this, Mamá." My voice is shaky and rough.

She places a hand on mine. "Don't you dare, Elaina. This is your home. And I'm your mother. Forever. No matter where you are or what's happening, darling."

I feel tears threatening to spill again, so I swallow hard and nod. "I really have to pee. I drove from New York without stopping."

Mom lets out a sigh. "Go. Use the bathroom down here. I'm going to draw you a bath upstairs. You're going to soothe those muscles and rest. We'll talk later."

A tear slips down my cheek, and she brushes it away with the back of her hand. I get up with her and when I walk upstairs after relieving my bladder, I hear the water filling the tub. She's putting lavender-scented salts into it. She has towels and my old robe hanging on the hooks on the wall.

"Relax, Lainey. Don't fall asleep in there. I'll come to check on you in a little while." She kisses my cheek and closes the bathroom door.

The water is hot. So hot it burns a little at first, but it gives me something other than the stabbing ache in my chest to focus on. I feel my muscles relax, but my mind and my heart are going a mile a minute. I can't stop hearing his words. *I love you. That's never going to change.*

I wish I believed him. I wish I could somehow guarantee that his love would never fade. That he would never leave me. But I can't. He can't.

Knock, knock.

"Hi, honey. You alright in there? You didn't fall asleep, did you?" Mom's soft voice comes in through the crack I left open in the door. The water is barely lukewarm, so I know I've been in here a while.

"I'm awake, Mom." Not alright, but definitely awake. "I'll be right out."

I dry myself off and put on the robe. I see the light in my old room is on, so I walk into it. The curtains are drawn, and the room is darkened despite the shining sun just outside. My mom brought up my suitcase and turned down my bed. She has a fresh cup of tea on the nightstand and a fresh muffin to accompany it.

I quietly get into my bed, and she tucks me in. All it does is remind me of Adam doing the same.

"Get some rest, *moro mou*. I'll just be downstairs if you need anything. Anything." I nod and she turns off the light, closing the door on her way out.

I lay there, staring up at my ceiling, in a room I haven't spent more than a full week in since I was eighteen. I sit up and see my mom has also left my cell phone on the nightstand. It's been on silent since I left New York, and I see I have a slew of missed texts and calls—two from Maeve and several more from Adam.

MAEVE

Call me. Please.

I need to know you're okay.

ME

I'll call soon, Maevey. Promise. I'm in Marblehead now. Please don't mention it to anyone. Love you.

MAEVE

I love you. So much.

Maeve knows I'm safe. Owen will probably eventually

hear what's going on, but I'll deal with that later. I move on to Adam's texts. He's sent one per hour since I left his apartment.

ADAM

Where did you go?

Are you safe?

Elaina, please. You promised.

It's been 4 hours. Please tell me you're okay.

Elaina, where are you?

Maeve hasn't heard from you. We're worried.

I'm losing my mind.

I'll be calling Owen next. You know he'll overreact. Please text me back.

Finally, I do. I hope he hasn't called Owen yet. That last text came in seventeen minutes ago.

ME

I'm sorry. I'm safe.

ADAM

I love you.

My heart sinks somehow lower than the canyon it's been buried under for the last eight hours. I turn my phone off. Otherwise, I'll sit here and read that last text until the letters all blur together.

Around noon, my mom comes into my room quietly. She's got a tray with soup and fresh bread on it. Another cup of tea.

"Did I wake you?"

"No, Ma. I was awake." I try to smile at her, but I'm sure it comes out more like a scowl than anything.

"You haven't slept. You haven't eaten or had anything to

drink. Elaina… please." She sets the tray down in front of me. The bread smells wonderful, but I'm not sure I can stomach anything.

I stare at the wall in front of me, wondering if I'm dehydrated because I don't seem to have tears left. Mom pats my hand and leaves the room, closing the door softly.

Three hours later, as I'm laying facing away from the door, staring at my curtains as the light tries to peek through the edges, Mom comes back. She must think I'm asleep. She replaces my tray with a fresh cup of tea and cookies.

At seven o'clock, she comes in and finds me sitting up in my bed, staring at my dresser. She sets down a tray on my lap. Chicken pot pie. She made my favorite. She turns on the lamp and cradles my face in her hands.

"Lainey, you need to eat. Please. I'm worried about you. I won't force you to talk to me, but you need to eat and drink something." I don't move. I blink and tears roll down my face. I guess I'm not completely dehydrated.

"Maeve called. She said your phone is off." I look up at her then. "She didn't tell me anything. And I didn't ask. But she said she's holding Owen off." I nod lightly, relieved. "But I won't for long, Elaina."

She gives me a kiss on the cheek and leaves the room again.

I eventually set the tray of food on the floor. My old alarm clock tells me it's midnight. It's been twenty-four hours since I left him. I bury my face in my pillow and cry.

———

"IT'S BEEN twenty-four hours since I found you sitting in a car." My mom is prying open the curtains and I see there's toast and yet another cup of tea on my nightstand. She sits on the edge of my bed. "What happened?"

I shake my head. "It's complicated, Ma."

"I have time. What are you running from?" She places her hand on my lap.

"Adam told me he loved me." She knows who he is. She knows how we met and that we've been friends for a little while. She does not know he started giving me orgasms in Hawaii.

"That's wonderful, honey." She smiles softly, waiting for the bad news.

"That's it, Mom. He said he loves me, and I ran away."

"You don't love him? Because based on the way you've talked about him, well…" She raises her eyebrows and when she sees the tears pooling in my eyes, I think she might be understanding. "So, you *do* love him. But you don't want to." I shrug. She's not wrong. I don't want to be in love again. Ever.

"I'm scared of what happens when he leaves. What will happen to me? I don't think I can survive another man leaving me." She opens her mouth as if to speak, then closes it again. "Andy left me. I know, I know. It wasn't my fault. But he didn't stay. He didn't tell me he needed help. He just left. I wasn't enough to keep him here." I sniffle, but there are no tears.

"Then, Daddy. He didn't want to leave, and he didn't mean to, but it still happened." My voice grows louder, and the roughness of my throat becomes more pronounced with each word. I attempt to swallow, but my mouth is so dry that nothing will go down.

"He's not here! Even Owen kept leaving, and we never knew if he'd come back." No matter how much the pain seems to seep through the cracks in my voice, no tears fall.

"How many times can a person watch the people she loves vanish before it finally breaks her?" It's like I'm asking an impossible question, of no one in particular, that I already know the answer to.

My mom's grip tightens on my lap. "Why would Adam leave you?"

I scoff. "The possibilities are endless! He falls out of love. He decides to move to the other side of the planet. He falls in love with someone else. We both change so much that we don't like one another anymore. He hits his head and gets amnesia and never remembers me. He could… he…"

"You're afraid he's going to die." Again, not a question.

"Of course, I am! I'm afraid of all of those scenarios and then some." I reach for the tray and take a slice of bread off the plate. I squish it in between my thumb and index finger before shoving it into my mouth.

"Weren't you afraid Owen would die every time he was deployed?" I take a bite of the bread and now I'm full-on talking with a mouthful. "And Dad! I still don't know how you survived losing Dad. I can't do that, Mamá. I can't build a life with someone only to lose them!"

I see tears streaming down my mom's face.

Shit. I should never have brought up Dad. I'm such an asshole.

"I'm so sorry, Ma. I shouldn't—"

"Elaina, I would feel the agony of his passing a thousand times, just to have the time I spent with him again. But even if I could, I wouldn't alter a single moment—it was all worth it just to get to love him like I did. To be loved by him. To be known in that way. To see him shine through my children's eyes."

Her gaze penetrates me, and with a heavy heart, I understand her pain. She looks into her late husband's eyes every time she looks at Owen and me, our grass-green eyes perfect replicas of Dad's. I'm sure it's both a reminder of the loss she suffered and the love she had.

"And I'm afraid something horrible will happen to you and Owen no matter where you are in the world. Even when you're right next to me. I have since the day I knew you existed in my womb."

She sniffles and takes my face in her hands again.

"But I would never let that fear keep me from letting you live your lives. I would never let it keep me from living mine. Your heart is so big and so capable of loving anyone it chooses. You love well and you love hard. Let yourself love him back. Don't cheat yourself out of your greatest love story because you're scared."

"I don't know if I can do that." She wipes the tears from my cheeks and smiles.

"You can do anything, my girl. Lean on your friends. Lean on your family. Let us help you get there."

She kisses my nose and leaves the room. This time the door remains open, and I think it's more as an invitation for me to leave than it is for her to come and go as she wishes.

I reach for my phone to call Maeve and see a text from Rafael.

RAFFY

Baby girl. I wish you'd stayed, but I know why you left. Where are you?

I might as well answer him. Everyone will know soon enough, anyway.

ME

I'm at Mom's. Haven't told Adam yet. I just need to figure this out alone for now.

Adam's name is next. My stomach flips and I regret the bread I just scarfed down.

ADAM

Where are you? Can I please come to talk to you?

I love you.

I feel sick. Those three words make me nauseous, and my

heart feels like it's beating out of my chest. I take a deep breath before I answer him.

ME

I'm with my mom. I need time. And space.

The three dots immediately come up and I hold my breath.

ADAM

I'll wait.

I love you.

I close my eyes tightly, willing myself to forget what his voice sounds like when he says those words to me. I can't. So, I pick up the phone and call Maeve. She answers on the second ring.

"Bon. What's going on? What happened?" Her voice is soft, but I can sense that she's anxious to hear what had me driving away from Adam and New York in the middle of the night.

"Adam... he told me... he told me he loves me." My voice cracks. I may as well be telling her he drowned puppies in the river based on the tone of my voice.

"And you took off." She takes a deep breath. "Have you slept? Or eaten?" Either my mom told her or she's a damn mind reader. Or she just knows me better than anyone.

"A little," I mumble.

"Bon, help me understand. Tell me with your words why you left." Her voice is soothing, and I feel the love in the gentleness of it.

"I don't... I can't... I don't know. I'm just so scared. I'm so scared of what will happen to me when he's not around anymore."

The shakiness in my voice reverberates in my entire body and I see my hands shaking, too.

"When? When he's not around?" She picked up on that. "Why when, my darling? You don't know that he will leave."

"Right. Yeah." I play with a loose thread on my quilt and Maeve says something else I don't hear.

"Bon? Did you hear me?" Crap. Is that a trick question?

"Ummm no, I'm sorry." Might as well be honest.

"When you're ready to talk, I'm ready to listen, alright?" I know she means well. I know she wants to be there for me, but I don't even know how to process everything that's happened yet.

"I know, Maevey. I love you." One hot tear falls down my cheek. Just thinking about my friends makes me teary.

We hang up and I go back to bed.

are you letting her go?

adam

I'M SLUMPED against the couch with my forehead resting on my palms. I don't even stir when Raf enters the room. He's bundled up in a hoodie, his hair sticking up at odd angles.

"Hey, man. Is there any coff—" He stops, taking in the look on my face, and his eyes widen with concern. "What's going on? Is Lainey sleeping? Are you alright?"

"Those are all questions I honestly can't answer right now." I go back to holding my head in my hands, rubbing my eyes. I haven't slept. I haven't even gone back to my room.

"Where's Elaina?"

A question I can answer.

"She left."

Raf takes a seat in a chair across from me and lets out a loud breath.

"Oh, fuck. What happened?" He's leaning in close, and I can hear the concern in his voice.

"I told her." I look up at him and he winces. I'm not sure if it's because I look like shit or because of what I just said. "I told her I love her. I told her that's never gonna change. She's it for me, Raf. She's everything."

"What did she say before she ran?" He's nodding. He called it. He knew she'd run.

"That it's not my fault. She let it go too far. That she can't do this." I swallow down the lump in my throat. "She said I needed to let her go, and I don't think she meant just leaving the apartment."

I get up and pace around the room. Repeating what she said to me makes me jittery. After what had happened just a couple of hours before, it's not right. Nothing is right.

"And what are you gonna do? Are you letting her go?" My head snaps up. Is he fucking serious right now?

"I'm never letting her go, Raf. I told you. She's it. I'm not giving up." I keep pacing, but I see him slowly get up from his chair.

"Good. Let's get some breakfast."

———

RAF TRIES TO DISTRACT ME. He really does. We work out, watch old episodes of *The Office*, and this morning he's making me breakfast again. But I can't think about anything except her. What she's doing. How she's doing. Whether she's sleeping or if she was staring up at the ceiling all night like me.

I've texted her the words *I love you* multiple times. I know telling her isn't enough, but I need her to know that I mean it. It wasn't just a spur-of-the-moment thing, though I can see how she might think that.

Raf turns around with a spatula in one hand and his phone in the other.

"She's in Marblehead!" He shows me his phone screen as proof.

"Yeah. She just told me too." Now, what do I do with that information? Do I go there? She said she needs time and I want to give that to her, but I also need to show her I'm not letting her go. I'm not walking away just because she's scared.

"You can't go." Raf puts the phone down. "Not yet." He turns around and plates the eggs he just finished making, wiping his hand on his apron. Just like he did yesterday, he sprinkles something green on them with a flick of his wrist and smiles down at the plates.

"We need a plan first. Sit. Eat." He puts the plates on the table and gestures for me to join him. "How much longer are you shooting? We're heading back to LA tomorrow, right?"

I sit, feeling a little confused by the repeat performance of Raf the chef I just witnessed. But I'm also a lot thankful for this guy who has seen me through pretty much every high and low in life and still wants to sit at the kitchen table and plan how I'm going to get my girl back.

"Yeah," I say with a sigh, "tomorrow. I should be done within the next two weeks."

"So we have two weeks to figure out what to do." He squints his eyes, waving a slice of bacon in the air as he talks. "That'll give her time to sort through some of her shit, too. Hopefully, Maeve, Charlie and Mrs. James will knock some sense into our girl."

"I'm just supposed to go two weeks without seeing her? Without talking to her?" I drop my fork loudly on my plate and Raf looks up, eyes intense.

"Yeah. You're supposed to give her as much fucking time as she needs to realize that not every man she loves will leave her. That it fucking sucks that Andy died, that her dad died, and that she had to live with the unknown of whether Owen would die for years. But that doesn't mean she has to be too scared to love anyone again." He takes a sip of his orange juice and shakes his head.

"She thinks she's broken, Adam. She thinks she can't love anyone. That she doesn't get to fall in love again because she already had that once." He scoffs, looking down at his plate.

"Can you believe that? Baby girl thinks all she gets in this life is a few months of being in love when she was eighteen. The girl who loves bigger than anyone else I know thinks she's maxed out on how much love she gets in this lifetime."

I hold my breath, my heart pounding in my chest as his words wash over me. Suddenly, it all makes sense—why Elaina always keeps her distance, never lets anyone outside of her circle get too close. I can understand why she loves so deeply, yet has such a hard time believing in the love of others. His revelations give me a newfound appreciation for my best friend and just how closely he pays attention to those around him.

"When I came back from my last tour, I knew I wasn't going back. Elaina was the first person I told. Do you know why?" I shake my head. "Because despite how scared I knew my mom was and how worried my family got, she was the one having night terrors. The fact that she loves me kept her awake at night more times than I'm sure she's admitted to. She loves with her whole heart, but she has a really hard time accepting that love back."

We finish our breakfast in comfortable silence, and I begin to consider new ways I can reach her—show her that I understand her need for space and still remain unyielding in my commitment to our love. Though I have no idea what that will look like, I'm determined to find a way.

———

WE'RE GETTING ready to board our plane and head back to LA when my phone pings with a text from Elaina.

TORNEROSE

Please stay at my house. I won't be there for a little while and I don't want you to worry about looking for another place to stay or going to a hotel. Please.

I don't know what to write back. I'm gutted that she's not going back to LA yet. I want to see her so badly. And I'm not sure if staying at her house will be comforting or torturous. I don't know how to respond, so I turn my phone off and get on the plane.

BY THE TIME WE LAND, I have a plan. I'm going to stay at Elaina's house, but only because it's the only way I can accomplish what I'm setting out to do. She has to come home, eventually.

I turn my phone back on and respond to her text.

ME

Okay baby. I love you.

On my way back to her house, I pick up Frankie at the dog sitter and head to her house. I have work to do.

IT'S BEEN two days since I last heard from Elaina. I've backed off from messaging her because I want to give her the time she asked for, but fuck, this is hard. I miss her. I miss everything about her. The constant music playing in the house. The smell of whatever delicious thing she's baking or cooking. The way she hums as she cleans or does yoga or pours her coffee.

Thank god we're almost done shooting. I've never wished time away as much as I do right now. I just want her to come back.

IT'S BEEN NINE DAYS. I've just finished on set and the light of my phone casts a bluish hue over my face and I scan the day's notifications, searching for her name amongst them.

When I see it, my chest tightens painfully, and I quickly shove my phone back in my pocket, willing the anxious beating of my heart to subside. I quickly take it back out to read her messages.

TORNEROSE

> I miss you. I miss you so much. But I think I need this time away to really be on my own.

> I hope you're taking care of yourself and resting. Maeve says you've been tired.

> I miss you.

She misses me.

The tiny seedling of hope I've been hanging on sprouts a delicate green shoot and unfurls its leaves.

ME

> I miss you, tornerose. More than I can say.

> I'm okay. Promise.

> I love you.

I stare at my phone, waiting. I know she's not going to write back and a part of me is thankful for it because I don't want just text messages. I want her. I want all of her. Here.

———

MAEVE and I are about to shoot our last scene together and it's an emotional one. It's set several years prior to the time-line of the rest of the movie so we've had to change our appearances slightly.

Raf and I stand in my dressing room, our eyes meeting in the mirror. I run my hands through my freshly cut hair, shorter than it's been in months. My face is now absent of the beard I'd grown over those same months. Beneath the harsh white lights, my face feels exposed and vulnerable.

"Your face is back!" Raf walks toward me and grabs my cheeks in his hands. "Look at this pretty mug. I missed it!"

"Dude, if you kiss me right now, I will punch you so hard." I break away from his freakishly powerful grip on my face as he laughs.

"How you holding up, man? It's almost over. What is it now, day twelve?" He knows I've been counting the days until shooting is done. Counting the days since Elaina left. Counting the days until I can leave LA and see her if I ever work up the nerve to do it.

"Eleven, actually. And I'm… fine." He shoots me a look that says he's not convinced. Someone walks toward us and lets me know we have to get going. "I'll see you soon. Let's have a drink once we're both off the clock."

"You got it." He hits me on the shoulder as I walk past him. That fucker is exactly as strong as he looks.

After endless comments on my cleanly shaven face and four hours of shooting, we're done. I shouldn't be needed on set for anything else. Finally, I can finish my project at Elaina's house.

"River!" I hear Maeve's voice calling out behind me and I stop in my tracks. Since Elaina had gone to stay with her mom, conversations between us have been brief and infrequent. Our talks only meander through the occasional check-in with one another, like passing information between us on behalf of our mutual friend.

"Before you go, I wanted to have a chat with you." Maeve has a tight line around her lips, her hands are white-knuckled as they grip each other in front of her. "Has Elaina told you anything about going to Betty's?" I shake my head in response. "Well, it's happening in a couple of days. She hasn't been back there since Andy died, but the diner and Betty were really special to her. She put it on her list and set a date to make sure it would get done. You know how she is…"

She smiles up at me and I smile back, thinking of Elaina nervously adding this to her list. "Anyway, we're all going. It's a surprise, but we're all going to be there to support her, so she doesn't have to do this alone." I nod in understanding.

They're doing the right thing. She would never ask for this, but it will mean the world to her.

"Owen was the first to suggest it, and we all agreed that you should be there." My gaze locks with hers, and I can see the hesitation in her smile. "Will you come?"

I pause for a few seconds, my stomach in knots. I want to be there for her. "Yes. Of course. Yes."

"It's just… you should be prepared. She might not be ready. But we know that your presence would mean everything to her." Right. She might not be ready to see me. I take a deep breath, steeling myself for what might come, and reply,

"I understand. I'm still coming." I scratch the back of my head and let out a long breath. I can't think about her reaction, only about the fact that I know I need to be there for her. "When do we leave?" She smiles brightly now, almost hopefully.

"Two days from now. I'll text you details later."

"Great. I guess I'll see you in a couple of days, then." My knees feel weak and my heart races as Maeve starts to leave. I manage to choke out, "Hey, Maeve?" She pauses and slowly turns to face me, the corners of her lips held in a tight line. "Thank you," I say, my voice barely a whisper.

Her eyes soften, and she gives me a single nod before turning away again.

I hurry back to Elaina's house. I have a lot of work to do.

why are you here?

elaina

DAYS GO by and I'm essentially a zombie. My mom tries to get me outside every day, so we go for a walk around the block, but beyond that, I'm laying on the couch or in my bed. I'm pretty sure she's getting sick of my bullshit. Maeve and Charlie call me every day. Raf and Owen text. Adam seems to be giving me space, which I know I asked for, but I look for his name to pop up on my phone every day. I asked him to stay at my house. I wouldn't be okay with him having to look for a new place to stay while he finishes shooting. I stare at that last message as new tears pool in my eyes.

ADAM

Okay baby. I love you.

It's been nine days since he said those words to me in person and I can't fight the urge to text him anymore. I need him to know that I miss him, that I am working through my shit, that I'm thinking about him.

. . .

IT TAKES a few hours for his reply to come in. I know he's probably had a busy day on set as they finish up, so when my phone vibrates while I'm in the shower, I reach for it with wet hands and all.

My heart constricts in my chest, and I read the words over and over and over.

ADAM

I miss you, tornerose. More than I can say.

I'm okay. Promise.

I love you.

After over a week away from him, I thought I would feel better about my decision to leave. I thought the hurt would fade. I thought all the reasons I said I can't be with him would start to make sense, but they haven't yet. I guess I just need more time.

I stand under the hot water of the shower until it runs cold. Once I'm out, I decide to set a date for visiting Betty and add it to my list. After all the silly things I set out to do this year, this feels like something substantial. Like it's something important.

A thrill courses through my veins as I pull on my jacket and sneakers and step out the front door. I know Mom is at the grocery store and won't be back for at least an hour, so I decide to take advantage of the time by going for a stroll by myself.

I don't know how long I've been walking, but I can feel that my hair has dried, so it must be a while.

"Elaina?" The voice is familiar, but I can't place it. I look up and don't see anyone, so I look around and when I turn back, I see her. Her hair has a lot more gray in it and the lines around her eyes are deeper, but she still looks younger than she is. She still has the same kind eyes.

"Mel. Oh my god." My feet move towards her on their

own accord, but when I reach the end of the driveway, a wave of memories crash into me. It's Andy's aunt. Seeing her is like replaying a movie I've seen a thousand times. I remember how she walked towards me with tear-stained cheeks and red rimmed eyes. I remember how my legs gave out beneath me and how I screamed when she told me he was gone. She must feel it too, because when she sees me, she hesitates. But then, she keeps walking and envelops me in a tight hug.

"Elaina, sweetheart. Look at you." She pulls back, tucking my hair behind my ears and smiling up at me. "You're so beautiful. You're so grown." She stands in front of me, her face a mix of understanding and sympathy, and gently wipes away my tears with her calloused thumb. I feel like I've been wandering aimlessly, searching for something I knew I would never find, and suddenly the sidewalk I had been blindly walking down opens up and reveals this moment. "Will you come in? I'll make us some coffee. Or something stronger, if we need it." I nod numbly and we walk towards the house together.

She enters the room in confident strides, her eyes fixed on the coffee machine. After it starts brewing, she plucks a bottle of Bailey's off the counter and places it on the small wooden table. She lowers herself onto a chair across from me, crossing her legs as she examines my features, a hint of a smile tugging at the corners of her mouth.

"You were always a beautiful girl, Elaina, but my god, what a beautiful woman you've become. It's so, so good to see you." She takes my hand and I seem to snap out of my numbness. I smile back.

"It's really good to see you, too, Mel. I didn't mean to end up here today, but I'm so glad I did." I look down at our hands on the table. "I'm sorry I haven't visited, I—"

"Oh, honey, no. None of that. You're here now." She pats my hand and gets up to get the coffee. "I've watched all your TV shows and movies. You're so talented!" Oh god, she's kept up with my career and I haven't even bothered to come to say hello to the woman the few times I've come into town. *I suck.*

"Thank you, Mel. That means so much."

She sits back down and sets a steaming mug in front of me, gesturing towards the sugar and cream next to the bottle of Bailey's.

"So. What's going on? You've been in Marblehead for over a week, and you haven't spent this much time here in years." Cutting right to the chase. Very much Mel's style.

"I needed some time away. To be alone. To think about some things." I pause, my fingers hovering inches away from the container of cream. Then, I snatch the Bailey's and pour it, glancing at Mel, who grins approvingly.

"What happened with the movie star?" she says into her cup of coffee. My head snaps up at her correct assumption that this is over a guy, and I laugh through my nose.

"Ugh, it's so predictable, isn't it? That I would be here, sleeping in my childhood bedroom, crying myself to sleep and wandering around town over a guy!" I'm so mad at myself for being such a walking stereotype.

"Oh, no, honey. We're not going to do that." She pours some Bailey's into her cup. "This is a judgment-free zone. He looks like he's a good kisser on screen. So... is he?"

Her candor catches me off-guard and in the state I've been in, I react to it all wrong. "What? You're really asking me that? Mel, I... I don't think I can talk to you about that."

"Then talk to me about what you feel you can talk to me about." She casually sips her coffee. "Why are you here?"

I stay silent. I don't want to answer her. I don't want to be here anymore. I don't know what to say.

"Why are you here?" She's relentless.

Why does she care? *I* don't even know why I'm here. I just started walking and ended up at her house. I didn't mean to. I didn't mean to come here.

"Why are you here, honey?" I can't talk about this. I can't

talk to *her* about this. This isn't right. What will she think? What would Andy think?

"Elaina, you can tell me. Why are you here?" As if she can sense me reeling downwards, her voice softens, and she holds my hand again while I sit still, stunned. She squeezes my hand and suddenly the dam breaks.

"Because I fell in love with a man, but I'm too scared to tell him. I'm scared to need him. I'm scared of losing him. I'm scared I can't handle another man I love not being there anymore. I'm so scared that I had a panic attack after he told me he loved me, and I left his apartment in the middle of the night and came here because I can't face going anywhere else. Because this place is where all of my hurts happened, and it felt like the most natural place to be when I'm so sad and broken. Because it's been ten years since I was in love and I don't know how to do it again, so I came back. There, that's why I'm here." My voice is sharp and I'm shaking. The real and ugly truth I've pushed deep down is now sitting on the surface for Mel to see, and it should be horrifying. It should be embarrassing. But it's liberating.

I take a deep gulp of my coffee, wishing I'd been more liberal with the alcohol. I pull in a deep, shaky breath, but I don't look at Mel. I can't. Not yet.

"That all makes a lot of sense, honey." She keeps holding my hand and somehow opens the bottle of Bailey's with the other. She tops up my cup and I squeeze her hand in gratitude. "What do you love about him?"

I sip my coffee, which is mostly Bailey's now, and think.

Everything. I love everything about him.

"He listens when I talk. He's gentle, but knows when to push me. He's generous with his affection. He tells me exactly how he feels. He's steady and dependable. He's insanely hot. And when he…" I don't finish my thought here because Mel doesn't need to know about *that*.

I look up to find her smiling. "He knows the way you

need to be loved. And something about the blush on your cheeks tells me that applies in the bedroom too." She laughs as I blush further. "I know I can't be the first to tell you this, but it's okay for you to love him. It's okay for you to be scared too, but don't let that stop you."

"You sound like my mom."

She laughs, tapping my hand and leaning back in her chair. "Well, your mom is a smart woman." Her face grows more serious. "And she knows a thing or two about grief."

I take a deep breath and nod. "She told me she'd do it all again. She'd live through the pain of losing Dad all over again as long as she got to have the time they had together."

"I believe that. Eva and Doug had a once-in-a-lifetime kind of love." I wince at her words, knowing they're true and wondering if the same is true for me. "But if she ever loved again, it wouldn't undo the love she had for him. It wouldn't change the connection they had. Do you know that?" She shakes her head gently before continuing. "If your mom ever loves another man, it won't undo, devalue, or erase the love she had with your dad. It would still be a once in a lifetime love. Do you agree?" I nod as I shut my eyes to hold back tears. "Do you understand that this is also true for you? You lost love once, but you've been lucky enough to find it again."

She knows. She knows I think Andy was my once-in-a-lifetime love. And, god, I feel so stupid because of course she's right. My mom had a whole life with my dad, and I know she could find love again. I hope she does. I had a few months with Andy, and I've lived the last ten years thinking I could never get that again. Thinking I didn't deserve it. Being too afraid to ask for it or want it.

"You know, Mel, I've been in therapy for ten years. I've talked to my best friends about my fear of relationships at length. Not once was I given this perspective. I could have saved myself a lot of sleepless nights if I had just come to talk to you." I let out a frustrated sigh, annoyed at myself that it took her a few sentences to put me in my place and get me to see what I'd been missing.

"Oh, honey, it wouldn't have mattered. You wouldn't have been ready. It had to be now. It had to be today when you unconsciously walked by my house." She smiles into her cup of coffee.

Mel wasn't just Andy's cool aunt who made herself scarce whenever Andy and I were watching a movie. He came to live with her for reasons I didn't know about when Andy and I were dating. It turns out it was because he was depressed and spiraling, and Mel offered to take him in. She was the person who told me of his death and held me up when my legs failed me. She stood by me at the funeral where no one knew who I was because Andy had never told his family and friends who lived hours away. She reassured me that he never told them because I was a treasure to him, not for any other reason. This woman, who was so deeply heartbroken herself, took time to see me and console me. She let me cry. Loudly. She let me release part of the pain I kept bottled in during those first few days.

"I don't know how to thank you. You have been monumental in my life, and I don't think I've ever told you." I feel tears threatening and bite my lip to keep my chin from wobbling.

"I was just thinking the same thing about you. You gave me a chance to see my nephew happy again. To hear him laugh. You gave him his first love, and I had a front-row seat as it unfolded." She wipes a tear from her cheek and sniffles. "What a gift you gave, sweet girl. To both of us." My own tears flow freely now as we sit and look at one another. If this isn't the exact thing I've needed to hear for a decade, I don't know what is.

"Can I give you a hug?"

She laughs as she stands, pulling me in. "You always did

give the very best hugs. The kind of hugs that say I love you without needing to say it."

I smile as I close my eyes and hug her tight. "I do, Mel. I do love you."

"I know, honey. And I love *you*." I nod as I commit this moment to memory. A new memory of Mel and me. A happy one.

We sit around the table for another hour as she tells me about how she's been running the bookstore in town and also the book club. She's fallen in love herself with the man who owns the coffee shop across the street from her store and she laughs when my jaw drops to the floor. It's almost too perfect to be true. But I'm thrilled for her, and I feel my heart beat steadily for the first time in nine days.

MEL DRIVES me home and by the time I get in, mom is home making dinner. She calls out to me when I step inside. "Elaina?"

"Hi, Mamá." I pause and take her in for the first time in a long time. Her brown hair is perfectly set in a low bun. The apron with mine and Owen's faded handprints that she's used since I was two. The warm smile she greets me with, no matter what. No matter how much she's hurting, and I know she's had many days when she probably didn't want to smile. I walk towards her and hug her tightly.

"Hi, darling. You doing alright?" She kisses my cheek and sets her wooden spoon down.

I nod, looking into her golden brown eyes. "I love you, Mom. And I appreciate you so much. And I'm sorry I haven't come home more. I'm sorry you've had to put up with my nonsense this past week."

"I love you, too, my beautiful girl. And you don't need to be sorry. You needed to do this on your own time." Her eyes sparkle with all the love and understanding she so willingly gives away.

"Can I help with dinner?" I kiss her temple, thankful for her love and her ability to give me space when I need it—something she would have struggled with ten years ago.

"I'd love that."

The sizzle of oil and the sweet aroma of mother's cooking fill the kitchen and it makes my stomach rumble. I share the conversation I had with Mel with her, a friend of my mom's thanks to the book club. She smiles at me, and I feel a warmth inside knowing that my mom and I have a friend in common.

That night I'm able to lay my head on the pillow without crying, though Adam is still on my mind.

————

ON DAY TEN, I cleaned up my room and made muffins with mom. I read more of my book and we went for a long walk around town.

ON DAY ELEVEN, I talked to Maeve and told her I set a date to go see Betty. She told me she's proud of me and that she'll support me no matter what happens.

ON DAY TWELVE, I made it to a steamy scene in my latest book while I was in the bath. When I touched myself, I thought only of him. And when I came, it was his name I whispered. I wanted to call him, to hear his voice, to hear him say those three words again so I could say them back. But I knew I needed to wait to do it in person.

. . .

NOW IT'S day thirteen and as I step out of Mom's car, my feet carry me forward even though I don't recall the movements. My heart is racing, and my palms are clammy as they clench and unclench. I can feel Mom's gaze behind me as I walk up the sun-bleached steps to Betty's Diner. The sound of a car engine idling follows my every move until I'm standing in front of the door, as if it's daring me to enter.

Great. I thought there might be a couple of customers, but did someone have to come right now?

"You got this, Lainey Banainey." It's Owen's nickname for me. It's Owen's voice. I turn around and see my brother stepping out of a car and three more heads I know and love popping out with big smiles on their faces. They came here. For me.

I jump off the steps that groan beneath my weight and run into them, feeling all eight arms wrapped around me.

I have the greatest friends in the world.

"We love you, Bon," I hear Maeve say.

"We're here for you," Charlie whispers.

"Proud of you, baby girl." Raf clears his throat as his words come out raspy.

I struggle to walk away, my feet feeling like they're stuck in mud. The sadness I expect to feel when I enter Betty's feels strangely absent.

There she is, sitting at her usual table, her smile lighting up the room like a beacon of hope. It was at this table where I first met Andy, and it's here that I feel a strange and powerful sense of peace.

"Well, if it isn't my Lainey girl!" Betty stands, and she somehow looks like she hasn't aged. Maybe that's because, to my mind, she had always been "old." She pulls me into a tight hug, and I know I learned the art of giving a good hug from this woman because I feel every ounce of love she has for me in this embrace.

She steps back and takes my face in her hands. "It's great to see you, kid."

"It's great to see you too, Betty. Really great." She pats my cheek and sits back down. I take the chance to look around the place and notice not much has changed. A few things have been repainted, but it's the same wooden tables and chairs, the same industrial lights, the same laminated menus.

Betty and I spend an hour talking. She tells me all about how Matt, who used to be the cook when I worked here, opened a coffee shop in town and fell in love with the bookstore owner. "He always was more passionate about coffee than he was about cooking," she says with a laugh. I can't help but think someone should write a book about Mel and Matt's love story.

We walk around the diner, and she holds my hand as we walk by the booth my dad and I used to sit at when we came here. When I try to apologize to her for not visiting sooner, she actually tells me to shut my mouth and we both laugh. No one does tough love quite like Betty.

When we circle back to the table, she says, "So are you going to invite your friends in and offer them something to eat? See if you still got what it takes to be a waitress here?" She points her chin over to the bar. "Your old apron is still back there."

Betty may dish out tough love, but she's also sentimental. I hug her again and step outside to call everyone in. As I round the corner, my heart skips a beat. There, perched on the front steps, is a figure in a familiar hoodie, their face illuminated by the sunlight. A wave of goosebumps cascades over me as I take in the strong arms that have held me tightly, the slightly shorter brown hair I'd run my hands through countless times. "Adam?"

He turns and stands quickly, his eyes roaming over my face and then body as if he's checking me for injuries. They're so blue, so intense.

I run to him and throw my arms around his neck. "You're here. Hi."

"I wouldn't want to be anywhere else," he says into my hair as he takes a deep breath. He steps back and I take in his face. His hair is shorter. His beard is gone, and my fingers automatically go to his jaw and I feel it tense beneath my touch. "Hi."

"Hi," I whisper. I want so badly to kiss him. To tell him how much I've missed him. How much I want him. Need him. Love him. But I can't find my voice and he speaks first.

"I wanted to be here for you today. As... as your friend. I wanted to come and…" He blows out a breath and I feel it on my cheek. "I'm here for you. Always. I wanted you to know that."

My heart sinks. He didn't kiss me. He didn't say he loves me. He came here as my friend. I push the melancholy aside and force a smile. "Thank you. It means everything that you came." I hug him tightly again and feel two tears slide down my cheeks. That's all I'll allow for now.

I glance over his shoulder and catch four pairs of eyes in the periphery—they're doing their best not to stare, but the fear and anticipation on their faces are plain as day. I try to take comfort in the fact that Adam is here for me, that my friends are here to offer love and support. It's the only thing that's certain right now.

I motion for the other four to come join us. "Where's Mom?" I link my arm with Owen as we walk inside.

"She said she didn't want to intrude, but that we all have to come by for tea after." He kisses the top of my head. "I'm proud of you," he whispers into my hair. My heart balloons in my chest and I squeeze his arm in gratitude. I will myself not to cry and somehow it works.

Betty is ready with my apron when we walk in. She motions towards the large booth in the corner. A table I have no particular memories at. Someplace new in this old diner.

Someplace for fresh memories. I put my apron on and find my old notepad and sparkly pink pencil still in the pocket. It feels like I never left, but I also recognize that I'm an entirely different person standing here in this familiar apron.

"Hi! I'm Elaina and I'll be serving you today. Can I get you all started with some drinks?" All sets of eyes are on me and they're all smiling. I take their orders, which consist mainly of coffee, and walk towards the bar, loading up a tray. I can feel their curious eyes on me at first, but as I joke with Betty and the new cook, everyone relaxes a little. I'm alright. This is okay.

"Have you decided what you'd like to order, or do you need some time with the menu?" I ask as I set their drinks down.

"I think we're all ready, baby girl." Raf's wide smile is contagious, and I smile back at him.

"Why don't you start us off, then?" I take out my notepad and get ready.

I go around the table, taking their orders. Adam is last. "What can I get you?" I look at him, knowing he has hardly glanced at the menu. He's been watching me the whole time.

"What do you recommend?" He lifts his coffee cup as he waits for my response.

"Everything is good here, but the pancakes are my favorite. And definitely splurge and go for the real maple syrup. It makes all the difference." My heart is lodged somewhere in my throat, and I can feel it pounding unsteadily.

Adam smiles as I speak and it's so casual, so easy, it takes me back to weeks ago when we were just two friends trying to get to know one another. "I'll take the pancakes then." His smile widens.

How is his face this *gorgeous? I wasn't prepared for a beardless Adam today. Or any day.*

His voice deepens. "With the real maple syrup, please." He hands me his menu and our fingers brush. I feel the too familiar spark between us, those fireworks in my chest threatening to go off.

Keep it together.

I close my eyes for a brief moment and take a breath. "Sounds great. I'll be back with your meals soon."

I walk away and put in their orders. There are only three tables currently with customers in the whole diner, so I know it'll be quick. I rush over to the bathroom and splash some water on my face, wondering if it's possible to fall in love twice in the same place with different people. I stare at my reflection and smooth my hair.

How are you so the same and so different?

It hits me then that I might feel a little like I did at eighteen. A little unsure, a little in love, a little scared of what's to come. But what's different is how I face my fears. This time, I want to face them head-on. I don't want to run away anymore.

33 /
did someone say chocolate chips?

adam

WHEN WE WALKED into the diner, all I could do was watch her. She seemed so at ease, so comfortable here. She put on her old apron and came to take our orders. And here she is now, telling me about the pancakes and to splurge on maple syrup. It's so natural, this thing between us and when our fingers touch as I hand her the menu, I have to hold my breath to keep from spontaneously combusting. It's impossible to ignore the gravity between us. We're pulled to one another always, no matter what.

Does she feel it, too?

She fills up a tray with plates and brings them all over with the cook behind her carrying some more. The plates look heavy, but she doesn't even flinch. Everyone smiles as they get their meals and Elaina finally sits down next to me, a giant plate of chocolate chip pancakes in front of her.

"You didn't say anything about chocolate chips," I joke, jabbing her lightly with my elbow.

"You didn't ask!" She shrugs and smirks at me as she takes a giant bite of chocolaty pancake. I resist the urge to lick the chocolate chip from the corner of her mouth.

She does it quickly anyway and I'm again left speechless at the sight of her tongue, especially now that I know what it feels like. What it tastes like.

Fuck.

She stabs one of my pancakes with her fork and puts it on her plate and before I can ask what the hell she's doing, she stabs one of her chocolaty ones and plops it down on my plate.

"Now you get the best of both worlds." She smiles brightly. She did this on purpose, knowing we'd be sharing.

WE ALL FINISH EATING, and there's happy conversation around the table though Elaina doesn't interact much with me. She hugs Betty tightly before we leave. Actually, we all end up hugging Betty because she's a sweet lady who seems to take everyone under her wing as unofficial grandchildren.

When we get to Eva's house, the whole place smells like tea and muffins. It reminds me of Elaina's house, except hers is coffee and muffins. Though we're all full, we immediately notice the stacks of muffins on the table. Blueberry, banana, chocolate chip, oatmeal, double chocolate, poppy seed and ones with red berries in them. All of our favorites.

"Hey, Ma. Wow, that's a lot of muffins!" Owen had already devoured two plates of food, but somehow, he's still hungry. He reaches for a banana muffin, breaks off a chunk, and closes his eyes as he savors the sweetness.

"Hi, darlings. Yes, Elaina's been busy making all your favorites. She made all of these except the lemon-poppy seed." She hugs and kisses Owen and Elaina tenderly, her eyes crinkling in the corners.

"Bon, you didn't know we were coming, did you?" Maeve walks over and smells the muffins as Owen watches her curiously.

"No. I just missed you all, so I made all your faves. Plus,

there was one I'd never made before, and I wanted to try out the recipe." Elaina looks at me as a blush creeps up her cheeks. She made my muffins. Tried a new recipe so she could make my favorite.

I feel a hand at my elbow and turn to see Eva smiling up at me. It's a smile I know well because it's Elaina's, too.

"You must be Adam." She pulls me into a hug. "Thanks for being patient with my girl and loving her so well." She says this so only I can hear and pats my cheek before turning away. The others are so enthralled with the muffins and their conversations that they miss the moment.

I excuse myself to go to the washroom and find myself standing in the hallway, staring at the photos on the wall. I hear Elaina's laugh and turn back towards the kitchen. Raf has his arm around her shoulders as he pretends to put her in a headlock, and everyone laughs. It feels so good to see her like this, but fuck, I'm scared she won't come back to me.

elaina

EVERYONE STAYED LONG ENOUGH for some tea, and Mom and I sent them all home with their respective favorite muffins.

Adam and I didn't talk. I didn't feel like I could. Not with so many people around. Not when all I wanted was to kiss him and tell him I love him. So Ma talked to him instead, and they seemed to hit it off. We kept goodbye hugs short and I promised them all I'd be back in LA soon.

I WAKE up the following morning with a smile on my face, and after two weeks of being here, sad, confused, and lonely, this feels so good. I'm done wallowing here and I know what I need to do... sort of.

There's not much of a plan. Basically, I'm going to go back to LA to pour my heart out to Adam and hope against all odds that he hasn't given up on me. On us. That's as far as I've gotten. Looking over my list one last time, it feels good to know I've taken chances, tried new things, and learned so much about myself.

~~Get a manicure and pedicure – this will make me feel pretty and even if no one sees my toes, I'll know they look nice.~~

~~Have more dance parties in the kitchen. Alone. With other people. Just generally dance more.~~

~~Host a dinner party. Make an extravagant meal. Enjoy every second of the chaos. This is for me because being around people brings me joy.~~

~~Visit Mamá in Marblehead. Tell her I love her. Hug her tightly. Lots.~~

~~Make a new friend? Just at least try. But only if it feels right and good and the vibes are impeccable.~~

~~Go on a trip just for fun. Pick somewhere I haven't been, or somewhere I have been and loved. Go and eat all the delicious things, see all the beautiful things and do whatever the hell I want.~~

~~Kiss someone. Make it someone really kissable. If they suck at it, stop and find someone new. Kiss because I love kissing and because it's fun.~~

~~Buy (and wear) sexy lingerie. Try to make it comfortable. Don't look at the price tags. Feel good about your little secret no one else can see.~~

~~Wax my lady parts. Just because I've always wanted to try it. Because it's new. Because I want to know what it feels like.~~

~~Spend more time with Owen. Show him the parts of my life he's missed and get to know the parts of his I've missed too.~~

~~Sing in public. Like Karaoke? Whatever. Just~~

~~sing. Sing all the songs I love most regardless of who's listening.~~

~~Get back to doing yoga. Because it feels so good to move my body that way and because my mind needs clearing.~~

~~Try a new recipe. Bake something new for me or for someone else. I already do this, but this is my reminder to keep doing it.~~

~~Do something that scares me. Not like skydiving or anything involving near or potential death, but something that scares me deep down. Something my soul will remember. Something I'll be glad I did when I'm old and wrinkly.~~

~~Have more than one orgasm in one day. Try to make it with something other than a plethora of toys, but no pressure. Just have more orgasms in general. I've gone long enough without them.~~

~~Masturbate in the bath because it sounds like fun. If it's not fun, don't do it. Bonus points for bringing snacks for afterwards.~~

I think I can safely cross everything off. Going into Betty's was scary, that's for sure, and thanks to having so much time on my hands, I've tried a few new recipes and I think I perfected the berry muffin for Adam. Now I need to add one more thing to this list. The one last thing I need to do, just for me. Because I need to audibly declare that my heart is ready and to face this fear once and for all.

·Tell Adam I love him. If words don't work, use

some sort of grand gesture so that he knows how
much he means to me, how he's changed my life and
that I was just too stupid to realize I've probably
been falling in love with him since the night we met.
Make sure to do something wonderfully romantic, like
the guy with the fake carollers in Love Actually or
maybe with a boombox like in Say Anything to really
drive the point home that it's always been him.
Perhaps add the perfect '90s pop song to the playlist
and play it for him. He just needs to know that it
doesn't matter where I go—when I enter a room, the
only eyes I ever want to see looking back at me are
his. The exact shade of blue when he's happy is my
favorite color in the whole world. His laugh is the
best sound I've ever heard, and I'd rather go
through life scared than live a single day without
him knowing how much I love him. I love him. I love
him. I love him. So much that it scares me and
makes me brave all at once.

I tuck the note away, pack my things and when I walk into the kitchen, I see Mom is already there with her tea and one for me.

"Hi, Ma."

"Hi, sweetie. Did you sleep well?" She pats the seat next to her.

"I did. Thank you." I pull her in for a hug. "Seriously, Mom. Thank you. For everything."

"Go and get your man, Elaina. He's a good one." Her eyes crinkle in the corners as she smiles.

I know she liked Adam even before meeting him, but

yesterday really solidified it for her. I caught them talking alone, smiling and the way my mom patted his cheek, well... that's her sign for *you're one of mine, now*. She's done it with the others, too.

"Yeah. He is. I just hope it's not too late." I sip my tea and say a silent prayer that I didn't wait too long.

"You have respect for one another, you're friends and you love each other. You'll be okay." She gives my hand a squeeze as she gets up. "Do you want to eat something before we go?"

"No, thank you. I don't think I could eat right now." I drink more of my tea and turn my body towards my mom.

"Ma?" She turns to look at me. "Do you think we could do Christmas here this year?"

A single tear rolls down her cheek, and a bright, warm smile stretches across her face as she looks at me. The tears in her eyes glisten in the sun's rays.

"I'd love that so much, sweetheart." We hold one another close, and no other words are necessary for us to grasp the depth of our love for one another.

The last few months have been transformative. I'm a different person. A person who made a new friend without first seeing him. Someone who actually likes getting her lady bits waxed so much she's done it multiple times—*who knew?* Someone who was finally able to let go of all my past hurts to fall in love with a wonderful, beautiful man. A man who may not even want me anymore, but who has changed my life nonetheless. I'm someone who likes sexy underwear because of how it makes *me* feel. It turns out I can love, despite my fears. Alongside my fears. Because I can share them with the ones I love and they can help me carry the burden. All this time, my friends have been doing that for me and I didn't really see it. Adam has been doing it, too. From day one.

When Mom and I pull apart, we both wipe away tears and laugh. I've cried so much these last two weeks, I can't believe I'm still capable of doing it at all.

"Let's get out of here before I decide to move back in." We laugh again and she wheels my suitcase out to her car.

We drive to the airport quietly and have another long hug when we get there. We say our *I love yous* and I walk towards the doors, feeling equal parts terrified and elated. I have no idea what the fuck I'm doing, but I need to go cross that last item off my list.

———

I ARRIVE at home and feel the weight of my worries melt away. I love it here and the sunny weather is definitely helping to lift my spirits, too.

When I open the front door, I'm greeted with loud music and the smell of something sweet and something savory in the air. "Cinema" by Harry Styles is playing and I smile.

Adam.

I walk straight to the kitchen, but I'm not prepared for the scene in front of me, so I gasp loudly before I can fully take him in. He's wearing workout shorts and an apron. No shirt. My mouth waters. He's loading the dishwasher so he can't see me, but he turns around anyway, sensing me.

"Oh shit! Elaina?" He stands there, frozen in his spot as my jaw drops to the floor. He's cooking. And baking. And the pink apron shouldn't be sexy, but it most definitely *is*.

"I'm home," I say dumbly. His face is still shaven, and I so badly want to touch it. Kiss it. But I seem to be frozen.

We finally move towards one another, and I hug him tight. "Hi."

His arms wrap around my waist tightly, his face in my hair as he takes a deep breath in. When we pull back, my fingers unconsciously go to his face.

"Hi," I whisper again. His eyes move over my face and when he licks his bottom lip, I almost don't have the self-control to not kiss him.

"You're home." He takes a small step back and swallows, looking around the kitchen. "I'm sorry about the mess. I was just... uh... trying something." His cheeks are flushed and he seems nervous.

"It's fine. You can do whatever you want. You live here too."

Even if it's temporary.

I smile at him, my eyes drawn to the plate of freshly baked muffins. But his gaze seems more focused on the paper lying next to them. I step closer and lean in, my eyes widening as I take in the handwriting on the sheet—*Elaina's Lemon Poppyseed Muffins*.

"This is... this is my mom's lemon poppyseed muffin recipe. How did you get this?" I lift it and start to read it, but he snatches it away from me faster than I can read the ingredients. "She has never let me have the recipe for this. Why do you have it?"

He tucks the paper into his pocket and the timer on the oven dings. I watch as he puts on oven mitts, and I choke on air as I feel every inch of my skin burn with desire for him.

Yes, this is incredibly sexy.

I want to take a picture of this moment. I want to frame the picture. Hang it up all over the house. I want to never forget how his muscles flex as he bends to take a dish out of the oven.

He's very careful to turn the oven off and gently pull a pie out, setting it on a cooling rack.

How did he know to use a cooling rack? Is that chicken pot pie? Oh my god is that chicken pot pie? Shit. Fuck. Breathe.

I look around the kitchen to see if I've missed anything else. What the hell is he up to? My ears ring and it sinks in that maybe he's doing this for me. Maybe he's making me my favorite things.

"Elaina!" I hear him nearly shout. I startle and turn back

to him. He's taken his apron off, and my eyes travel over the hard ridges of his body.

Cheese on rice. I'm not gonna make it.

"Yeah, what?" I shake my head, wondering if I've walked into the twilight zone.

"Didn't you hear me? I asked if you're alright. You look a little pale." I'm having a very hard time concentrating on breathing right now, let alone formulating actual thoughts and words.

"What are you doing, Adam?" He's on the other side of the island from me. Too far away.

He clears his throat. "I was, uh… trying to make your favorite foods." He reaches into his pocket absentmindedly, where he just put the muffin recipe.

"Why?" I can tell my tone is all wrong by the way he winces when I ask this.

I am fucking this up so badly.

"Because I lo—because you matter to me. Because you do these things for other people all the time like it's not a big deal, but it *is*." His cheeks flush and he reaches for a T-shirt on one of the stools. Sadly, he puts it on.

Probably for the best. Maybe getting some blood flow back to my brain will help me actually think through what the hell I'm saying.

"How did you get my mom to give you the recipe for the muffins?"

Nope, I'm still fucking this up. Why does that even matter right now?

"I told her I wanted to make them for you, and she said alright, as long as you never set eyes on the recipe because, and I quote, 'she should have someone who loves her make her favorite comfort foods for her.'" His eyes never leave mine and he's taken a few steps closer to me, but we're still too far to touch.

"And that person is you?" My voice cracks and I think I'm sweating.

"Yes. Always," he answers simply.

"But… you said… in Marblehead, you said you were there as my friend." I begin pacing. I wasn't prepared for this, and the words come flying out. "I flew here to make a big… a grand… I was supposed to brainstorm a whole thing. Maybe finally get you that basket of strawberries. I came to show you… to tell you…" His hands are on my shoulders, holding me still, steadying me like only he can.

"Slow down. Show me what? Tell me what?" His brows are furrowed and his blue eyes swirl with worry.

"That I'm in love with you. I came home to—" His lips crash into mine as he holds my face tenderly in his hands. As our kiss deepens, his fingers grip the back of my head.

"You love me?"

I nod.

"Tell me again," he whispers against my lips. His ocean-blue eyes hold mine and I don't dare look away.

"I love you, Adam. I'm in love with you." My heart expands in my chest as I finally say these words out loud.

"Again?" His forehead rests on mine, his eyes intent on my lips like he needs to both see and hear what I'm saying.

"I love you. I never want to be without you." He kisses me again, more urgently now, pulling me up on the countertop so he's standing between my legs.

"One more time," he says as his lips move against mine, a small smile across his lips.

"I love you. So much." We're forehead to forehead for a few seconds until he stands straighter, his blue eyes finding mine.

"I love you, Elaina." He kisses my cheek. "I love you." Then my jaw. "I love you." My neck. "I love you." He kisses my lips again and wipes the tears from my cheeks. "Only you. Forever." The fireworks burst inside my chest, their sparks lighting me up from the inside and the warmth blazing through every inch of my body.

Our kiss becomes more frantic, and I feel his hands scoop me up as he walks us out of the kitchen and down the hall to my bedroom.

He sets me down on the bed, and as if knowing exactly what I'm thinking, he undresses himself. I make quick work of removing my jeans and T-shirt. This is nothing like last time. He's not controlled and calm and neither am I. We're frantic for each other.

I don't take my eyes off of him. He's unfairly beautiful. All taut muscles with a scattering of dark hair on his chest and arms, and that trail down to his perfect cock. I could never want anyone else like this. I unclasp my bra and remove it. Then he's on top of me, his mouth on my breast, his teeth grazing my nipple, making my back arch off of the bed.

"Tell me what you want, Elaina." I smile at his request, loving how much he likes to hear me say it.

He grasps the waistband of my panties and quickly pulls them down, then his lips are trailing up my body. His lips are gentle yet firm, and I feel a wave of goosebumps ripple up my skin as he brushes my neck with a feathery kiss.

"I want you. Now." I wrap my fingers around his erection and line him up. God, he feels so fucking good.

He makes quick work of moving my wrists above my head, trapping them beneath one of his large hands while the other travels down my body, exploring every curve. I tremble and shake my head in refusal, but he just chuckles knowingly.

"We can take it slow, baby."

"I don't want slow, Adam. *Please!*" I'm desperate and panting now as his fingers travel below my belly button. "Not your fingers. I want *you*. I need you to fuck me right n—"

He pushes himself fully inside me and I moan so loudly I'm sure the neighbors can hear me.

"Again," I whimper. He slowly pulls out and rams himself into me again and I nearly come on the spot. Nothing feels as good as this. As good as him. Us.

"Yes," I whisper as I kiss him.

"More," I say into his mouth.

My legs are wrapped around him and when he lets my wrists go, my hands find his hair, tugging his mouth to my breast, asking him without words for what I want. What I need.

He groans his approval as he licks and sucks, leaving kisses everywhere as fucks me wildly. "Fuck, I've missed these perfect tits. Missed your taste. Your smell. Missed your pussy gripping my cock like this. I missed every single thing about you, my love." I could come just from hearing him talk like this. The mix of dirty and sweet talk drives me wild.

And here I thought I was the one with the filthy mouth.

His breathing is heavy, and his eyes are steady on me. He pulls almost all the way out and pushes into me hard and fast, picking up the pace. My eyes drift closed.

"Eyes on me, Elaina." The stern tone of his voice mixed with the love I see in his eyes is like a rolling wave that takes me under. My orgasm rolls through me in slow motion and seems to last forever.

As I finally come down, he pushes into me one last time and I feel him empty himself inside of me. He grunts and whispers my name, and I've never seen anything more beautiful.

He collapses on me, careful not to set all of his weight on top of me, and rolls us over so my head is on his shoulder.

"I'm sorry that only lasted like a minute," he says through quick breaths.

"Best minute of my life." I giggle and he laughs that low, deep laugh from his chest that I feel inside my own. I know in my heart there could never be another man for me.

WE FALL asleep for a short time and when I wake, I feel one arm under my head and the other tight around my waist. I feel his warm breath land on my neck as he exhales slowly. His chest is warm and hard across my back. I smile, gently wiggling my ass as I feel him stir. He kisses my neck and my shoulder, and I feel him harden.

"What do you want, baby?"

"Make love to me, Adam." He groans as he runs the head of his cock along my wetness and I moan, arching into him. He's slow and gentle this time, kissing up my neck and biting down on my earlobe. We stay like this for a while as he touches and kisses me all over.

His words are gentler now, too as he whispers to me. "You're so beautiful. I missed you so much. I'm going to love you forever."

And the swirl of emotions in my chest is enough to make me feel as though I'm floating.

"I need to see you," he says in my ear, and I turn to face him.

I wrap my leg around his waist and sit up to straddle him, settling down slowly as he fills me completely. I lean down to be closer to him, our eyes never leaving one another's.

"I love you, Elaina."

My heart threatens to burst out of my chest.

"I love you, Adam." We find a comfortable pace as I ride him and his grip on my hip tightens. I can tell he loses control when he slams my body down onto his and as I start to come, he flips us over, bringing my ankles to his shoulders. He's so deep that I another quick orgasm hits me, then his body stills as he comes inside of me.

As we settle down, he kisses me deeply, tucking my hair behind my ears, and we both roll over on our sides slowly, facing one another.

"You're incredible. Do you know that?" His voice is so tender. I shake my head, closing my eyes. After years of feeling like there was something wrong with me, like I was broken somehow, it turns out I just needed to find him. "You are, my *tornerose*. My Lainey. My girl. My love." I couldn't fight the wide smile taking over my face, even if I tried.

"Well, that I am. Yours. All yours." We stare at each other for a while. Him drawing circles on my shoulder or playing with my hair. Me with my hand over his chest, feeling his heartbeat. Eventually, and as the stickiness of my thighs sinks in, I speak up. "I should go shower."

"Want company?"

More than anything, says my brain.

Not on your life, screams my sore vagina.

"Only if you promise to keep that giant crotch snake of yours away from my lady bits."

He laughs, throwing his head back, and the sight of him steals all the breath out of my lungs. He reaches out to tickle me.

"You love my giant crotch snake."

I squirm, giggling. "Yes. Yes, I do, but I won't be able to walk for a week if we do this again right now."

"Just a shower. Promise." He gives me a Scout salute.

"You dork," I laugh. "Let's go."

I'M JUST PUTTING on fresh panties when he walks into my closet. He's standing in the doorway, leaning on his forearm and looking all kinds of delicious.

"I have something to show you," he says, smiling.

"Can I get one of those yummy-looking muffins first? I've worked up an appetite for some reason." I smirk at him, and he laughs. It feels so good to be back like this with him that I almost want to avoid the conversation I know we need to have. I need to explain myself.

"Yeah. Come on, my little comedian." He walks away and for the second time today I feel the disappointment of seeing him put on a T-shirt.

I get dressed and before Adam hands me a muffin, I take

the piece of paper with my list out of my purse and tuck it into the waistband of my leggings.

Adam takes my hand and leads me back the way we came, then takes the stairs up to my office. When he opens the door, I nearly choke on my muffin.

The walls are painted. There's a big white desk underneath the window and a deep sofa off to the side in the perfect natural linen color. The rug is worn and looks to be vintage. There's a basket filled with wool blankets, my yoga mat is rolled next to them, and the bookshelves have been stocked with my books and pictures.

"Oh my god," I whisper. "Oh, my god... Adam." I look around and tears run down my cheeks. He did this. He did this for me. "How did you... when did you..."

"I watched some YouTube videos on the best wall-painting techniques. Googled the best white paint colors. Researched the best writing desks and most comfortable couches. The internet is super handy, you know?"

He walks over to me and wraps his arms around my waist from behind. He rests his chin on my shoulder so casually, as if he didn't just do the sweetest, most romantic, most beautiful, and most wonderful thing in the world. As if him researching how to decorate my office wasn't making me fall even deeper in love with him.

"Have you ever used Pinterest before? It's... intense!" I have no words for this man. "With my training done and without you here, I had a lot of time on my hands, so this seemed like the best use of it."

I turn around in his arms and he swipes my tears away with his thumbs, holding my face in his hands.

"Do you like it?" The uncertainty in his voice cracks my heart wide open.

"Like it? Oh, Adam... I... this is... this is the most special thing anyone has ever done for me." I swallow, trying to find the words and letting this simple fact sink in: Adam

River Holm loves me, and he loves me well. Better than anyone else could. And I don't know what I did to deserve this love or even if I do, but I'm not letting it go. Not ever again.

I pull the piece of paper out of my leggings and hand it to him. He lowers his hands and takes it from me, scrunching his nose as he opens it.

"Is this your list?" He reads on. "Wow, you crossed almost everything off." I watch as his facial expressions change as he goes down the list. The smirk as he gets to the lingerie and waxing line items. The smile as he reads about singing in public. Another smirk as he gets to the orgasm one.

"Did you… in the bath, did you?" I nod. He swallows hard. It's amazing to me that the man who makes me come multiple times and dirty talks like he was born for it blushes as he reads about me masturbating. "What did you think about?"

"Oh my god, Adam. I thought about you, obviously, and I came in like thirty seconds. I forgot the snacks. Now, can you please focus?" I laugh and push his head back down towards the paper.

Such a guy.

I can tell when he gets to the last one because his eyes fill with tears and his Adam's apple bobs, but he doesn't swallow.

I stand frozen still as he takes in the words on the paper. His expression is unreadable now, and I'm freaking out a little.

Is this stupid? Does he hate this? I need to say something.

"I wanted to come home and think of something special to do for you, to show you how much you mean to me. Then I get here and you're baking and cooking my favorite things, and now you went and did the most romantic thing ever and finished my office for me and it's perfect. It was supposed to be me with the grand gesture."

He walks over to my desk and takes a pen out of the cup. He sets the paper down and draws lines on it.

"I... I don't know how I'll ever be able to show you that you make me better. I don't know how I can thank you. I'm still not entirely sure I deserve you, but I want to try to. Every day, I want to try."

He walks to the corkboard on the wall and pins the sheet up and I keep going. "It just... it shouldn't have been you doing all of this. I'm the one who fucked up. I walked away. I hurt you. I should be the one out there with the boombox, playing a sappy song."

Finally, he walks back towards me, takes my face in his hands again and kisses me. Our tongues perform that perfect dance and my knees wobble.

All thoughts are erased from my mind, and I wonder if this is normal. If everyone feels this when they kiss their person, except I don't have time to wonder because my brain ceases to function.

By the time he stops kissing me, I'm convinced all the blood has rushed to my vagina, leaving me braindead.

"I need you to hear me, Elaina." He keeps a hold on my face so we're eye-to-eye. "There's no 'should' with us. There's no deserving. There's no comparison. You have made me feel loved and heard since the first night we met. You've shown me what selflessness looks like. You've made *me* better just by being who you already were."

Great, now I'm crying again.

"'It's easy to halve the potato where there's love', right?" Yep. Cue the ugly crying because he just quoted my dad's favorite saying. He sweetly wipes at my tears with his thumbs, his aquamarine eyes shining with a love as deep as the sea itself.

"All I've ever needed is for you to love me."

"I do. I do love you. So, so much," I whisper.

"I know. And now I get to be one of those lucky people.

Lucky to be loved by you. I don't need anything else, *tornerose*. Only you. Forever." He kisses me one more time then pulls back just far enough for me to see his eyes. "Are you happy?"

This time I answer honestly, with eyes wide open and not an ounce of hesitation.

"So happy, my love." I can't believe this is my life. I can't believe this is my man.

epilogue

a few months later

elaina

"YOU KNOW, you really are going to have to learn to not leave all of this to the last minute. For someone who's always so punctual, this is the one thing you can't ever seem to do ahead of time. And also think about better hiding spots. I found a polka dot scarf under the couch last week and Frankie nearly ate it!"

I'm at Maeve's helping her with her Christmas wrapping two days before the big holiday because she just cannot ever manage to have things wrapped on time.

"Oh, you found that? Thanks! That's for your mum, actually. It's cashmere and should keep her well warm in those Massachusetts winters." She walks over to the couch and pulls out the scarf box and I laugh. I fucking love her. "Are you all ready? You have a lot more people to celebrate with this year." *What a difference a year makes!*

"Yep. I think I've been wrapping since October. I got Emma the cutest princess costume, and I had to wait in line to get Liam his new Lego set. I nearly fought a lady for it. I grabbed the last one, and she tried to claim it was hers when she already had one in her cart. Not a chance, lady. That shit was mine!" Maeve laughs as she sips her wine.

"Those kids are lucky to have an auntie like you, Bon. I can't imagine ever getting into a fight over Legos!"

"I'm not their aunt!" I raise an eyebrow at her.

Adam and I aren't married. We know it'll happen eventually and that we both want kids, but we have this movie that will start shooting next year and that's our baby for now. And I'm happy with that.

He officially moved in with me about two weeks after I came back from Marblehead. The damage to his house ended up being a lot more effort than it was worth, and he sold it to someone who wanted to rebuild, anyway.

It was fast, but we knew moving slowly and doing things the typical way was never our style, so we took the leap. And we haven't looked back.

"Not yet!" Maeve wiggles her eyebrows at me as she butchers the poor wrapping paper on the present she's wrapping.

"And honestly, I had to do it. The kid has been talking about it for like four months! I can't wait to see his face when he opens it!" And it's true. I love Gwen and Callum's kids. I babysit as often as possible, and I love every second. The old guest room is now a room for them to stay in.

"You're adorable. You two will definitely be back for the party, though, yeah?" She looks up at me hopefully.

"Oh, definitely. We wouldn't miss it. We'll be there early." I wink at her, and she smiles. As if Adam and I would miss her New Year's Eve party. It's the one-year anniversary of the night we met!

———

AFTER TWO CHRISTMAS CELEBRATIONS, one on each coast and one with each side of our families, and a quiet birthday celebration for Adam, we're back in LA for New Year's Eve. Charlie opens the door to Maeve's house as she hears me honking on the way up the driveway.

"Lainey," she says, smiling. We haven't seen one another for a few weeks. "I'm having a bit of déjà vu here." We both laugh as we hug. "But it's great that you can actually see this year. Let's go in and grab a drink."

I walk into the kitchen with Charlie. Adam is already here, helping Raf with something. Char bounces around, finding us glasses and pouring us some champagne. Before we have time to clink glasses and drink, someone calls her down the hall so she leaves the glasses on the island.

"I'll be right back, love." She scurries off, and I put away the muffins I baked for the girls to have at breakfast tomorrow, dancing along to the music as I go. I hear someone clear their throat and turn quickly, smiling widely as I see my favorite person in the entire world.

----

adam

I stand in the doorway watching her sway her hips to the music as she sets muffins down. I see her dancing in the kitchen almost every day and as often as I can, until I get caught, I stand and watch her before I join her.

I'm nervous as all shit this time though, and thinking back to a year ago, how fucked up everything seemed, it's crazy that we're here now. This girl. She makes everything better.

I swallow hard and she swivels around after I clear my throat. Her face lights up like a firework and her mouth spreads into a grin that I've come to recognize as the one she reserves for me. It's a smile that turns her eyes into crescent moons and fills her cheeks with dimples. Before I can take another breath, she wraps her arms around me, melting into me like a hug was invented for us.

"Hi," she says into my neck, kissing me there, then turning to kiss my lips. "Hi," she whispers again. None of it ever gets old. This greeting, this kiss, this girl.

"*Tornerose*. Fancy catching you dancing in a kitchen." She giggles as we sway to the music. "Let Me Love You" by Mario. I wonder if she's noticed. "You know, this is exactly what I wish I had been doing a year ago."

She smiles up at me, running her fingers through my hair.

"In fact, this is what I want to do every day. Forever. What do you say, Lainey? Will you dance with me forever?"

Her lips curl into a gentle smile, her eyes glimmering with love. "Only you," she says. "Forever."

I pull the ring I've had hidden in my sock drawer for six months out of my pocket and hold it between us. Her gasp is barely audible as she takes in the band of gold, a substantial yellow diamond sparkling in its center. The world around us suddenly stills, and I whisper the two words that will bind us together for all eternity.

"Marry me."

Her eyes well with tears as I slip the ring onto her finger.

"Yes," she whispers back. "Oh my god, yes. I love you. I love you so much." Our lips collide hungrily, and she melts into me. Our hands roam each other's body as if by instinct. I can feel the heat radiating from her, and it makes my head spin. Her curves fit my frame like a glove, and if it wasn't for our friends waiting eagerly to celebrate with us, we'd be doing some very dirty things on this kitchen counter.

As if on cue, I hear Maeve's voice. "Can we celebrate before you two start shagging in my kitchen?"

We both turn, laughing. "You all knew?"

"Of course, baby girl." Raf walks over and hugs us both.

"Your boy needed our help to make sure your little meet-cute was recreated properly. Down to the song."

Everyone is hugging and laughing, and it feels good to know that the six of us are all family to one another. Chosen or otherwise.

THE END

acknowledgements

Writing Elaina's story was a wild experience. I had my very own Andy once, and it altered almost every single aspect of my life, both for the better and worse. Though Elaina and I don't share all the same life experiences that came after, the feelings of guilt, of not being enough, of hurt and shame that came with that kind of loss were with me for a really, *really* long time and it meant that romantic relationships became something I both desperately wanted but also feared.

That being said, this book has been equal parts therapeutic and frustrating to write. I learned a lot about how I processed loss by writing it, and also about the level of support I wish I had during that time in my life.

I know I'll look back on this book one day with both fondness and perhaps a touch of embarrassment, because if you don't look back at the very first thing you created and feel a little embarrassed, it probably means you haven't grown, right?

I could never, ever have written this story without the support of my amazing husband. When I told him I had decided to write a book, he didn't even flinch. He encouraged me every day and celebrated with me when I finished the very first draft on the day of our tenth wedding anniversary. Babe, you're the reason I can write and share this story. You healed my heart in ways I didn't think would ever be possible. You're the inspiration for every book boyfriend I'm ever going to write. You're the reason I'm on the other end of being a broken-hearted girl. You're the reason I believe I actually *can* do anything. You're forever my favorite person and I love you. A lot a lot a lot a lot a lot.

Not many people knew about this project while it was still in its baby stages, but to those of you who did and who cheered me on, I will never have enough words to thank you. Ashley and Sabrina, you were my sounding board, my first responders when I felt like I was losing it, the OG alpha, beta and ARC readers for this book and your friendship is not something I take for granted. When I grow up, I want to be as cool as Ashley and as sassy as Sabrina. Thank you from the bottom of my heart.

Meg, I will think back on your notes and commentary often because they make me smile so, so big. I still don't know how you guessed the major plot theme in Owen and Maeve's book, but it must be because you're made of magic. Thank you for being my friend and writing my first unofficial book review and making me feel like I can actually do this crazy thing.

To Natasha, Jermaine, Sarah, and literally anyone else I said the words "I wrote a book" to and heard nothing but lovely encouragement after the fact, you are a priceless gem and I adore you. You have no idea how many times I thought back to the kind words you've shared with me as fuel to keep going when the nights were long and the early mornings were dark.

And now to you, my dear reader. Thank you for reading this story. I had no idea what I was doing when I started this (I probably still don't), but I knew I couldn't go on any longer with this story living only in my brain. It had to come out. Every part of me hopes that you enjoyed it, and if you didn't, I'm still glad I got it out for myself.

xoxo,
-Cristina

about the author

Cristina Santos is a mom of two little boys who hopefully will never read this book. She is married to the man of her dreams and lives lakeside with all her wild boys (pup included) in Nova Scotia, Canada. She loves a good sunset and will forever and ever and ever believe in the power of playlists, 90's romantic comedies and love stories.

This is Cristina's first book.

cristinasantosauthor.com

instagram.com/cristinasantosauthor
tiktok.com/@cristinasantosauthor

also by cristina santos

Please note that though these are interconnected, they can all be read as standalones. Remember to check content warnings.

there's more...

Want to read Elaina and Andy's story? The whole prologue (more of a novella) is available to newsletter subscribers.

Or maybe you want the 90's and 00's playlist Adam and Elaina created in the book?

Head to cristinasantosauthor.com to get all the goods!

———

Flip the page to read chapter 1 of *Sparks Still Fly*

sparks still fly

part one - then

1 / fuck me sideways.

maeve

may, 10 years ago

TODAY, I met the man I'm going to marry. Of course, he doesn't know, and I certainly won't be telling him or anyone else right this second because he's my best friend's older brother. But he's the one. I feel it with every fiber of my being. I may only be nineteen, but once I know what I want, nothing can stop me. And what I want is Owen James.

Some may call me dramatic, and they would be right, but the moment I saw his 6'4" frame walk through the door of our dorm, I felt it. A bolt of electricity ran right through me, and I saw sparks fly. It's not just because he's the hottest man I've ever seen, though that certainly doesn't hurt. It's because he's meant to be mine, and I'm already his. It's as inevitable as the sunrise.

WE'RE SITTING in a booth at our favorite Thai restaurant, close to where I live with my roommates—Elaina, who I call Bonnie, and my twin sister, Charlie. Owen is directly across from me, and he's been so polite, asking me and Charlie about how our first year at NYU has been, what we love most about the city, and what we miss about living in London.

I've been taking in every detail about him. The way his blond hair is cropped evenly all around his head, the way his throat moves when he swallows, the muscles in his arms moving as he brings his chopsticks to his mouth. His cheeks are perfectly smooth, and my fingertips tingle as I imagine what it would feel like to touch them, kiss him there.

I've done little except smile and occasionally ask a question as I fidget with my chopstick wrapper, turning it into a mini origami swan. It's something I started doing as a way of distracting myself during dinners as a child. My mum's third husband insisted we should try different foods and be exposed to all cuisines, and I always loved going to the restaurants that had chopsticks so I could practice making things like boats and hearts. But I always loved the swans most of all—there's something about how graceful they look, even in paper form.

Once I've successfully made four swans out of all the discarded wrappers, I allow myself to glance at Owen, my eyes pausing where he's twisting one of my swans around the table with his index finger and thumb as if the tiny bird is swimming along calm waters. It's soothing, watching the way his fingers move my little creation, and eventually, I allow my gaze to move back to his unfairly sharp jaw.

He seems more comfortable with Charlie because she smiles just about as much as he does, which is not very much at all. Ever the opposing twin, I've constantly got a smile on my face. I like to be happy, and I like to make other people happy, too.

Char is very direct with her answers. That's always been her style, and she's not one for theatrics. I, on the other hand, absolutely live for theatrics. It's why I'm going to become an actress. I love becoming someone new, thinking of new ways to express myself and really getting into my characters' minds. So, when Owen addresses me, I give him the full Maeve, which amounts to big smiles, loads of eye contact and pauses in all the right places. He smiles politely back at me, but it's the same smile he's given Charlie—small and tight— so I know he hasn't realized we're meant to be just yet.

That's fine, I can learn to be patient. Maybe. Hopefully. I mean, I've never done it before, but how hard can it be, right?

He pays for dinner, and we start the walk back to our dorm. Char and Elaina are happily chatting ahead of us, and that allows me to hang back a bit with Owen.

"How are you liking New York so far? Has it met all of your expectations?" I raise an eyebrow and look up at him as I ask this, and he glances at me quickly before staring ahead again.

"It's fine. I've visited before, but it's nice to see Lainey feeling so at home here." He shrugs as he says this, then looks down at me. "Thanks for being a good friend to her. She always writes about how great you and Charlie have been, especially after everything that happened at home."

The earnestness in his eyes knocks me off my game, and my *Maeve the actress* persona falls away faster than a car explosion in a movie after someone shoots the gas tank. I swallow hard as I think of everything my new best friend has been through in the last year. She fell in love and lost that love tragically. It took her weeks to open up to us about it, and she's finally smiling a little more these days.

"Oh." Suddenly, my eyes fill with tears for a reason I can't explain. I'm not a crier. I control my emotions like I control my eyeliner—with the precision of a brain surgeon. But when it comes to my girls? My sisters? I'm a goner.

Owen touches my arm, and I'm certain I stop breathing. "I'm sorry. I didn't mean to upset you. It's just nice to know she's got good people around her. I worry about her, you know?" He moves his hand away, and I stare at it for a moment too long, watching the imaginary sparks as they flutter around us.

"Of course. She's doing so much better, though, and you don't have to worry. We've got our Bon no matter what." I smile weakly up at him, and when he returns the motion with a deliciously crooked smirk, my step falters. My hands instinctively go out, and Owen's massive arm is there to catch me.

"You all right, Maeve?"

Oh god, he said my name. He said my name. It was the first time he's said it and I'll forever remember this moment as the first time he said my name, and I nearly fell on my face into a disgusting New York City sidewalk.

"Yep. Thanks!" There's far too much pep in my tone, considering I'm not sure I've taken a breath yet since he touched me.

Thankfully, Owen is much smoother than I am at this moment and diffuses the situation brilliantly. "Why do you call Lainey Bonnie? Or Bon? Where does that come from?"

"Oh, well, it's a nickname. It means beautiful. Because Elaina is beautiful inside and out, and that's easy to see from the moment you meet her." This is a fact. I have known Elaina for eight months, and she's one of the best people I've ever met. "She's a bonnie lass, that one. Charlie and I had this elderly Irish neighbor who used to babysit us sometimes, and she always called us that. I guess it felt natural to pass on to Elaina."

His rumbly chuckle makes my pulse race. "That's...very cute."

Cute? Oh, bollocks. Cute is no good. Not when I need him to see me as his future wife, or, at the very least, his next shag who will turn into his future wife.

"Well, you've been good for her. So...thanks. Again." One more time, the sincerity of his voice rocks me.

"No need to thank me. She's been good for me, too. And for

Charlie." We lock eyes for a few seconds. His eyes are green, like his sister's, but there's something deeper about them. They remind me of fir trees in winter on a sunny day after a snow-fall. The light bounces off them, and they nearly sparkle.

I'm so caught up in thinking about his eyes that, for the second time today, Owen keeps me from slamming my face into something. This time it's the back of Charlie's head as they've come to a stop in front of our building.

His hand is firm and warm against my belly, and it drops away quickly, but not quickly enough for me to miss the warmth of his fingers as they wrap around my waist.

"Okay?" And that word. That one whispered word turns my brain into soup inside my skull. I don't respond. I can't. I'm floating away, and the only thing keeping me tethered to the ground is Owen.

"All right, Maevey. Why don't we let Elaina and Owen say their goodbyes?" Charlie takes my hand and looks at Owen with a small smile on her face. "Thank you for dinner, Owen. It was nice to meet you."

"Right. Thanks." Those are my parting words to him. To my future husband.

Crap on a cracker.

———

september, 10 years ago

I haven't told Bon and Charlie about my feelings for Owen because they'll surely think I've gone off my rocker, but Charlie instinctively knows. A twin always knows.

It's been a few months since that first meeting, and I've dreamed about him every night. I think of him often, which is why I've taken up working out to Zumba videos. I need the distraction.

The music is so loud, and the dance moves are so outrageous that it makes me forget about his bright green eyes and that reluctant smile. With that thought, I put on my headphones and push our minuscule coffee table out of the way to make room for my awkward arse shaking.

Sweat pours down my back and chest halfway through the class and I throw my fist in the air, congratulating myself for finally nailing the hip thrusts in 'Gasolina.' I turn around to find Bon twisted in her chair at the kitchen table; a slackjawed Owen on her laptop screen. I throw myself on the floor, hiding from their prying eyes and hope I can just live here forever. I don't need to move ever again. I'll just go ahead and die of embarrassment right here on our shit-brown carpeted floor.

"It's too late. He already saw you." Bon's voice is so full of mischief, it makes me want to pinch her right on the nipple. She deserves it. She couldn't have taken her call with Owen elsewhere? She had to do it here? While the camera faced my arse?

Ugh.

"Don't let us stop you. I can see that the class isn't over yet." The low timbre of his voice has the butterflies in my stomach all taking flight at once and my skin breaking out into goosebumps even though I'm a sweaty mess. Every word is laced with amusement, but not in a way that makes me feel embarrassed. It makes me feel shy, and that's not a feeling I'm comfortable with. At all. I obviously don't mind an audience —I'm constantly on stage in front of crowds. So why do I feel like this?

His voice breaks through my muddled thoughts. "Come on. At least come say hi if you're not gonna keep shaking your ass for us."

My body reacts to his words quicker than my brain and before I can stop myself, I'm on my feet, waving at the screen.

I feel like Jim Carrey in *The Truman Show* with one hand awkwardly high above my head. "Hello, Owen."

His smile is wide and makes his dimples pop. I'm drawn to the sight of it like a moth to a flame. I know it'll be my demise, but I can't be stopped. Can't be helped. Wouldn't want to be, either.

"Hey there, tiny dancer." His voice is clear, but the deep baritone always hits me in the same spot. Right between my thighs.

I hover over Bon, smiling right back and hoping it looks casual, not frenzied. "Glad you enjoyed the show, O."

"Ew, you're sweating all over me. Here. Sit. I'm running late for class, but Owen should talk to someone other than me and Mamá, anyway. Not like he ever has a girlfriend he can call." She pushes my shoulders down so I'm sitting on the chair, then wipes her hands on her jeans, not masking her horror at my sweat on her palms, completely unaware of how many times I'm going to overthink that girlfriend comment. "Bye, O. Love you!"

"Love you, Lainey Banainey!" The nickname makes me melt, which only reminds me I actually *look* as though I'm melting right now. There's sweat everywhere, and my hair is stuck to my face and neck.

I clear my throat, attempting to wipe my forehead with the back of my arm. It's not helping. Everything is sticky.

His chuckle brings me back to the moment, and I remember he can see me.

Is this your first time on a video call? Of course he can see you, you twat!

Oh, fuck me sideways.

His laughter gets brighter, the sound bouncing around in my chest like a ping-pong ball. "I said that out loud?"

"You sure did." He cocks his head to the side, taking me in. I take a moment to do the same, noticing that the room he's in is dark. His hair is buzzed even shorter than when I met him. His brown uniform seems to be covered in some sort of pixelated camouflage pattern, a black T-shirt peeking out beneath the collar. A million questions hit my brain all at once.

What time is it there? What does the air smell like? Are you sleeping enough? Eating enough? Will you come back to New York to see us? To see me?

"You wanna go get some water? That was an intense workout, and you seem a little out of it." He's joking, though the smile is gone from his face. Even so, the pesky belly butterflies flutter at the fact that he thought to ask.

"I'm fine. I'd rather talk to you, anyway."

Fuck. Nooooo! Why did you say that? Idiot.

I clear my throat in an attempt to delete that last comment. I know. It doesn't work that way. "Where are you?"

He clicks his tongue. "Can't tell you that, sunshine. But it's really hot and dry here."

Sunshine? Did he just nickname me? Is it like a cute, flirty thing or a sisterly thing?

I can't think about it, and I don't want to ask him about his deployment. I'm sure he doesn't want to talk about that. He needs to think about happy things, so I naturally ask about the thing that always cheers me up.

"Do you ever watch *The Office*? I don't mean while you're deployed, but like when you're home?" I haven't a clue where this is going.

"Yeah, I love that show. And we watch it here sometimes." He shrugs, a small smile playing on his lips. "But we are talking about the American version, yeah?"

"Oh, god, yes. Of course. I mean, I love Ricky Gervais, but Steve Carell is a comedic genius." His smile widens. "I'm sad the show's ended, but I feel like I'll rewatch it over and over, you know? It just feels like one of those shows you never get sick of."

He keeps looking at me, smile still on his face, head still slightly cocked.

"The episode where Jim dressed up like Dwight has to be one of my favorites." I clear my throat and deepen my voice. 'Fact: Bears eat beets.'"

I pause, and when I get going again, I can't hide the delight on my face as we say in unison, "'Bears. Beets. Battlestar Galactica.'"

We both burst into laughter. I will quote every single line from this show if it gets him to laugh like this again. He looks so... light. Free. Nothing like the serious and stern guy I first met. Elaina has said that he makes a terrible first impression because he's not super friendly to strangers, but that once he warms up to a person, he's a big teddy bear, and maybe I'm starting to see that.

We're both nearly recovered, and he looks like he's about to say something when he looks off to the side, the smile immediately erased from his handsome face.

"Sorry, Maeve, I have to get going. But, uh...thanks. For staying and talking to me."

"Don't mention it." We're both quiet and unmoving, staring. He's completely still, and it seems as if the video is frozen, so I say the thing at the forefront of my mind.

"Please stay safe." Then I kiss my fingertips and touch them to the screen, where his lips are. I hit the red button to end the call, and half a second before the screen goes black, his eyes move to the camera, so it's as if he's looking right at me. My stomach dips faster than The Tower of Terror ride, and I clutch my chest in actual horror. "Noooo!"

Did he see me do that? After he saw me shake my uncoordinated arse all over the living room? After I sat here like a sweaty beast talking about a TV show? Did he see me do the kiss thing?

Charlie runs into the room with a giant textbook in her hands, holding it like a baseball bat, though I'm certain she wouldn't know the difference between a bat and a lacrosse stick.

"Get off her, you filthy beast!" I swear, ever since Charlotte saw her first NYC rat while leaving the subway, she's convinced they're out to get us.

"There's no rat, Char. Just a giant wanker." I close the laptop and walk toward the bathroom. I desperately need a shower and to forget whatever that was that just happened.

I hardly hear Charlie's "Ew! What? Why? Where? When? And whose?" She really just gave me the 5 W's. I cannot with this girl.

"It's me, Char. I'm the wanker!" I slam the bathroom door before she can reach it and immediately turn on the shower, drowning out the noise, but not the visions of two wide green eyes staring right into me.

————

Sparks Still Fly is available on e-book, Kindle Unlimited and paperback.

Printed in Great Britain
by Amazon